CHRISTMAS CAROLS & YULETIDE PERILS

A SOUTHERN PARANORMAL CHRISTMAS COZY MYSTERY

A DARKLY SOUTHERN MYSTERY
BOOK THREE

TAM LUMIÈRE

BOOKS BY TAM LUMIÈRE

A NOTE FROM TAM

If you would like a free novella to this series, you can sign up for my newsletter and receive a copy of **Conch & Circumstance**, the one where Win and her friends visit the merpeople living off the coast of Cradlerock at the bottom of the ocean.

Free Book Here 👉 https://tamlumiere.com/bonus-book-1

CHAPTER 1

*T*he shiny red sleigh brushed past a snow-covered bough, and there it was—Greywolf Manor, every gable and turret glittering like a castle in a fairytale. The sleigh bells fell silent as Whisper, the magnificent undead mare from Lila & the Piggles Sanctuary, came to a graceful stop beneath the *porte-cochère* of the manor, steam curling from her nostrils in ghostly spirals. Frost clung to her hollow eye sockets, and when she stomped a bone-white hoof, it echoed like a warning from the grave. A stable boy hurried over, taking Whisper's reins with the careful deference of someone who wasn't entirely sure she wouldn't hex him simply because it tickled her fancy.

"Easy girl," I murmured as Whisper huffed cold fog from her nostrils and gave the poor boy a baleful stare and a subtle skeletal clink.

I turned toward the mansion and paused, appreciating the sheer spectacle.

Greywolf Manor had dressed to dazzle, every inch dripping in Christmas magic. Frosted garlands twisted up the wrought iron railings, lanterns dangled from the bare trees like stars caught mid-fall, and the enormous front door wore a wreath so large it could've comfortably housed a family of Christmas elves. A cluster of Wentworth students in lopsided elf hats belted out carols beside the carriage porch, their voices wobbly with enthusiasm and just enough magic to keep the snowflakes dancing.

Another young man, lanky with a shock of blond hair and a bowtie half undone, hurried around to open our door. "Welcome to Greywolf," he said, when Keir stepped from the sleigh.

I tucked my one-eyed feline familiar, Pyewacket in my arm, accepted the boy's hand, and stepped down onto the snow-cleared path.

Keir Bane—alpha of the Silverfang Clan, all quiet strength, sharp warmth, and my boyfriend (a word that still felt strange and sparkly every time I thought it)—took my hand and pressed a kiss to my knuckles. Snowflakes clung to his dark wavy hair and the shoulders of his black tuxedo, which fit him with maddening precision.

"Windsor Ebonwood, you are absolutely gorgeous tonight," he said in a low voice meant only for me.

I gave his hand a light squeeze.

I had my close friends Chase Abernathy-Wyatt and Lorenzo de Zavala to thank for that.

Chase had worked his magic, sweeping my hair into an elegant twist with soft tendrils framing my face. But I had his husband Ren to thank for the smokey eyes and pouty lips that made me look far more glamorous than I had any right to. I wore a crimson Zuhair Murad ballgown from my New York days— low-cut, shimmering, and impossible to ignore—and twinkling Christian Louboutin sandals, also relics from the Big Apple, now spelled to handle snow like a dream.

The valet's head abruptly turned toward the forest. "Wait. Y'all hear that?"

Everyone froze.

I listened for a moment then adjusted the holly-red velvet

ribbon around my neck and brushed my fingers over the protection charm, a gift from my great-aunt Sibella, tucked beneath it. Just feeling it there helped steady my nerves.

That's what solving two murders in a town full of magical weirdos will do to a girl.

Between being nearly unalived in the Darkly Cemetery and almost taking a flight to my death, I'd learned to pay attention when things felt off. Add in the emotional hurricane of discovering I had a half-sister I'd never known about—thanks, Mother—and I had every right to scan the tree line like a paranoid Christmas elf.

As I slid my hand in Keir's once more, one of the valets twitched and turned toward the woods. "Okay. I heard it that time."

For a breath, all was still. Snow fell in lazy spirals, landing on shoulders and hair with soft whispers. Even the carolers had quieted.

Then, just beyond the tree line, a sound drifted through the snow—low and strange.

"There!" one of the valets said, moving off toward an approaching sleigh. "Was that...growling?"

"No worries, Windsor, love," Keir murmured against my ear, guiding me past the carolers who were launching into a decidedly off-key "Rudolph the Red-Nosed Reindeer."

Despite his assurance, a whisper of unease brushed my thoughts.

When I reached the doorway, I turned. Beyond the glowing lanterns and garland-strung archways, at the edge of the woods, a figure stood half in shadow beneath a snow-laden tree. Too tall for a child. Too still for comfort. The figure raised one hand, as if in greeting.

I blinked.

Gone.

Just trees. Just snow.

3

I shook it off and stepped inside, where warmth and light and the hum of celebration wrapped around me like a spell.

THE BALLROOM of Greywolf Manor shimmered with enchanted elegance. Tall arched windows framed in evergreen garlands and silver ribbon lined the walls, while chandeliers dripped with mistletoe and glowing icicles, casting a soft, icy glow over the room. Couples whirled across the marble floor, their gowns and tuxedos catching the light in glints of crimson, emerald, and saffron. Along the edges of the hall, ice sculptures—reindeer poised mid-leap, delicate snowflakes frozen in flight, twisting garlands of crystalline ivy—shifted imperceptibly, catching the light in ripples and sparkles. Miles Everhart and Moonlight & Brass's silver-toned rendition of "Moonlight Serenade" floated beneath the soaring ceiling, dreamy and romantic.

Keir slid the velvet wrap from my shoulders, handing it to the coat check attendant with a polite nod. Pyewacket, done with being held, launched from my arms and scampered off toward the massive Christmas tree, a tree sparkling from bottom to tip with enchanted pearls and old-world ornaments—glass birds, nutcrackers with jointed jaws, hand-painted baubles gleaming with tiny scenes of Darkly winters past. At the base, gift boxes wrapped in rich velvets and embossed gold foil encircled the tree in a dazzling display of holiday splendor.

I watched him go with a flicker of unease. Knowing Pye's track record with shiny objects, I could only hope the towering fir would still be upright by evening's end.

I looped my arm through Keir's and we made our way toward our table—prime real estate next to the dance floor. Chase, Ren, and Tzazi Strangeland, another very dear friend, had already settled in with a handsome man I didn't recognize, all of them cracking up at whatever outrageous thing Chase had just said.

Leave it to Tzazi to find the fun before I'd even had my first glass of champagne. The dhampir attorney had a talent for that.

Greywolf's ballroom was full of the people and characters of Darkly. I waved to Gertie Briar, the well-meaning elderly witch who lived above Hathaway & Strangeland law firm and spent most days leaning out her window to shout greetings, gossip, and commentary at everyone on Tataille Street below. Next to her sat our Mayor, Fernando Mayór, a full-blooded leprechaun, and his wife Lilith, an exotically beautiful axolotl demon. Fernando managed to make a lime-green velvet tuxedo with sequined lapels and a bow tie covered in tiny glittering Christmas trees look like the height of sophisticated elegance. At least in his own mind.

An elderly man with a shock of white hair sticking straight up like he'd been electrocuted stepped into our path. "Sir Keiren. Dr. Ebonwood." He nodded kindly to me and extended his hand. I felt Keir tense beside me at the formal title, but he shook the man's hand with practiced courtesy.

To his side stood three people, obviously important judging by the way others inclined their heads to the trio as they passed. A striking woman in her late thirties wore a sculptured black Dior gown, its geometric neckline and severe lines transforming elegance into something almost weaponized. Beside her stood an older man with piercing blue eyes and silver hair swept back from a face that spoke of effortless command. The kind of man who'd never needed to raise his voice to be heard. The third figure was austere in a way that made the others look warm by comparison, his mere presence creating a pocket of silence that rippled outward through the gala like a black jewel dropped in still water.

"Evening, Selvin," Keir said, his arm slipping around my waist, warm and reassuring.

Selvin gestured to his companions. "Allow me to introduce Alexander...er...excuse me, Lex Lavallette. And Eudora Quenleigh and her husband, Eliaz Quenleigh."

"A pleasure," Lex Lavallette said, his voice smooth as aged

whiskey. His smile was polished and warm in a way that somehow didn't quite reach those calculating blue eyes. When he extended his hand to me, I noticed the rings adorning his fingers. Dark stones glinted against precious metals.

"Lovely gala," Eudora murmured as she inclined her head with practiced elegance. Her hand rested lightly on her husband's arm, her expression pleasant but carefully neutral. The kind of face that revealed nothing and promised less. Up close, I could see the precise architecture of her makeup, the strategic positioning of each piece of jewelry. Everything about her looked like it had been selected with ruthless precision.

Eliaz Quenleigh said nothing at all, merely offering the slightest nod of acknowledgment. When he extended one slim, pale hand in greeting, I caught a glimpse of a small black signet ring on his finger—simple, understated, but somehow significant in its very plainness.

Seemed black rings were very much in style.

"Mr. Lavallette's company is quite remarkable," Selvin continued with the enthusiasm of someone determined to impress. "Lavallette Global is a Phantom 500 company. Wonderful work they're doing."

A server approached with a tray, and I caught Eliaz Quenleigh accepting a glass of champagne with a slight frown. He murmured something to the server and waved him off with one pale hand.

"You're too kind, Selvin," Lex said, though his tone suggested he agreed with the assessment.

"And Eliaz here serves as primarch of the Eldritch Council," Selvin added.

Keir's hand tightened almost imperceptibly at my waist. I felt the shift in his energy—a heightened awareness, like a wolf catching an unfamiliar scent.

When I glanced back at Eliaz, he was sipping from a glass of deep red wine.

Had the server come back? I must have missed it in the conversational shuffle.

"Current primarch," Lex Lavallette interjected smoothly. "Never forget, Selvin—I'm the past primarch of the Eldritch Council. The distinction matters."

His tone was pleasant, almost teasing, but something underneath it suggested the correction was anything but casual.

"Of course, of course," Selvin said quickly. "Well said, Lex."

"Are you enjoying your evening, Mrs. Quenleigh?" I asked, partly out of politeness and partly because I had no idea how to navigate whatever power play was unfolding.

"It's lovely," she said, her smile never quite reaching her eyes. "Though I understand this is your first major Darkly event, Ms. Ebonwood. You must find it all rather...overwhelming."

My eyebrows pulled together in a confused frown, though I couldn't quite suppress a flicker of amusement. Nothing like being patronized by a complete stranger to start the evening.

"Actually, I'm finding it quite captivating," I said, matching her pleasant tone. "So many interesting people—and such carefully curated company. One hardly knows where to look first."

"I—yes, well, curation is rather the point, isn't it?" Eudora said, her voice losing some of its polish. "One can't just...I mean, these relationships take time to..." She trailed off, then recovered with a stiff smile. "In any case."

Keir's thumb brushed against my hip as he gave me a wink.

"Indeed," Eliaz Quenleigh said, speaking for the first time. His voice was surprisingly soft but carried the weight of absolute certainty. "Captivating."

The single word somehow managed to sound like both agreement and dismissal.

"Windsor's a book conservator," Keir added, his Scottish burr more pronounced than usual. His tell when he was being deliberately charming to mask calculation or annoyance. Though I'd noticed it thickened under more pleasant circumstances too.

"She's been working miracles with some of the town's historical documents."

"How useful," Eudora said, her tone making it clear the word was anything but complimentary.

"Come now, *l'gamine*. The Eldritch Council maintains quite an extensive library," Lex said, those blue eyes studying me with renewed interest. "Perhaps you'd be interested in consulting sometime. We have several volumes in need of expert attention."

"I'd be honored," I said carefully.

"Excellent." Lex's smile widened fractionally. "I'll have my people reach out. It's always valuable to establish connections with talented newcomers to Darkly."

"Well, we mustn't monopolize your time any further," Selvin said, already beginning to edge away. "Enjoy your evening. Keir. Windsor."

The group continued on, leaving behind the faint scent of expensive cologne, designer perfume, and old money.

I looped my arm through Keir's as we moved toward our table.

"What exactly is a primarch?" I asked quietly. "And why is it so important to Lavallette?"

Keir's took a sip of his scotch. "The primarch commands the Eldritch Council—every magical law, every binding, every judgment in the Isles flows through him. Even the queen treads carefully around that seat."

I leaned in. "And Selvin. He's one of the town elders?"

Keir confirmed, voice low. "The longest-standing since Minta…"

"Died," I finished for him.

Minta Ebonwood—my grandmother. The lineage ran through her: the power, the responsibility, and the Magically Enchanted Travel shop (MET, for short, and now my responsibility). I barely knew her growing up. My dad had made sure of that, keeping me at arm's length from anything Ebonwood-related. My mother, Genevieve, left us when I was still small, slipping back to Darkly and into a world I'm only now beginning to understand. Since arriving on the island, I'd been piecing together her story—shards of truth buried under layers of rumor and grief. And the deeper I dug, the darker it got.

As Keir and I wove through the glittering ballroom toward our group's table, Tzazi intercepted us with a platinum-haired blur of excitement—unusual for someone who typically radiated nonchalant cool, even in a sleek black gown that left her rose-tattooed arms gloriously on display.

"Finally!" She grabbed my arm and tugged me toward a tall, athletic man in a perfectly tailored tuxedo. "Win, this is my baby brother, Zavier. He's home from the Isles for the holidays. Zav, this is Win Ebonwood."

Zavier's grin was instant and disarming, revealing just a hint of fang. His short dreadlocks were styled with the kind of effortless confidence that probably took considerable effort, and his deep brown eyes sparkled with the same mischief I'd seen in Tzazi—though his came with considerably less restraint.

"The famous Win." He clasped my hand warmly. "Tzazi won't shut up about you. It's either 'Win did this' or 'Win solved that' or 'Win's dating the alpha'—"

"I do not sound like that," Tzazi cut in, shoving his shoulder.

"You absolutely do." Zavier dodged her second swat and turned to clasp forearms with Keir in that distinctly masculine greeting. "Good to see you, Bane. Keeping the island in one piece?"

"Barely," Keir said with a warm chuckle. "How's the hexbee season treating you?"

"Three wins, no broken bones. I call that a success."

We made our way toward our table where Chase and Ren had already claimed seats, Chase resplendent in a burgundy velvet jacket, his hands gesturing wildly as he told some story that had Ren, dapper in his classic black tux, wiping tears of laughter from his eyes. Whatever the punchline was, we'd missed it, but Ren's quiet joy was infectious enough that I found myself smiling before we'd even sat down.

BANG!

The side doors leading to the sculpted gardens flew open. A blast of icy air swept through the ballroom, curling around ankles and lifting hems, chased by a tangle of teenagers half-screaming, half-scrambling over one another. They spilled inside in a whirlwind of heavy footsteps, shouting, and breathless panic.

"The Christmas witch! We saw her!"

Guests nearest the door let out startled gasps, clutching their pearls or drinks with wide eyes. One woman yelped as her champagne sloshed onto her satin dress. A waiter dropped a tray of macarons with a tragic crash.

Chase clutched his chest and staggered a half-step backward, eyes wide with mock horror. "Well, butter my biscuits and hang the stockings! We've got ourselves a holiday haunting!"

Ren rolled his eyes, and I laughed, giving Chase a slight nudge.

I looked around for Pyewacket and with relief found him beneath the Christmas tree, watching the hubbub with interest. Whatever was going on wasn't his doing. For once.

Reaching out instinctively, I caught the arm of a familiar figure stumbling past—Evon Frick, one of the teens who'd been caroling earlier. His curls were wild, his coat buttoned wrong over his gala clothes, and his bow tie hung askew. One of his dress shoes was missing entirely.

"Evon, what's going on?" I steadied him as he swayed.

He opened his mouth, but only a wheeze came out. His chest heaved as he struggled to catch his breath, eyes darting back toward the open doors.

Keir stepped forward and rested a calming hand on Evon's shoulder. "Breathe, aye? Yer not out there anymore. What'd yeh see, lad?"

Evon's eyes turned to Keir, wide and darting.

"The Christmas witch," he gasped. "I swear. She was in the garden. Near the Mab sculpture."

Chase stopped mid-sip, his cocktail glass frozen halfway to his lips. "Now, hold up there, *mon ami*." His piercing blue eyes locked onto Evon's face, reading the terror written there, the way his shoulders shook despite the warmth of the mansion. The humor drained from his features completely.

"Good gracious," he breathed. "You're not joking, are you, *chèr*?"

He glanced at Keir, who didn't speak, but the grim shift in his expression said enough.

Evon nodded, voice shaky. "Perchta," he whispered, like saying her name might summon her all over again. "I need to find Mom."

With that, the terrified teen bolted into the chaotic crowd.

I turned to Keir, keeping my voice low. "Christmas witch?"

We all settled into our seats.

He took a slow sip of his scotch, his eyes meeting mine over the rim, sharp and steady. "Aye. But probably not the kind you're imagining."

"No, she's not exactly known for her generosity," Ren added dryly.

Tzazi leaned in slightly. "But she *is* known for punishing the wicked by ripping them open and stuffing their bodies with straw and rocks. Super merry."

I shivered, thinking of the figure I had seen at the forest line. "And here I thought the Brothers Grimm were terrifying."

A gust of wind moaned through the cracked doors behind us, and for a beat, the scent of pine and cold earth curled through the warmth of champagne and vanilla. I didn't say anything else, but Evon's wide-eyed panic didn't feel so theatrical.

Keir reached for my hand. "Belleclaire's about somewhere. Likely just one o' the bairns pullin' a fast one, but...I'll be back in a tick."

He kissed my cheek, and I watched as he disappeared into the glittering crowd, swallowed by tuxedos, champagne flutes, and the low hum of nervous chatter.

But my thoughts lingered on Evon's face. That wide-eyed fear, the way his voice had caught on her name. That wasn't sugar panic or a teenager trying to stir up drama. That was real. And whether the figure in the garden had been cloaked in tattered skirts ruffling like feathers or a gala attendee wrapped in shadows and bad timing, something had scared those kids enough to burst into a ballroom full of donors, ice sculptures, and rosemary-tied pastries.

I turned back to the doors, still cracked open to the night. The music sputtered back to life, the band weaving a festive melody that felt just a shade too bright. Chandeliers cast their amber glow across the polished floor, but the laughter rippling through the crowd came in stutters. Quick and nervous, dying too fast.

Pyewacket leapt up onto a table beside me, ears angled toward the doors. "Someone's idea of festive mischief got out of hand."

"Or," I murmured, eyes trained on the dark stretch beyond the glass, "someone's out there who's not playing tricks at all."

I stepped away from the warmth and hum of the ballroom, toward the doors still bumping gently on their hinges in the wind, the cold slipping in like a warning.

Chase raised his champagne glass. "Darling, if you're about to go chasing witches, do take a beignet for the road. And if you disappear, just know I will throw you the most spectacular memorial service Darkly has ever seen. Open bar, naturally."

I SLIPPED out the side doors of Greywolf Manor's ballroom and onto a half-moon terrace. The concrete steps below led into a moon-drenched garden, the snow glowing pale and soft beneath the sky's silver gaze.

The terrace, however, looked like it had hosted a stampede. Snow was churned and trampled in a chaotic, haphazard trail.

Evidence of the teens' panicked charge back into the house. Shoe prints, scuffs, and something that looked suspiciously like a broken heel created a clear path from the tree line.

Behind me, the heavy doors creaked wider.

Pyewacket appeared, slipping through the doorway, gracefully leaping onto the concrete railing.

"We now arrive at the entertainment portion of the evening," he announced. "If you insist on getting murdered in the woods, at least I'll have a front row seat."

He launched himself neatly onto my shoulder, his tail coiling around the back of my neck like a living scarf.

I took a breath and flicked a snow barrier spell into place, the charm humming faintly around us. The temperature eased slightly—less biting, less brittle—and the sting of snow against skin dulled to a tolerable chill.

Then, carefully, I stepped off the patio and into the garden, following the path carved by fear and teenage footwear.

I followed along the trail and paused at the threshold, peering into the trees. The woods beyond were unnervingly still, the wind fading at their edge. I didn't dare go any farther.

Beside my neck, Pyewacket shifted and snorted softly. "Chicken."

"You know," I said, "you don't have to come. You could've stayed inside, pawing open the empty Christmas presents under the tree."

"You saw that, did you?" He had the audacity to look thoughtful rather than guilty. "Fascinating tradition, wrapping empty boxes. Is it meant to teach children about disappointment early, or is it simply poor planning?"

"Pye," I said, my voice a warning.

"Honestly, do collect yourself," he sniffed, each word clipped. "I've long been curious to meet Perchta. Cats, she practically venerates. Other witches?" He paused to lick one paw with infuriating nonchalance. "Barely tolerates, I'm afraid. Do try not to irritate her."

My jaw tightened. He was trying to poke at me, to get a rise, but his words lodged in the back of my mind all the same.

"Another word, and I'll charm that cute little bowtie to cling to your throat for the rest of your days."

He gulped and tapped his tail once against my shoulder.

"You wouldn't."

"Try me."

We moved forward, crossing into the trees. The garden path disappeared behind us in seconds. The deeper we went, the more the world changed. Sounds dulled. Light thinned.

Ahead, something darted across our path.

I stopped short.

A rabbit. Small, white, quick.

A few more yards, and we stepped into a small clearing. Moonlight filtered down, pale and harsh on the snow, turning the ground to glass. The air didn't move here. Even the trees surrounding the space seemed to lean inward, heavy with silence.

We stood still.

A crow swooped low over our heads, startling us.

Then—

"What's that?" Pyewacket whispered.

"Where?"

He raised a paw, pointing toward the edge of the clearing.

I followed his gaze.

There, in the snow near the tree line, was a single, deep indentation.

We approached slowly. The print was large, oddly shaped. A wide Y. Three toes splayed outward in a fan, with a smaller mark behind it, like a heel or weight press. There was a faint drag line curling through the snow, connecting the toes in an uneven arc.

I crouched to get a better look.

"That's not a shoe print," I said.

"Brilliant deduction," Pyewacket murmured. "You have an incredible ability to notice even the smallest details."

I rose to my feet, heart ticking faster now, gaze scanning the clearing and the trees beyond.

"It's definitely not rabbit," Pyewacket said, voice a touch tighter now.

After a few moments of silence, we turned back to the print.

"Turkey?" Pye asked, squinting at the print with his one eye.

"Nay. That'd be goose," a deep voice rumbled behind us.

I jumped. Pyewacket squealed.

I spun around.

"Keir!"

I smacked his chest. "You nearly gave me a heart attack."

Keir grinned, entirely too pleased with himself. "Chase said yeh'd gone out witch hunting."

"More like teen-terror investigating," I said.

He nodded and moved past me toward the odd track in the snow, crouching down with the ease of someone born to woods and wild things. He sniffed the air, his gaze roaming the edges of the clearing, reading a language I couldn't decipher.

"So this is a goose print. Just the one?" I asked, standing beside him. "Are you trying to tell me a one-legged goose hopped through the forest and scared a bunch of teenagers into a dramatic ballroom entrance?"

Keir looked up at me, lips twitching.

"Tell me," I demanded.

"It's definitely a goose print," he said. "But not just any."

I raised a brow.

He stood and dusted snow from his hands. "Perchta's been known to leave a goose footprint behind."

I blinked at him. "You're kidding."

"She's no' dangerous," Keir added, glancing around the clearing. "At least, no' anymore. She's mellowed, she has. Comes through Darkly near every winter. Doesnae bother anyone."

"No deaths by straw stuffing?" I asked.

He took a step toward me, expression softening. "Not a single one."

His smile warmed the chill from my cheeks. It was unfair, really. How quickly he could shift the mood just by existing.

I folded my arms but couldn't quite hide my grin. "So you came out here just to check on me?"

"Yeh've a habit of driftin' further than's safe. Came to keep an eye, is all."

"You know me. Always walking the line between curiosity and poor judgment."

He stepped in close, brushing a stray curl from my face. "Next time yeh go chasing legends, give us five ticks so I can come with yeh."

Pyewacket groaned and jumped to the ground. "Unbelievable. You two are one flirt away from writing poetry in the snow."

Keir leaned just a little closer. "At least you brought backup."

I glanced down at Pyewacket, who licked a paw and carefully ran it over the fur on his face. "Technically."

Keir chuckled and tilted his head toward the path ahead. "Come on, then. Even if Perchta's still around, she won't mind us."

I wasn't sure what we'd find deeper in the woods but with Keir beside me, the dark didn't feel quite so heavy anymore.

A sudden snap echoed through the trees. Keir's smile dropped. His head turned sharply toward the sound.

"Stay here," he said, his voice low and clipped.

He moved deeper into the forest, each step deliberate and silent. Naturally, I followed.

I did my best to match his stride, but the forest floor had other plans and none of them involved keeping me upright. A branch snagged my shoe and I stumbled. Keir glanced back with a frown, steadying me with one hand. I gave him a sheepish wave as Pyewacket launched himself back onto my shoulder.

Another rustle. Then a sharper crack, then a rush of movement to our right.

Keir whipped round and moved to my side, his body tense, movements silent.

I froze. My breath caught. I couldn't pinpoint the source. The trees all looked the same. Trunks, shadows, bark. No path. No landmarks. Just depth. I could see how people got lost out here. How they disappeared.

Then I spotted it.

A footprint pressed into the snow. Another print lay further ahead. Wait, was that a—?

I shook my head. I must've been seeing things. My imagination running wild in the eerie quiet.

I forced my attention back to the closer track, my breath misting in the frigid air.

Not goose, the pads too distinct.

Wolf.

I turned to Keir. His expression was dark now, all amusement gone, jaw clenched as he sniffed the air again.

I tried to do the same but caught nothing beyond cold leaves and wet bark.

"You're so cute," Pyewacket muttered against my ear. "Really trying."

"Quiet," I hissed.

Keir's hand found the small of my back, firm and insistent, steering me back the way we'd come.

"Move," he said quietly.

"What's wrong?" I quickened my steps to match his suddenly urgent stride.

"You said Perchta doesn't hurt anyone."

"She doesn't."

"Then what—?"

"Rougarou," he said, eyes still scanning the dark, his head tilted to the side as he communicated with his pack. "Pick up the pace, love."

My breath hitched.

Pyewacket let out a strangled squeak and dug his claws into my shoulder. "Move, Win! I am entirely too charming and debonair to be digested by anything smelly and drooling."

Rougarou. The cursed ones. I'd heard the recent whispers. Stories of them creeping too close to town, pacing the edge of properties, getting bolder.

When we broke through the tree line and hit the edge of Greywolf's grounds, I nearly stumbled in the sudden openness. The manor glowed like a beacon in the night, windowpanes lit, laughter still floating faintly from inside.

On the terrace, Ava Nguyen and Pup Bane stood waiting. Silverfang Enforcers. Deadliest members of Keir's shifter clan, the Silverfangs. Ava's deep blue evening gown didn't dull her intensity one bit. Pup's tuxedo looked like it might rip at the seams if he took a single step forward.

Keir tilted his head, sharp and wordless.

Both of them leapt from the patio without hesitation, landing in the snow and shifting mid-stride. Fur replaced fabric. Bones cracked. Limbs lengthened. Within seconds, they were gone. Black shapes tearing through the forest with perfect, terrifying grace.

From the front of the house, another wolf approached. Larger. Slower. Measured. He met Keir's gaze, gave a single nod, and then vanished into the trees after the others.

We stepped onto the porch. My pulse hadn't slowed yet. I dropped the snow-barrier charm from Pyewacket and myself. My breath came in short, clouded puffs. I turned to Keir and let out a nervous giggle.

He was covered in leaf litter, his tuxedo soaked from the knees down, dirt smudged across his shoulder and collar. His bow tie hung limply to the side.

I lifted an eyebrow and flicked a little magic toward the disaster that was his formalwear.

He looked down at himself, then back up at me with a grin. "Aye. Thanks, lass."

His hand found mine, our fingers locking as we stepped back inside. The warmth of the manor hit us like a soft wave. Music drifting in, laughter rising again from the ballroom.

Keir guided me around the edge of the dance floor, past

couples who held each other just a little tighter than before. We slipped into our seats, and I let out a breath I hadn't realized I'd been holding.

Keir leaned toward me, elbows on knees. "Rougarous aren't like Silverfangs," he said softly. "Rougarous are cursed. They don't shift at will; they're driven by impulse. Hunger. Fear."

"The ones who can't control themselves," I said quietly.

"Aye," Keir confirmed. "And this one's venturing a little too close."

A sudden loud guffaw caused us both to turn abruptly.

CHAPTER 2

*N*ext to us, a greasy man in a cheap suit held court at a table loaded with overfilled wineglasses, loudly spouting tales that drew more stares than laughs. The sharp click of heels striking marble cut through his braying, and a woman strode from the opposite side of the ballroom. Her velvet wrap snapped behind her, earrings sharp as drawn steel. Every eye followed her as she glided to his side, and even the braggart, mid-story, faltered.

"Well, if it isn't the pawn scum slash real estate leech himself, Michey Lowlife Stramm," the woman said, voice syrup-slick and heavy with disdain.

Michey didn't stand but he grinned up at her through silver hair with a face smug enough to deserve its own slapping rotation.

"Miss Mari DeLongpre," he said, words loud and slurred, drawing attention. "You clean up nice for someone still cryin' over a cottage."

"You stole our family's land."

"Papers were signed. Your grandpapa didn't know the first thing about contract negotiations. Not my fault he left his reading glasses in the truck."

"That's not what happened and you know it!"

She jabbed a finger in his toady face. "He couldn't read the contract because you spelled it to blur the ink."

Michey lifted his wineglass in mock salute. "Guess that's one lesson in legacy magic your folks forgot to pass down."

The table chuckled. One man choked on a canapé and lowered his face.

Mari's jaw tightened. Her eyes scanned the faces around the table, all of them pretending not to enjoy the show.

"You may sleep under its roof," she said, smiling without warmth, "but peace won't follow you through the door."

"Don't worry, doll, I sleep fine. Big feather bed. Views of your grandmother's oak tree with the rope swing. Real peaceful."

Mari didn't respond. She turned, cloak billowing as she stalked away.

She reached her own table, grabbed her clutch, and slipped out a wand, slender and polished like a piece of carved bone. She turned her head ever so slightly, pointed it low across the room, and mouthed a string of words that shimmered through the air so faintly they looked like heat rising off pavement.

My apprehension rose.

At the table next to us, Michey laughed at his own joke and nearly spilled crab dip into his lap. His shoulders shook with glee as he slapped the man next to him on the back.

I blinked. The man looked perfectly fine—flushed from drink, absurdly loud, and proud of whatever nonsense he'd just spouted.

Mari tucked the wand back into her wrap like nothing had happened, then picked up her wineglass and took a long sip, eyes glittering with mirth behind the rim.

Keir paused, raising a finger and canting his head slightly, his eyes distant.

Then he exhaled. "Ava, Pup, and Skoll picked up the scent of the rougarou. It circled around to the trees on the opposite side of the house. It's gone now."

Then he grinned—and just like that, my legs nearly gave out. That damn smirk.

"Forget the rougarou," he murmured. "It won't be back tonight. Let's enjoy ourselves."

A full-figured woman in a black sequin gown stepped to the front of the bandstand and took the mic in her gloved hands. Her voice, smoky, slow, and full of longing, rolled through the room as she began a haunting rendition of Billie Holiday's "I'll Be Seeing You."

Keir drew me onto the dance floor with a firm hand at my waist. Around us, the gala blurred into candlelight and shimmer. The band softened, the saxophone stretching each note like a memory, and Keir moved in time with it. Confident, grounded, steady.

Despite Keir's reassurances, I couldn't shake the sense of foreboding. I felt for my charm again, my instincts prickling like someone had tucked a warning spell under my skin.

As THE FINAL note lingered in the air, the room held still for half a breath. Then the horns picked up with a bright, familiar blast, and "In the Mood" swelled to life beneath a ripple of applause as waitstaff in crisp black and white began directing guests toward the candlelit tables. Keir didn't let go immediately. His hand stayed at my back a moment longer, thumb brushing once before he pulled away with a smile that made my pulse trip.

He offered his arm, and I tucked my hand into the crook of Keir's elbow as we made our way back to our table.

I slid into my seat beside Tzazi, who leaned close to her brother, both of them bent together in laughter over some whispered joke.

"Win! Keir!" Jessamin Wilde, owner of Grewolf Manor and proprietor of the Green Gator Tavern and another best friend, swept up to the table with her date, Jaime Mayór. She hugged me as her eyes roamed around the table and landed on Tzazi's brother.

"ZAVIER!" She lunged forward to wrap him in a hug, and he laughed, returning it with the warmth of someone who'd known her since childhood.

The mayor along with his wife Lilith sauntered up to our table. Lilith's cranberry red satin ball gown showed off her voluptuous curves and shiny black hair beautifully.

"Wonderful party, Jessamin," Fernando said, with a wink at his son.

He took a sip of champagne as his wife leaned in.

"It is exceptionally glamorous," she said with a smile.

"I agree," I said as Lilith and I exchanged cheek kisses.

Suddenly Michey Stramm pushed Lilith to the side and stuck his hand in Fernando's face. I reached out to stop her from falling as she turned a dagger stare in Michey's direction.

After a slight hesitation, the mayor accepted Michey's hand, shook it once, and then wiped the hand on his velvet trousers.

During the evening, Michey's vest had become unbuttoned and he was now visibly fighting to keep his jacket closed over a very large protruding belly. His face was flushed, sweaty, and smug.

"Mayor Mayór," Michey slurred with a too-wide grin, "Your gonna love this. Gonna love it. Just picture this." He raised his hands, pantomiming a screen. "Waterfront. Classy. Discreet. High-end gator-view suites, private boardwalk, maybe a boutique haunted hammam…"

His expression twitched like his mouth suddenly got ideas of its own. "I've always had a crush on you."

The words dropped like cannon fire.

I covered my mouth with my hand to halt the release of a surprise expletive. Keir didn't hold back and laughed loudly next to me.

Fernando blinked. "Pardon?"

"I mean—" Michey's face flushed crimson as he struggled to

regain control. "The profit margins—I have feelings for you—NO! The investment opportunity—"

Mayor Mayór lifted one eyebrow, his sharp green eyes gleaming with barely concealed amusement behind his tiny gold glasses. "How...unexpected, Mr. Stramm."

"You're so handsome," Michey blurted, his eyes widening in horror. "I can't stop thinking about—" He slapped a hand over his mouth, his face now the color of a fire engine.

His belly gave a loud, ominous gurgle.

Then a button shot off his straining vest like a tiny missile, pinged across the space and struck someone's champagne flute with a perfect crystal *ting*.

Across the room, Mari grinned wider.

"Good heavens, I haven't seen this much public unraveling since a poltergeist wreaked havoc at Gumbo Fest," Chase murmured, fanning himself with a canapé plate. "This is better than vaudeville."

As Michey turned, red-faced, and stomped back to his seat, Jess stood, pushing back a laugh and smoothing her gown with a practiced hand. "Well. Time to get this show on the road," she said with a quick smile.

She wove her way to the front of the room, her shimmering emerald gown resplendent against her bright red hair. She climbed the steps to the stage with the poise of someone who'd done it a hundred times before. Miles Everhart and Moonlight & Brass lowered their instruments in respectful silence as she turned toward the mic, the room dimming slightly as the chandeliers shifted to a cool, soft glow.

Jess looked out over the audience, not speaking right away, letting the hush settle. Then she smiled, and her voice rang clear across the room. "It's my honor tonight to introduce someone who has helped shape the minds—and occasionally test the humility—of some of the brightest magical youth in the Charming Isles," Jess said, her smile tugging a few knowing chuckles from the room.

"A scholar, a disciplinarian, and a man who once turned an entire dormitory invisible for a week just to prove a point about 'unseen consequences,' please join me in welcoming the Headmaster of Wentworth Academy, Dr. Landravedon Truegaze."

A ripple of polite applause moved through the room as a tall man in formal evening wear ascended the stage with measured steps. He shook Jess's hand with courteous restraint, then faced the crowd with quiet authority.

Pyewacket hopped into my lap for a better view of the stage.

Jess returned to our table just as Headmaster Truegaze cleared his throat. "Good evening," he began, his voice crisp and formal. "It is a rare privilege to address such an—"

His words broke off, gaze snapping to the ballroom entrance. His pale gray eyes widened, not with anger or annoyance, but something closer to disbelief.

A collective gasp swept through the crowd as heads turned.

Alone in the grand entrance stood a tall man dressed in a black tuxedo so sharp it looked etched against the ballroom's soft glow. His presence rippled through the room like a struck bell, freezing conversation mid-sentence. Glasses hovered, forgotten, in midair. Somewhere behind us, a plate crashed to the floor.

"Hey, Arty! Over here!" Stramm pushed his chair back noisily and rose, swaying slightly, waving his hands ridiculously over his head.

The man he'd called Arty didn't move as he pointedly ignored Stramm, gazing out over the seated crowd, a tight smile on his face.

Tzazi shot to her feet, her chair scraping sharply against the marble, and very nearly sprinted across the room. She threw her arms around the man with a cry that broke the stunned silence.

At our table, Jess stared, her face frozen in shock. "You've got to be kidding me," she muttered, her voice low and tight.

I turned, scanning the faces around me. Jess, Keir, Chase, Ren, Jaime, even Zavier—each one locked in the same stunned silence, caught between disbelief and something that felt dangerously close to awe.

I could hear Stramm mumbling incoherently at his table next to us.

What in the bayou blazes was going on?

As the energy in the room shifted back to the stage, Tzazi tucked her arm through the man's and steered him toward our table. Her smile was wide, almost too bright, as if she hoped it would resonate with everyone seated there, and it only made my confusion knot tighter.

"Win," she said, voice light but a little rushed. "I'd like to introduce you to my old Wentworth pal, Arthur Vanderholt. Arthur, this is Windsor Ebonwood."

The man—Arthur—inclined his head slightly. "Good evening, Windsor."

I offered my hand. His handshake was firm, but there was a tension in the way his fingers tightened briefly around mine before letting go.

"Nice to meet you," I said, keeping my voice steady even as the silence at the table pressed in.

No one else moved. The stillness was sharp, unnatural. Stramm's mumbling becoming louder, more obnoxious.

Finally, Keir rose, jaw tight, and shook Arthur's hand. "Good tae see you, Arthur. It's been a while."

"Bane." Arthur gave a smile, but it strained at the edges, too careful to be easy.

A fog of cheap cologne hit me before Michey Stramm swayed into view. "Well, well, well," he said, resting his hand on the back of my chair. I shifted forward, putting distance between us.

Stramm took a long drink of champagne, his eyes steady on Arthur. "Too good for the likes of me now, huh, Arty? You didn't think so at the Academy." He then literally swayed in place, laughing loudly, drawing attention from the neighboring tables.

Both Keir and Chase stood.

"C'mon, mate. Let's head back to yer table," Keir said, as he and Chase escorted Stramm away. He popped another button as he plopped down in his chair.

I saw Chase's mouth moving, hopefully spelling Michey to remain in his seat until he calmed down.

Pyewacket hopped into Tzazi's empty seat, his golden eye fixed on Michey with the kind of hard, measuring stare he usually reserved for people about to receive a claw or two.

Keir and Chase had just returned to their seats when Zavier shot up from his chair, fists clenched at his sides, his face dark with fury and disbelief. When he spoke, his voice was low and sharp enough to slice through steel.

"How dare you, Vanderholt."

The table snapped into a tense stillness once again.

"How dare you come back here." His voice was low, threatening.

Tzazi whipped her head toward him, her voice a harsh whisper. "Zavier!"

But Arthur just raised a hand, a flick of dismissal. "It's okay, Tzazi," he said, as if he'd expected this reaction. He turned back to us, his voice smooth but the tightness around his mouth betraying him. "Good to see y'all. Nice to meet you, Windsor."

Without waiting for another word, Arthur lifted two fingers to catch the attention of a nearby hostess. She approached quickly, and after a murmured exchange, escorted him to his table.

Arthur seemed like a perfectly nice man. Yet ever since the man arrived, almost everyone in this room looked like they wanted to rearrange his face.

Waiters moved through the room, setting plates before each guest as Headmaster Truegaze continued speaking from the stage, his voice smooth and deliberate as he listed Wentworth Academy's many accomplishments and thanked the attendees for their generosity. At our table, no one was listening.

A tight current had settled over us. Tzazi kept shooting sharp, silent glances toward Zavier, who was studiously pretending she didn't exist. Jess, in turn, kept her eyes on Tzazi, each look a degree cooler than the last. The rest of us had turned our attention to our plates, forks clinking in practiced distraction.

But all around us—whispers. Sharp breaths. Gasps. Fragments drifted past: *Arthur...decency...the nerve...* But more and more, the murmurs carried a different name.

Perchta.

~

AFTER TRUEGAZE'S PRESENTATION CONCLUDED, light conversation resumed at our table, though tension still hummed beneath the surface.

Tal Prescott, liaison officer for the Silverfangs, clapped Keir on the shoulder in greeting.

"Tal!" Keir stood and pulled him into one of those brief, back-slapping hugs men do.

Tal's gaze swept the table, brightening the moment it landed on Jess—but before he could even offer a smile, Jaime materialized at her side with eager energy.

"Care to dance?" Jaime was already reaching for her hand, the question more formality than request.

Jess blinked, startled, but let him sweep her onto the dance floor with a surprised laugh. Behind them, Tal watched them go, his half-formed smile fading. Then he straightened his jacket, squared his shoulders, and disappeared into the crowd like he'd never been heading her way at all.

Keir reached for me, his hand warm and sure. "Yeh care to show 'em how it's done, love?"

I smiled and slid my arm into the crook of his elbow.

The music wrapped around us as we stepped onto the dance floor. Keir spun me into his arms with an easy, practiced grace. His hand settled firm at the small of my back, guiding me through the first few steps before pulling me closer.

I hooked my arms around his neck, feeling the steady beat of his heartbeat against mine.

"I never figured you for a dancer," I teased, breathless.

Keir gave me a mock scowl. "Yeh think we just trot around in the woods all day?"

"You do kinda give off that vibe," I said, smirking up at him.

He huffed and twirled me again just to prove a point, sending my gown swishing around my legs.

"Rhythm's in the blood, sweetheart," he said, voice low, smug. His hand slipped a little lower on my back.

It felt perfect to be right there, tucked against him while the rest of the world blurred away. Music swelled around us, bright and golden, the room alive with laughter and the tap of shoes on the polished floor.

Keir pulled me in tighter and we danced for a few more slow turns, the music soft around us, the lights catching little glints off the decorations overhead. As we moved, I noticed the smiles that followed us, quiet nods of approval and small, knowing looks from the people we passed.

And, for once, I didn't mind their stares.

WHEN DUKE ELLINGTON'S "Prelude to a Kiss" floated up from the band, Keir caught my hand and led me toward the bar. We lifted two glasses of champagne off a tray, then wound our way back to our table, the festive night pressing on around us in a haze of laughter, music, and gold light.

A blur of iridescent wings whizzed past us. I turned just in time to see Dianthe Petalsigh, the pixie who owned Oopsie Daisies flower shop, darting across the ballroom at eye level, her delicate wings blurred with speed. Her normally gentle face was twisted with fury. The raw anger radiating from someone so typically shy stopped me cold.

I followed her movement through the ballroom until the crowd swallowed her whole.

"It's warm in here." I lifted my champagne glass, determined to focus on something normal. "All that dancing."

"Not enough dancing, I'd say." Keir leaned back in his chair, one ankle crossed over his knee.

"You've got stamina I can only dream of."

His mouth curved. "Aye, I've been told that before." He caught my hand, turning it palm-up before pressing his lips to my wrist. His thumb traced a slow circle against my pulse point. "Though I suspect yeh could keep up if properly motivated."

Heat bloomed under my skin, as Keir leaned over and kissed the tip of my nose, his smile brushing warm against the cool air between us.

He ran his thumb along my arm. "Come with me to the terrace."

Before we reached the doors, Keir shrugged out of his jacket and draped it over my shoulders with a wink. The warmth of it sank into my skin, still carrying the faint, wild scent of him.

He pushed open the door and a gust of cold air tumbled inside, rattling a few glasses on the nearest tables.

I stepped forward—and my foot bumped into something solid.

Keir caught me around the waist before I could stumble.

"What is it?" he asked sharply.

In the middle of the concrete terrace, lightly covered in the new-fallen snow, lay Michey Stramm.

A scream tore through the night.

The sound snapped the crowd into silence just as the Darkly bells began to toll.

CHAPTER 3

*H*ands clamped down around my arm, and I struggled to free myself until I realized it was Jess. She let out a second, more guttural scream as the bells continued to toll—those dismal, cursed chimes that reverberated straight through bone. The crowd shuddered beneath the sound, everyone shrinking into themselves, unsure whether to run or freeze.

"Shh, shh, shh," I said, patting Jess's arm while gently prying her fingers loose. "Stay here."

She didn't respond, just clutched her chest and stared with wide, unblinking eyes. I stepped closer to the body alongside Keir.

Pye leaped onto my shoulder and gazed down at the scene. "Not all that terribly shocking, I must say."

Michey Stramm's lips were tinted a deep, ugly shade of blue. His eyes—bulging and open, tiny red dots speckling the whites—locked on something no longer there. Surprise? Fear? A bit of both.

His mouth was crammed with stones and brittle straw. White, downy feathers lay around his head like a broken halo, eerie against the frost-slick terrace stones. Across the snow-dusted ground, silver coins glinted coldly

A woman in a soft mauve gown beautifully flowing over her round figure suddenly pushed through the crowd, her light brown hair escaping from its low twist. She stopped short when she saw the body, one hand flying to her mouth.

For a heartbeat, she simply stared—her expressive brown eyes going impossibly wide, the color draining from her warm, round face until she looked almost gray in the lamplight.

But it wasn't just horror that twisted her expression. It was recognition. And with it, a bone-deep fear.

Her gaze darted from the body to the crowd, then back again, her free hand clutching at the fabric of her modest gown as if anchoring herself to reality.

I started toward her, concern overriding everything else.

But she was already moving, spinning on her heel with surprising speed for someone who looked like she might collapse. She disappeared into the glittering throng of ball gowns and tuxedos, swallowed by the crowd before I could even finish forming the question on my lips.

I stared after her, my skin prickling with unease. That woman hadn't just been shocked by Michey's death.

She'd been terrified of what it meant.

Keir dropped to his knees beside the body, face grim. He pressed two fingers to Michey's wrist and gave a faint shake of his head.

"Ava," he said, voice low. "Belleclaire."

The Silverfang Enforcer I hadn't even noticed next to me moved without a word, melding into the stunned crowd.

Behind me, the hush fractured. Gasps and murmurs shivered through sequined gowns and tailored coats. People surged forward and then shrank back just as quickly, repelled by what they saw.

Gertie Briar elbowed her way through and halted with a strangled gasp.

"Frau Perchta..." she breathed, eyes enormous behind her rhinestone-studded glasses. Then, to the wide-eyed man beside her, she said louder, voice quaking, "It's Frau Perchta! She's here!"

She spun around, nearly toppling over in her heeled boots, and bolted back into the ballroom. A crowd of rustling taffeta and expensive suits pushed up behind me.

"Gertie!" I called after her. "Wait!"

Too late. The scent of patchouli and the rustle of skirts trailed after her as she disappeared.

Frantic whispers spilled across the terrace and bled into the ballroom, words twisting with each retelling like a game of deadly telephone.

The air left my lungs with a whoosh. Ransom Belleclaire, Darkly's royal inspector, and Boddy Grim, our coroner appeared on the terrace.

"Back into the ballroom," Boddy said, his voice gliding over the chaos like a scalpel.

The crowd obeyed, one uneasy step at a time. I stayed rooted.

Boddy Grim's unnerving red eyes found me. They flickered with that unreadable look of his. Normally this would be the part where he accused me of yet another murder. After all, I did have an unfortunate habit of stumbling over bodies.

But tonight, he didn't say a word to me.

Instead, he turned to Michey.

"How long's he been dead?" Ransom Belleclaire asked, stepping up beside Boddy. His tailored coat had a fresh dusting of snow on the shoulders, and his eyes lingered on me a beat too long.

"I just saw him," I stammered. "Not fifteen minutes ago."

Keir, still crouched, gave my hand a squeeze before rising and sweeping the terrace with a sharp, protective glance. I could practically feel him reaching out with his senses, trying to catch the tail end of whoever—or whatever—had done this.

"What's happened?" Tzazi stormed through the doors and on to the terrace. Her voice rang with steel.

She froze as she saw the body. Her features tightened.

"Good goddess. So that's why everyone's whispering about Perchta," she murmured.

Boddy's head canted slightly, bones clicking with the movement. He regarded her the way a crow regards a viper.

"Miss Strangeland."

"Bodderick." She didn't flinch, just dipped her head in return.

I always got the feeling he was half-terrified of her, though he'd never admit it. Frankly, I didn't blame him.

Ransom cleared his throat.

"Time of death was nine minutes ago," Boddy said crisply, as though that would make any of this feel procedural. Normal.

Boddy rose, his joints giving an eerie creak. As a former grim reaper, Boddy didn't need instruments or tests—he just knew. Grim reapers could tell when and how someone died, but not who helped them along.

"You discovered Michey out here?" Ransom directed that question at me.

I let out a sigh. "I...actually Keir and I stumbled over him on our way out to the terrace."

He canted his head, examining me with those light blue elven eyes of his.

"Did you see anyone?"

I thought about it for a second. "No. Although my eyes were on Michey, to be honest. I didn't think to look around."

His eyes traveled over the expansive back lawn and its array of footprints as Keir jogged back up the steps, brushing frost off his sleeves. I flicked a drying spell his way to clean him up.

"Thank you, love," he murmured, his voice barely a breath.

"What'd you find out there, Bane?" Ransom asked, their voices fading as the men moved to the other side of the terrace.

A murder of crows perched in the bare branches of a snow-dusted oak, their black bodies stark against the white like macabre Christmas ornaments. One tilted its head, releasing a soft caw that sounded almost like a warning.

"Charming," Tzazi said dryly, her breath misting in the cold air. "Nothing says 'crime scene' like an audience of corvids."

Keir, Ransom, and Boddy were deep in tight conversation, voices low enough that none of them noticed as I caught Tzazi's elbow and steered her back through the doorway.

Jess stood just beyond the threshold, her wings trembling faintly—not the usual shimmer of fairy magic, but the fine vibration of barely controlled panic.

I put an arm around Jess and began leading her through the mass clustered at the garden doors. Tzazi shadowed us—close enough to help if needed, far enough to give space.

By the time we reached the doors to the drawing room, Pyewacket had appeared from wherever he'd been lurking. He wove between my feet with feline precision, then miscalculated and stepped squarely on the hem of my gown.

I stumbled. Caught myself.

Jess never broke stride. One hand pressed against the hollow of her throat, her breathing shallow and quick. She hadn't looked back at Tzazi once.

BEFORE I COULD FOLLOW them through the massive double doors of Greywolf Manor's drawing room, Keir pulled me aside, the muffled din of fear and confusion still pulsing behind us. He tilted my chin, forcing my eyes to meet his.

His gaze anchored me. Steady. Fierce. Warm.

"Yeh okay, love?" His voice dropped low, but it still cut through the noise with ease.

I nodded once. My throat was tight. Words would've snapped whatever thread I was hanging from.

He studied me for a heartbeat longer, jaw clenched, then brushed his lips across mine. It wasn't showy. Just enough to hold me together.

"Stay in here. Until I return." He paused for a moment. "Please, love."

Then he turned, shoulders already braced for whatever storm waited in that ballroom and vanished into the crowd.

Placing my hand on the doorknob, I pushed the door open and did a silent headcount as I surveyed the room.

Jess had settled stiffly beside Jaime. His hand rested on her arm, the smallest attempt at comfort. Tzazi perched in the window seat, a brandy glass clutched to her chest.

The opposite sofa from Jess and Jaime held three of my grandmother's closest friends. Maybelle and Dewey Hathaway occupied one end, their shoulders touching in that comfortable way of long-married couples, while Conny Verity settled into the other corner. In the high-backed rocker near the fireplace sat Hildegard Orso, Fernwood's longtime guardian and the closest thing to a mother I'd had since—well, ever. Her knitting needles clicked a steady rhythm, and I couldn't begin to guess where she'd produced that project from. Beside her, my great-aunt Sibella gnawed thoughtfully on her unlit pipe, eyes narrowed, surveying the room and everyone in it.

I caught Hilde's eye.

"You all right, honey?" Her voice was both gruff and warm, a comforting blanket amidst the rising tension.

"Or should we go ahead and summon the emergency flask and a salt circle?" Sibby added brusquely.

An emergency flask sounded just right.

As she rocked, Hilde's barely-contained energy pulsed, as if she might transform into her bear form at any moment.

I crossed the rug, my legs heavier than they ought to be, and sank into the damask chair closest to Sibby. Between us sat a drinks cart—crystal decanters, silver tongs, and an array of bottles. Definitely Sibby's doing.

"Where's Zavier?" I asked.

Sibby passed me a glass without a word, poured stiff and neat.

Pipe between her teeth, she finally muttered, "Left early."

I gripped the glass tighter. "What does everyone know that I don't?"

Silence settled over the room like a dropped sheet. Thick. Suffocating. Even Hilde's needles had stopped their clicking.

The only sounds were the wind scraping across the roof and the rhythmic tick of the mantle clock, counting down to something we couldn't see yet but all felt coming.

Dewey exhaled slowly, the sound drawn out and heavy. "Undoubtedly Simone Petalsigh."

"Petalsigh?" I asked. "Any relation to Dianthe?"

"Cousins," Conny said, her lips pressed into a tight, bitter line.

My mind slipped back to Dianthe zipping across the room right before all hell broke loose.

I frowned, trying to piece it together. "If you're saying Zavier and Michey fought over the same woman, I don't see it."

Across the room, Chase reached for the decanter and topped off his bourbon with a splash.

"Let me tell you a story about the darker side of our quaint little island. The side everyone avoids mentioning."

He settled back on the sofa, one leg crossed, the picture of ease —but the shift in the room was immediate.

"You already know Mason ran with a bad crowd back when he was at the Academy with Tzazi and Jess."

Ah, yes. Mason Beckworth. Tzazi's ex, presumably my half-sister Elspeth's former lover, and the lawyer who'd sued Jess on Elspeth's behalf. A necromancer with sharp cheekbones and sharper instincts, all devil-may-care charm wrapped around a dangerous core. He looked like trouble because he was trouble—the kind that apparently started back at the Academy.

"And he wasn't even the worst of them," Jess said softly, dabbing her eyes with a delicate handkerchief. A single stitched "W" winked at me from the corner.

"That would've been Arthur Vanderholt," she added pointedly.

"Arthur?" I blinked. "The man I met tonight?"

Sibby removed the pipe from her mouth and scoffed. "Known as Party Arty back then."

"Seriously?" I almost laughed, but the look on their faces cut that short. Stone silence. No one else even cracked a smile.

Well. That explained the drop in temperature the moment he walked in.

"Jess, that's not fair." Tzazi finally spoke up from her seat at the window. "We don't know what happened."

"Don't we?" Jess countered, her voice cold.

Tzazi turned to see us all staring at her. With a shake of her head, she strode out of the room, slamming the door behind her.

I stood to run out after her when Chase's words stopped me cold.

"His partying was the least of it," Chase went on. "Arthur and his crew were the kind of bullies who didn't just push buttons—they crushed them. Picked on anyone they thought was weak."

I eased back into my seat. "That couldn't include Zavier."

I knew Tzazi's brother had been a star hexbee player since he was barely out of diapers. No way bully cowards would've dared to go after him.

I took a gulp of bourbon, relishing the shock of heat as the rest of my body felt close to numb.

"Not Zavier," Chase said. "Simone."

"Such a sweet and quiet girl," Maybelle murmured from her place near the fire. "Wouldn't hurt a fly."

"And a brilliant sculptor," Conny added. "I have one of her pieces. Keeps watch over my sunroom."

"Exactly the kind of person they'd zero in on," I muttered.

"Exactly." Jess's voice cracked on that one word, her face blotched red and streaked with tears.

Jaime watched her, concern etched deep on his face. She wouldn't meet his eyes. She truly needed to have a conversation with him. The longer she waited, the harder it would be for him.

Chase tapped the rim of his glass. "One night the island

experienced one of the worst snowstorms in its history. Simone was found the next morning outside her dorm. Frozen."

The room stilled again.

"There is some debate over why she didn't just go back inside."

The air was yanked from my lungs.

"No."

Chase nodded once. "Those cursed bells rang for sixteen days. One day for each year Simone lived."

That stopped me short. How horrific for the entire town!

"What happened to Arthur and the others?" I asked, already knowing I wouldn't like the answer.

"Nothing," Dewey said, his voice was low, his Southern accent drawing heavily upon each word. "They weren't there when it happened. There was no proof they were involved in any way."

"But everyone assumed it was Arthur," Sibby added darkly.

"But what does Zavier have to do with what happened?" I asked.

"He and Simone were friends," Jess said. "He hates Arthur. And Mason? Let's just say he's not a fan after what happened with Tzazi at the Academy. You know, the obsession potion."

I turned back to Chase. "So Michey was picked on by Arthur and Mason too?"

"Michey Stramm was *friends* with Arthur and Mason," he said.

I rolled my glass between my palms. I did *not* see that coming. Clearly, any friendship they'd had was now a distant memory.

"There's one thing I still don't get." I narrowed my eyes. "Why would Tzazi run up and hug someone like that?"

Jess slammed her glass down on the side table. "That's exactly what I'd like to know."

Her voice was sharp now, stripped of sorrow and full of fire.

No one moved. The wind hissed outside, and the fire cracked once, sharp as a warning.

The silence was louder than any answer we could give.

~

AFTER A MOMENT, Tzazi threw the door to the drawing room open, startling us all, and thrust her head into the room. She didn't glance at anyone—just barked, "Ransom wants everyone back in the ballroom."

We followed her without a word. The celebration was done. Guests stood clustered in tense knots around the edges of the room, their faces etched with confusion, fear, and something quieter. Dread maybe. The music had stopped. Glasses sat untouched. Every eye turned toward us as we stepped back into the room, looking for something to focus on.

Then Ransom's voice rang out, amplified by magic.

"Attention!"

The ballroom stilled. Heads turned, conversations dropping mid-sentence.

And then—pain.

A sharp sting pricked across my chest, like a needle threaded straight through my sternum. Gasps rippled outward.

"Ow!"

"Ouch!"

"What the—!"

Someone shouted, "Belleclaire! Why'd you go and do that?"

"I've applied a bindling," Ransom called out. "I've marked all of you as witnesses so I can easily find you again if needed."

More groans, a few muttered curses.

"You may all return to your homes. Thank you for your assistance this evening."

I winced. A bindling thread. Subtle but invasive. A magical breadcrumb trail. It would buzz faintly against the skin until released by the caster.

Marked. In more ways than one, I feared.

CHAPTER 4

*J*essamin Wilde stood in the middle of the sitting room of my family's ancestral home, Fernwood, her arms crossed tight, ballgown rumpled from the night's unraveling. She'd kicked off her heels after we arrived, slipping into Sibby's Harry's House slippers, which were two sizes too small, their bright pink a jarring contrast to our moods.

"I don't need a fuss," Jess said, voice tight, fraying at the edges.

"You're at Fernwood, chile. Fuss done seeped into the floorboards" Hilde said, looping an arm around Jess and steering her toward the library doorway that led to the guestrooms. "I done laid fresh pajamas out for you."

Jess blew out a breath and looked at me. "You sure?"

"Jess, c'mon. You know you're always welcome here," I said, giving her a slight grin. "Unless you'd rather bunk at Tzazi's and get your friendship back on track."

That earned me a bitter smirk. "Back on track? We're past tracks now. We're full-speed derailment."

Jess nodded her thanks and turned toward the library.

Sibby entered the room with an armful of quilts, dropping two onto the sofa in a flurry of soft cotton. A bottle of Hennessey and four glasses floated behind her like a well-trained family of ducks and came to rest on the coffee table.

I was already curled up on the couch in burgundy and charcoal plaid flannel pajamas, one leg tucked under the other, trying to make sense of the night. Perchta showing up in the woods. Michey dropping dead in the middle of the gala. Jess and Tzazi not speaking. All in one night.

One.

I waved a hand toward the hearth, and the fire jumped to life, casting sharp light and the faint scent of scorched cinnamon bark across the room.

Jess returned a few minutes later, quiet-footed, her face soft with a calm sadness. She'd changed into my old Smurfs Christmas pajamas. The colors had dulled to a gentle blur of green and white, the fabric thinned in places. Soft and comfortable. Exactly what she needed.

I poured us each a glass of cognac, and she accepted hers with a nod and sank into the far end of the sofa without a word, dragging a quilt up to her chin. The fabric bunched at her sides, heavy and comforting, a small barrier against everything outside this room. Pyewacket appeared a breath later and leapt into her lap, circling once before settling in. Jess rested a hand on his back, fingers moving in slow, absent strokes.

She stared into the fire, eyes fixed and distant, as if the events of the night might turn to ash in the flicker of the flames. After a long stretch of silence, I shifted, the cushion sighing beneath me. The fire cracked, soft and steady, filling the space.

"Jess," I said, keeping my voice low, "what did you mean when you said Simone died because of Arthur?"

Her eyes didn't leave the flames.

I pressed on, careful. "She died because she got trapped outside in a snowstorm…right?"

The wind sighed against the windowpanes, and somewhere in the kitchen, something clinked, probably Hilde's kettle demanding attention.

"I don't believe he physically killed her," Jess finally said. "Not directly."

She twisted her fingers together, dark green nails tipped with tiny gold moons catching the light. "Simone'd been arguing with Arthur earlier that day in the quad."

"What about?"

"I don't know. I was too far away to hear. But I do remember the look on her face. Whatever Arthur'd said, it hurt her." Jess paused, brows drawing together. "Come to think of it, Michey was lurking nearby. At least until Arthur spotted him and told him to get lost." A dry laugh escaped her. "That part the whole quad heard."

The room went still.

"Michey was a runt with a nasty streak," Jess added flatly. "He shadowed bigger dogs and nipped ankles when no one was looking. He didn't have the spine for anything else."

I thought of his oily smile, his self-importance at the gala, and the way he'd tried to insert himself into conversations without ever truly being welcome. A shadow, never quite reaching that status of power he craved. And then, of course, the buttons that kept pinging off his straining vest one by one while he yanked the fabric down over his gut, convinced no one had noticed, while half the ballroom snickered behind their champagne flutes.

"What do you know about Mari DeLongpre?" I asked, as Sibby and Hilde reappeared.

Sibby set down a plate of Azalea's Tranquili-tea tarts— lavender and white with scalloped edges, delicate but packed with intention, chamomile, and whatever secret magic Tzazi's mom wove into everything she touched. Azalea's baked goods never missed.

I picked one up and took a bite. Jess did the same. Warmth moved through me, low and steady, quieting the static under my skin.

Jess chewed in silence for a moment, eyes on the fire. "She's loud. Sharp as broken glass and proud of it. Most people keep their distance, unless they want a hex that makes their hair fall out in the shape of cuss words across the back of their head."

I laughed and after a moment, Jess joined in.

Sibby sank into her favorite chair with its overstuffed arms and a high-back and popped her unlit pipe into her mouth. "She once cursed my second cousin's ex to hiccup every time he told a lie. He almost passed out during a deposition."

I really needed to map out the Ebonwood family tree one day. With warning labels.

"She hexed Michey at the gala," I said.

"Yeah, I saw," Jess said, wiping a crumb from her lip.

"When Michey told the mayor he had a crush on him, I nearly ruined my gown," Hilde added, settling into her chair, cradling a mug of hot cocoa spiked with a little Hennessy and a dollop of cream. "Then he marched right up to Gertie and told her the same thing. She threw her champagne in his face and called him a pervert."

Jess snorted. "That was the only time I've ever known him to be entertaining."

"But what if that spell wasn't harmless," I said. "Not entirely."

Jess's brow knit, thoughtful now. "Mari doesn't usually cross a line. She embarrasses. She doesn't injure. At least, not on purpose."

Hilde gave a slow nod of her head. "Mmm-hmm. Mari's got a mouth on her and a spell for every mood, but she don't strike me as someone lookin' to do real harm. She's no killer."

I leaned back, eyes on the flames again. "Could her magic go wonky? Mine does."

Sibby gave a snort. "Peanut, Mari's got over a century of magic under her belt. You've got less than a year. Your magic's gonna be— What'd you call it? Wonky?"

Jess and Hilde didn't hesitate to laugh. I narrowed my eyes at Sibby, but I didn't really mind. The tension cracked just enough to let a little air in.

Hilde took a large sip from her mug. "Now that you say that,

Mari's magic sure does skate close to the edge though. Don't think it'd take much for it to tip right on over."

Jess flicked a look my way. "You think Mari did it?"

I gave a small shrug. "He stole her family's land. If anyone had cause for revenge, it's her."

The fire had burned low. Most of the tarts were gone, Pyewacket was asleep on Jess's lap, and the snow drifted down in a settled hush.

I stared into the embers. "Tell me about the Christmas witch."

Sibby looked up first, then over at Hilde. Neither of them laughed. Jess didn't either.

"Perchta," Hilde said, the name falling like a door creaking open. "She's older than the calendar. Older than Yule logs and candle songs."

"Older than Pyewacket's first nine lives," Sibby muttered.

From Jess's lap, Pye cracked his eye open. "I liked the second one best. Plenty of sunshine, no indoor plumbing, and I was worshipped properly."

I cocked my head at my arrogant familiar. "Well, that sure explains the attitude. You've been coasting on divine entitlement ever since."

Sibby snorted with laughter and offered a quick translation for Hilde and Jess. Only those with Ebonwood blood could understand Pye when he spoke.

The room settled again, shadows stretching long across the walls. The fire popped once, then went quiet. I looked between them. "Have y'all ever seen Perchta?"

Hilde nodded. "Every now and then. Never up close. She walks the woods 'round Darkly most winters—quiet and slow, like she's taking stock. Don't speak. Don't stop neither."

Jess shifted, brushing a crumb from her lap. "I've never seen her, but I've never heard of her hurting anyone. Some folks swear she leaves blessings. A pouch of silver coins. Something lost turning up just when you need it. Others she's a warning."

I raised an eyebrow. "You're telling me she's come to Darkly all these winters and never once punished a single greedy man?"

Hilde's voice was quiet but sure. "She's ain't wrath, honey. She's balance. Brings folks what's earned, good or bad. And she don't always hand it over in ways folks understand."

The wind picked back up, whirling around the eaves in a low, steady howl. Out back, the lagoon shimmered under a light sweep of snow, the cedars on the far bank dusted white. I couldn't help but wonder if she was out there, watching.

"Perchta's tied to the Twelve Nights," Sibby said. "In some German villages, folks used to leave her offerings—porridge, wool. They believed she visited homes while they slept. If the house was tidy and the children behaved, she'd leave silver coins or small gifts. If not…"

"She opened your stomach with a blade and filled you with straw," Jess said flatly.

A chill ran down my back. I didn't like how easily she said it. Or the reason I could picture it so clearly.

"Anyway," Hilde said with a grin. "Perchta's nothing to fret over. She's been walkin' these woods since before I was born. Probably before Minta was too. She didn't kill no Michey Stramm."

I hesitated. "When Keir and I got to the gala, everyone outside heard singing, growling, bells ringing. Seemed like everyone heard something different. Was that Perchta?"

Sibby stood to refresh her drink. "That was probably her followers."

Jess stiffened. "The perchten were at my house?"

I glanced at her. "The *what*?"

"Demons," Jess said with a shiver. "Shaggy, horned. I've heard they're terrifying."

Sibby sat back into her chair. "I ran into one of her perchten once at a train station in Bavaria. Ugly little thing with antlers and a fondness for pretzels. Tried to bite my ankle. I hit it with an umbrella."

Jess blinked. "That...sounds made up."

Sibby sipped her cognac. "Wasn't."

I stifled a laugh. "Then I guess I should tell you—Perchta was definitely at Greywolf tonight."

All three of them looked at me.

"I think I saw her in the trees when Keir and I first arrived. She was in the forest, no question. She left a goose-print in the snow."

Jess stared at me. "You're sure?"

I nodded. "Keir caught her scent. He wasn't worried—not even a little."

Pyewacket stretched in Jess's lap, tail flicking. "But he *was* worried about something else."

Sibby's head snapped up. "What's that supposed to mean?"

I hesitated. "Keir tracked something else in the forest that night too. He said it was a rougarou."

Jess straightened. "And now a *rougarou*? Near Greywolf?"

The mood in the room shifted, sharp and alert.

Hilde's voice dropped low. "You sure 'bout that?"

"Well, I didn't see it," I admitted. "Just the prints. Keir picked up the trail, and whatever it was moved fast. Strong. He said it was a rougarou, and I trust his nose."

Jess pressed a hand to her thigh like she needed the contact to steady herself. "I've got wards up around the house. If something got that close..."

"You know there've been sightings lately," Sibby offered. "Could've just been passing through."

Hilde gave a slow nod.

"So now we've got a dead man," I said, "a Christmas witch walking the woods, furry demons trailing behind her, and a rougarou prowling near Greywolf the same night Michey died."

I leaned back against the cushions. The popping of the fireplace and the shrill bite of the wind outside wrapped me in a cocoon of warmth and safety—but out there, someone was doing everything they could to shatter it.

"I think I'll pay Mari a visit tomorrow after work," tumbled out of my mouth before I could think better of it.

"I'm coming too," Jess said. "Trust me—you'll want backup."

Pyewacket yawned, long and slow, then flopped back across Jess's lap. Hilde rose, shaking her head, and started gathering dishes, humming a tune I didn't recognize, soft and low. Sibby gave me a pointed look over the rim of her mug.

"Better get some sleep, Peanut," she said. "That witch you're visiting? I doubt she'll be in a holly jolly mood. Never can tell with Mari."

CHAPTER 5

*S*now pressed gently against the windowpanes, turning the trees into crooked towers of white. A crow flew past the porch and vanished into the woods. The light filtering through the kitchen was winter-pale, the kind that pressed softly against the walls and counters.

"Morning," I said, voice gravelly.

Sibby stood by the stove in a floor-length robe patterned with moons and holly leaves, tapping her spoon against the side of her mug with slow, thoughtful clinks. Hilde had commandeered the counter, rolling out dough that looked like the beginning of Krampus-shaped sugar cookies.

I slid onto the stool closest to a mug that was already steaming with a foamy swirl of chai. Bless Sibby and her psychic beverage timing.

"Is Jess awake?"

Pyewacket draped himself across the stool next to me. "She left before sunrise," he said with a yawn.

Sibby snorted. "Probably checking on the manor."

"Poor chile had a rough night," Hilde said, patting my arm. "She said she'll see you this afternoon."

Popping the newspaper open, I braced myself. Beatrice

Snarkle's name was sprawled across the top like a headline in its own right. My eyes flipped to the article, took a sip of chai, and read silently while Hilde cut dough into tiny horned shapes and arranged them on a baking sheet.

Death Crashes the Cold Moon Gala
By Beatrice Snarkle, Senior Correspondent of Unsettling Affairs

DARKLY, LA—What began as an evening of elegance and goodwill ended in blood-chilling fashion at last night's Cold Moon Gala, when the body of Michey Stramm was found dead on the snow-dusted terrace of Greywolf Manor.

The glittering event—hosted by local society icon and tavern proprietress Jessamin Wilde—was intended to raise funds for Wentworth Academy's magical enrichment programs. Instead, it was brought to a standstill by a scream that sent guests rushing outside, where they discovered Stramm's lifeless body sprawled on the terrace outside the ballroom. One shaken attendee commented, "One minute we were sipping champagne, the next it was like Agatha Christie crashed the Nutcracker."

Stramm's corpse bore eerie hallmarks that appear to mimic the modus operandi of known murderess, Frau Perchta: a mouth stuffed with straw and stones, a trail of goose feathers in the snow, and a scattering of silver coins. Several guests claim they spotted movement in the woods earlier in the evening—including Leidy Alvar, a local teen who insists she locked eyes with the Christmas Witch herself.

The investigation is now in the hands of Royal Inspector Ransom Belleclaire and coroner Bodderick "Boddy" Grim, who formerly served as Darkly's sheriff. Rumors of a "Perchta curse" are spreading like frostfire across town.

Stramm, though hardly a household name, had built a profitable reputation flipping questionably obtained properties and fleecing the naïve and/or desperate from his Graves-based pawnshop, Pawn of the Dead. Known for his oily charm, suspect ethics, and a snorting laugh said to curdle eggnog, Stramm was no stranger to enemies. Fitting, perhaps, that his final moments were spent surrounded by coins—the only things he ever truly valued.

Headmaster Landravedon Truegaze of Wentworth Academy was seen leaving early, described by onlookers as "visibly shaken."

As for Frau Perchta, the Christmas crone at the center of local legend, she refused comment. Instead, she sent her perchten after this humble journalist. (Luckily, I'm light on my feet.)

As of this morning, no arrests have been made.

So the question remains: was this the work of a judgy witch— or someone using an old legend to mask a very modern murder?

I finished the last line and set the paper down, resisting the urge to reread the quote about Stramm's laugh curdling eggnog.

Hilde set a small tin of star anise on the counter. No sooner had it landed than Pyewacket swatted it over with one paw, sending the fragrant stars skittering like little wooden shurikens across the marble.

He pounced on the nearest star as Hilde stepped back, arms crossed and mouth pinched in the way that usually meant she was counting to ten in bear. We all watched in silence as he pranced across the counter like a spice-fueled menace, swatting each star anise to the floor with the uncontainable glee of a toddler on a sugar high. As soon as the last one had clattered off the edge, he flopped back down in the center of the counter, tail curled smugly around his paws.

"Another battle won for House Paw," he purred.

I translated.

Hilde didn't blink. "House Bear would like a word."

He gave a lazy wave of one paw, utterly unbothered, as Hilde yanked the broom from the closet and threatened to brush him off the stool.

"Perchten," he sniffed, returning to the matter at hand. "Honestly, the dramatics of it all."

"Is it dramatics, though?" The terrace flashed in my mind—the hush, the snow, the bone-deep wrongness of it. "Stramm wasn't a good man. It makes just as much sense for someone with a grudge to kill him as it does for some creature out of folklore."

The kitchen fell into a companionable hush, broken only by Pyewacket's contented purring and the soft scratch of Sibby filling in the daily crossword. From the lagoon, our guardian alligator, Greta Garbo, bellowed into the wind, her voice echoing through the frost-laced air.

I took another sip of chai.

Hilde wiped her hands on a towel and gave me a look that held more care than comment. "You and Jess still planning to stop by Mari's?"

I nodded. "After work."

Sibby didn't look up from her crossword. "Wear shoes you can run in."

MARAIS, my enchanted flying broom, carried us into downtown on a smooth arc of magic, the spellwork smooth and sure beneath us. A warmth bubble shimmered around us, keeping the wind's bite and scattered flakes from creeping under my coat. Below, rooftops were dusted white and wreaths glittered in shop windows. Pyewacket lounged in his enchanted bed near the bristles, tail fluffed like a feather duster, his golden eye half-lidded in sleepy approval—first class travel all the way.

"Stop leaning away in the turns," I muttered, nudging the broom upright. "You've got to lean into them. Trust me."

He snorted. "Trust you? Need I remind you—broom, tree, *bam!*"

"Okay, yes," I said. "But that only happened once."

I could practically feel his eye roll behind me.

We skimmed above Tataille Street, where the cobbled lane had been overtaken by the Christmas market. The air was thick with cinnamon and fir needles, warm and sharp in equal measure. Ribbons snapped in the breeze, twining around lampposts and merchant carts like they were holding the town together. A child tore past in a pair of felt antlers, dragging a spark-spitting toy that trailed smoke and chaos behind her—and no one seemed the least bit alarmed.

I passed a trio of goblins belting out off-key holiday tunes in front of the Sugarloaf display windows, where a mechanical sugarplum fairy repeatedly wacked the rat king with her tiny sequin purse.

Pyewacket frowned. "You'd never know someone dropped dead in a ballroom less than twenty-four hours ago."

Marais coasted to a stop outside The Magic Cup, hovering just long enough for me to slide off. Pyewacket leapt from his spot in the bristles to the cobblestones, his eye bright with the thrill of flight.

The moment my feet touched down, Marais shimmered—wood grain dissolving into golden sparks that winked out like spent fireflies.

"Everyone's trying not to think about it," I said, and pushed open the door to The Magic Cup.

THE MAGIC CUP smelled like cardamom and honey, with a back note of warm eggnog and cinnamon. Steam fogged the windowpanes, turning the street outside into a blur of gold tinsel and bobbing Santa hats. Inside, the place was packed to the rafters. Azalea hadn't had the courtyard enchanted yet, so everyone had crammed inside, crowding into mismatched chairs and nursing mugs the size of mixing bowls.

Azalea was behind the bar, sliding a tray of gingerbread scones into the case. Tzazi sat at a table near the front, sharp-lined and composed in a velvet jacket of merlot and knee-high leather boots, her platinum blonde pixie smoothed to perfection and glinting like frost in the café lights.

I made my way over, and Pyewacket veered off course, beelining for the pastry case and smushing his nose against the glass with a long, exaggerated sigh.

"Morning," I said as Azalea approached the table. "Either of you seen Jess today?"

Azalea shook her head and handed me a steaming chai latte. "Not since the gala." She smiled sadly at her daughter and then returned to the counter.

Tzazi lifted her cup, took a slow sip, then set it down with deliberate precision—like someone keeping a tight grip on their thoughts.

"Is that a no?" I asked, sliding into the chair across from her.

"That's a no," she said.

Pyewacket launched himself into the empty chair beside me and immediately began kneading the cushion, claws flexing in slow, deliberate rhythm as he settled in.

I watched Tzazi over the rim of my cup. She held herself the same as always—shoulders back, chin lifted—but there was a tightness around her mouth that hadn't been there yesterday. I didn't push.

"You mind if I sit for a bit?"

"You're already sitting."

"Great," I said. "Love when we have these heart-to-hearts."

Tzazi's mouth twitched. "Careful. Azalea's brewing one of her special blends. Says it's for clarity and communication."

"Let me guess," I said. "Lavender, mint, and a big old nudge."

"She's calling it "Make the First Move (or I Will)." Tzazi blew across her cup. "She's not subtle."

Tzazi and I sat in a comfortable hush for a few beats, the buzz of the café filling in the background. I wrapped my hands around my mug, letting the warmth soak in, and leaned forward just enough to close the space between us.

"So," I said. "Arthur Vanderholt."

Tzazi's gaze cooled. "Still alive. Much to the horror of some." She took another sip of her tea. "He's sorry, you know. Arthur. Not just for appearances. I can feel the sadness in his voice."

I let that sit. Then: "Jess told me Michey used to run with Arthur, Mason, and their crew. Hard to imagine."

She gave a dry, humorless laugh. "Michey Stramm wanted to be Arthur so badly he damn near erased himself trying. Started copying Arthur's clothes, his way of talking. Even grew his hair long the same as Arthur's. People thought it was funny. Arthur didn't."

"Jess said they were friends."

Tzazi shook her head. "Not really. Arthur and Mason barely tolerated him, if I'm honest. Michey wasn't exactly subtle, and Arthur never liked being idolized. He just liked being the one in control. What happened to Simone changed him."

She leaned in slightly. "Win, Arthur didn't have anything to do with what happened to Simone. I honestly believe that. I've had years to sit with it. And while Arthur was reckless, he wasn't cruel. Not deliberately. I never understood where the bullying rumors came from."

She paused. "And Jess knows that. She's letting her anger over the unfairness of Simone's death cloud what she knows is true."

It was a messier story than I'd expected. I'd imagined Arthur as a straight-line villain—relentless, arrogant, the kind of boy who fed on the weak. But I trusted Tzazi's judgment as much as I trusted Jess's.

So where did that leave the truth?

I took a long sip of chai, the warmth steadying me. "Tzaz, have you ever noticed how much Arthur and Michey look alike? Especially from behind. Same build. Same hair. Even similar suits at the gala."

Tzazi let out a soft laugh, but it cut off fast. Her eyes flicked to mine, and something shifted. She leaned back slowly, fingers tightening around her mug, the quiet between us suddenly louder than the rest of the café.

"Win," she said, voice low, "do you think the killer mistook Michey for Arthur?"

I nodded, heart thudding. "I think maybe Michey wasn't the target at all."

Pyewacket, who had been curled in the seat beside me and pretending not to listen, let out a long sigh. "Dilettantes," he muttered, "Can't even murder the right man. Though I suppose mistaking one pompous academy boy for another is quite understandable. Rather like a flock of peacocks, really."

I didn't bother to translate that one, but his observation about the similar appearance wasn't wrong.

Tzazi and I sat for another minute or two, as we both quietly let the realization sink in. The sounds in the room seemed louder, more grating. Azalea clinked a spoon behind the counter, and at the table next to us, someone's familiar let out a squeaky snore.

"I should head out," Tzazi said, rising and pulling her coat tight. The gesture reminded me of armor, wrapping herself in protection before stepping back into the world. She paused at the edge of the table, her fingers drumming once against the wood. "Tell Jess I hope she's okay."

"I will."

I caught her wrist before she could turn away completely. Her skin was cool under my touch, that vampire trait she couldn't quite hide.

"Tzaz. Want to come with me to The Graves to visit Benicio Kim? I want to know more about Michey Stramm."

For the first time since I'd joined her in the café, her entire face lit up. Not the tense, sorrowful smile she'd been wearing, but something genuine and pleased. "Hell yes." She checked her platinum watch. "I've got a deposition this morning, then I can meet you back here around ten?"

Relief flooded through me. Having Tzazi along meant having someone who could read people the way I read old manuscripts—carefully, thoroughly, and with an eye for what was hidden between the lines. Plus, The Graves was exactly the kind of place where you wanted a dhampir watching your back. Those cobblestone streets had a way of swallowing people whole, and Tzazi's particular brand of supernatural intimidation might be the only thing keeping us from becoming permanent residents.

"Perfect."

I watched Tzazi hurry out in the cold and then finished up my chai and turned toward the door myself. But movement caught my eye—a familiar figure tucked into the back corner. Hood up, legs stretched out, coffee in one hand, and the sports section of *The Daily Shade* spread out in front of him. Zavier Strangeland.

I made my way over, dodging a tray of floating scones and the ghost of someone's grandmother muttering at a biscuit display.

"Morning," I said.

Zavier looked up and gave me that lazy, crooked smile I was already beginning to recognize as his default expression. "Morning, Win."

He folded the paper in half but didn't set it down—just kept one finger tucked in to save his place. The headline was something about hexbee standings in the coastal leagues.

I glanced toward the headlines. "Hexbee season still going?"

"Always. The regional leagues never sleep." He shrugged. "And I like knowing how the younger teams are stacking up. Keeps me humble."

I slid into the bench opposite him. "How long are you in Darkly?"

"Just through the holidays. Got roped into family things. Not that I'm complaining." He lifted his coffee. "Figured I'd at least enjoy the perks."

"Caffeine and sarcasm?"

"And the occasional tranquili-tea tart."

"Those do come in handy quite often." I laughed, then let the levity fade. "I take it you don't like Arthur."

Zavier's face didn't change, but the air around him seemed to cool a degree.

"Or Michey," I added.

His jaw tightened just enough to notice. "I didn't like any of them. Arthur, Mason, Michey. Whole pack of golden boys. They were cruel—and smart enough to get away with it."

He thought for a moment. "What happened to Michey was a long time coming."

I blinked. There wasn't heat in his voice, just a low steadiness that made it clear. This wasn't old school drama. This was something that hadn't quite scabbed over.

"Arthur couldn't have been all bad, could he?" I asked. "Tzazi seems to think highly of him."

Zavier shrugged, folding the paper with one hand and setting it aside. "I just don't want people acting like he was some misunderstood soul. Arthur knew exactly what he was doing back then. I'm just surprised someone finally caught up with one of them."

"Aunt Sibby said you left early."

His brown eyes flashed with something sharper than annoyance. "Hours before Stramm took his last breath, Windsor. Check with the valets if you don't believe me." He leaned back, arms crossed. "Besides, killing that pompous fool would've been a waste of perfectly good magic."

He held my gaze for a second longer, then looked down at his coffee. "Tell Jess I said hi."

"You should go see her yourself. You two are like family."

His thumb traced the rim of his mug. "Maybe I will."

But we both knew he wouldn't. Not yet. Not with Jess and Tzazi locked in their stubborn standoff.

Honestly, what a mess.

CHAPTER 6

*M*idmorning we left the streets of Darkly behind, Marais gliding smooth and steady beneath us. The air had thickened since dawn, snow swirling above the rooftops. Tzazi rode behind me, straight backed and wordless. Pye crouched in his comfy seat on the bristles, his tail wrapped tightly around his paws, gaze locked forward.

Marais descended through the curling mist with the grace of a swan landing on still water, her cypress bristles barely whispering as they touched down on the frost-slick cobblestones between two crumbling columns.

We dismounted. Tzazi pulled her coat tighter around herself without a word. Pyewacket leapt from the broom, landed without a sound, and shook himself from ears to tail like he was settling his fur after the flight.

The moment my feet hit the ground, Marais vanished with a soft pop, leaving behind only the faint scent of orchids and swamp moss.

The Graves welcomed us as we crossed the threshold with its usual blend of cold stone, low mist, and the press of half-seen watchers. Fog crawled over the cobbled path, clinging to boots and trailing behind like a second shadow. The air carried the faint scent of old wax and funeral flowers left too long in stagnant water.

Snow fell softly in thin, deliberate flurries, muffling sound and sharpening the edges of everything else. Black poinsettias hung in planters, their petals veined with silver. Poison ivy garlands twisted through the wrought-iron fences, each leaf glossy with frost. Someone had spelled them to chime—low, metallic notes that rang whenever the wind passed.

A spectral carriage clattered by just ahead of us, wheels never touching the stones. No driver, save for a top hat floating at exactly the right height for a head that wasn't there. The horses were bone-pale and translucent, breath curling like grave fog in the winter air.

As the carriage passed, a row of gas lamps flickered to life in perfect succession, their blue flames dancing behind warped glass. The light they cast was cold and oddly beautiful, turning the falling snow into tiny diamonds before it hit the ground.

Tzazi's platinum hair caught the gaslight as she glanced around warily. "I hate this place," she muttered, though she kept her voice low, as if the very buildings might be listening.

I only nodded, not wanting to hear my voice in the fog. A shadow that might have been a cat—or something else entirely—disappear into a slim passage between two brick buildings that leaned against each other like drunken friends.

We passed shops with half-visible names—The Dagger's Tongue, Mourning & Co., Hollowthread. A spirit drifted overhead, pausing at the awning of a haberdashery before vanishing straight through the roof. Bells jingled from somewhere I couldn't pinpoint. The Graves earned its name honestly. The dead rarely left.

We turned down a narrow side street where the fog grew heavier, wrapped tight between the buildings, and then took a left next to a wrought-iron fence where stone angels wept into the mist. Ahead, Benicio's brownstone came into view—three stories of haunted elegance, all clean brick, iron balconies, and enchanted windows that shimmered faintly with magic. A wreath hung on the door, made from dried blackthorn and gleaming bones. The gas lanterns on either side lit themselves as we stepped forward, the ever-present mist coiled around our ankles like curious cats.

I lifted my hand and knocked. Once. Twice.

The heavy black door opened before the third.

A figure glided forward from the shadows—Lucasta, materializing like smoke given form. Her feet made no sound against the hardwood floor, and when she smiled at us in greeting, a smile held just a beat too long, I caught the glint of teeth that were just a touch too sharp.

Her eyes flicked to me first, then landed on Tzazi. She didn't blink.

"Miss Ebonwood, wonderful to see you again," she said with another unsettling smile. She cocked her head and gazed at Tzazi.

Tzazi didn't offer a smile. She shifted the weight of her stance, chin lifted.

"Lucasta," I said, keeping my tone cordial but clipped. Now that I knew what she really was—a penanggalan—I couldn't help noticing the little things. The faint wet click behind her teeth when she smiled too long. The way her feet hovered ever so slightly above the floor when she moved.

"Is Benicio in?"

The door swung wider of its own accord.

"Of course, dear. He's expecting you."

Pyewacket slunk in first, tail twitching as he skirted the edges of the hallway rugs.

Benicio's brownstone was as decadent as I remembered— ornate dark wood, thick brocade drapes that shimmered with faint enchantments, and ancestors' oil paintings whose eyes tracked our movement through the hall. Sconces lit with steady witchlight cast the space in amber warmth, the kind that made you forget the bone-deep chill of The Graves waiting just outside.

"Darling Windsor," came a voice like aged whiskey poured over velvet.

Benicio Kim appeared at the top of a curved staircase, wearing a black silk dressing robe. His hair was tousled in a deliberate way and a coffee cup steamed in a delicate porcelain cup in his hand. He descended the stairs with theatrical elegance, barefoot but somehow regal, and swept toward the parlor.

"Come in." Benicio motioned us into the sitting room, then turned to Lucasta, hovering in the doorway. "Luca, please bring our guests some coffee. Make it a pot. I could use a refill myself."

His eyes shifted to Tzazi, and I caught the subtle shift in his expression—interest sharpening into something more appreciative. "Miss Strangeland," he said, giving Tzazi a slight bow. "Your reputation precedes you, though I confess it doesn't do you justice."

Tzazi raised an eyebrow—his charm offensive wasn't landing. "Benicio Kim. Your reputation precedes you as well."

"All terrible, I hope," he said with a laugh.

Tzazi's sharp gaze tracked Lucasta as she drifted away into the shadows once more.

Benicio gestured for us to sit on a wine-dark velvet sofa while he settled into a matching armchair with the fluid grace of someone used to being in control. A fire crackled in the marble hearth, casting everything in shades of gold and amber.

"I took the liberty of having something prepared for your demon-furred sidekick," he said, nodding toward a side table where a blood-orange tart sat on a fine china plate, steam still rising from its glazed surface.

Pyewacket's ears perked forward with interest. "Now this is proper hospitality," he announced, scampering toward the table with more enthusiasm than dignity.

"You spoil him," I said, though I was smiling as Pye settled himself at the table with the satisfied air of a small, furry king.

"Excellent familiars are rare," Benicio replied, sipping his coffee. "They should be treated accordingly."

Tzazi remained standing, her platinum hair catching the firelight as she surveyed the room with the calculating gaze of

CHRISTMAS CAROLS & YULETIDE PERILS

someone cataloguing exits and potential weapons. "We want to know about Michey Stramm."

He smiled wider, delighted. "I do so enjoy a woman who skips the foreplay."

I rolled my eyes.

Lucasta drifted back into the room just then, setting a tray with a carafe of coffee and two cups onto the table. She quietly poured, and I accepted the Turkish coffee she handed me—dark and sweet as sin. Tzazi declined hers with a measured smile, her tone polite but distant. Benicio's smile deepened with quiet amusement. He extended his cup to Lucasta, never breaking his focus on Tzazi, as though the refusal only made her more intriguing.

"What do you want to know?"

"Who killed him." Tzazi crossed her arms around her chest, glaring at the warlock.

"Ah. Straight to the point again. That—I don't know."

Then Benicio's expression shifted, the lazy charm dimming as something sharper took its place. He set down his coffee cup with deliberate care. "Michey was many things—most of them unpleasant—but he'd been acting strange even by his standards these past few days."

"Strange how?" Tzazi asked, finally settling onto the edge of the sofa like a cat ready to bolt.

"He came into The Lucky Lounge three nights before the gala, practically preening." Benicio took a sip of his coffee and stared at the fire for a moment. "Talked about a 'big score' he had in the works. Said he was about to make more gold in one night than he'd made all year."

"Did he say what kind of score?" I asked.

"That's just it. He was being coy about the details, which was not Stramm's way." His head suddenly pivoted in Tzazi's direction. "You should try Lucasta's coffee. It's really very good today."

I held back a laugh as he turned back to me. "Stramm kept

hinting that he had 'insurance' on someone important. Someone who'd gotten away with something for too long."

Benicio's jaw tightened as he stared out at the street, watching snow bury the cobblestones below. "Stramm wasn't clever enough to be subtle, so when he started playing mysterious, I knew he was in over his head."

Tzazi and I exchanged glances. Insurance sounded suspiciously like blackmail.

"Any idea who he might have been targeting?" Tzazi pressed.

Benicio stood and moved to the window, gazing out at the fog-shrouded street below. "Stramm collected secrets the way other people collected coins. But he was also a coward. He wouldn't have gone after anyone truly dangerous unless he thought he had a guarantee."

"What kind of guarantee?" I asked.

"The kind that gets you killed when you miscalculate," he said softly. "Which, given the circumstances, appears to be exactly what happened."

The fire crackled in the silence that followed, and somewhere in the distance, the sound of spectral bells echoed through The Graves like a funeral dirge.

"I don't suppose you'd let us have a look at his pawnshop?" I ventured.

"Why such interest in the death of Michey Stramm?" Benicio's skeletal fingers drummed against the armrest. "By all accounts, the djinn will not be missed. Some might even consider his demise a...civic improvement."

"Simone Petalsigh."

"Ah." Benicio turned back to us with eerie grace, a slow smile spreading across his features.

"Pawn of the Dead is still sealed, but..." He reached into his robe and withdrew an ornate bone key that seemed to gleam with its own inner light. "I might be persuaded to give you a guided tour." He set his cup down and rose in a single smooth motion. "Give me five to become socially presentable."

As he disappeared up the stairs, Lucasta appeared in the doorway without a sound.

I watched her until she turned and vanished into the hallway, silent as snowfall.

A few minutes later, Benicio reappeared, dressed in a coat and gloves that shimmered faintly with wards. He adjusted his collar and smiled.

"Shall we?"

He opened the door with a flourish and extended one hand into the darkness, ushering us into the tomb-quiet streets of The Graves.

THE ALLEY NARROWED as we turned into it, the fog thickening with each step. Rusted wind chimes clinked somewhere above, and an unseen cat yowled deep in the mist. At the end of the lane, wedged between two slumping buildings, was a single crooked door with a dirty window sign painted in dripping silver:

Benicio produced the bone key with a flourish, its surface carved with symbols that shifted and swirled, vanishing the moment I thought I could see them clearly. "Skeleton key. Opens any lock in The Graves." He smiled down at me. "Being me has its advantages." The moment it touched the lock, the door swung open with a groan that sounded almost human. Dust and shadows spilled out in welcome.

"After you, ladies," he said with a bow that was somehow both gallant and mocking.

The interior smelled of mildew, old candles, and stale air. Dust motes hung in the air like suspended secrets, barely stirred by our entrance. The space was cramped and cluttered, every surface covered with objects that seemed to watch us with malevolent interest.

"Charming," Tzazi muttered, as Pyewacket immediately began investigating a skull of a very large animal that hissed back at him from a glass box.

Display cases and low shelves crammed the pawnshop. Narrow aisles wound through displays of forgotten and forbidden things. I passed a box of enchanted teeth, a mirror with claws scratching behind the glass, and a pair of white gloves pinned upright to a corkboard. One glove flexed when I leaned in to look.

"He always did have exquisite taste," Benicio said dryly. He lingered near the door, arms folded, eyes glinting in the low light. "Stramm specialized in items with...personality."

I moved deeper into the shop, past shelves lined with scrying mirrors that reflected other worlds and a collection of mourning jewelry that wept actual tears. Near the back wall, I spotted something interesting—a curated display shelf labeled "Darkly Oddities."

Among the collection of island memorabilia, one item caught my attention: a jeweled hairpin in the shape of a rearing unicorn. Its gems had dulled with age, the horn worn smooth over time by loving fingers.

Benicio stepped forward, eyes narrowing as he examined the barrette. "This wasn't here a few days ago."

I looked over at him. "You sure?"

He pointed at the box beneath where the hairclip had lain. "I gave Stramm the phonograph. Kept playing 'All I Want for Christmas is You' at 3 a.m. every morning. Lucasta threatened to quit if I didn't get rid of it. Not much of a Mariah fan."

Turning the jeweled unicorn over in my palm, I searched for any trace of magic. Nothing hummed beneath its surface, no whisper of enchantment. So why was it here, sparkling like something from a child's jewelry box, absurdly out of place in this tomb of forgotten things?

I set it down, then circled around the back counter, chipped oak with deep gouges and burn marks that spoke of a business that didn't deal in ordinary merchandise. The air back here felt heavier—thick with old magic and something meaner. The paper chaos Michey left behind—receipts curled at the edges, half-finished real estate contracts, ledgers with coffee stains bleeding through the pages—looked ordinary enough, but a shimmer near the baseboard caught my eye. I knelt down, brushing aside a veil of cobwebs. A cloud of dust rose in the air. A spider skittered away when I ran my fingers along the grain.

There. A cabinet panel not quite flush.

I pressed on the edge. It clicked open with a soft snick. Inside the hidden compartment lay a single ledger book, its cover black as coal, even darker than the shadows surrounding it.

"Tzazi! I think I've found something." She was at my side in seconds, having crossed the shop with that preternatural vampire speed.

The ledger was bound in worn, mottled leather, its cover etched faintly with symbols I didn't recognize. Cold leached into my fingertips the moment I touched it. Not the chill of the pawnshop. This was deeper, coiled and unnatural. Dangerous.

I opened it carefully.

Blank pages.

Every single one.

"It's empty," Tzazi said leaning over my shoulder.

Benicio arrived behind us, his footsteps unnaturally silent. He reached past my shoulder, fingers brushing the edge of the book. "No, not empty. Glamoured." He narrowed his eyes, turning it toward the light from a flickering lantern. "And not by Stramm. He didn't have the talent for this level of spellwork."

I ran my hand along the book's spine, and the leather seemed to pulse beneath my touch like a sleeping heartbeat. "Can you break the glamour?"

"Perhaps," Benicio said. "But it will require time. This type of spellwork doesn't yield its secrets easily."

I handed the ledger over.

Benicio gave a small bow, sliding the book into his coat.

"My money's on blackmail," Tzazi said, her voice grim. "Michey wasn't smart enough for anything more sophisticated."

I thought of Michey's bragging at The Lucky Lounge, his talk of big scores and guarantees. "What if he got too greedy? Used whatever information he had to demand more than they were willing to pay?"

"Then he signed his own death warrant," Benicio said quietly. "Blackmail only works when you're smart enough to know when to stop."

"Greed and stupidity," Pye muttered to me, barely audible. "The twin pillars of every poorly planned demise since King Midas."

We stood in the dusty silence of the pawnshop, surrounded by cursed objects and broken dreams. Somewhere behind us, a music box began playing a funeral dirge all by itself before abruptly falling silent.

"I'll be in touch once I've had a chance to examine this properly," Benicio promised, patting his coat where the ledger rested. "But I suspect what we find won't paint dear Michey in a particularly flattering light."

On the way out, I cast one last glance down at a display case. A plain silver locket caught the dim light, and for just a heartbeat, my mother's face stared back at me from its tarnished surface.

I blinked. Nothing but shadows and smudged silver remained.

I hurried after the others, desperate to be free of that dark and cursed place.

THE FOG HAD THICKENED during our time in the pawnshop, turning the world into a maze of gray veils and muffled sounds. We walked slowly toward an old wishing pool that marked the center of The Graves' main square, where flickering lanterns cast wavering circles of blue witchlight.

The pool itself was ancient, gouged from black stone and filled with water so dark and still it might have been a sheet of obsidian. Three hedge witches in rotting moss-green robes crouched at its rim, their arthritic fingers breaking the surface as they keened in voices that belonged to things long dead. Silver coins flashed in their withered palms before they let them fall, each one disappearing without disturbing the water, as if the pool itself opened to swallow them whole.

All three heads swiveled toward us at once, their faces hidden in shadow except for the pale gleam of spying eyes. One of them hissed, showing blackened teeth.

Pye sprang onto the stone rim with feline grace, positioning himself between us and the witches. His fur bristled slightly, making him look twice his normal size. "Ladies," he said coolly. "Personal space, if you please."

Benicio's hand rose in a sharp gesture, and the witches slithered backward into the shadows on the pool's far side.

Tzazi reached into her coat and pulled out a gold coin. For a moment she held it up to the blue-flamed lantern light, watching it gleam like captured starlight.

Then she closed her eyes and flipped it into the pool.

The coin disappeared into the dark water without a sound, but the air around us seemed to hum with potential—as if her wish had weight and wings, ready to take flight.

When she opened her eyes, they were brighter than they'd been all day.

Benicio adjusted his cuffs, watching Tzazi with quiet interest, but I knew his question was directed at me. "You think Michey knew something worth killing for?"

"Maybe," I said, watching the still water. "Or maybe he was just the wrong man in the wrong place."

"He was always the wrong man," Benicio said. "He double crossed nearly everyone he ever worked with. The only thing he valued more than coin was leverage."

Tzazi's jaw worked, tight and tense. "So his death might've had nothing to do with Simone."

"Or Arthur," I said, my breath forming clouds in the unnaturally cold air. "Could've been money. Could've been revenge."

The silence stretched.

I watched one of the witches toss another coin into the pool. "Whoever did this wanted it to look supernatural. They wanted people to think the Christmas witch had come for Michey."

"Maybe Perchta did come for Michey," Pye stated flatly. "She's eviscerated much nicer folk than him for much lesser crimes than his."

I shook my head at Pye. "I really don't think she did it."

"You don't believe Perchta had anything to do with the murder?" Tzazi asked grimly.

I shook my head.

Benicio finally spoke, voice smooth but low. "This isn't Perchta. I don't care what the townspeople believe. My guess? That ledger will show Stramm got himself into something he couldn't handle."

"Thank you," I said. "You'll let us know when it gives up its secrets?"

"Of course." Benicio gave a slight bow, then turned toward the square's outer edge. His fingers swept a lazy arc through the air, silver trailing behind his hand like a veil being pulled back. A shimmer split the fog ahead of us. The spellveil he cast was unlike anything I'd seen before—not the usual portal magic, but something that folded space itself.

"Until next time," he said, already turning back toward the dark.

The world rippled around us like heat shimmer, and suddenly we were stepping through a curtain of silver static onto solid cobblestones outside The Graves' main gate. The transition left my ears ringing and my stomach slightly unsettled.

Beside me, Tzazi swayed once before steadying herself against a lamppost, her usual composure cracking just enough to show that even vampires weren't immune to dimensional displacement.

The heavy fog that had clung so persistently to The Graves couldn't seem to follow us past the boundary stones. Here, in the space between districts, the air was crisper, cleaner, carrying the scent of swampy, salty air instead of candle wax and decay.

I sat down on Marais, though my thoughts kept circling back to the locket in Michey's shop and the way my mother's face had seemed to flicker in its surface.

"Win." Tzazi sat gingerly on my broom. "Since we still don't know for sure whether Michey was the real target—"

"Then Arthur could still be in danger," I finished.

As I pushed off into the air, I found myself looking back over my shoulder at the fog-wrapped district with its blue-flamed lanterns and watching shadows.

None of us spoke on the way back to Darkly.

The truth had shifted.

And it was no longer clear whose story we were chasing.

CHAPTER 7

The air inside the MET felt thick and expectant, like the moments before a storm breaks. I settled into one of the deep armchairs near the fireplace, my fingers wrapped around a mug of spiced chai that had gone lukewarm. The fire crackled softly, but its warmth couldn't quite chase away the chill that had settled in my very being.

Across from me, Tzazi sat with perfect posture, her platinum hair catching the firelight as she stared into the flames. The glamoured ledger rested heavy in both our thoughts, along with the uncomfortable realization that perhaps someone skilled in advanced magic had wanted Michey's records hidden badly enough to kill for them.

Pyewacket claimed the third chair and sprawled across the velvet cushion with the satisfied air of someone who'd had an excellent adventure. His golden eye tracked the dancing flames while his tail twitched with residual energy from our morning's escapade to The Graves.

The comfortable silence stretched between us, broken only by the whisper of turning pages from somewhere in the gallery above and the occasional pop from the hearth.

I found myself thinking about the silver locket I'd seen in the pawnshop.

Had I really seen my mother's image ripple across its surface?

The rattle of the doorknob pulled both our eyes toward the front of the MET. Through the frost-etched glass, I could see Jess approaching, her breath forming small puffs in the cold air.

The door chimed as Jess entered, and the warmth seemed to drain from the room when Jess's gaze swept past Tzazi without acknowledgment, landing on me with forced brightness.

"I thought it was just you and me going to visit Mari," Jess said, her voice carrying an edge I rarely heard from her. Her eyes flicked between Tzazi and me with barely concealed irritation. "Why's she here?"

Tzazi's spine straightened, but her response was measured, calm. "That's okay. I'm not staying."

Tzazi rose from her chair with fluid grace, wrapping herself in her leather coat like a shield. As she moved toward the door, she gave me a look—half sorrow, half reluctant support—that spoke volumes about the fractures running through our little group.

"We just got back from The Graves," I said, hoping to jump start a conversation, but it was too late. The door chimed again as it closed behind her.

"Jess," I started, but she was already shaking her head.

"Don't." Her voice was quiet but firm. "Just...don't."

Pyewacket lifted his head from the cushion, golden eye assessing the tension with the shrewd intelligence of someone who'd witnessed too many human dramas. "Well," he said dryly, "this is awkward."

I didn't disagree.

Jess finally unwound her scarf and moved toward the fireplace, but she chose the chair farthest from where Tzazi had been sitting. The distance felt deliberate, calculated—like she was trying to erase any trace of the vampire's presence from the space.

"Are you still going with me to see Mari?" I asked carefully.

"Yes." Jess pulled off her gloves with sharp, precise movements. "That hasn't changed."

But something fundamental had shifted between us, and we both knew it. The easy camaraderie that had always existed in our little group now felt fragile, cracked like ice too thin to bear weight.

I watched her settle into the chair, noting the way she held herself—shoulders rigid, jaw tight with unspoken words. The fire cast dancing shadows across her face, highlighting the exhaustion that makeup couldn't quite cover.

"Jess—"

"Win, please." She closed her eyes briefly. "I know what you're going to say. But I can't...not yet. What she did at the gala, going to him, defending him, bringing him to our table..." Her voice trailed off, but the hurt was unmistakable.

I nodded, though my chest felt tight with the weight of watching two people I cared about tear each other apart over old pain and newer betrayals. Outside, the snow continued to fall, each flake adding to the blanket of silence that seemed to be settling over everything.

The moment stretched between us until Pyewacket finally broke it with a pointed yawn. "If we're going to visit the formidable Mari DeLongpre before the roads get worse," he announced, "we'd best be off."

The drive to Mari's cabin wound through hills that seemed carved from winter itself—bare trees reaching skeletal fingers toward a pewter sky, their branches heavy with snow that looked like lace against the gray afternoon light. The windshield wipers worked steadily against the flakes that gathered at the edges of the glass, their rhythmic scraping the only sound breaking the silence that had settled between Jess and me like a physical presence.

I kept my eyes on the winding road ahead, where tire tracks from earlier travelers had already been softened by the falling snow. The isolation of the drive—stretches of white emptiness broken only by the occasional glimpse of a distant farmhouse or the dark line of a fence disappearing into the woods—seemed to mirror the distance that had opened between my two closest friends.

"Mari's place is about a mile up this track," Jess said, guiding us onto a narrower road that disappeared into heavy woods.

The trees closed in around us as we climbed, their snow-laden branches creating a cathedral of white and shadow that seemed to muffle even the sound of our engine. The mailbox that marked Mari's property was a work of art—wrought iron shaped into twisting vines and thorns, with her name spelled out in letters that seemed to writhe in the corner of my vision.

As we pulled into the clearing, I caught my first glimpse of Mari DeLongpre's cabin and understood immediately why she chose to live so far from town.

THE CABIN CROUCHED in its snow-covered clearing like something out of a fairy tale—the kind where the witch might give you wisdom or turn you into a newt and you wouldn't know which until it was too late. Half-swallowed by drifts and wrapped in the arms of ancient pines, it seemed to pulse with its own inner warmth, golden light flickering behind frost-etched windows like captured fireflies.

Smoke curled from the stone chimney in lazy spirals that defied the wind, and I could smell woodsmoke mixed with something else—herbs and spice and the faint, wild scent of magic being worked.

The front door opened before we'd even cut the engine, and Mari DeLongpre appeared in the doorway. Tall and regal in a way that made queens look common, she wore a dark purple velvet wrap that flowed around her like liquid shadow. Her feet were bare despite the snow, and her silver-streaked hair hung in loose waves around her shoulders.

"Well," she called, her voice carrying that syrup-laced drawl I remembered from the gala, now sharpened with amusement. "Y'all planning to sit in that car all day or are you coming in before you freeze your pretty little assets off?"

Jess and I exchanged glances before stepping out into the cold. The snow crunched beneath our boots as we made our way to the porch, where Mari stood watching us with dark eyes that seemed to take our measure and find us...interesting.

"Mari," Jess said with careful politeness.

Mari's laugh was rich and dark as molasses. "Honey, save the good manners for people who give a damn. You're here about Michey Stramm, and frankly, it's about time somebody with sense started asking questions." She stepped aside, gesturing us into the warmth of her cabin. "Come on in. I've got cider mulling and bread in the oven."

The interior of Mari's cabin was a study in controlled chaos—every surface covered with books, crystals, dried herbs bundled and hanging from exposed beams, and cats. So many cats. They wove between furniture like living shadows, some ordinary, others clearly touched by magic. One had stars in its fur that actually twinkled. Another seemed to be partially translucent, existing somewhere between dimensions.

The hearth dominated the room, its fire burning with flames that shifted from gold to green to deep purple. The flames rippled and bulged outward, and suddenly a small face pressed through the fiery curtain like someone pushing through a beaded doorway. A tiny body followed, all sharp angles and liquid movement, dancing with manic energy—a fire sprite. Above the mantle, antlers from some massive creature stretched toward the vaulted ceiling. Christmas ornaments dangled from their points. A cauldron hung over the fire on an iron hook, bubbling with something that smelled of cinnamon and nutmeg.

"Tea? Cider? Something stronger?" Mari asked, moving with fluid grace to a sideboard loaded with bottles and jars. "I find conversations about murder go down easier with proper lubrication."

"Cider sounds perfect," I said, taking in the overwhelming sensory feast of the space. Every breath carried new scents—sage, vanilla, something that might have been vetiver smoke, and underneath it all, the wild green smell of growing things despite the winter outside.

Mari poured steaming cider from a copper pot into thick ceramic mugs that looked like cooled lava stone—dark gray with veins of burnt orange running through them, rough-textured and primal. She handed them over with a flourish, rings glittering on every finger—silver, gold, and stones that seemed to pulse with their own inner light.

"Now then," Mari said, settling into a chair beautifully carved from a single piece of oak. She tucked her feet beneath her, and the velvet wrap shifted of its own accord, draping and tucking itself around her like a contented cat. "I assume y'all want to know about my little dust-up with the late, unlamented Michey Stramm."

The fire sprite in the hearth sparked higher at the mention of his name, sending a shower of purple sparks up the chimney. One of the cats—a massive orange tom with intelligent green eyes— hissed softly before stalking away.

"Even Mr. Whiskers had better sense than to trust that man," Mari observed dryly, watching the cat disappear behind a bookshelf. Her voice softened. "I wish granddad had seen through him."

Jess leaned forward slightly, cradling her mug between her hands. "Mari, we need to know—did your hex on Michey have anything to do with his death?"

Mari's expression sharpened, and the fire in the hearth flared so suddenly that shadows leaped across the walls like startled birds. The cauldron above the flames began to bubble more violently, sending wisps of aromatic steam curling toward the ceiling.

"You asking if I killed him?" Her voice had gone deadly quiet, but there was no fear in it—only a dangerous kind of amusement.

"We're asking if your magic could have gone wrong somehow," I said carefully. "If what was meant to embarrass him might have—"

"Child." Mari's laugh cut through my words like a blade through silk. "When I hex somebody to embarrass them and show what a putz they really are, that's exactly what happens. Nothing more, nothing less."

She took a long sip of her cider, her dark eyes never leaving our faces. "Now, did I want to see that thieving weasel suffer? Absolutely. Did I kill him? No. But I'll tell you straight—I'll be damned if I shed a single tear over his passing."

The cauldron bubbled over, hissing against the flames and filling the cabin with the sharp scent of scorched herbs. Mari waved one ring-laden hand, and the mixture settled back to a gentle simmer.

"He stole your family's land," Jess said.

"Stole it, hell." Mari's voice turned bitter as winter wind. "He bought it for a song when my granddad was dying and desperate to pay for healing magic that never came. Waited until the old man was too sick to think straight, then swooped in with spelled contracts and clauses that would make the devil's lawyer proud."

The pain in her voice was raw, immediate despite the years that had passed. I watched as she gripped her mug tighter, her knuckles going white beneath the rings that caught the firelight.

"That land had been in our family for almost two hundred years," Mari continued, her drawl thickening with emotion. "My great-great-grandmother built the first house there with her own hands after she escaped slavery. Every generation added to it, blessed it, made it home. And that snake took it all for the cost of a fancy dinner."

One of the cats—a sleek black female with white markings—leaped into Mari's lap, purring loudly as if sensing her distress.

Mari's hand automatically moved to stroke the cat's fur, and some of the tension left her shoulders.

"My granddad died three weeks after signing those papers," she said quietly. "Broken heart, the healing woman said. But I knew better. He died of shame."

The fire sprite in the hearth burned lower, its flames shifting to a deep, mournful blue, responding to its mistress's grief.

"I'm sorry," I said, and meant it. The theft of ancestral land was a wound that never fully healed, passed down through generations like a scar on the family soul.

"Don't be sorry for me, honey." Mari's voice regained its steel. "Be sorry for Michey He lived his whole miserable life thinking money could buy him what my family *had*—respect, belonging, a place in this world that meant something. But all he ever bought were enemies."

She looked directly at me then, her dark eyes holding mine with uncomfortable intensity. "Now, I did see something suspicious that night. Interested?"

I nodded, suddenly very aware that we were about to cross into dangerous territory.

Mari set down her mug and leaned back in her chair, the velvet wrap falling away from her shoulders to reveal arms that bore faded tattoos—protection sigils and family marks inked in gold and silver.

"I saw Dianthe Petalsigh screaming at Arthur Vanderholt like a dragon with a belly full of flame. Right there in the vestibule, where anybody could hear." Mari's voice dropped to almost a whisper, but it carried clearly in the cabin's enchanted atmosphere. "She was shaking, crying, pointing her finger at him like she meant to curse him where he stood."

My breath caught. "What was she saying?"

"'How dare you show back up here after what you did to Simone!'" Mari's voice took on a mocking falsetto as she quoted Dianthe's words. "'How dare you walk around like nothing happened, like she didn't die because of you!'"

The cauldron began to bubble again, responding to the magical tension that had suddenly filled the room. Steam rose in spirals that formed shapes—faces, perhaps, or memories given form before dissolving back into mist.

"And Arthur?" Jess asked, her voice tight.

"Looked like a man who'd seen his own ghost. White as fresh snow. Kept trying to calm her down, saying it wasn't his fault, that she knew better than anyone what really happened that night." Mari's eyes glittered with something that might have been satisfaction. "But Dianthe wasn't having any of it."

I exchanged glances with Jess, both of us processing this new information. If Dianthe had been that angry, that publicly confrontational...

"Plenty of people saw it," Mari continued, as if reading our thoughts. "Half the gala was gawking by the time Bane's Enforcers came to break it up. Girl was beyond caring who heard her."

"Where was Michey during all this?" I asked.

Mari's laugh was sharp as broken glass. "Following along behind Arthur like a pathetic little bootlicker, as usual. Trying to insert himself into the drama, probably hoping to pick up some gossip he could use later. That man collected secrets like other folks collected stamps."

The fire sprite flickered higher, casting dancing shadows across Mari's face that made her look ancient, otherworldly. "But here's what I find interesting, sugar. If Dianthe was that mad at Arthur, mad enough to make a scene in front of half of Darkly society, why would she kill Michey instead?"

The question hung in the air like smoke, heavy with implications. The cats had all gone still, as if sensing the weight of the moment, and even the fire sprite's flames burned steady and low.

"Unless she didn't mean to," Jess said slowly. "If she was that upset, that angry—"

"Maybe Michey wasn't supposed to be the target at all," I

finished, voicing the theory that had been growing stronger in my mind since our conversation with Benicio.

Mari's eyebrows rose, and she leaned forward with sudden interest. "Now that's a thought worth chewing on. Those boys always did look alike, especially from behind. Same build, same way of holding themselves like they owned the world."

She stood abruptly, moving to the window that looked out over the snow-covered clearing. Her reflection wavered in the frost-etched glass like a ghost superimposed over the winter landscape.

"Simone Petalsigh," she said quietly. "Poor little thing. Sweet as honey and twice as fragile. Dianthe loved that girl like a sister —hell, more than a sister. Losing her the way she did... The guilt..." Mari shook her head. "Some wounds never heal. They just rot from the inside."

The cauldron bubbled once, softly, as if echoing her words. One of the cats—the translucent one I'd noticed earlier—materialized more fully and began winding around Mari's ankles, purring in frequencies that seemed to resonate in my bones.

"You think twenty years of grief could drive someone to murder?" I asked.

Mari turned back to face us, her expression grim. "Honey, I've seen grief do worse things than that. Grief mixed with guilt? With blame that's been festering for decades?" She shrugged, the velvet wrap shifting around her shoulders. "That's a poison that can make people do things they never thought possible."

A new scent drifted from the cauldron—something dark and complex, like earth after rain mixed with the metallic tang of old blood. The fire sprite's flames shifted to deep crimson, casting the entire cabin in shades of wine and shadow.

"Another thing that troubles me," Mari continued, leaning toward us with predatory grace. "If someone was angry enough to kill for what happened to Simone, why wait twenty years? Why now, at a Christmas gala where half the island could see?"

She settled back into her chair, the movement causing several cats to rearrange themselves around her feet like furry sentinels. "Either something happened recently to stir up old pain, or..." She paused, her dark eyes calculating. "Or someone's been planning this for a very long time and finally found the perfect opportunity."

The weight of that possibility settled over us. A murder planned for decades, waiting for just the right moment, the right circumstances. It painted a picture of patience that was almost more chilling than sudden violence.

"So what do you believe happened to Michey?" I asked.

Mari stood again, moving to tend the cauldron with practiced motions. She stirred it with a long silver spoon, muttering something under her breath in what sounded like French mixed with older languages. The bubbling settled, and the oppressive scent of dying roses faded.

"I think," she said without turning around, "that someone's been carrying a twenty-year-old wound, and it finally festered enough to poison everything around it. I think someone was destroyed by what happened to Simone. And they're not going to stop until they've had their revenge."

She faced us again, her expression grave. "And I think y'all are chasing a ghost through a graveyard, not realizing that the real danger is still very much alive and walking among us. Sometimes it's best to stay out of the graveyard."

The fire sprite dimmed to barely glowing embers, plunging the cabin into deep shadows that seemed to reach toward us with grasping fingers. Outside, the wind picked up, howling through the pines like something wild and hungry.

We thanked Mari for her time and stood.

THE DRIVE back down the mountain felt heavier than our ascent, weighted with everything Mari had revealed. Darkness had fallen while we'd been in the cabin, and snow drifted through our headlights like confused spirits trying to find their way home.

I watched the lights of Darkly grow brighter as we approached the edge of town. The familiar silhouette of the bell tower and Creole rooflines emerged from the snow like old friends welcoming us home, but even their comforting presence couldn't shake the feeling that we were walking into something much larger and more dangerous than a simple murder.

"I should talk to Dianthe," I said finally. "Face to face. If she's carrying this much pain, this much anger, maybe she'll tell me what she knows about what really happened that night."

Jess nodded slowly, but I could see the worry lines deepening around her eyes. "And if she's the killer?"

"Then we deal with that when we get there." I settled back in my seat, watching the snow continue its lazy dance through our headlights. "But I have a feeling there's more to Simone's death than anyone's been willing to admit."

CHAPTER 8

*J*ess and I stopped off at The Gator for dinner, and by the time she dropped me off at Fernwood, the snow had thickened into a proper magical Southern snowfall, the kind that transformed the familiar landscape into something enchanted and strange. The ancient magnolia wore a mantle of white that made its branches look like the arms of sleeping giants, and the Spanish moss hung heavy with frost that caught the porch lights like captured starlight.

The enormous Christmas tree in the sitting room sparkled through the window, dressed in red velvet bows and glowing white bulbs. Light danced across glass ornaments and gilded branches, spilling across the glittery-wrapped gifts scattered beneath the branches.

I stood on the front steps for a moment, breathing in the crisp air and trying to process everything Mari had told us. The real estate con, Dianthe's confrontation with Arthur, the possibility that Michey hadn't been the intended target at all—it all swirled through my mind like the snow swirling around the estate's lampposts.

The front door opened before I could reach for the handle, spilling warm light and the scent of Hilde's cooking onto the porch. But instead of my bear-shifter housekeeper, Keir filled the doorway—tall, broad-shouldered, and looking at me with those storm-gray eyes that never failed to make my pulse quicken.

"You're home," he said, and there was relief in his voice that made something tight in my chest loosen.

"I'm home," I agreed, stepping into his arms without hesitation.

He pulled me close, and I melted into the solid warmth of him, letting the stress of the day drain away.

"How did it go with Mari?" he asked softly, his accent carrying that slight Scottish lilt that always made me want to listen to him read poetry.

"Complicated," I murmured against his chest, not ready to move away from the safe harbor of his embrace. "She gave us some information, but it just raised more questions."

His arms tightened around me slightly. "Questions that can wait until tomorrow?"

I tilted my head back to look at him, taking in the concern etched around his eyes and the way his dark hair was mussed as if he'd been running his hands through it while waiting for me to return.

"They can wait," I said softly. "What are you doing here? Not that I'm complaining."

A slow smile spread across his face, transforming his expression from worried to something warmer, more intimate. "I had a feeling you'd had a long day and might need some looking after."

"Did you now?" I arched an eyebrow, though I was fighting my own smile. "And what exactly did you have in mind?"

"Well," Keir said, closing the door behind us and helping me out of my coat, "How about hot cocoa, *Midsomer Murders*, and absolutely no thinking about Michey Stramm for at least two hours."

The foyer felt different with him in it. Warmer, more awake somehow. Melted snow from my boots pooled quietly on the hardwood, and deeper in the house, I caught the low hum of voices—Sibby and Hilde in the kitchen, laughing as Hilde washed up the dinner plates and Sibby got in the way.

"Hot cocoa and my favorite show sounds perfect," I said, letting him take my hand and guide me toward the living room. "But I should warn you. I'm terrible at not thinking about things."

"Lucky for you," Keir said, pausing to brush a strand of hair away from my face with fingers that were surprisingly gentle for their size, "I'm very good at distraction."

The living room had been transformed in my absence. The fire in the massive stone hearth burned low and steady, casting dancing shadows across the Persian rugs and antique furniture. Someone had arranged thick quilts and oversized pillows on the sofa facing the fireplace, creating a cozy nest that looked like an invitation to forget about the outside world entirely.

"This is nice," I said, settling onto the sofa and tucking my legs beneath me. "Very...domestic."

Keir laughed, the sound rich and warm. He moved to stoke the fire. "Don't sound so surprised. I can do domestic when the situation calls for it."

"The mighty alpha, master of domestic comfort," I teased, watching the way the firelight played across the strong lines of his shoulders. "Your pack would be scandalized."

"My pack," he said, turning back to face me with poker still in hand, "wants their alpha to be happy. And apparently, according to Pup, you make me 'disgustingly happy.'"

I laughed, the sound bubbling up from somewhere deep in my chest, the first genuine laugh I'd had all day.

Keir set the poker aside and moved toward the kitchen doorway. "Hilde got everything ready. Don't move. I'll be right back."

I watched him disappear down the hallway, admiring the easy way he moved through my home like he belonged here. Which, I was beginning to realize, he did. Somewhere between investigating murders and navigating magical crises, Keir Bane had become as essential to my sense of home as the ancient oaks outside or Pyewacket's sarcastic commentary.

Speaking of which—where was my familiar?

As if summoned by my thoughts, Pyewacket appeared in the doorway, his golden eye gleaming with satisfaction and what looked suspiciously like powdered sugar on his whiskers.

"Successful raid on Hilde's baking supplies?" I asked.

"A gentleman never tells," he said primly, settling himself on the hearth with his back to the fire. "Though I will say that her snickerdoodles are approaching perfection."

"And you're in here...?"

"To say goodnight. Hilde threatened to use me as a testing subject for her new catnip-free treats if I didn't make myself scarce for the evening." He began grooming his paw with elaborate nonchalance. "Something about 'young people needing space to be romantic.'"

I felt heat rise in my cheeks. "She didn't actually say that."

"She used more colorful language, but that was the general sentiment." Pyewacket paused in his grooming to fix me with his penetrating stare. "Win, dear, you do realize you're practically glowing, don't you?"

"What?"

"Magic responds to emotional states," he said matter-of-factly. "And right now, you're radiating contentment like a small, besotted sun. It's quite nauseating, actually."

Keir returned carrying a tray laden with two oversized mugs of hot chocolate topped with whipped cream and a dusting of cinnamon, along with a plate of Hilde's famous gingersnap cookies. The rich, sweet scent filled the room, mixing with the woodsmoke from the fire to create something that smelled like Christmas and comfort combined.

I accepted one of the mugs with grateful hands. The ceramic was warm against my palms, and the first sip revealed layers of flavor—dark chocolate, a hint of vanilla, and a touch of bourbon.

"Hilde's secret recipe," Keir explained, settling beside me on the sofa close enough that our knees touched. "She made me swear a blood oath not to reveal the ingredients."

"Mmm," I hummed appreciatively, taking another sip. "I can see why."

Pyewacket snorted delicately from his place by the fire. "If you two are quite finished being precious about beverages, I'll be in the library. Try not to get chocolate on the antique upholstery."

With that pronouncement, he stalked from the room with his tail held high, leaving us alone with the crackling fire and the soft whisper of snow against the windows.

I translated for Keir.

"He's protective of the furniture now?" Keir asked, amused.

I laughed, shifting slightly so I could curl into Keir's side. His arm came around me automatically, and I felt the last of the day's tension finally begin to drain away. "Just be thankful he's giving us privacy. In his own dramatic way, of course."

Keir switched on the TV and navigated to *Midsomer Murders*, settling in as DCI Barnaby solved his ten-thousandth murder in the quaintest village in England.

We sipped our cocoa in companionable silence, his arm wrapped around my shoulders, warm and comforting. Outside, snow continued to fall, blanketing the lagoon and cypress trees in white. The old house creaked around us, settling in for the night.

"Keir," I said finally, setting my mug on the side table and turning to face him more fully. "Can I ask you something?"

"Always," he said, his gray eyes serious in the firelight.

"How do you do it? Handle all the pack responsibilities, the leadership expectations, the weight of other people depending on you, and..." I gestured between us, struggling to find the right words. "...and still make room for this?"

His expression grew thoughtful as I sipped my cocoa and waited for him to answer. When he finally spoke, his voice was soft, reflective in a way I didn't often hear from the formidable alpha.

"I used to think I couldn't," he admitted. "For years, I believed that being alpha meant sacrificing everything personal for the pack. That caring about someone outside the clan was a weakness, a distraction. I guess that's why I only dated women I knew I'd never want to…stay with."

He reached for my hand, his fingers intertwining with mine with practiced ease. "Then you came to Darkly, lass. Stubborn as they come, brilliant, and utterly fearless when danger calls. Everything I thought I knew about duty and sacrifice crumbled the moment I met you."

I felt my breath catch.

His thumb tracing circles across my knuckles. "You taught me that being a good leader doesn't mean cutting yourself off from joy, from love. It means being whole enough, happy enough, that you can lead from a place of strength instead of emptiness."

The fire popped softly, sending sparks up the chimney, and somewhere in the house a clock chimed the hour. But all of that seemed distant, unimportant, compared to the intensity in Keir's eyes as he looked at me.

"You make me a better alpha," he continued. "Not despite loving you, but because of it. The pack sees that I'm happy, and it gives them permission to find their own happiness too."

Did he just use the "L" word? Does he know he just used the "L" word?

He took my face in his hands, that stubborn lock of hair falling into his face as usual. Firelight flickered warm against my closed eyes as we kissed, snow hushing the world beyond us, and the tight knot of worry in my chest finally began to unravel. Keir's lips were warm and familiar, tasting of chocolate and something indefinably wild that was purely him. When we finally broke apart, he rested his forehead against mine, his breathing slightly uneven.

"Better than hot cocoa," I murmured, and felt rather than saw his smile.

"Much better," he agreed, his voice low and rough in a way that sent warmth spiraling through me.

"Tell me something about you," I said, settling more comfortably against his side. "Something that has nothing to do with murders or magic or pack politics."

Keir was quiet for a moment, his fingers absently stroking through my hair. "When I was small—maybe eight or nine—I used to sneak out of the den during the full moon gatherings. While the adults were running and hunting, I'd find the highest hill I could and just...sit. Watch the moon and listen to the pack singing in the distance."

"That sounds lonely," I said softly.

"It wasn't, though. That's the thing." His voice carried a note of wonder, as if he was rediscovering the memory. "I felt connected to all of it—the moon, the pack, the forest. Like I was part of something bigger than myself, but still completely free."

I tilted my head to look at him. "Is that why you accepted the position as alpha? To protect that feeling?"

"Maybe." His smile was thoughtful. "Or maybe I just wanted to make sure other wolves could have that same sense of belonging without having to choose between duty and freedom."

The way he said it, so matter-of-factly, made my heart squeeze with affection. Here was this powerful, respected leader, and at his core he was still that little boy who'd climbed hills to watch the moon.

"What about you?" he asked. "Tell me something about you before you moved to Darkly."

I considered that, sipping my hot cocoa and letting the warmth of both the drink and his presence settle into my bones. "When I was in graduate school, completely buried in my dissertation about medieval manuscripts, I used to take these long walks through Central Park at dawn. The city would be so quiet, just me and the joggers and the occasional dog walker."

"Sounds peaceful," Keir said, his fingers still moving gently through my hair.

"It was. But one morning when I was feeling completely overwhelmed—questioning everything, wondering if I was smart enough, if my research mattered—and I found this tiny folly tucked away in the trees. It wasn't even on the park maps."

He raised his hand to my lips and kissed my fingers. "Folly?"

"Mmm. Probably some kind of magical sanctuary, though I didn't know it then. I sat on the steps and just...breathed. And suddenly I could feel this sense of purpose, like all those old books and forgotten stories were calling to me. Like I was meant to be their guardian."

I laughed softly. "I thought I was just being dramatic. Turns out it was probably the first stirring of my Ebonwood magic, trying to tell me what I was really meant for."

"Your magic knew before you did," Keir said wonderingly.

"Sometimes I wonder if that's how I ended up here. If some part of me was always supposed to find Darkly, find the MET." I paused, then added more quietly, "Find you."

The words hung in the air between us, heavy with meaning. Keir's arm tightened around me, and when I looked up at him, his eyes held that storm-gray intensity that never failed to make me feel heard.

"I've been thinking the same thing," he admitted. "About fate, about how everything seemed to align to bring you here. The pack has a concept—true mates—but it's more than just romance. It's about finding the person who makes you more yourself than you ever thought possible."

My breath caught.

"I'm not asking for anything," he said, his voice dropping lower, rougher. "And you know it must be your choice. But Win..." His fingers traced a slow path up my arm, leaving heat in their wake. "You feel like fate to me. Like where I belong."

The fire crackled, low and steady. I didn't say anything else, just stared at the twinkling fairy lights on the Christmas tree and let myself breathe, let myself *feel*—the solid warmth of him behind me, the way his chest rose and fell against my back, the way my pulse quickened in response.

He took both our mugs and set them down on the table with

deliberate care. The movement shifted me slightly, and when he settled back, his arms encircled me completely.

Then he leaned in, his breath warm against my skin, and pressed his lips to the curve of my neck.

My breath hitched. His mouth moved slowly, deliberately, tracing the line from my shoulder to just below my ear. One hand splayed across my stomach, fingers pressing gently, possessively. The other slid up to tuck my hair aside, giving him better access.

"Keir," I whispered, though I wasn't sure if it was a question or an answer.

His lips curved against my skin—I could feel the smile. "Right here, darlin'.

Murders—Midsomer or otherwise—became the furthest thing from my mind. There was only this: the crackle of the fire, the scent of pine and cinnamon, and Keir Bane slowly, thoroughly, making me forget everything but us.

CHAPTER 9

I walked into Oopsie Daisies, the delightful flower shop next door to the MET, owned by Dianthe Petalsigh, the next morning with the scent of snow still clinging to my coat. The bell above the door chimed softly as I stepped into the humid embrace of the flower shop, where Christmas had exploded in shades of crimson and gold.

Pine garlands draped every available surface, their needles releasing that sharp, clean scent that spoke of winter forests and holiday magic. Poinsettias in impossible shades—deep burgundy, cream with pink edges, and one variety that seemed to shimmer between gold and silver—crowded the front displays.

But it was the more unusual blooms that caught my attention. Glass roses that chimed softly when the blast from the heating vent touched them. Winter jasmine that bloomed in spirals of white and blue, each petal edged with what looked like real frost. A hanging basket of silver bells—actual flowers shaped like tiny bells that rang with crystalline notes when brushed against.

"Those are moon chimes," came Dianthe's voice from behind the counter, where she was arranging white lilies in a crystal vase. "They only bloom during the darkest part of winter and only ring when touched by someone pure of heart."

I glanced up at the delicate flowers, which had fallen silent at my approach.

"Oh, come on," I said. "What do I have to do, rescue orphans? Because I'm really more of a 'solve murders and pet my cat' kind of pure."

Dianthe's laugh was soft but strained, and when I looked at her properly, I could see the exhaustion etched around her eyes. Her usually pristine appearance was slightly disheveled—hair escaping from its careful twist, mascara smudged as if she'd been crying.

"What can I help you with this morning, Win?" she asked, but her voice carried a wariness that had never been there before.

"I need some arrangements for the MET," I said, moving closer to the counter. "Christmas flowers to brighten the space for holiday travelers."

She nodded, but her hands shook slightly as she reached for an order pad. "Of course. What sort of arrangements were you thinking?"

I watched her carefully as I described what I needed—centerpieces for the reading nooks, garlands for the staircase, something festive for the front counter. But my mind wasn't really on flowers. It was on the way her fingers trembled when she wrote, the dark circles under her eyes, the way she kept glancing toward the shop door as if expecting someone.

"Dianthe," I said gently when she finished jotting down notes, "are you all right? You seem...upset."

Her pen stilled on the paper, and for a moment the only sounds were the soft chiming of the moon bells and the whisper of the heating system. When she looked up at me, her eyes were bright with unshed tears.

"I heard you were asking questions," she said quietly. "About Michey. About...about what happened at the gala."

My pulse quickened, but I kept my voice calm, sympathetic. "People are worried. Scared. It's natural to want answers."

"Is it?" Her laugh was bitter, hollow. "Or are you just stirring up old pain for no reason?"

The air in the shop seemed to thicken, heavy with the scent of too many flowers and unbearable grief. One of the glass roses chimed softly, a sound like breaking crystal.

"Dianthe," I said carefully, "I know you and Simone were close. I can't imagine how difficult it must be to have Arthur back in town."

Her hands clenched into fists on the counter, crushing the order pad beneath her fingers. "You don't know anything about Simone. About what she went through. What they did to her."

The words came out in a rush, raw with twenty years of suppressed grief and rage. Around us, the flowers seemed to respond to her emotional state—the poinsettias' leaves rustling without any breeze, the winter jasmine's blooms closing slightly as if seeking protection.

"Tell me," I said softly. "Help me understand what really happened."

I kept my expression gentle, encouraging, as Dianthe struggled with whatever memories were clawing their way to the surface.

"Simone was my cousin," she said finally, her voice barely above a whisper. "We grew up together, shared everything—secrets, dreams, even clothes." A small smile ghosted across her lips before disappearing. "She was the sweetest person you'd ever meet. Gentle as a lamb and twice as trusting."

She moved away from the counter, her hands trailing along the garlands as if seeking comfort in their texture. "When we got our letters to Wentworth, we were so excited. Two little girls from Darkly, going to the most prestigious magical academy in all the Isles."

"But it wasn't what you expected," I prompted gently.

Her laugh was sharp, brittle. "Those boys—Arthur, Mason, and that whole group—they ruled that place like little princes. And Simone...she was different. Quiet, studious. An easy target."

The winter jasmine in the hanging basket began to droop, its frost-edged petals losing their shimmer. The very air seemed to darken as Dianthe's pain filled the space.

"They tormented her daily. Spelled her books to combust during lectures. Hexed her robes to change colors in the middle of formal dinners." Her voice grew harder with each word. "The professors did nothing. Their families had too much influence, too much money."

"Did you actually see Arthur bully her yourself?"

Dianthe's jaw tightened. "Who else would it have been?"

Grief had turned her into someone I barely recognized—all sharp edges and blame.

"And the night she died?"

Dianthe's hands stilled on the garland. "They said it was an accident. That she'd fallen asleep outside during a winter storm and simply...froze. But I knew better."

"What do you think really happened?"

She turned to face me then, and the expression in her eyes was devastated, haunted. "They spelled her. Made her unconscious somehow, then left her outside in the snow like she was nothing. They might not have meant to kill her, but they did."

The shop fell silent except for the soft whisper of petals falling from the winter jasmine. Even the glass roses had stopped their gentle chiming, as if the flowers themselves were holding their breath.

"That's a serious accusation," I said carefully.

"Is it?" Dianthe's voice cracked. "When you know what those boys were capable of? The way they looked at girls like Simone— like we were toys for their amusement?"

She stared out at the snow-dusted cobblestones of Tataille. "The worst part was afterward. How everyone closed ranks. The faculty, the other students, even some of the families. They all wanted it swept under the rug, forgotten. A tragic accident, nothing more."

"But you couldn't forget."

"How could I?" She pressed her palm against the glass, her breath fogging the surface. "Twenty years, Win. Twenty years of watching them go on with their lives while Simone mouldered in the ground. Arthur traveling the world, Michey making his dirty deals, Mason building his career on the backs of other people's misery."

The pain in her voice was raw, immediate despite the decades that had passed. I could see why Mari had been concerned about infected wounds. This kind of grief didn't heal; it festered.

"I'm so sorry, Dianthe. I honestly don't know how you and your family got through it."

Dianthe's smile was soft, genuine. "The Charlottes saved my life after Simone died. After Simone's death, they asked me to join. I knew how much she liked those girls. Made me feel close to her. We were a unit. No one touched one of us without touching all of us. That kind of loyalty, that bond...it's rare."

"The Charlottes? Who were they?" I asked, trying to sound casually interested rather than like I was interrogating her.

"The Char-*lottes*," Dianthe said, correcting my pronunciation.

"Who were the Char-*lottes*?" I asked correctly.

"Were?" Dianthe's laugh landed somewhere between wistful and bitter, like biting into a perfect praline only to find it had gone stale. "Once a Charlotte, always a Charlotte. That was our motto."

She drifted back toward the counter, her fingers trailing across ribbon spools, setting them spinning in small, hypnotic circles. The silk whispered against her skin. "We were a social group—a sisterhood, we called ourselves. Simone was a member." Her hand stilled on a spool of deep purple velvet. "After she passed, they invited me to take her place. I suppose they thought I could fill the hole she left."

I waited, letting the silence stretch. Sometimes people needed space to decide what to share.

"There was Coralie Chevalier—brilliant girl, transferred to

some prestigious academy in the Ethereal Reaches right after graduation. Haven't heard from her since." Dianthe moved to adjust a display of silk flowers, though they looked perfectly arranged to me. "Letha Marsh. She's the Director of Willow Haven now, that crisis support center in Strawbridge." Dianthe's voice softened on the name. "She was in here earlier. It was nice to see her."

She paused, and I caught something flicker across her face— pain, maybe, or regret.

"And Tamsin Kettlewell who married into the Blackwater family. Runs a crystal shop up in Wychwood. New age stuff, mostly. We exchange Christmas cards."

She selected a length of burgundy velvet ribbon and ran it through her fingers like a worry stone. "Then there was Dora Lavallette. She was our leader, really. The one who held us all together when everything fell apart."

My pulse quickened at the name, though I kept my expression neutral. "Dora Lavallette? Is she related to Lex Lavallette."

"His daughter," Dianthe said, her voice growing distant. "The Lavallettes left Darkly not long after Dora's graduation. Family business in the outer territories. Rosewood, I think. But Dora..." She smiled, a real smile that transformed her face. "Dora was fierce. Protective. When Simone died and I thought I might die myself from the grief, she wouldn't let me give up. Made me eat, forced me to attend classes, held me when I cried myself sick, and asked me to join the Charlottes."

The shop fell quiet except for the soft rustle of pine needles and the distant chiming of the moon bells.

"They sound like good friends," I said.

"The best." Dianthe's expression grew wistful. "We swore we'd always be there for each other, no matter what. That's what real friendship is—standing by someone even when the world turns against them."

The way she said it made something cold settle in my stomach. There was an intensity to her words, a fervor that suggested the

Charlottes' bond had been about more than just teenage friendship. What exactly had they sworn to do for each other? And did "standing by someone" include burying secrets? My mind spun with possibilities—secret societies, blood oaths, the kind of magical bindings that—

"—at the gala," Dianthe was saying, and I realized I'd missed part of what she'd said. Something about seeing old friends again? "It was good to reconnect."

I shook myself back to the present conversation. Whatever wool gathering I'd been doing could wait.

"Dianthe," I said carefully, "at the gala, when you confronted Arthur..."

Her entire body went rigid, the velvet ribbon falling from her fingers to pool on the floor like spilled wine. "What about it?"

"People heard what you said. About Simone's death being his fault."

"Because it was." The words came out flat, matter-of-fact, but I could see the tremor running through her hands as she gripped the counter's edge. "All those years of torment, all those cruel spells and humiliations—it built up to that night. He killed her spirit long before her body gave out in the snow."

The winter jasmine above us began to shed its petals in earnest now, tiny blue and white fragments drifting down like tears. The very air seemed to thicken with Dianthe's anguish.

"Why would they do that?" I asked.

Dianthe's laugh was hollow, bitter. "Because boys like that don't need a reason. Just a target." She looked up at me then, her eyes bright with unshed tears and something fiercer. "They thought they were untouchable. That their names and their families' money made them gods among mortals."

"And now?"

"Now Michey's dead." Her voice was soft, but there was something in it that made the hair on the back of my neck stand up. "Funny how the universe has a way of balancing the scales."

Before I could respond, she turned away sharply, moving to

wrap a winter bouquet with mechanical precision. "Your arrangements will be ready by this afternoon. I'll have them delivered to the MET."

The dismissal was clear, but I couldn't leave it there. "Dianthe, if you know something about what happened to Michey—"

"I know that some people get what they deserve," she said without looking up from the flowers. "And I know that the past has a way of hurting people all over again."

The silver bells swayed in their woven basket, releasing a cascade of delicate chimes but even their magical song did nothing to lift the darkness that had suddenly fallen over the shop.

I hesitated, then gently pressed, "Someone told me they think Arthur Vanderholt might be in danger."

She didn't blink.

"Good," she said simply, eyes fixed on the wrapping ribbon as if it held every secret she'd ever sought.

The silence stretched between us, heavy and brittle. Then she turned, the steel set in her jaw softening just enough to let the weariness in.

"After all these years, it's about time for some justice."

I STEPPED out of Oopsie Daisies into the crisp air, my mind churning with everything Dianthe had revealed. Her pain was evident, but could she have killed Michey? Did she have it in her to kill anybody?

I gazed around Darkly's downtown area, where Christmas decorations hung from every lamppost and storefront window. Garlands of pine and holly draped the wrought-iron balconies, while enchanted snow fell lightly from the sky. The festive atmosphere should have been comforting, but something about the brittle cheer felt forced, desperate—as if the town was trying too hard to maintain normalcy in the face of growing unease.

I passed clusters of people huddled in conversation, fearful looks creasing their faces. Fragments of worried discussions drifted on the winter air: "...saw Perchta watching from the treeline..." "...my sister swears she heard singing in the middle of the night..." "...getting home before dark, just to be safe..."

Fear was spreading through Darkly like frost across a windowpane, and I couldn't shake the feeling that we were all balanced on the edge of something much larger and more dangerous than Michey Stramm's murder.

I stepped into the MET's warm glow, its stained-glass dome casting jeweled patterns across galleries of books. I slipped out of my coat and scarf, tossing them onto the metal stand next to the front doors and picked up the box of garland I'd abandoned earlier.

A group of teenagers clustered in front of the *Twilight* books, giggling and whispering.

The bells on the door jingled and I turned to find Keir walking in the door, wearing a thick wool sweater that made his shoulders look impossibly broad. Snowflakes melted in his dark hair, He carried two steaming cups from The Magic Cup. His eyes traveled over me with undisguised affection.

"How's my beautiful witch?"

The young girls' chatter died mid-sentence as they turned to stare at Keir, practically swooning in unison. He had that affect— devastatingly handsome, exuding confidence, and completely oblivious to the trail of sighs he left in his wake. The boy with them cleared his throat loudly, looking distinctly annoyed.

"Your beautiful witch is having a terrible day," I said, accepting the cup he offered. The scent of chai and cinnamon rose with the steam, but it was the way he was looking at me—like I was the only thing worth seeing in the entire shop—that made my chest tight.

He reached out to tuck a strand of hair behind my ear, his fingers lingering. "Then I'm glad I'm here. Want to talk about it?" I glanced around the MET, noting the scattered customers browsing among the shelves and the soft murmur of conversation that filled the space. "Upstairs."

Keir followed me to the spiral staircase that led to the gallery level.

We climbed the wrought-iron steps, up to the gallery where reading nooks tucked between towering bookshelves offered quiet spaces for contemplation. Keir chose a secluded alcove near the dome's edge, where the afternoon light filtered through glass in patterns of blue and gold.

"So," he said once we'd settled into the comfortable chairs, "what's troubling you?"

I told him about my conversation with Dianthe, about the Charlottes and Dora Lavallette helping her after Simone's death.

"Did you say Lavallette? As in Lex Lavallette?"

"The same." I thought for a moment. "Dora is his daughter."

Keir took a sip, his amber-flecked eyes studying me with an intensity that made my stomach flip, even when we were just standing in my bookshop drinking coffee.

"Huh," he murmured, but his gaze had sharpened, shifting from warmth to wolf-sharp focus as he processed what I'd told him.

Keir was quiet for a long moment, his expression thoughtful. The light from the dome cast shifting patterns across his face, highlighting the strong line of his jaw and the way his dark, wavy hair caught the colored light.

"There's something else," I said, setting down my chai. "The way Dianthe talked about the Charlottes. How she became a member after Simone's death. That group—it wasn't just friendship. It was something deeper. More...ritualistic, maybe. Like they'd bound themselves together somehow."

Keir's expression grew more serious. "Magical bonds between group members aren't unheard of, especially when formed during times of intense grief or trauma. But they can be dangerous if they're not properly balanced."

"Dangerous how?"

"Shared emotion becomes amplified. One person's pain becomes everyone's pain but magnified through the bond." He leaned forward slightly, his voice dropping. "Like if someone in that group was planning mischief, the others might feel compelled to help, even if it's something they wouldn't normally do."

Keir paused, then added quietly, "Pack bonds work similarly. The alpha's emotions and intentions influence the entire group, sometimes in ways they don't even realize."

I thought about Dianthe's fierce protectiveness when she'd spoken about her friends, the way her eyes had lit up when she'd mentioned Dora's name. Even after decades, the connection was clearly still strong.

"If this is all about Simone, why wait twenty years?" I asked. "Why not seek revenge immediately after Simone's death?"

"Maybe they needed time to plan. To gain resources, influence, the ability to move without being detected." Keir's expression was grim. "Or maybe something happened recently to trigger them. Some catalyst that brought all that buried grief and anger back to the surface."

We sat comfortably in silence. Then Keir pulled me into a hug. "I need to head back to the Cairns, love. Pack meeting tonight," he said, standing and taking my hand, pulling me up with him. "The rougarou's been passing closer to the village. We've started up twenty-four hour patrols."

Right. The rampaging swamp creature. I'd almost managed to forget there was still one of those on the loose.

Keir leaned in and kissed me. "I enjoyed last night."

I blushed. Last night had been…well, magical.

"Me too."

We walked down the stairs, our fingers brushing until the last step. At the front door, he gave me a wink before vanishing into the snowy street like a wolf-shaped phantom.

~

THE AFTERNOON SHADOWS were lengthening by the time I finished decorating the MET's main floor, draping garlands along the spiral staircases and arranging the winter bouquets Dianthe had delivered as promised. The shop hummed with quiet contentment as the last few customers of the day browsed among the shelves, their voices mixing with the soft whisper of turning pages and the gentle crackle from the reading nook fireplaces.

"That should do it," I said, stepping back to admire the effect of the enchanted garland I'd just finished hanging. The pine boughs sparkled with tiny lights that pulsed gently like captured fireflies, and small silver ornaments chimed softly when touched by the warm air rising from the heating vents.

"It looks beautiful," came a voice behind me.

I turned to see an older woman approaching from the rare books section, her silver hair perfectly styled and her winter coat suggesting both quality and careful maintenance. She moved with the measured grace of someone who'd spent a lifetime observing and judging, and when she smiled, I caught a glimpse of the kind of steel that hid behind Southern politeness.

"Thank you," I said, trying to place her face. She looked vaguely familiar. Maybe I'd seen her at community events or passing on the street.

"Can I help you, Mrs.—"

"Lorinda," she said. "Just Lorinda."

I smiled. "Lorinda, how are you this evening?"

"Oh, surviving the winter as best I can," she replied, her voice carrying that particular cadence of old Darkly families— measured, musical, with consonants that had been softened by generations of careful breeding. "Though I must say, all this talk about Perchta and Christmas witches has me quite unsettled. In my day, we knew better than to speak such things aloud."

Her eyes, sharp with intelligence, locked with mine and I

realized she wasn't making idle conversation. "Some people think decorating's disrespectful after a death," she continued, her gaze settling on the twinkling garland. "Me, I think joy honors the dead better than all the mourning in the world."

"I agree," I said carefully, paying attention to her expressions.

Lorinda nodded approvingly. "Michey Stramm was a small, petty man who spent his life collecting other people's misery. The best way to honor his passing is to fill the world with a little more light."

She moved closer, ostensibly examining the silver ornaments. "Of course, some folks are saying his death was just the beginning. That old debts are coming due at last."

The casual way she dropped that observation made my pulse quicken. "What kind of old debts?"

"The kind that accumulate when you think your money and your family name make you untouchable." Her smile was pleasant, grandmotherly, but her eyes held a gleam that reminded me of a hawk spotting prey.

Lorinda selected a leather-bound volume from a nearby display, running her fingers over its gilded spine with reverence. "Beautiful binding work. The old craftsmen certainly knew how to make books that would last centuries." She glanced up at me with those sharp eyes. "Rather like grudges, I suppose. Some things are built to endure."

The weight of her words settled over the conversation like a fine layer of dust.

"Lorinda," I said carefully, "do you know something about what happened to Michey?"

Her laugh was soft, musical, but there was something brittle underneath it. "Child, I know that some chickens take twenty years to come home to roost, but when they do, they arrive with talons sharp enough to draw blood."

She set the book back in its place with careful precision. "You be careful now, dear. Winter nights in Darkly can be treacherous, and you know how folks around here feel about too much prying."

With that cryptic warning, she glided toward the front door, her footsteps silent on the hardwood floors. The bell chimed softly as she departed, leaving behind only the faint scent of lavender and the echo of words that felt more like prophecy than advice.

CHAPTER 10

That night, after my favorite dinner of pot roast, cheese grits, and sweet tea (yes, even in the winter) followed by a large slice of chess pie, I drifted into the library and picked up *Wuthering Heights*. I'd been trying to read it for months but was still barely a few chapters in.

I curled up on the chaise and watched as shadows fell over the meadow beyond the tall library windows. The last amber light bled across the grass before fading into dusk, turning the distant oaks into dark silhouettes. I shifted in the plump chaise, pulling the chenille throw higher over my lap. *Wuthering Heights* lay open in my hands, but I'd read the same paragraph three times without absorbing a word.

The warm fire crackling in the stone fireplace was making me drowsy. I focused my gaze on the large opening, wide enough to accommodate a large witch's cauldron above the fire. The mantel and surround were intricately carved with fern fronds, alligators, and dragonflies.

My eyelids grew heavier with each pop and hiss from the hearth. The book slipped lower against my chest as I sank deeper into the chair's embrace, Brontë's words blurring into dreams.

The book slid onto the floor and I jerked awake when it thudded on the antique wood.

Sometime during my sleep, Pye had joined me in the library and was now curled up at the end of the chaise. I could hear Sibby and Hilde in the sitting room laughing at something on TV.

I reached out to wake Pye so we could go to our own room when a blinding pulse of light caused me to fall back. I blinked, searching the room for its source. Nothing obvious—no lamp knocked over, no candle flaring. Just shadows and the soft glow of moonlight through the curtains.

I rubbed my eyes, wondering if exhaustion was playing tricks on me.

"Pye, c'mon. Let's head to bed." Another flare of light—only this time I saw where it was coming from.

I crept to the fireplace. The blaze within suddenly exploded, shooting up about four feet. I fell back and stared at the enormous fireplace.

"Pye! Pye! Wake up!"

Pye stretched, then hopped down to join me on the rug in front of the fire. "Now. What exactly are we doing?" he asked and yawned.

"Hush. Just watch."

"Just watch. Okay. I am watching and—"

The fire suddenly sprang to life, surging up the throat above the firebox.

"Blimey!" Pye screeched, jumping straight up into the air, fur bristling, claws clinched tight. "What is that?"

"I was rather hoping you knew."

We edged up to the fireplace.

"Look at that, Pye. The andirons."

Two green glass balls rose up on the metal andirons on either end of the fireplace, almost as if the metal pieces were clutching the spheres and holding them up in the air. Each one was topped by a red stone. As I drew closer to examine the green finials, the heat grew almost unbearable and I was about to give up on getting any closer when the heat suddenly…disappeared.

I knitted my brows. "Pye, this fireplace must be enchanted. Come see."

"Yeah. I'll pass. I'll let you check it out."

Pye suddenly became very interested in cleaning his hind leg.

I spun around on my rear and faced him. "I thought one of your duties as my familiar was to protect and look out for me."

"We're in Fernwood. Nothing is going to happen to you," he said, still concentrating on that leg.

"If that's true then why aren't you coming with me?"

He sighed, "Fine," and pranced up to where I sat by the fireplace.

I spun back around. "See? Not hot—despite the fire."

Pye stepped back a few steps, then forward a few steps, back again, forward again. He frowned up at me. "You're right."

"And look at this," I said, drawing his attention to one of the green glass balls. "It looks like there's ink floating around in there." Ribbons of black twirled and swirled endlessly within.

"This one too," Pye said, pointing to the other glass ball at the end of the andiron.

I raised my index finger and cautiously moved it bit by bit toward the glass ball.

"You don't think you might be pressing your luck here?" Pye hissed.

"There's no heat. None," I countered slowly moving toward the ball, ready to scoot out of the way if the fire or heat suddenly flared in my direction.

When my finger was only a few inches from the glass, the black tendrils inside stopped randomly swirling about the ball. Instead, they moved with purpose and congregated at a spot directly in front of my finger.

I moved over to the other glass ball and tentatively moved my finger close to the glass. The tendrils on this side also converged in front of my finger. Biting my lip, I pushed my finger up until it was touching the glass. A feeling of power moved through my finger and into my body and as I moved my hand away, the tendrils moved with my finger, creating a line of swirly dark smoke from my fingertip to the ball. Wherever I directed my finger, the tendrils followed. It was as if I had a string connecting me to the andiron. I shook my hand, trying to dislodge the connection but the tendrils moved with it. My efforts were like trying to shake sticky spider webbing off fingers.

"Back up," Pye said," See if that will break it."

I took a few steps back to no avail.

"Argghh!" After shaking my hand until I thought it would fall off, I gave up and flopped onto the sofa in front of the fireplace. The second my rear hit the cushion, the connection dropped.

"Do you have any idea what this is?" I examined my finger, but it appeared to be perfectly normal.

"Obviously, it recognized your Ebonwood ancestry and tried to connect. Did you feel anything?"

"Not really. But, when I first touched the ball, it was like a brightness, a power of some kind flowed through me."

I rose and returned to the fireplace, reaching for the other green globe. The moment my finger touched its surface, the connection snapped into place.

"What is this supposed to be?" I watched my magic ripple across the glass. "All it does is spark when I touch it—like a plasma ball responding to static."

"Hmm." Pye stared into the fire and looked up at me. "What happens if we connect them?"

I stared into fire. "Using me as the link, you mean."

"Brilliant. She's earned her cookie for the day." He leaped onto a side table and then launched himself at the carved wooden mantel.

"Goodness. There's no heat up here either." He stuck a paw over the edge. "Here neither."

I waved a hand through flames that felt like soft flowing silk lapping against my skin.

He sat on his haunches, a bemused look creasing his face.

"This is quite bewildering. Anyway, let's try connecting the two."

"You're awfully brave when I'm the guinea pig," I grumbled.

"Oh, I *do* like guinea pigs." Pye ran his tongue over his teeth. smacking his lips

"Stop it. You know I hate it when you say things like that."

"Why do you think I continue to do so?"

"Anyway." I stood in the middle of the fireplace and spread my arms wide as I could and placed a finger on each glass ball. The power surge was immediate, but again, not painful.

"Do you see anything?" I asked Pye as he still perched on the mantel. His eye darted back and forth between the two balls until it widened and I jerked my head to see what he was looking at. The red stone on the tip top of each andiron was glowing brightly as if lit from within.

"I wish I'd paid a little more attention to those," I grumbled. "I thought they just held the andirons together."

"Actually, I think the red stones are the mechanisms. Pull your fingers off the green balls and place them on the stones."

I narrowed my eyes at him.

Pye sighed. "I don't feel anything untoward. Do you?"

He was right. The ol' female intuition, along with my witchy senses, wasn't detecting anything dangerous. Although, I *was* feeling a nervous sense of adventure.

I released my fingers from the balls and held them directly above the red stones. Before I could change my mind, I pushed down on the stones.

A whoosh filled the room as the fire flared up once more then died down. A scraping sound reverberated through the room. A stone wall at the back of the fireplace slid out of sight, revealing a set of stairs leading up and out of sight.

Pye and I looked at each other and screamed:

"Hilde!"

~

AUNT SIBBY SQUATTED in front of the fireplace, her body a black silhouette against the flames. I couldn't help but think she looked like a giant toad. She grunted and stood.

Even sounded like one.

"Hmm," Sibby grunted. "That is one humdinger of a hole."

She finally turned, curlers hanging limply from her head and pulled her fluffy robe tighter around her middle.

Sibby grinned when she saw me watching. "I sleep commando-style. Let's the good bits air out, you know."

I shook my head, dislodging the unfortunate image that had parked there.

Hilde sat on the sofa, arms crossed. "I knew Fernwood had enchanted areas—I've come across some myself—but this! Right here under our noses! Pyewacket!"

His head jerked around from his perch on the mantel.

"Did you know anything about this?" Hilde grumbled.

"I'm as baffled as you," he said, his voice tight and small. "How did I not know of it? The magic needed to create it had to have been enormous."

"It's enchanted to present itself when needed," Sibby said. "Minta might not have even known about it."

"I wonder where it leads?" Hilde leaned forward, gazing into the shadowy opening.

"Only one way to find out," Sibby said with a mischievous grin.

After a short discussion and plenty stomping of the feet on my part, it was "decided" I would be the first to venture up the stairs.

After all, as I pointed out, the passageway had presented itself to me, hadn't it?

"Besides, nothing in Fernwood can harm me," I said.

"We don't know where that—" and here Hilde jabbed her finger in the direction of the fireplace— "goes."

I turned to the woman who felt like family to me. "I promise I'll be careful and won't do anything stupid."

Pye snorted.

"What he said," Hilde grumbled.

Sibby gave me a wink.

I stepped through the silky flames and found myself on a small stone landing. On one side was a gothic-style window and on the other, a set of grey stones curving upwards. Small slitted windows and flickering gas lamps curved along the outer wall, creating an atmosphere of medieval magic.

I gazed down at the vista spread beneath us—a small village blanketed in pristine snow, looking like something from a storybook. Sibby stepped in behind me, followed by Pyewacket.

"Well, I'll be," Hilde's voice came from behind us, filled with wonder.

I turned to see her ducked just inside the entrance, her eyes wide while she took in the narrow stone walls. Dancing shadows played across her face, and she moved fully into the space, running her hand along the ancient stone wall.

"You okay?" I asked, noticing her slightly dazed expression.

"More than okay," Hilde said, a smile spreading across her face. "Just...surprised to find this. And to be honest, surprised the wards let me through. I've been with the Ebonwood family for all my life, but I'm not blood."

Sibby stepped closer, examining the entrance thoughtfully. "The wards must recognize more than just bloodline," she mused, a knowing look in her eyes. "Loyalty, perhaps. Or love. The Ebonwood magic has always been...intuitive."

"Well, whatever it is," I said, squeezing Hilde's shoulder, "you belong here. The magic knows it even if you doubted it."

Hilde's eyes glistened for just a moment before she cleared her throat gruffly. "Stop with the sentimental crap and let's see what we've got here."

But I caught the pleased smile she tried to hide while she herded us up the steps.

"It's freezing in here," Pye complained, shivering and padding up to my side.

"It should be. The land outside is covered in snow," I said. I began a slow ascent into the tower. "Aunt Sibby? Do you have any idea where we are?"

Sibby huffed while she followed us up the stairs. "Oh, let me think. Stone tower? Freezing cold? Mountain air thin enough to make a leprechaun wheeze? I'd wager we've landed ourselves in one of the royal family's vacation castles—probably the drafty one in the Aerie Mountains nobody uses because it's colder than a vampire's heart in January."

"Vacation castles," Hilde muttered from behind us, her heavy footsteps echoing in the stairwell. "Of course, the royals have vacation castles."

Beyond the glass, snowflakes spiraled down in slow, looping pirouettes.

I was dumbfounded. "Do you mean we're in the Charming Isles?"

Pye hopped onto a sill of one of the small, curved windows pressed into the exterior wall of the turret. "Hmm. I'd agree with Aerie Mountains. Do you see that village? I don't recognize it. Do you?"

Sibby and I joined Pye at the window, Hilde leaning over our shoulders to peer out.

"Can't say I do." Sibby chewed on her bottom lip and squinted at the landscape below. "But I think you're right." She tapped lightly on the glass. "That might be one of the villages high up in the Aeries."

"Minta never mentioned Fernwood connecting to the Charming Isles," Hilde said, her voice carrying a sharp edge of reproach. "Told me every other blessed thing about this house, or so I thought."

We climbed higher, the stairs curving around the turret. Cold stone met my fingertips as I steadied myself. Outside, a chilly wind blustered and moaned, rattling glass in its wake.

But in the building itself, I heard not a sound. The eerie silence set my nerves on edge. I glanced back at Sibby who had her wand out and ready. Hilde's dark eyes were alert, scanning every shadow.

I pulled out my magic and felt it buzz around my fingertips. After what seemed to be hours of endless looping up the turret steps, we reached a door. A plain wooden door with a curly "E" carved into the wood.

"Well now," Hilde said, stepping forward to trace the carved letter with one thick finger. "That's Ebonwood, sure enough."

I reached for the antique doorknob and pushed the door open. A fluttering of warm air and the smell of old books flowed from the room. And was that...?

"Chocolate," Hilde said with a grunt. "Minta's favorite. Dark chocolate with sea salt."

Even though the room felt inviting and safe, we all crept in, afraid to let our guards down. Sibby put up her wand and looked at me.

"I feel Minta in here," she said. "We're safe."

"Absolutely. The chocolate gave it away," Pye said hopping up on a small desk covered in papers and tan letter-sized boxes.

A fire whooshed into existence in the stone fireplace at the center of the room. Its flames reflected in the tiered shelves built around it, shelf after shelf spiraling upward, stacked with boxes and books all the way to the ceiling.

Hilde stood frozen in the doorway, her imposing frame blocking most of the light from the stairwell. Her dark eyes swept across the room, and for the first time since I'd known her, she looked genuinely shaken.

"Mother of..." she breathed.

Everything in the room was round. The walls. The rug beneath my feet. The enormous circular panes of glass set high into the stone, at least fifteen feet up. Even the fireplace curved in a perfect arc.

I gazed around in wonder. The turret soared at least two

stories tall, its upper reaches dotted with four round alcoves—each fitted with cushioned benches perfect for reading. But there were no stairs. No ladder. No way up at all. You'd have to sprout wings to reach those cozy perches.

A small desk was pushed up against the lone window in the lower half of the room.

Pye jumped up on a low table with plump sofa and chairs clustered around it. "Another library?" he asked. "Why do we need another library?"

"It's not a library," I said, taking a look at the loose documents scattered on a coffee table. "It's an archive."

"Archive," Hilde repeated, finally stepping fully into the room. She moved slowly, reverently, as if afraid the space might vanish if she walked too quickly. "All the years I've lived in this house and not once did Minta—" Her voice cracked slightly before she caught herself.

Sibby jangled a chain connecting one of the boxes to the shelf it sat on. "What's the difference between an archive and a library?" She moved over to Pye and plopped down on the sofa.

"Basically, an archive is a record of human or paranormal existence. I would guess this archive contains the history of the Ebonwood witches."

Hilde crossed her arms over her broad chest. "So, while I was scrubbing floors and cooking meals and protecting this estate with my life, Minta was keeping secrets. Perfect."

"Hilde—" I started.

"Don't." She held up one hand. "I understand duty. I understand keeping the family's business private. But this?" She gestured at the walls of boxes and books. "This is our history too. Mine and Pye's. We've served this family for generations."

Pye's ears flattened against his head. "I quite agree. Most distressing to discover one's loyalty was not reciprocated with trust."

Sibby hopped back up and perused the books and boxes along the walls. She picked up a box and set it on the coffee table.

Pye joined us as Sibby lifted the cardboard lid. I surveilled the outside of the container but there were no labels or markings.

Sibby rooted around and pulled out some of the documents inside.

"I'd say it contains more than just Ebonwood history." Her stubby finger poked at the papers. "This here's a box on Lord Lazarus."

"Ruler of Nocturnelle," Hilde clarified.

Hilde moved closer, peering over Sibby's shoulder. "Now that's interesting." She frowned. "Minta had dealings with him back in the sixties."

"Tzazi's father," Pye said to me.

I had no idea Tzazi's father lived on Darkly Island, much less that he was a ruler over one of the Darkly Island parishes. The way she spoke of him gave me the impression she hadn't seen him since she was young.

"Why is there information on the ruler of Nocturnelle here? Why exactly is there a secret archive in Fernwood?" Pye asked.

I moved to one of the shelves and pulled out a random box. Again, no identifying markings or labels on the container. I rustled through the documents inside.

"The marriage of Princess Ermione to Prince Gelron," I muttered, reading through the faded document.

Pye cocked his head. "Perhaps this is a vessel of information concerning not only the Ebonwood family, but also anyone who they may have dealings with."

"Intelligence," Hilde said bluntly. "That's what this is. Minta was collecting intelligence on everyone who mattered—allies, enemies, everyone in between." She pulled down another box, handling it with surprising gentleness for someone with such large hands. "Smart woman. Paranoid, but smart."

"It looks like someone's been doing a lot of research in here," I offered.

Books and papers lay scattered on every available surface.

Hilde picked up a leather-bound journal from the desk, flipping it open. "This is Minta's handwriting."

"Look at this," Sibby said, showing us a newspaper article. "Our Windsor had quite the career."

University Names New Leadership for Preservation and Conservation Dept

The New York Times

The Department of Preservation and Conservation announces a leadership transition following the retirement of longtime Director Alberto Botero.

Lucas DeWinter has been named the new Director of the department, while Dr. Windsor Ebonwood has been promoted to Assistant Director. Dr. Ebonwood will retain her existing titles as Senior Book Conservator and Head of Book and Paper Conservation.

Dr. Botero, who mentored both DeWinter and Dr. Ebonwood throughout their careers at the university, expressed confidence in the department's future leadership. "I leave the collection in extraordinarily capable hands," he said in a statement.

Dr. Ebonwood, recognized nationally for her expertise in rare book preservation and paper conservation techniques, has been instrumental in several high-profile restoration projects during her tenure at the university.

The appointments are effective immediately.

Pictured: Dr. Windsor Ebonwood (center) with retiring Director Alberto Botero (left) and incoming Director Lucas DeWinter (right).

That image. Me grinning wildly, flanked by my mentor, Alberto Botero, and my boss and fiancé, Lucas de Winter.

Seeing Lucas again brought an unexpected ache—not for us, but for who he'd been before everything went wrong. Bertie, though. My throat tightened. I'd give anything to hear his laugh one more time.

I took a deep breath to settle myself and examined the scattering of newspaper articles and photos on the desktop, arranged as if someone had recently left them there.

Dr Ebonwood scores funding to preserve one of last Gutenberg bibles

Ebonwood assists in care of Louvre's water damaged artifacts

Dr. Windsor Ebonwood promoted to Head of Book and Paper Conservation

Hilde stood at my shoulder, reading over the articles. When she spoke, her voice was softer than I'd ever heard it. "She was so proud of you. Used to read these to me at breakfast, pretending she'd just stumbled across them in the paper." She cleared her throat roughly. "I always knew better. She sought them out. Kept every single one."

"I had no idea," I whispered.

"'Course you didn't. Minta didn't want you to know. Said you had to make your own way without the weight of family expectations." Hilde's large hand landed briefly on my shoulder. "But she watched. Always watching."

Pye hopped onto the desk, careful not to disturb the articles. "I served Minta for decades, and she never once mentioned this archive. Did she think I'd gossip about it to the neighborhood cats?"

"It wasn't about trust," Sibby said quietly, still examining the boxes. "Minta trusted both of you with her life. This was about protection. Some knowledge is dangerous."

"Dangerous how?" Hilde demanded. "Dangerous enough that the people who'd die for this family couldn't know about it?"

"Maybe," I said slowly, looking around at the walls of information, "she thought that not knowing would keep you safe. If someone came looking for information, they couldn't torture it out of you if you didn't have it."

Hilde's expression darkened. "I'd like to see someone try to torture information out of me."

"That's precisely the problem," Pye said. "You'd fight to the death rather than betray the family. Minta knew that. Perhaps she wanted to ensure you'd never have to make that choice."

Hilde was quiet for a long moment, her dark eyes moving from shelf to shelf, taking in the magnitude of what Minta had built in secret. Finally, she sighed. "Well. She's gone now, and the secrets are yours, Win. What are you going to do with them?"

"Right now?" I said, looking at the three of them—Sibby, Pye, and Hilde, all of whom would give their lives to protecting the Ebonwood legacy. "Right now, I'm going to stop keeping secrets from the people I trust. Starting with showing you everything in this room."

Hilde's lips twitched—not quite a smile, but close. "Good. About time someone in this family had some sense. Now let's get back to Fernwood proper, before the house decides to transport us somewhere else. I've got empanadas waiting to go in the oven, and I'll be damned if they'll go to waste."

"Always thinking with your stomach," Pye muttered, but there was affection in his tone.

"Says the cat who ate half a pound of salmon this morning."

I looked around one last time before we headed toward the door. I couldn't wait to explore my new treasure trove properly. Here, I may be able to finally get some answers about my mother.

And now, with Hilde, Sibby, and Pye knowing about it too, maybe we could find those answers together.

"I STILL CAN'T BELIEVE IT," Hilde said for the umpteenth time as we settled back into Fernwood's familiar kitchen. "All my life in this house, and there's a whole archive I never knew about."

She sat back into her rocking chair and picked up her cup of cocoa. "Why in the world would she not tell me about it? Minta told me everything. We trusted each other." Her head fell. "At least, I thought we did."

Watching the feelings of hurt and sadness flick across Hilde's usually stern countenance, a part of me wished I'd never discovered the blasted place.

Pye leaped into her lap, startling her, and then curled up in a furry ball to provide comfort. He rarely did that for anyone besides me, and it made me love the cantankerous beast even more.

"Listen," Sibby said, her loose curlers now hanging dismally around her head." Minta loved you like a sister...as do I, I admit."

I chuckled at these two taciturn, strong women uncomfortably sharing their feelings with one another. There's every chance I was witnessing a once-in-a-lifetime event!

"You know Minta. She would not have kept that from you unless she had a dang good reason," Sibby finished, stuffing her pipe back into her mouth, and mumbled, "And to be fair, I think we should be careful in that place. Maybe not go in there alone. At least at first."

Their heads turned in unison toward me.

The grandfather clock suddenly bonged three times startling us into silence.

"It's time for you to be in bed," Hilde said sternly to me. "I can't believe we're all awake at this time of night."

"And I need my beauty sleep." Sibby patted down her curlers and shuffled back into the library to the guestroom she was using.

I gathered up Pye from Hilde's lap, and we all made our way to our beds. Pye immediately curled up on one of the pillows and began softly snoring. I threw on a pair of pajamas and climbed in next to him.

The soft, cool sheets calmed my excitement at the discovery of the archive, and I tumbled into dreamland.

THE NEXT MORNING, I wasted no time heading back into the secret archive.

I'd had a realization last night that not only might the archive contain information regarding my mother but wasn't there every chance it could help us solve Michey Stramm's murder? I just needed to figure out how to access the information I needed. It didn't make much sense to randomly pull out boxes to see what they contained.

Before the sun had even risen above the giant mangroves against the far side of the pond, I was standing in front of the library fireplace, coffee in hand, staring at the flickering flames.

Setting my cup down on a table, I stepped toward the hearth and began to lift my arms. The secret door disappeared instantly and I could see the dark stone wall of the turret. I felt a tingle of excitement.

I ran up the steps of the cold turret when I realized I'd forgotten my coffee and jogged back down to retrieve it. As I reached for the cup, preparing to immediately bound back up the stairs, someone cleared their throat.

"Whatcha doing?" Pye said, his tail swishing back and forth behind him. He sat on the arm of the sofa looking terribly irritated.

"Oh. Well, to be honest, I thought I might find something in the archive to help me figure out who killed Michey."

"Uh huh. You heard Sibby and Hilde last night. Until we know why Minta kept this a secret from everyone, no one should go in there alone."

"Okay. Well, you're here now. Let's go!" I turned back toward the fire.

"Stop. By any absurd chance, did you notice there is only one way in or out of that room? If anything…um…appeared, we'd be trapped in there."

"The only way in is from Fernwood."

"We don't know that, do we?" he said sternly.

"Pye, that archive has answers."

"This is probably true. Answers that Minta obviously didn't want anyone to know."

I took a sip of coffee and folded my arms. "Don't you want to know?"

"Yes... No," he stuttered "I don't know."

Instantly, I got it.

"I'm afraid too, Pye," I said gently, sitting down next to him on the soft rug. I scratched under his chin, setting off a steady hum of purrs. "But I have to know."

He stretched his neck out, enjoying the scritches, and purred even louder.

Pye looked up at me and nodded. "Fine. Let's go."

THE MOMENT we stepped into the archive, a crackling fire roared to life in the circular fireplace.

I stopped and looked around. Something was wrong. I grabbed Pyewacket before he stepped further into the room.

"Someone's been in here," I whispered.

Rather than the cluttered mess we had witnessed a few hours ago, the room was neat as a pin, not a loose paper or unshelved book in sight. I backed up, ready to haul our rears back to Fernwood. I was not ready to meet a Charming Isles-style boogeyman. No doubt it'd put our human-style boogeyman to shame!

Pye pushed out of my hands and trotted over to the desk, leaping easily onto the surface.

"I don't think so, Windsor," he said as he moved around the desk and pawed at a small piece of paper. "Look at this."

On a sheet of parchment was a single word handwritten in an elegant script: Welcome.

Pye and I looked at each other.

"That's Minta's handwriting," Pye said, wonder evident in his voice.

"Do you think she's here?" I looked around, hoping to see

Grandmother step forward but there really wasn't any place to hide in the turret.

"It's an enchantment. She knew you'd discover this room."

"Then permission to explore!" I laughed and pulled out the closest box and examined it. Unfortunately, the enchantment didn't include labeling the document boxes.

After returning the box to the shelf, I sat in one of the plush chairs in front of the fireplace. Pyewacket jumped into my lap.

"It's like the newspaper morgue at *The Daily Shade*," I said quietly as I ran my hand down Pye's soft far. "I just need to tell the archive what I want."

"Hmm. I do believe you may be correct, *chère*. Give it a try. But don't stop running your hand down my gorgeous fur," he added when I withdrew my hand.

Taking a deep breath and making sure my voice didn't quiver, I announced, "Please provide me with all documents concerning my mother."

Nothing happened.

I scrunched up my brow, shocked at the lack of response.

"Maybe you were too rude," Pye whispered.

"How was I rude?" I hissed back.

"It's an enchanted room in a cold turret. I don't know how it thinks. Now if we're talking about a can of tuna on a kitchen counter, I can tell you exactly what that tuna thinks."

"Hush."

"Maybe you need to say her name," Pye finally whispered.

"Of course!" I whispered back.

I had no idea why we were whispering. It just felt prudent under the circumstances. While the archive hadn't responded to my request, I felt the magic permeating the air, as if it was waiting, listening, the enchantment poised to take action if I asked in the manner required.

"Please," I said firmly, "may I have all records and documents concerning my mother, Genevieve Ebonwood?"

Again, my non-rude request was met by silence. No soft

whooshes as the records sailed through the air, nor gentle thuds as they stacked themselves on the desk.

We both sat quietly. I finally shook my head. "I don't know what else to do."

"What exactly did you say at *The Shade*?"

"I don't remember exactly. Something like,"—I clapped my hands for the third time that morning—"please bring me all the records you're storing concerning Simone Petalsigh."

The room moved into action as a few file folders, newspapers, and leather-bound books deposited themselves on the desk.

I raised my hands, palms up in front of me.

"What did I do differently?"

Pye thought for a moment. "I'm not sure. Ask again."

Again, I clapped twice and asked to see any records concerning my mother.

Nothing.

Pye nodded, a look of understanding in his eyes. "Minta added a spell to not allow the retrieval of anything concerning Gen."

"What? But why—"

He raised a paw silencing my grumbling immediately. "Do you want the good news or the bad news first."

"The good. Always the good first."

"How very positive thinking of you."

I rolled my eyes.

"Spells can be reversed."

"And the bad?" I asked, not sure I wanted to know.

"A spell conjured by Minta is going to be extremely tough to undo."

I sighed and fell back into the chair.

"But that doesn't mean we can't figure out who killed Michey while we work on breaking the spell." I think he grinned. Or maybe he snarled. The expressions looked the same.

∿

"It's freezing in here," I whined, only a few minutes into my research. Yes, whined. The air turning into clouds of vapor in front of my mouth as I spoke gave me the right.

I shivered slightly as I sat down at the desk and pulled the chair in tight.

But I had to admit the view outside was lovely—bare white aspens interspersed with tall evergreens dotted the hilly landscape below, the entire scene covered in a blanket of whiteness so bright it almost hurt my eyes.

"You knew it would be." Pye pawed at the newspaper spread out in front of him on the coffee table as he read the text. "You should have brought your coat. As I did."

"Hah-hah. Funny."

"Well, I bet you don't forget it next time."

"I wish I'd brought it this time!" I sighed and shivered.

Before the words were even out of my mouth, a chunky soft sweater appeared next to me, sliding up each arm.

"Pye!"

"Huh?" he said, never taking his eyes off the document he was reading.

"Look." I held my arms out and crooked one finger toward the fluffy sweater already warming my body.

"Holy smokes!" Pye scrambled off the table and leaped into my lap. "You conjured a sweater out of thin air? That's highly advanced magic."

"I don't think it was me. It was the room." I looked around in awe, more curiouser than ever about the history of this turret and what all it could do.

Pye cleared his throat. "Great turret in the sky..."

"You don't think that's a bit much?"

"...I am quite faint with hunger since Windsor here dragged me into this archive before my breakfast. May I please be granted a tin of mackerel? Removed from the packaging, of course, and placed on a plate of porcelain china."

I pointed as a small delicate plate materialized on the table filled with four silver colored fish.

Pye dove for the table.

I wrinkled my nose. "Bleh." Mackerel wasn't my thing.

I turned back to the documents on the desk. "Once I've made some headway into Michey's death, I want to know more about the history of this room."

Pye smacked his lips, bits of fish fillet stuck in his whiskers. "Ah darn care 'bout the hith'ry. Ah juth' wan' more fith," he said, brine running down his chin.

I ignored him and returned to the meager documents in front of me, putting them into separate piles.

I finally sat back and pulled my "turret" sweater tightly around me. On my left lay all the newspaper articles pertaining to her death that, while interesting, provided little more than I already knew.

On my right sat a much smaller stack—documents detailing Simone's life before her death. I picked up the first page, a grade report from elementary school showing neat rows of A's and B's and set it aside. Beneath it lay a small leather journal, its cover plastered with stickers of orchids—cattleyas, phalaenopsis, lady slippers—their once-vibrant colors faded but still discernible. The leather itself had darkened from brilliant blue to something closer to twilight, its edges soft and worn from countless handlings.

I gently opened the leather journal, its cover softened with wear but still supple. The pages had taken on a faint cream tinge with age, and a subtle scent of old paper and pressed flowers drifted up as I cracked the binding. My fingers brushed the first page, the ink still surprisingly dark despite the years.

The early entries were written in looping, careful handwriting, the kind that comes from a girl trying to make her thoughts look as pretty as her words.

October 10
   Mrs. Thunderwell announced the Winter Gala today and everyone is

already freaking out about dresses. Honestly, I'm more excited about the food. Last year they had those little chocolate eclairs that were absolutely perfect. I hope A asks me to go with him (as friends, of course. BUT STILL!) ♡

I smiled despite myself. This girl sounded so normal, so alive. Not like someone who would end up frozen to death a few months later.

I flipped forward, skimming through entries about herbology practicals and hexbee games with friends, each one capturing small moments of teenage life.

October 25

The Halloween dance is this weekend and I still haven't figured out my costume. Everyone else seems to have theirs planned already. A is going as a vampire (of course—so original. NOT.) but he'll probably still look amazing because that's just how life works. I'm thinking maybe a woodland fairy? Or is that too childish?

Then, on the very next page, everything changed.

The handwriting was the same, but the words made no sense. Strings of letters that looked like gibberish, symbols I didn't recognize, clusters of numbers. After the Halloween entry, it was page after page of cipher.

"What in the world?" I muttered, tilting the journal toward the light as if that would somehow make the code reveal itself.

Whatever happened at the beginning of November, Simone'd hidden it all. Every secret from those final weeks of her life locked away behind an impenetrable wall of symbols and scrambled text.

Arching my back and stretching my arms above my head, I felt the tightness that had settled throughout my body begin to relax. Twisting my head from side to side, the muscles in my neck popped as they relaxed back into place.

"I'm done for today. I need to figure out how to crack this

code." I closed the journal carefully. "Maybe there's a cipher key somewhere else in these boxes."

I looked to the other side of the room and found Pyewacket lolling on his back in a small hammock swinging gently in front of the fireplace.

"You've got to be kidding," I muttered.

Pye rolled to his stomach. "Why not ask the turret to help you search?"

"Oh!" Not used to having a magical archive at my disposal, I hadn't even thought of it.

I was going to do one better. "Please decode the cipher in this journal without damaging the book." I winked at Pye and held up the book. The coded pages remained stubbornly unreadable. "Oh, come on," I said spinning around in my chair and pointing at Pye. "You gave him a hammock."

"That swings itself." Pye sighed contentedly and fell back into the hammock.

"Now, how is that fair!"

A laugh reverberated around the stone room, startling us both.

Great Aunt Sibby leaned against the stone wall.

"I told Hilde this is where I'd find y'all. Any luck?"

"I got a hammock," Pye quipped.

Sibby frowned. "What do you mean?"

"Watch this," I said. "I'll need some tools. Can you please provide me with a variety of fine picks and probes, feeler gauges, a jeweler's loupe, and tweezers?"

A rounded hutch pushed up against the wall disappeared and a long, curved table appeared in its place, the requested tools displayed to the side.

"Well, well," Sibby thought for a moment, rolling her eyes to the ceiling and pursing her lips. "Oh, I know. I'd like a Mars bar."

"Ooh, good choice," Pye said.

I shook my head. It was like trying to build a house with Ren and Stimpy. One slept, one ate, and nothing got done.

Sibby ripped the packaging from the chocolate bar and crammed half in her mouth.

"Mmm!" She pointed at her mouth and then gave me a thumbs up.

Hilde's voice suddenly rolled into the room from Fernwood below. "Breakfast is ready! And if there's a candy dispenser up there, can someone bring me down a Butterfinger?

Forget Ren and Stimpy. I lived with the Three Stooges.

CHAPTER 11

*S*eemed the murder hadn't dimmed Darkly's holiday spirit; if anything, it burned brighter. Perhaps tragedy had a way of reminding people what mattered most.

I could see the proof of it when Keir and I rounded the corner onto Tataille. The Darkly Christmas Market had transformed the street into an enchanted chaos of red Santa hats, gleeful tots, and garlanded streetlight poles. Vendor stalls zigzagged down the cobblestones in delightfully crooked rows, each one twinkling with fairy lights that bobbed and swayed in the winter breeze. The air smelled of cinnamon, fried dough, and the spicy-sweet scent of fresh beignets dusted with cayenne instead of powdered sugar.

Keir laced his fingers with mine as we strolled past families bundled in scarves, their arms laden with shopping bags and wrapped packages. A group of children darted between the stalls, shrieking with laughter as they chased each other through the falling snow. One little girl stopped to press her mittened hands against a display of snow globes in the windows of Sugarloaf's that swirled with actual miniature blizzards, her eyes wide with wonder.

I paused at a holiday booth where wreaths hung from every

available space, my attention snagged by one that seemed to shimmer in the late afternoon light. Spanish moss draped like silver-green lace between clusters of crystal orchids that caught the sun, while waxy magnolia leaves formed the base—pure Louisiana Gothic elegance.

"I'll be over there when you're done, lass." Keir brushed a kiss to my temple, his warm breath stirring loose tendrils of my hair. He gestured toward The Gator, where Tal, Laurent Rivier, and Pup Bane stood clustered outside, mugs of hot spiced cider in hand and grins already spreading across their faces at the sight of their alpha approaching.

He flashed me that devastating smile. Then he strode away with that easy, confident swagger, his broad shoulders cutting through the crowd like he owned the very cobblestones beneath his feet.

Something about the way he moved—all power and masculine grace wrapped up in a protective, loving nature—made my heart stumble over itself.

I pressed a hand to my chest, willing my pulse to behave.

It didn't listen.

As I turned my attention back to the wreath, it began to sing.

Not the cheerful, bright rendition you'd hear piped through a department store, but something older. Darker. The melody of "God Rest Ye Merry, Gentlemen" drifted from the wreath in a minor key, the harmonies layered and discordant, as if three different centuries were singing at once. The crystal orchids chimed like distant bells, while the moss added a deep, resonant undertone that seemed to pulse with ancient magic. The magnolia leaves rustled in rhythm, though there wasn't a breath of wind.

"The wreath sings on its own," a melodious voice said from behind the booth's counter.

An elf with silver-blue hair and pointed ears stepped forward, her elegant, delicate features arranged in an amused smile.

"The crystal orchids respond to ambient energy—joy, curiosity, even a good strong wind," she continued, gesturing to the display with one graceful hand. "The moss carries memory of old songs, and the magnolia leaves...well, they just like to join in."

I studied the wreath as it continued its haunting carol, the eerie harmonies somehow perfectly suited to Darkly's particular brand of Christmas spirit.

"It's perfect for Fernwood," I murmured, already imagining it hanging in the kitchen, greeting visitors with its uncanny song. The woman tucked it into a bag for me, and I hurried to join Keir and the shifters as snowflakes drifted down like sifted confectioner's sugar, dusting the cobblestones with white.

"Let's see more of the market," Keir said. He nodded to his shifters. "We'll be back in a few." They raised their glasses in salute.

A young couple ahead of us stopped to steal a kiss beneath one of the floating lanterns, their laughter bright as bells. Nearby, an older woman balanced three shopping bags while trying to corral a toddler who seemed determined to touch every single enchanted ornament within reach.

"This is what I love about Darkly," I said, pausing to admire a display against the bricks of The Magic Cup—hand-carved wooden toys that moved on their own. A tiny wooden alligator snapped its jaws at me playfully, making me laugh. "Everything is always over the top. Nowhere else would have Christmas decorations that bite back."

Keir's laugh rumbled through his chest, warm as whiskey. "Wait until you see the Papa Noël offerings. Last year someone left him a live chicken."

"No way. Did he take it?"

"Aye. Though the debate about whether he ate it or kept it as a pet raged for weeks."

A cluster of shoppers—three women arguing good-naturedly over the best hot sauce blend—shifted to the side and there it was. In the very center of the market like a shrine to culinary chaos, sat the children's offering table. A hand-painted sign in glitter glue declared:

The display overflowed with Louisiana Christmas treasures. A wooden bowl filled with sweet, creamy pralines. Miniature pecan pies arranged in the shape of a pirogue. One ambitious child had contributed gumbo in a mason jar with a note that read: "Warm before flight." Several small bottles of hot sauce had been tied with green ribbon and tucked between the plates like party favors.

And there, right in the middle of the chaos, sat a towering platter of beignets stuffed with andouille sausage and drizzled with pepper jelly—sitting on a very recognizable platter.

I laughed, spotting the tray. "Sibby contributed to the children's table?"

"Well, she is a child at heart," Keir said, eyeing the beignets with obvious interest.

A father hoisted his daughter up in the air so she could add her contribution—a carefully wrapped praline she'd clearly made herself, the wax paper slightly wrinkled from small hands. The little girl's face glowed with pride and excitement.

"I hope Papa Noël likes pecans," the little girl announced to the crowd at large, holding up her praline. "I picked the pecans myself!"

"Oh, *ma petite*." An elderly woman stopped, her cane tapping the cobblestones as she bent down with a grandmother's ease. Her fingers, gnarled but gentle, patted the child's arm. "Papa Noël adores pralines. And ones with pecans picked by such careful hands? Those will be his favorites, I guarantee."

The little girl's smile stretched impossibly wider, revealing a gap-toothed grin. With both hands, she placed the praline on the offering table—gently, deliberately—nestling it between a jar of fig preserves and a bundle of dried lavender.

The sweetness of the moment settled warm in my chest. This was Darkly at its best—strange and wonderful and full of heart.

We continued down the cobblestones, weaving between more families and groups of friends. Two teenage girls giggled over a display of charmed jewelry that changed colors with your mood. A man with gray-streaked hair examined a set of carved wooden nutcrackers with the serious concentration of a true collector.

I stopped so abruptly that Keir nearly bumped into me.

The brown-haired woman from the gala stood near a booth selling candles—bayou-scented, smelling of cedar and moss and orchids. The same woman who'd reacted so strangely when she'd seen Michey's body. Horror, yes, but threaded through with recognition. The kind that turns your stomach because you'd been expecting it.

Our eyes met.

For a heartbeat, neither of us moved. Then she offered a small, tentative smile before turning back to the candle display.

"Win?" Keir's voice was low, concerned. He followed my gaze to the woman. "Everything all right, love?"

"Yeah," I said, trying for casual as we started walking again. "I'm fine."

But I wasn't fine. Not really.

I shook off the stab of fear.

"Bonny night for a market," Keir said, his accent softening the words. "Though it's the company that makes it perfect."

Heat rose in my cheeks despite the cold. "Smooth talker."

"Would I lie?" He drew my hand to his lips, his brown eyes

never leaving mine as he pressed a kiss to my knuckles. Then he tucked my arm into the crook of his elbow, and we continued our stroll like something out of a Victorian romance novel—if Victorian romance novels included vengeful Christmas demons, enchanted hot sauce, and beautiful, loving alpha shifters.

Ahead, a crowd had gathered around a juggler who kept five flaming torches spinning through the air while standing on one foot. Children sat cross-legged on the cold cobblestones, their faces tilted up in awe.

"Win! Keir!" Maisie Marlowe waved us over to her booth, which glittered like an open jewelry box under the fairy lights. Mooncharms Jewels & Gems sparkled with jeweled ornaments that caught the candlelight like captured stars—ruby cardinals with emerald tail feathers, crystal icicles that chimed softly in the breeze, and a silver ornament shaped like a crescent moon.

I couldn't help the small sound of delight that escaped me when I picked up a miniature golden reindeer. The moment my fingers touched it, the creature sprang to life—hooves tapping an invisible rhythm, head tossing as it pranced in place. Magic hummed beneath the gilt surface. "Maisie, this is exquisite." I held it out to her, the reindeer still performing its tiny, eternal dance. "How do you capture so much life in something so small?"

"Family secret," Maisie winked, carefully wrapping it up in festive tissue paper. "But between you and me, a little bit of Christmas magic goes a long way."

Keir selected a wolf-shaped ornament carved from moonstone, its surface shimmering with an inner light. "For the Cairns' tree," he said, a faint blush coloring his cheeks, obviously embarrassed at the thoughtful gesture. The Silverfangs were so lucky to have that man. As was I.

"That's one of my favorites," Maisie said, wrapping it carefully. "The moonstone responds to pack bonds. It'll glow brighter when family's near."

We paid for our treasures and slipped back into the festive throng. Santa hats bobbed everywhere I looked, worn at jaunty angles by elves and shifters and humans alike. A chihuahua pup in a tiny reindeer sweater pranced past on a leash, his tail wagging furiously. His owner carried enough shopping bags to stock a small store.

My eyes followed the cute pup through the crowd until it passed by a pair of black Bruno Magli boots below an obviously expensive suit. Lex Lavallette. He stood near the edge of the market, his slick silver hair catching the fairy lights as he examined a display of rare whiskeys. Even in the chaos of the Christmas market, he moved through the space like he owned it, that particular brand of confidence that came from genuine power rather than posturing.

A few stalls down, among the jostling crowd, we came across the booth of Mr. Creech, Darkly's one and only zombie, where Christmas poppets hung from tiny wooden gallows—a delightfully macabre twist on holiday decorating that was so very Darkly.

He waved when he saw us, a slow deliberate act. "Listen to them carefully and pick the one that speaks to you loudest," Mr. Creech advised in his papery voice. His gnarled fingers adjusted the poppets with surprising gentleness and care. "They choose their humans as much as you choose them."

I nodded, leaning over his display, examining each unique poppet. "These are amazing. The detail!"

Pride flickered across his weathered features.

I found myself drawn to a poppet with wild hair made of Spanish moss and a tiny amethyst sewn over its heart. When I touched it, warmth spread through my fingers, and I could have sworn it hummed with contentment.

"Wise choice," Mr. Creech nodded approvingly. "That one's got protective magic woven in. Old bayou blessing from my old friend Tonton Filou, the Laughing Man."

The name flitted across my conscious—like a greeting—then was gone. I shivered and tugged my coat tighter around me. Keir noticed and pulled me closer, wrapping his arms around me.

"Will it protect me from swamp imps?" I asked, only half-joking. "Or maybe Frau Perchta if she decides to put me on her naughty list?"

Mr. Creech's laugh sounded like wind through autumn leaves. "The imps, yes. Perchta?" He shook his head. "Child, nobody's got magic strong enough for that."

Ooh. Not the answer I was hoping for.

Keir paid for my poppet and we moved on, past a vendor demonstrating enchanted snow globes that played music when you shook them. Each one contained a tiny scene from Darkly—miniature versions of the Darkly Falls, a raised wood home in the middle of the swamp, even the cursed cemetery tower, all rendered in exquisite detail. People crowded around, oohing and ahhing as the vendor wound up a globe showing Tataille Street in summer, complete with tiny people walking along the cobblestones.

"Look at their little faces!" one woman exclaimed, peering closer. "I swear that one just waved at me."

The market pulsed with energy and joy. Music drifted from a fiddle player tucked into a corner, his bow flying across the strings in a spirited rendition of "Grandma Got Run over by a Reindeer" with a distinctly Cajun flair. A few people had started dancing, their boots tapping against the cobblestones.

I glimpsed Mrs. Quenleigh near a high-end boutique booth, examining a display of designer scarves with the focused attention of someone who knew quality when she saw it. She moved with that particular grace of the extremely wealthy—unhurried, confident, as if the market existed for her convenience rather than the other way around. When she noticed me looking, her expression remained perfectly neutral before she turned her attention back to the scarves.

More children ran past, their voices high with excitement. One boy waved a wooden sword he'd clearly just purchased, declaring himself the "Knight of Christmas" while his friends groaned and laughed. Their parents trailed behind, laden with packages and wearing expressions of patient exhaustion mixed with genuine joy.

The snow kept falling, gentle and persistent, transforming the market into its own giant snow globe. Fairy lights reflected off the white-dusted cobblestones, creating pools of amber and sapphire and ruby red light.

By the time we circled back to the Gator, our group had claimed a sprawling table on the temporary patio Jess had set up outside the tavern and multiplied considerably since we'd left the shifters earlier. The seating arrangement told its own story of alliances and tensions. Jess sat next to Zelda, who was holding open a shopping bag that seemed to have a life of its own, squirming and occasionally emitting faint musical notes.

Tzazi occupied one end of the table with Zavier, her platinum pixie cut catching the fairy lights as she pointedly ignored Jess.

On the other side of the table, Tal, Laurent, and Pup had forgotten their mugs entirely, caught up in whatever tag-team story Chase and Ren were spinning. Laurent shook his head in disbelief while Tal wiped tears from his eyes. Pup just stared, mouth hanging open.

Just as Keir and I approached, his sister Quinn emerged from the crowd, her voluminous afro adorned with a single sprig of holly and her golden arm bands glinting in the candlelight. She gave me a wink and slid into the empty seat beside Laurent with the easy grace of someone who belonged everywhere she went, her amber eyes taking in the scene with a beta shifter's keen assessment.

Jess waved us over, her wings shimmering faintly in the fairy light. "You're just in time! Zelda brought...something."

"Entertainment," Zelda corrected, beaming. "I brought entertainment."

Tzazi groaned.

We joined the group as servers brought out platters of hot food —fried oyster po'boys, jambalaya that steamed in the cold air, and baskets of hush puppies. It was all elbows and arms as we grabbed bowls and plates and dug in.

Once everyone had been served, Chase raised his mug. "To Christmas in Darkly," he toasted.

"Christmas in Darkly," we echoed and clinked our mugs together, the sound bright and cheerful despite the close of the day. Around us, the market continued its festive chaos. More vendors called out their wares. More children shrieked with joy. More couples stole kisses under the floating lanterns.

For a moment, everything felt normal. Safe. Like maybe we could enjoy Christmas without perchten and murder and ancient magical threats.

That's when Zelda pulled out the mushrooms.

They looked innocent enough at first glance—delicate white fungi about the size of silver dollars, each one dusted with what looked like powdered sugar. Zelda held them up proudly.

"Snow-shrooms!" she announced. "They sing Christmas carols when they come in contact with real snow. Uncle Jovial's using them for an upcoming catering job. I thought they'd be perfect for the market!"

The snow, which had been falling gently all evening, chose that exact moment to intensify. Fat flakes drifted down onto Zelda's outstretched hands, settling onto the snow-shrooms with delicate precision.

A sudden commotion erupted from the woods. The market fell silent instantly—song and laughter snuffed like a flame.

The sound came first—branches snapping, heavy footfalls crashing through underbrush, and men's voices raised in terror. Then a group of men in flannel shirts and boots, axes hanging from their hands, erupted from the forest onto Tataille Street like demons were chasing them.

Which, as it turned out, wasn't far from the truth.

Alvar Vache led the stampede, his face bone-white with terror, eyes wide and wild. Behind him, the other men stumbled and shoved, their axes and ropes abandoned in their haste to escape.

One man tripped and fell, scrambling on hands and knees until his companions hauled him upright. Their lanterns swung wildly, casting crazy shadows across their panic-stricken faces.

"RUN!" Alvar bellowed, his voice cracking with fear. "THE PERCHTEN! THEY'RE COMING!"

The festive atmosphere shattered like glass. People who'd been laughing moments before now fled toward the safety of nearby shops. Shopping bags hit the cobblestones as parents scooped up children and ran. The fiddle player's bow screeched to a halt mid-song.

Then, to add to the pandemonium, the snow-shrooms began to SCREAM.

Not sing. Not hum. Not even perform an off-key but charming rendition of "Jingle Bells." They screamed like someone had taken a Christmas carol, dipped it in acid, and set it on fire.

"What the—" Tzazi started, then cursed as Pyewacket launched himself under the table with a yowl of protest.

"They weren't supposed to scream!" Zelda wailed, looking genuinely distressed as the snow-shrooms continued their ear-splitting performance. "The enchantment was meant to create gentle harmonies!"

"Well, they are harmonizing," Chase said grimly, hands pressed over his ears. "Just not gently."

"MAKE IT STOP!" Quinn shrieked, her hands clamped over her ears. "Wolf hearing is sensitive!"

The shrieking tore through the Christmas market. The perchten sighting had rattled everyone; the mushrooms pushed them over the edge. Vendors' booths erupted in confusion as customers scattered. Children began crying, their candle lanterns wobbling dangerously.

Several of the more sensitive magical creatures in the area responded with their own alarmed noises. A pixie vendor started hiccupping sparks, and somewhere nearby, a hellhound puppy howled in distress.

The juggler's flaming torches clattered to the cobblestones, quickly extinguished by snow covered cobbles. The fiddle player clutched his instrument to his chest and bolted.

Keir rose in one fluid motion as the men stumbled toward us. He caught Alvar's elbow, keeping him upright. "Steady now, mate. Tell me what you saw."

I wrapped an arm around Alvar from the other side before his legs gave out. He sagged between us, trembling violently enough that I could feel each shudder.

"Horned—" one of the tree-cutters answered, clutching his chest as he tried to catch his breath. "Horned masks—"

"Those weren't masks!" Alvar cut him off, his voice shaking with conviction. He grabbed Keir's arm with trembling hands. "I'm telling you those things were real as the winter itself. Seven feet tall if they were an inch, with antlers like ancient trees and eyes that burned red as hellfire!"

"Dragging sacks," gasped another man, pointing back toward the dark tree line with a shaking hand. "Chains clanging like death bells. They came out of nowhere—shadows with horns and faces like demons—"

"We were just cutting down our Christmas trees," another man interrupted, his voice high and panicked.

"Just like we do every year. Then the temperature dropped so fast I could see my breath turn to ice, and the woods went dead silent. No birds. No wind. Nothing. Like the whole forest was holding its breath."

"We weren't doing nothing wrong," another man said before rushing to grab his children and wife and disappearing, veilshifting to safety.

"And then we heard them," Alvar continued, his face gray as ash. "Bells. Those awful bells, getting closer and closer. We turned to run and there they were—emerging from the shadows like they'd been standing there the whole time, just waiting for us to notice."

Chase leaped up so quickly his chair toppled backward, his hands already weaving a hasty protection sigil around our patio.

Golden light shimmered into existence, forming a barrier just as Pyewacket poked his head out from beneath the table, his fur standing on end. He scrambled onto the tabletop and launched himself at my shoulder, claws digging in through my coat.

"Did they follow you?" Chase demanded, his sorcerer senses already scanning the edge of the forest.

"I don't know!" Alvar shouted. "We didn't stop to check!"

Zelda finally managed to stuff the screaming snow-shrooms back into their bag, muffling the worst of the noise. But the damage was done—the cheerful Christmas market had already transformed into something out of a winter nightmare, with vendors hastily closing their booths and families fleeing toward the warmth and safety of their homes.

"Everyone, get inside," Keir commanded, his alpha voice brooking no argument. "Home if you can."

Our group scattered like leaves in a storm. Tzazi vanished with a soft pop, replaced by a small bat that flapped urgently toward the darkening sky. The Silverfangs transformed into massive wolves—larger than should be possible, their hackles raised and teeth bared. Without a sound, they turned and loped toward the woods, heading straight for where Alvar's group had emerged.

Jess's wings flowed out behind her in a shimmer of iridescent orange, and with a quick kiss blown to the group, she soared through the air toward the safety of Greywolf Manor. Chase, and Ren had veilshifted home, most likely, getting to safety while they could.

The Christmas market lay empty. Shopping bags littered the cobblestones alongside trampled packages. The only movement came from the falling snow and one small candle lantern, bouncing down the empty street.

But I lingered at the edge of the patio, Pyewacket's claws still embedded in my shoulder, searching the treeline with a growing sense of dread.

Keir's hand found mine, his fingers warm and steady.

As we hurried toward his Land Rover, I took a chance look behind. The joy of the market had soured into something else entirely. The threat was no longer theoretical. Whether perchten or pranksters, something was stirring in the woods around Darkly.

And whatever it was, it was getting bolder.

The snow continued to fall as Keir drove us to Fernwood, each flake catching the streetlights like tiny white warnings scattered across the night. Behind us, the market square stood empty except for Papa Noël's abandoned offering table, the children's carefully prepared gifts now dusted with snow and silence. Sibby's beignets sat untouched in the center, steam still rising from the platter like smoke signals to an absent saint.

In the distance, barely audible above the wind and the Land Rover's engine, those strange bells clonked a few more times—closer now, and somehow hungrier—before fading into the winter dark.

CHAPTER 12

*T*he familiar rhythm of book repair usually calmed my mind, but today my hands moved automatically through the motions while my thoughts churned elsewhere. I pressed a bone folder along the spine of a water-damaged folklore anthology, trying to lose myself in the methodical process of restoration, but the Christmas market chaos kept replaying in my mind—those strange, hollow-sounding bells echoing in my head. The empty market.

Keir had sworn Perchta was harmless, but what about her perchten? Those creatures weren't just causing mischief—they were hunting fear, feeding on it. Every rattling chain, every bestial growl echoing through the streets of Darkly felt purposeful. Designed to unsettle. To terrify. If Perchta was so harmless, why did her minions turn our Christmas market into a nightmare?

"Your technique is abysmal today," Pyewacket observed from his perch atop a stack of vintage Charming Isles travel guides. He regarded me with the sort of withering judgment only cats could master. "That poor book deserves better than your distracted fumbling."

I paused, realizing I'd been pressing too hard with the folder, leaving an unwanted crease in the delicate paper. "Sorry. My mind's elsewhere."

"Obviously." Pye tilted his head—and yes, even one-eyed and judgmental, it was devastatingly adorable—his yellow eye narrowing to a slit. "The perchten have rattled you quite thoroughly."

"I thought they were supposed to leave people alone," I said, gesturing vaguely toward the chaos beyond my lab. "Instead, they seem hell-bent on terrifying the entire town."

"So it would appear." Pye leaped down to the worktable with the fluid grace only cats possess, picking his way carefully through the scattered conservation tools and materials spread across its surface. His tail swished once, precisely, as if punctuating his point. "Though I suspect there's more to their presence than simple mischief."

I set down the bone folder and looked at him properly. "So does that mean Perchta actually is the one behind Michey's murder then?"

But before he could answer, the shop's entrance bell chimed with unusual intensity, cutting through our conversation like a blade through silk.

Benicio swept through the front door without ceremony, winter air and snowflakes following in his wake. He moved with more purpose than his usual theatrical grace, and the black silk bundle in his gloved hands commanded immediate attention.

"I cracked the glamour," he announced without preamble, his dark eyes bright with satisfaction.

I emerged from the conservation lab, brushing paper dust from my sweater. "The ledger?"

"The very one." He held up the silk-wrapped bundle like a trophy. "Took me most of the night and a few favors I'd rather not specify, but the secrets are finally visible."

Pyewacket materialized beside me, his whiskers twitching with interest. "This should be illuminating."

"Let's hope so," I said, gesturing toward the fireplace seating area. "What did you find?"

We settled into the plush chairs near the crackling fire, the wrapped ledger on the small table between us like a dark omen.

His gaze drifted to my poppet on the mantle, lingering on the amethyst heart embedded in its chest. "Abimilech does excellent work. Commanding guards."

Benicio turned back to the ledger and unwrapped it with reverent care, his long fingers working at the knots as if he were handling something holy. The black silk whispered as it fell away, revealing the worn leather cover I remembered from the pawnshop, cracked and age-darkened, smelling faintly of dust and old magic.

I opened the book, half-expecting the same blank pages that had taunted me before.

Instead, faint writing shimmered across the cream surfaces, appearing and disappearing like moonlight on water. The script seemed to breathe, pulsing with a silvery luminescence.

"Any chance of a coffee?" Benicio asked, pushing back a lock of dark hair that had fallen across his eye.

"Of course," I said, and a cup of Turkish brew materialized on the table beside him, steam curling upward in lazy spirals.

He lifted it to his lips, took a long sip, then touched his heart with his free hand. "Wonderful."

Setting the cup down with a satisfied sigh, he leaned forward. "The glamour was more complex than I initially thought." His fingers hovered just above the open book, close enough that I could see the shimmer of magic responding to his proximity.

"Multiple layers, designed to hide different information from different eyes. Casted by Malachi Muck. A mercenary conjuror who lives in The Graves. Absolutely no conscience or scruples."

"How did you crack it?" I leaned forward, squinting at the revealed text. The handwriting was cramped and hurried, as if whoever had written it was always looking over their shoulder.

"Magic invariably leaves a trail so one must follow it down the rabbit hole, removing enchantments, layer by layer. Digging down to the base object. Had to roll up my sleeves for this one."

"And now we can read it all?" Pyewacket asked, jumping onto the table for a better view.

I translated.

"The majority," Benicio said. "Some entries remain partially obscured, but enough is legible to understand the meaning. The most recent ones are perfectly clear."

He turned to the final entries, and my breath caught as I read the last line written in Michey's distinctive scrawl:

One-of-a-kind unicorn hairpin. From LG.

"That's got to be the hairpin I saw in his pawnshop," I whispered, my heart hammering against my ribs.

Benicio nodded grimly. "Undoubtedly. And, interestingly, this entry is dated just two days before the gala."

Pyewacket's tail lashed once.

"And 'LG'?" I asked.

"That," Benicio said, "is where things become interesting." He flipped back through several pages, his finger tracing various entries. "The initials 'LG' appear throughout the ledger, going back years. Whoever this person is, looks like they've been doing business with Michey for a very long time."

I studied the cramped handwriting, my conservation experience helping me decipher the sometimes faded text. Each entry represented a transaction, but many hinted at dealings far darker than simple pawnshop business.

"Look at this pattern," I said, pointing to a series of entries from the previous year. "Jewelry, personal items, small valuables —all from 'LG,' and all described as 'payment for services rendered.'"

"Services," Benicio repeated, his voice thoughtful. "Not items pawned for cash, but payment. As if LG was settling debts."

"Or paying for silence," Pyewacket observed darkly.

The fire crackled in the silence that followed, popping and hissing as a log shifted in the grate.

"How far back do these LG entries go?" My voice sounded hollow in the quiet.

Benicio carefully thumbed through the ledger, the shimmer-script dancing under his fingertips as he turned page after page. "The first payment appears..." He paused, tracing a line with his finger. "Nineteen years ago. Almost a year after the death of Simone Petalsigh."

I'd been staring at the pages, at Michey's cramped, greasy handwriting documenting transaction after sordid transaction, when something that had been scratching at the edge of my conscious broke through.

The breath left my lungs in a rush.

"LG" My voice came out strangled, barely more than a whisper. "Oh my god. I know who LG is."

Both Benicio and Pye swiveled toward me. Benicio's ebony hair caught the firelight as he straightened, his expression sharpening with sudden intensity. Pye's eye fixed on me with that unnerving focus that always made me feel like he could see straight through to my bones.

"Lavallette Global." The words tasted bitter. "It's Lex Lavallette's company."

For a moment, no one moved. No one spoke.

The fire popped again, louder this time, and a log shifted with a shower of sparks that painted the room in dancing orange light.

"Well," Pye said from his perch on the arm of the sofa, his tail flicking once, twice. "That does complicate matters, doesn't it?"

"Complicate?" I turned to stare at the cat. "Pye, Lex Lavallette is one of the most powerful people on Darkly Island. If he's connected to Michey's operation—"

"Then we're not just dealing with a two-bit pawn shop operator anymore," Benicio finished grimly. He ran a hand through his hair, disrupting its usual perfect arrangement. "We're dealing with someone who has the resources, the connections, and the influence to make problems disappear."

I took a deep breath and flipped back through the ledger,

scanning earlier entries. Years of transactions stretched across the pages, Michey's cramped handwriting documenting deal after deal. The ink changed—sometimes black, sometimes blue, occasionally a brownish sepia that looked like it had been mixed with something I didn't want to think about. The handwriting shifted too, evolving from the careful script of someone just starting out to the hasty scrawl of a man who'd stopped caring about appearances.

I wasn't just holding a record of transactions. This was a history. A chronicle of every desperate soul Michey had exploited, every shady deal he'd brokered, every magical object or service he'd traded for profit.

And Lex Lavallette and the initials LG appeared again and again, woven throughout like a dark thread in an already rotten tapestry.

"Here," I said, my voice tight with anger as I found what I was looking for. "Mari's grandfather's land."

Benicio leaned closer to read over my shoulder. The entry was detailed and damning:

Riverbend tract - 847 acres prime agricultural land. Acquired from E. Boudreaux via special contract. 100% ownership acquired. Matter closed.

Benicio's finger traced down to the next damning record. His jaw tightened as he read it aloud:

"Sweetwater Springs homestead - 34 acres waterfront property with natural mineral spring. Acquired from M. Hathaway via 'health remedy contract' - traded property deed for 'guaranteed cure' of terminal illness. Cure delivered as specified (extended life by 2 1/2 months). Full transfer completed per contractual terms. Owner relocated to mainland hospice facility."

I felt my stomach turn. "He gave someone with a terminal illness false hope, took their family land, and technically fulfilled the contract by giving them less than three more months of life?"

Benicio's eyes had gone cold. "That's exactly what he did.

Legal enough to hold up under magical contract law, evil enough to condemn him in any moral court."

The third entry made my hands shake:

"Bellweather Orchards - 156 acres heritage pecan groves, established 1847. Acquired from the Bellweather Family Trust via 'prosperity spell agreement.' Clients requested financial success for eldest son's business venture. Spell delivered as contracted - business thrived for exactly 13 months before natural collapse. Family defaulted on property payments (triple compound interest clause, paragraph 47, subsection D). Foreclosure completed. Full ownership transferred 5x market price to Lavallette Global. Original family now residing in rental housing in The Hollows."

Benicio's voice was taut and quiet. "I knew Michey was a horrible person. I just didn't realize how truly horrible he was."

"Bastard," Pyewacket hissed, his fur standing on end. "He documented his crimes."

"And the crimes of others." I continued reading, my hands trembling slightly with rage. "There are names here—people who he sold the land to for four or five times the market value."

"Michey kept records of everyone involved," Benicio observed quietly. "Insurance policies of his own."

"Which means someone on this list had a very good reason to want him dead," I said, scanning the familiar surnames. "Seems Mari was telling the truth about everything."

THE SHOP HAD TAKEN on a different character in the evening light, the front glass now glowing from the streetlamps outside rather than filtering daylight. The space felt both protective and vulnerable, a sanctuary that could easily become a target if the wrong people discovered what we'd learned.

"So what's our next move?" I asked, closing the ledger carefully and wrapping it back in its black silk covering. I carefully laid it on my desk.

"First," Benicio said, rising from his chair with fluid grace, "I'm going to place some additional wards around this place. If someone killed Michey for this information, they won't hesitate to come after anyone else who's seen it."

Pyewacket nodded approvingly. "Sensible."

I felt the weight of what we'd uncovered settling over me like a heavy cloak. The ledger wasn't just evidence of blackmail; it was a roadmap to decades of corruption that reached into some of Darkly's most established families.

I stood and moved to the window, watching the last of the Christmas market vendors packing up their stalls. The cheerful holiday lights seemed grotesquely out of place now that I knew what darkness lurked beneath Darkly's festive surface.

Benicio moved toward the door, his fingertip tracing a ward sigil along the frame—ancient symbols that pulsed faintly gold before fading into the wood. I felt the magic take hold—a subtle hum as the MET's shadowmen added their power to his. The beauty of these wards was their discernment—a lost traveler at midnight would find the door swinging open, while someone with ill intent would find it decidedly...far less welcoming.

"Be careful, Benicio," I warned. "If the people in those ledgers realize someone's been breaking through them..."

"They'll know exactly who to come looking for," he finished with a wry smile. "Don't worry, darling. I've survived much worse than angry Darkly Island conspirators."

As Benicio disappeared into the winter evening, I turned to find Pyewacket watching me with his golden eye, his expression unusually serious.

"You realize what this means, don't you?" he said quietly. "We're not just investigating murders anymore. We're threatening to expose a conspiracy that's been in place for generations."

I nodded, feeling the full weight of that truth settle in my chest. "I know. But we can't unknow what we've learned, Pye. And we can't let them get away with it."

"Even if it means putting ourselves directly in their crosshairs?"

I looked around the MET—at the warm firelight dancing across the walls, the towering shelves of books that represented knowledge and truth, the stained-glass windows that had witnessed so many secrets. This place had become my sanctuary, my home, my purpose. But more than that, it represented everything those conspirators sought to destroy—transparency, justice, the preservation of truth.

"Especially then," I said firmly. "Minta didn't leave me this place just to maintain portals and stay safe. The Ebonwoods have always been guardians of truth, even when it's dangerous."

Pyewacket purred softly, a rumbling sound of approval. "Then we'd better make sure we're ready for whatever comes next."

CHAPTER 13

*T*he rest of the morning passed quietly until just before noon, when Mrs. Quenleigh appeared among the stacks like a well-dressed ghost. I hadn't heard the door chime, hadn't seen her enter, but suddenly she was there perusing the rare books section.

"Mrs. Quenleigh," I called out, injecting politeness into my voice. "Finding everything you need?"

She glanced up from a leather-bound volume of Charming Isles history, her smile perfectly calibrated to appear friendly while revealing nothing. "Just browsing, thank you. You have an impressive collection."

Her movements were elegant and measured as she replaced the book on its shelf. The woman struck me as the type who acquired books for status rather than substance or travel.

"Is there something specific I can help you find?" I persisted, moving closer but keeping the central aisle between us.

Before she could answer, the door chimed again, and Letha Marsh rushed in. Her cheeks were flushed from the cold, and there was something urgent in her manner that made Pyewacket's ears perk forward with interest.

Letha stopped dead when she saw Eudora. The two women

stared at each other across the shop, and the silence that fell was sharp enough to draw blood.

"Letha. How lovely to see you."

"Eudora."

Letha's response was neutral, but I caught the hardness beneath it.

Mrs. Quenleigh straightened, smoothing down her expensive coat with deliberate precision, her hands twirling in the air between strokes.

"Well," she said brightly, "I should let you get to your business. Miss Ebonwood. Thank you for your time."

She glided toward the door with the same silent grace with which she'd arrived. The door chimed softly as it closed behind her, but the echo seemed to linger longer than it should have.

Her hands were trembling as she pulled off her gloves. "I'm Letha Marsh. In town for the gala. I was hoping to catch you before you got busy. There's something I need to tell you," Letha said, her voice barely above a whisper. "About Simone Petalsigh."

My pulse quickened. "What about her?"

A group of teen girls piled into the shop, giggling and whispering. Leidy Vache gave me a wave as they headed up the stairs.

"Not here," Letha said quickly, casting a nervous look around the shop. "Too many ears, too many eyes. Could you meet me tonight? At The White Hart Inn bar, after seven?"

The fear threaded through her words was contagious. "Letha, if you know something—"

"I can't. Not here." Her brown eyes darted to the shop door, the shadowed corners between the bookshelves, anywhere but my face. "Please. Just meet me tonight. It's important."

When I hesitated, Letha whispered, "If you don't, someone else could die."

The weight of her words settled over the shop like a blanket of snow, muffling everything except the crackle of the fire and the distant sound of wind against the windows. I found myself studying her face, noting the dark circles under her eyes, the way her fingers worried at the strap of her handbag.

"Seven o'clock," I agreed. "I'll be there."

Relief flooded her features. "Thank you. And Ms. Ebonwood? Be careful who you trust. Not everyone is who they seem to be."

She left as quickly as she'd arrived, the door chiming behind her with a note that sounded almost mournful. I watched through the window as she hurried down the cobblestone street, her figure quickly swallowed by the swirling mist.

"Well," Pye said, leaping onto the counter with fluid grace. "That was delightfully vague and foreboding. I do hope she provides more details this evening. Shall we spend the day wildly speculating?"

THE AFTERNOON DRAGGED by with the weight of waiting. Every time the door chimed, I expected to see Letha returning with second thoughts or Mrs. Quenleigh coming back to finish whatever business had brought her here in the first place.

Why won't people just tell me what they want?

But the customers who wandered in were ordinary—a hedge witch looking for a book to transport her to her sister's home in Wychwood, a nervous young strigoi vampire in a black cloak asking in hushed tones if we had anything that could get him to Nocturnelle before the next sunrise, and a ghost who kept flickering in and out while trying to book passage to a haunted castle in Rosewood.

By six o'clock, I was ready to close early.

Thirty minutes later, I headed out. Perhaps a glass of wine as I waited would help calm my strangely frayed nerves.

"You're uneasy," Pye observed, leaping onto my shoulders in one graceful movement and burrowing into the warmth of my scarf.

"Shouldn't I be? Two people dead, corporate corruption, and now Letha Marsh acting like she's carrying state secrets."

"Perhaps you should bring backup to this meeting," he suggested.

I considered it. Keir would come without question, but his protective instincts might overwhelm Letha before she could share what she knew. Tzazi would be formidable in a crisis, but her sharp edges might put Letha on the defensive.

"I think this one requires a gentler touch," I said finally. "Besides I've got you."

"How reassuring," Pye drawled. "Your track record with 'gentler touches' is truly inspiring."

The wind picked up as I left the MET and made my way toward The White Hart. The winter darkness had settled over Darkly like a heavy quilt, and the streetlamps cast wavering pools of light that did little to chase away the shadows gathering between buildings.

When I reached the corner where Tataille Street met Bayou Boulevard, I couldn't shake the feeling that I was being watched. I glanced back over my shoulder, scanning the empty street behind me. Nothing moved in the lamp-lit fog except shadows that could have been anything—or anyone.

I pulled my coat tighter, listening for bells and growls, and hurried toward the inn, where answers waited in the gathering dark.

THE WHITE HART INN wrapped around me like a familiar embrace as I pushed through its heavy oak doors. Pine garlands swooped gracefully along the pristine whitewashed walls, their needles releasing the sharp scent of winter forests. Red velvet bows adorned the clusters of elegant tables and chairs, while the stunning painting of the white stag—its golden laurel now entwined with holly—presided over the main room like a benevolent guardian.

Cinnamon and mulled wine perfumed the atmosphere, while a gentle, jazzy rendition of "Silver Bells" drifted through the room.

I entered the bar and claimed a table near the windows, perfect for watching both the door and the misty street beyond. A waitress materialized and I ordered a chardonnay, settling into my seat. The leather beneath me had been worn butter-soft with age, and sprigs of holly peeked from behind the brass fixtures on the walls. The inn radiated warmth and welcome, but tension coiled in my chest, refusing to ease.

Seven o'clock came and went. Then seven-fifteen.

By seven-thirty, Trixie Frick, the owner of The White Hart Inn with her husband Boone, appeared at my table in a swirl of sequined gold and holiday cheer. Her voluminous mane of bright red hair was teased to perfection, catching the warm lights of the restaurant, and her signature red lipstick gleamed as she hummed along to the Christmas music playing softly in the background.

"Rockin' Around the Christmas Tree" gave way to "Holly Jolly Christmas," and Trixie did a little shimmy, her sequined top catching every flicker of candlelight as she slid into the seat across from me.

"Win, honey, please tell me you're on a case."

I grinned, despite my concern. Trixie had that effect on people.

"Something like that," I admitted, glancing toward the door again. "Letha Marsh asked me to meet her here. At seven tonight."

Trixie's expression shifted, concern replacing her natural sparkle. "Letha? I didn't realize y'all were friends. She's usually punctual to a fault."

"You know her well?" I asked, trying to keep the worry from my voice.

"Well enough." Trixie settled back in her chair, her rings catching the firelight as she gestured. "Ran in some of the same circles at Wentworth Academy." She paused, studying my face. "Same time as Jess and Tzazi. Eudora Quenleigh…"

My attention sharpened. "Eudora Quenleigh was at Wentworth at the same time as you?"

"Oh yes," Trixie nodded. "Though she went by her maiden name back then. Dora Lavallette."

Dora Lavallette! Well, my, my, my.

"Trixie," I said slowly, "do you know what happened to Simone Petalsigh that night?"

Her face went pale beneath her carefully applied makeup. "Poor girl froze to death outside our dorm. Horrible business."

"Wait! You lived in the dorm where it happened?"

Trixie drew a breath, her lips pursed. She nodded. "The official announcement from the Academy reported it as an accident, that she'd gotten confused in the storm and couldn't find her way back to the dorm."

"You sound doubtful."

Trixie was quiet for a long moment, her fingers worrying at the edge of her sequined top. "We were young," she said finally. "And scared. When the school authorities and police tell you something is an accident, you want to believe them. Especially when the alternative is..."

"What?" I pressed gently.

"That someone let a girl die," she whispered. "That someone you knew, someone you were in school with was capable of something so cruel."

Then she lightened up and waved a hand. "But it was just rumors, dear. Nothing but teenage fanciful gossip."

Trixie's response gave me pause.

"What aren't you telling me?"

I knew Trixie Frick couldn't resist a whiff of mystery. She fancied herself a homegrown Miss Marple, armed with peppermint lip gloss and an overactive imagination. If she knew something, she'd spill it faster than cocoa on Christmas pajamas.

She stared at the table so long even the carols seemed to hold their breath—something I wished a few of the singing angels on the mantel would try. When she finally looked up, her eyes were bright with unshed tears.

"My suspicions have grown over the years," she whispered. "Because of what I saw that night."

My heart started beating faster. "What did you see?"

She sighed. "I was up late, working on a paper due the next morning that I'd put off, typical me." She attempted a small smile. "I came down to the kitchens and saw Letha and a few other Charlottes…"

"Trixie, were you a Charlotte?"

"Goodness, no, honey. My tinsel was too shiny for those girls. But many of them were friends." She waved a hand in the air. "Anyway, they were in the common room, whispering about something. They looked upset, guilty. When they saw me, they scattered like startled birds."

"Did you ask what was wrong?"

"No, but it was on my mind. Then the news came about Simone, and everything else seemed so trivial." Trixie's voice cracked slightly. "I never put it together until years later, when I realized the timing. They were acting strange right around the time when Simone must have been…"

She couldn't finish the sentence, but the implications hung in the air like smoke from the fireplace.

"Was Eudora one of the girls?"

Trixie thought for a moment, then shook her head. "I don't think so."

"But Letha was?"

"Absolutely."

After a few more minutes of casual banter with Trixie, I finished my wine, donned my coat and cat scarf, and headed back to the MET.

～

SOMETHING HAD SHIFTED in the MET during my absence. I felt it the moment I stepped inside—a tension in the air, a weight pressing against my chest. Pyewacket sensed it too. He launched from my shoulder without his usual commentary and melted into the shadows between the stacks.

I'd barely hung up my coat when the door chimes shattered the silence—frantic, discordant notes that set my teeth on edge and raised the hair on the back of my neck.

Jess exploded through the entrance, bringing winter wind and raw panic with her. Her normally immaculate hair flew wild around her face. Her eyes were too wide, glassy with fear.

"Oh, Win!" she gasped, clutching the doorframe for support. "I was hoping you were still here."

"What's wrong?" I was already reaching for my coat again, adrenaline flooding my system at the sight of her face.

"It's Letha Marsh," Jess said, her voice breaking. "She's hurt."

The bell tower answered before I could—one deep, resonant toll, then another, the sound heavy with portent.

Jess's face lost all its color.

We rushed into the night air, our footsteps echoing off the cobblestones as we ran toward whatever horror waited in the darkness behind the inn.

I FOLLOWED Jess behind the buildings lining Bayou Boulevard, the woods towering in the dark behind us. A cluster of people stood next to the brick buildings, chattering quietly and hugging themselves in the cold.

But it was the figure lying in the snow that drew my attention like iron to a magnet.

Letha Marsh lay crumpled a few feet from the brick wall like a discarded doll, her body arranged with the same terrible precision I remembered from Michey's crime scene. Her mouth had been stuffed with straw and stones, the ancient punishment for liars and those who broke their silence. Her eyes stared sightlessly at the winter sky, empty of the fear that must have filled them in her final moments.

Keir spotted me and cut through the organized chaos of the crime scene, his expression tight with concern.

"Don't come any closer," Ransom called out to the crowd from where he crouched beside Letha's body.

I nodded, my feet rooting to the ground. I understood about contaminating crime scenes, about protocols and procedures. But I couldn't look away from Letha's still form, couldn't stop seeing her nervous hands twisting together in the MET, couldn't stop hearing her whispered confession that someone else might die if she didn't speak.

Keir reached me and pulled me into his arms without a word. The dam broke. Tears I'd been holding back since I saw her crumpled body spilled over, hot against my frozen cheeks.

"Keir," I managed through the tears, my voice cracking. "Letha and I—we were supposed to meet. At seven. At the White Hart."

His body went rigid. He pulled back just enough to look at my face, his hands gripping my shoulders. "Why?"

"I don't know exactly," I stammered, swiping uselessly at my tears. "Something to do with Simone. She was scared, Keir. So scared. And I—I should have—"

"Oh, love." He pulled me back against his chest, one hand cradling the back of my head. "This isn't your fault."

But it felt like it was.

Jess materialized beside us, her earlier panic replaced by fierce protectiveness. She slipped an arm around my waist, anchoring me. "I've got her, Keir."

He studied her face for a long moment, some silent understanding passing between them. Finally, he nodded. He pressed a kiss to my temple, his lips warm against my cold skin, then gave my shoulders one more squeeze before releasing me.

I watched him stride back through the lamplight to where

Ransom stood beside Letha's body conferring with Boddy Grim. The Christmas decorations strung along the buildings—twinkling and cheerful—seemed obscene in the face of such violence.

A commotion near a group of townspeople drew my attention. Eudora Quenleigh was pushing through the crowd with tears streaming down her perfectly made-up face.

Eliaz appeared beside her instantly, wrapping a protective arm around Eudora's shoulders as she swayed on her feet.

His eyes met mine and sharply turned away.

The wind picked up, sending snow swirling around the crime scene like ghostly dancers. I pulled my coat tighter and tried to process what I was seeing—not just the body, but the reactions of everyone around it. Tzazi stood near the brick wall, Mason and Zavier beside her, with her arms wrapped around herself, her usual confidence shaken. A few other people I recognized from the gala huddled together, whispering in hushed tones.

But it was Eudora's anguish that held my attention. She clung to her husband like a lifeline, her sobs echoing off the brick walls of the alley. The bond of the Charlottes fully on display.

"Win," Ransom called softly. I looked up to find him approaching, his expression carefully neutral. "Keir told me you had plans to meet with Ms. Marsh tonight."

I nodded, not trusting my voice. "Seven o'clock at The White Hart. She said she had something important to tell me about Simone Petalsigh."

Ransom's jaw tightened. "Did she give you any indication what that might be?"

"No. Only that it was urgent. And that someone else might die if she didn't speak." The irony of my words hit me like a slap. "She was right, wasn't she? Someone killed her to keep her quiet."

"We don't know that yet," Ransom said, but his tone suggested he was thinking the same thing. "Did anyone else know about your planned meeting?"

I thought back through the evening. "Trixie knew I was

TAM LUMIÈRE

waiting for her. And Letha seemed nervous about being overheard in the MET when she asked me to meet her."

Ransom nodded grimly, his enchanted pen scribbling furiously on a notepad floating in the air between us. "Thank you, Win." He glanced meaningfully toward Letha's body once more. "Keep your eyes open. Trust your instincts."

As Ransom hurried back over to the crime scene, I looked up at the winter sky, where clouds obscured the stars like secrets waiting to be uncovered, and wondered who would be next.

CHAPTER 14

*T*he pale winter sunlight streaming into the MET felt weaker than usual, as if the world itself had dimmed since Letha's death. I hadn't been able to sleep that night. Tossing and turning, unsettling Pye, until I finally gave up, got dressed, and went to the MET, my comfort space.

The first edition Agatha Christie slid into place with a satisfying whisper of leather against wood. Before I could reach for the next volume, the brass bell chimed. Eudora Quenleigh rushed inside, snowflakes clinging to her dark hair and coat, more flurries swirling past her into the warm shop. They drifted toward the nearest shelves like curious spirits. I made a quick gesture, drying the air with a breath of magic before the moisture could damage the precious portals.

She looked every inch the grieving friend—elegant black coat, her dark hair swept into a perfect chignon despite the December wind. But it was her eyes that caught my attention. They were red-rimmed, genuinely so, and when she spotted me, her composure cracked.

"Windsor?" Her voice carried that particular tremor of someone holding back tears. "I hope you don't mind me coming by unannounced. Do you have a moment?"

Pyewacket, who'd been dozing on a stack of Stephen King books, opened his eye and fixed it on Eudora with unmistakable suspicion. His tail gave a single, pointed twitch.

"Of course not," I said, signaling for her to follow me. "Please, come sit by the fire. Can I get you some tea?"

She nodded gratefully and settled into one of the velvet armchairs, her movements precise despite her obvious distress. "Thank you. I'm sorry to bother you during business hours, but I didn't know where else to turn."

As we sat before the fire, warm cups of tea materialized on the table between us.

"Letha was one of my dearest friends from Wentworth," Eudora said, accepting the steaming cup with both hands. "We'd grown apart over the years, as people do, but those bonds..." She stared into the tea, watching the steam rise. "They don't just disappear."

"I'm so sorry for your loss." I settled into the chair across from her, cradling my own chai.

The woman sitting across from me bore little resemblance to the carefully composed socialite from the gala. Her makeup was minimal, her expression unguarded. Grief had a way of stripping away pretense.

I let the silence stretch for a moment before speaking. "I couldn't help but notice the tension between you and Letha. Here at the MET. Yesterday."

Eudora's hand stilled halfway to her mouth. She set the cup down carefully, as if it might shatter.

"Stupid childhood jealousy that never quite died." She looked away, jaw tight. "Letha had feelings for Eliaz. Back at Wentworth. He was everything—handsome, ambitious, from the right family." A bitter smile crossed her face. "He chose me instead."

"That must have been complicated."

"It ruined our friendship." Eudora's fingers traced the rim of her cup. "And now we'll never have the chance to fix it. Never get to have that conversation we should have had twenty years ago."

I watched her carefully, noting the way her throat worked, the slight tremor in her hands.

"This must be incredibly difficult."

"It is." Eudora's fingers tightened around the teacup. "But it's more than that. I'm frightened, Windsor. Truly frightened." She leaned forward, her voice dropping to barely above a whisper. "You see, this isn't the first tragedy to strike our old circle. Twenty years ago, another dear friend—Simone Petalsigh—died in what everyone called an accident. Now Letha..."

Pyewacket's ears pricked forward, though he maintained his pose of casual disinterest.

"You think the deaths are connected?" I asked carefully.

"I don't know what to think." Eudora set down her cup with a soft clink. "It's been so long. But both women had something in common beyond our school days. They'd both been part of a group I founded during our time at Wentworth—a sisterhood of sorts, for young women who felt lost or alone."

I decided to play this like it was the first time I'd heard of the Charlottes. "What kind of sisterhood?"

A wistful smile crossed her features. "We called ourselves the Charlottes. It started small, just a few of us who understood what it was like to feel...displaced. You know how cruel teenage girls can be, especially in an environment like Wentworth. We wanted to create something different—a source of support and belonging."

The way she described it painted a picture of noble intentions, but something in her tone didn't quite ring true. Or maybe I was just letting Pyewacket's obvious dislike color my perception.

"Both Simone and Letha were members of the group," Eudora continued, her voice catching. "And I can't shake the feeling that someone is targeting us. Targeting the Charlottes.

"I find it suspect that both Michey and Letha are killed after a gala for Wentworth twenty years after the death of Simone."

I studied her face, noting the micro-expressions that flickered beneath her carefully maintained composure. "Have you taken these concerns to Royal Inspector Belleclaire or your husband?"

Eudora's laugh was bitter, almost harsh. "Eliaz? Not his jurisdiction, I'm afraid. And the local authorities?" She shook her head. "Twenty years ago Simone's death was ruled an accident—a terrible case of exposure during a winter storm. And now with Letha..." She gestured helplessly. "I don't trust them to take this seriously."

She thought for a moment, her eyes fixed on the cobbled street outside, the people bustling by.

"So that's why I'm here," Eudora said, her voice taking on a note of desperate hope. "I've heard about your talents. Your ability to see things others miss, to find truth where others see only tragedy." She leaned forward again, her perfectly manicured hands clasped together. "Would you help me? Would you investigate these deaths? I'm terrified that whoever is doing this isn't finished."

The vulnerability in her voice was compelling, and I felt that familiar tug of sympathy that always got me into trouble.

"Tell me about the Charlottes," I said. "Beyond the general description. What exactly did the group do?"

For just a moment, something flickered across her features—too quick to identify, but it made my pulse quicken. Then her expression smoothed back into grief-stricken earnestness.

"Oh, the usual things young women do," she said with a dismissive wave. "Study groups, social gatherings, philanthropical endeavors, emotional support. We had our little rituals and traditions, of course—what group doesn't? But nothing sinister, if that's what you're wondering.

"I'm willing to pay whatever fee you require," she continued. "Money is no object when it comes to finding justice for my friends."

"I appreciate your confidence in me," I said carefully, "but I'm not actually a private investigator. What happened with previous cases was more...circumstantial involvement."

"Nonetheless, I can tell you have a gift." Eudora released my hand and sat back, her composure sliding back into place like a well-fitted mask. "Please, Windsor. I feel so vulnerable, so helpless. If there's someone out there hunting the surviving Charlottes..." She shuddered delicately. "I could be next."

"Tell me more about Simone's death," I said. "What made it seem suspicious to you?"

Eudora's hands stilled on her teacup. "It was during a terrible snowstorm. She was found outside our dormitory the next morning, frozen. The official explanation was that she'd become disoriented in the storm and couldn't find her way back inside."

"But you don't believe that?"

"Goodness, no. She was right outside the door and, besides, she knew the grounds like the back of her hand. She'd lived at Wentworth for years by the time of her death." Eudora's voice hardened slightly. "And there were...other circumstances...that the investigation never properly explored."

"Like what?"

"The time she went outside. We saw her at dinner so when did she leave the dorm? The disappearance of the pin she *always* wore. The student she argued with the very day she died."

I needed more to go on than cryptic hints, but she stood abruptly, smoothing down her coat. "I've taken up enough of your time. But please, consider what I've asked. The thought of facing this alone..." She let the sentence hang, her vulnerability on full display once more.

After Eudora left, Pyewacket jumped onto the arm of my chair, his tail swishing with obvious disapproval. He fixed me with his penetrating amber stare.

"She's a snob," he announced between licks, his British accent particularly crisp.

I laughed. "Hello, pot!"

His paw froze mid-lick. "I beg your pardon?"

"Pot. Kettle. Black."

"Are you having a stroke?" He abandoned his grooming to

peer at me with genuine concern. "Should I fetch someone? Do you smell toast?"

"It's an expression. You're calling someone else a snob when you're—"

"I," he interrupted with magnificent dignity, "am discerning. There's a difference." He began grooming one black paw with exaggerated delicacy. "Quite a significant one, actually."

I scratched behind Pye's ears until he purred despite himself. "I want to see Wentworth. The place where Simone died. The school that birthed the Charlottes."

"'Birthed the Charlottes?'" He rolled his eye so hard I worried it might stick. "How delightfully dramatic. Shall we bring flowers? Perhaps hire a string quartet?"

"You in?"

He stretched, claws flexing against the upholstery, then gave me a look that somehow managed to be both long-suffering and conspiratorial.

"Naturally."

TRACKING down Wentworth Academy took the better part of an hour and three different inquiries. The blasted school refused to stay put, drifting across Darkly Island whenever it pleased—a building straight out of Howl's Moving Castle, if Howl's home had been a temperamental academy with a flair for dramatic relocations.

The last confirmed sighting placed it on the old road to Strawbridge in that desolate stretch just before the crossroads. My stomach tightened at the thought. The crossroads were ancient, marked by a weathered stone that pointed travelers in two very different directions: left to the charming market town of Strawbridge, right toward the fog-draped borders of Necropolis.

Necropolis. The parish of the zombies. Where the dead walked freely and the living tended to keep their visits brief.

I gripped the steering wheel a little tighter and pressed on, hoping the Academy hadn't developed any ideas about relocating even further down that particular road.

Pyewacket sat perfectly still in the passenger seat of Tzazi's Jeep, only the rapid twitch of his tail betraying his excitement as Wentworth Academy finally materialized through the swirling mist ahead.

And what a sight it was.

The building seemed to defy every law of architecture and physics I'd ever learned. Victorian towers jutted at impossible angles from a foundation that appeared to be part stone manor, part Gothic cathedral, and wholly something you'd expect to see in a Dracula movie. Turrets spiraled upward into the gray sky, their copper roofs green with age. Gargoyles perched on impossible ledges, and one turned its head to watch our approach.

But it was the legs that truly captured the imagination—or the horror, depending on your perspective. The entire massive structure balanced on a framework of enchanted supports where clockwork mechanisms tangled with ancient tree roots, creating something simultaneously organic and mechanical. They shifted and adjusted as we watched, the building settling itself more firmly into the earth like a great beast making itself comfortable.

A gangplank extended toward us with a sound like grinding gears wrapped in velvet—magic smoothing the mechanical edges. It unrolled across the frost-brittle grass, old wood reinforced with brass fittings that gleamed despite the gray day.

"Now why are we going to all this trouble to talk to Headmaster Truegaze?" Pye asked as I eased the Jeep onto the swaying gangplank. Beneath us, through the gaps in the planks, I caught glimpses of those impossible legs and the dark space beneath the Academy.

"Scene of the crime, Pye." I paused, then corrected myself. "Well, scene of Simone's death."

Pye snorted, his whiskers twitching. "If it was a crime."

"And *that* is exactly what I expect to find out."

I parked the Jeep in what I hoped was an appropriate spot—a courtyard of sorts, though "courtyard" seemed too mundane a word for the space. Flagstones arranged in a spiral pattern radiated outward from a central fountain that had been caught mid-performance—water frozen solid in graceful arcs, suspended in the act of dancing upward toward the gray sky.

The moment I cut the engine, silence descended like a heavy curtain. Even the wind seemed to hold its breath here.

Pye settled onto my shoulder as I stepped out, and the cold hit me immediately, sharper here than it had been on the road, as if the building generated its own microclimate. My breath plumed in front of me as I approached the massive double doors that dominated the entrance. They were easily twelve feet tall, constructed of dark wood bound with iron straps that had been worked into intricate Celtic knots. The handles were brass shaped like coiled serpents, their eyes set with what looked like amber.

Or maybe they were real eyes. With magical architecture, it was hard to tell.

I reached for one of the serpent handles, half-expecting it to hiss or bite. Instead, before my fingers could make contact, both doors swung inward with a groaning creak that echoed through whatever vast space lay beyond.

Warm air rushed out to meet us, carrying with it the scent of old books, burning wood, and beeswax.

"After you," Pye murmured against my ear, his claws tightening slightly on my shoulder.

I stepped over the threshold into Wentworth Academy.

The entrance hall stole my breath. It soared upward at least three stories, maybe more—the ceiling was lost in shadows that even the dozens of floating candles couldn't quite penetrate. Students rushed everywhere. Some taking the grand staircase of dark polished wood that swept upward directly ahead, others simply flying up to the galleries on broomsticks or levitating themselves with casual flicks of their wands. The staircase split at a landing into two curved branches, and a group of laughing teenagers raced each other up opposite sides, their footsteps thundering through the space.

Portraits lined every available wall space, their subjects—witches and wizards from centuries past—watching our entrance with expressions ranging from curiosity to stern disapproval. Some of them shifted in their frames, whispering to their neighbors and pointing, while others shouted advice or warnings to passing students who largely ignored them.

"She's Genevieve's girl," a voice rang out from one of the portraits. "See that hair."

I turned toward the sound, but at least a dozen painted faces stared back at me, impossible to tell which one had spoken.

The floor beneath my feet was an elaborate mosaic of colored tiles that formed a massive compass rose, its cardinal points marked with symbols I recognized as elemental markers. Banners hung from the upper galleries—house colors, I assumed—in jewel tones of emerald, sapphire, ruby, and amethyst. Someone had added garlands of holly and ivy for Christmas, strung between the banners and wound around the staircase railings.

To my left, an enormous fireplace crackled with flames that burned in shades of blue and green rather than orange. High-backed leather chairs had been arranged before it, and several students lounged in them, textbooks spread across their laps while they debated something with animated gestures. On the other side, an archway led to what appeared to be a corridor lined with more portraits and flickering sconces, students disappearing down it in twos and threes.

And directly ahead, standing at the base of the grand staircase as if he'd been expecting us, was a figure in deep purple robes trimmed with silver.

Headmaster Truegaze.

He was tall and impeccably dressed in a waistcoat under sweeping academic robes, his salt-and-pepper hair combed neatly back from sharp, refined features. His face was all angles and quiet authority, but it was his eyes that held me—pale gray and intense, shadowed underneath as if he hadn't slept properly in weeks. Perhaps had become ill since the gala. Those eyes fixed on me with a penetrating intelligence that made me want to take a step backward.

"Miss Ebonwood," he said, his voice carrying effortlessly across the vast space without him raising it. "Welcome to Wentworth Academy. Though I confess, I did not expect this visit."

I plastered on my best professional smile and moved forward, my footsteps echoing on the mosaic floor. "Headmaster Truegaze. Thank you for seeing me on such short notice."

"I don't know that I had much of a choice, did I?" One silver eyebrow arched upward, and I couldn't tell if he was amused or annoyed. "The Academy opened its doors for you. It tends to make its own decisions about visitors these days."

"I appreciate the Academy's hospitality nonetheless," I said, stopping a respectful distance from him. Up close, I could see that his robes were embroidered with moving constellations, stars shifting across the fabric in slow, eternal patterns. "I was hoping we could discuss Simone Petalsigh."

Something flickered across his stormy eyes—grief, maybe, or guilt. It was gone before I could be certain.

"Of course," he said quietly. "I've been expecting someone to come asking questions. Though I imagined it would be Inspector Belleclaire, not a travel agent." His gaze dropped to Pye. "Even one accompanied by a familiar of considerable power."

Ah. So we were starting with intellectual superiority wrapped in polite condescension. I'd dealt with much worse in the human academic world.

I smiled and gave him a slight nod.

A flicker of respect crossed his features before his expression smoothed back into careful neutrality. He studied me for a moment longer, as if recalculating his initial assessment.

Truegaze abruptly turned toward the right-hand archway, his

robes swirling around him like liquid shadow. "Come. We'll speak in my office."

He swept down the corridor at a pace that forced me to hurry, portraits blurring past in a gallery of disapproving faces. The passage seemed to stretch impossibly long, stone walls giving way to wood paneling, then back to stone again—the architecture as restless as the building itself.

Christmas decorations appeared sporadically along our route —a wreath of enchanted mistletoe that whispered as we passed, crystal icicles that chimed soft discordant notes, a small tree in an alcove adorned with ornaments that rotated slowly without wind. But even these festive touches felt oppressive here, as if the Academy's ancient stones refused to embrace anything as cheerful as the holiday season.

We reached what looked like a solid stone wall—no doors, no windows, just ancient rock veined with something that might have been silver or simply old magic made visible. Truegaze stopped, raised his right hand, and traced a complex pattern in the air. His fingers left trails of pale light that hung suspended for a moment before sinking into the stone like water absorbed by parched earth.

The wall shimmered, reality bending like heat waves rising from summer pavement. Colors bled and swirled—deep purples that reminded me of winter twilight, imperial blues shot through with silver, flashes of white like fresh snow catching starlight— coalescing into a portal that hummed with barely contained power.

"After you, Miss Ebonwood." He stepped aside, one hand gesturing toward the swirling gateway. His expression was unreadable, but there was something in his pale eyes—a flicker of wariness—that spurred my curiosity.

"It's *Doctor*, Mr. Truegaze."

I exchanged a glance with Pye, felt his claws tighten slightly on my shoulder—a small gesture of solidarity that steadied my nerves—and stepped forward. The portal's surface felt cool against my skin, like walking through a waterfall made of winter itself. The world tilted sideways, colors streaming past too fast to identify, my stomach lurching as I was flung upward a great height—

And then I was through, standing on solid ground again. A curved wooden door rose before me, set into stone walls that looked far older than the corridor we'd just left. *Headmaster Truegaze* had been carved into the dark wood in flowing script, the letters filled with what looked like actual liquid gold.

A small wreath hung on the door—not the cheerful sort one might expect for Christmas, but something twisted from blackthorn and winterberry, its red berries bright as drops of blood against dark branches. It gave off a faint scent of cinnamon and cloves. At least it smelled festive.

Truegaze emerged from the portal behind me, his arrival silent and dignified, as if stepping between spaces was no more remarkable than crossing a threshold. The portal collapsed behind him with a soft sound like wind through winter trees, leaving nothing but solid stone wall.

The headmaster's office occupied a corner of the building's top floor, offering a commanding view of the snow-dusted grounds. Through the mullioned glass, I could see the gardens, imprisoned by the Academy's buildings, transformed into a winter wonderland—bare trees etched in white, frozen fountains, and snow-covered statues that looked like sleeping sentinels.

When Truegaze ushered me inside, I was struck by the room's imposing atmosphere. Dark wood paneling rose to a coffered ceiling painted with the constellations of the night sky. Leather-bound volumes lined built-in shelves that stretched from floor to ceiling, their spines stamped with gold lettering, some in languages I couldn't identify. Oil portraits of stern-faced former headmasters glared down from their gilded frames with expressions of permanent disapproval.

A fire crackled in an enormous stone hearth carved with Celtic knots and winter symbols—bare branches, snowflakes, sleeping animals. But despite the flames, the room held a bone-deep chill—the kind that settled in your marrow and refused to leave, no matter how close you stood to the fire.

I settled into one of the leather chairs facing his desk, the old leather creaking beneath my weight. Pyewacket leaped into the other with his usual air of feline authority, his eye fixed on Truegaze with unblinking intensity.

The headmaster moved behind his desk and lowered himself into the high-backed leather chair with careful precision, as if the act of sitting required all his concentration. He folded his trembling hands on the desk blotter as beads of sweat trickled down his temples.

"What can you tell me about the Charlottes?" I asked, watching him carefully.

Something flickered across Truegaze's features—too quick to identify, but definitely there. Surprise? Fear? Guilt? Whatever it was disappeared as quickly as it had come, replaced by a carefully neutral expression. "A social group here at the school. Been around for ages."

"Well," I countered, keeping my voice pleasant but firm. "More like twenty years."

"Why do you ask?" His fingers began to drum against the desk blotter—a slow, rhythmic tap that suggested barely controlled nerves.

"They may have something to do with the death of Letha Marsh."

He adjusted the papers on his desk, aligning them with practiced precision. "Letha Marsh." A small sigh escaped him. "Brilliant student. One of our best, truth be told. Hard to believe it's been nearly twenty years since she graduated."

"Around the same time as Simone Petalsigh's death.

The color drained from Truegaze's face so quickly I thought he might faint. His hand moved instinctively to his wrist, where I noticed faint scarring beneath his shirt cuff—multiple thick lines.

"Simone Petalsigh," he repeated, his voice barely above a

whisper. The name seemed to cost him something to speak aloud. "Now there's a name..."

"You remember her well?"

"Of course. Tragic accident." His words came out too quickly, like he was reciting a memorized script he'd repeated so many times the edges had worn smooth. "Terrible storm that night. Students were warned to stay indoors..." He shrugged helplessly, but the gesture seemed forced, mechanical.

"Dr. Truegaze, I believe Letha and Simone's deaths are connected. Perhaps even Michey's."

If I thought Truegaze had gone pale before, now he looked positively ashen—the kind of gray-white that suggested a man on the verge of collapse. His eyes narrowed, and for just a moment, something feral flickered in their depths—something that made Pyewacket's fur stand on end. His hand moved again to that scarred wrist, rubbing at it absently, compulsively. "I'm not sure what you're implying, but I find this line of questioning rather inappropriate."

I watched him for a moment, cataloging every tell—his nervous gestures, his dilated pupils despite the dim light, his constant tapping on the desk that had begun like a metronome counting down to something inevitable. A single drop of sweat ran down his temple.

"I believe they knew something about the Lavallette family. Something that would have destroyed them," I said, laying my cards on the table.

"Preposterous!" His voice exploded across the room, the sudden volume making me jerk back in my seat. His eyes flared yellow—animalistic and wild. "The Lavallettes are a highly respected family. Numerous ancestors have passed through these doors. Five headmasters were Lavallettes. Wentworth Academy does not associate with 'corrupt families,' Dr. Ebonwood."

The fury in his voice made the very air vibrate. The fire in the hearth flared higher, casting wild shadows across the walls. One of the portraits, a particularly stern-looking former headmaster, actually flinched.

Pyewacket hopped over into my lap, his claws digging into my thighs through my slacks.

I stroked his back to calm him, feeling the tension thrumming through his small body.

Professor Truegaze visibly settled himself down, taking long, controlled breaths that suggested years of practice at containing something that wanted very badly to break free. His eyes faded back to their normal pale gray, though his hands still trembled as he resumed that incessant tapping on the desk—tap, tap, tap, like a clock counting down to midnight.

"You'll have to forgive my outburst." His voice came out hoarse, like he'd been shouting for hours. "The Lavallettes have been generous patrons of this institution for generations. I won't have their name dragged through unfounded accusations."

"Unfounded?" I kept my tone level. "Two women are dead, Professor. Both connected to this school, both Charlottes, both carrying secrets about that family."

"Where is your proof, Dr. Ebonwood?"

The question settled between us, and I watched those strange yellow flashes return to his eyes—brief as lightning, but unmistakable. His fingers drummed against the desktop, faster now, almost frantic. Another bead of sweat traced down his temple despite the coolness of his office.

The ledger sat in my messenger bag, its secrets suddenly feeling dangerous.

Everything in me screamed not to mention it. Not to this man who'd lost his composure twice already in our short conversation, whose eyes betrayed something prowling beneath the surface. Whatever was happening to Headmaster Truegaze, whatever was making him unravel at the seams, I didn't trust him with more ammunition.

Until I knew he could be trusted, I was keeping the ledger to myself.

He looked away first, his attention shifting to the snow-covered grounds beyond the window. When he spoke again, his voice had gone rough around the edges. "That period of my life..." He paused, swallowed. "I have no desire to excavate old pain for the sake of speculation."

"You were here when Simone died?"

The headmaster stood abruptly, the sudden movement sharp and jerky, and moved to the tall windows that overlooked the academy grounds. Snow fell in sheets now, obscuring the view, turning everything beyond the glass into a world of white and gray. He stared out at it as if seeing something other than the present moment—some ghost from his past, perhaps, some memory he couldn't quite escape.

"I was assistant headmaster." When he turned back to me, his eyes had returned to normal, although his back was rigid, shoulders held with the kind of tension that spoke of barely contained panic. Or barely contained something else. "Dr. Ebonwood, I think this conversation has run its course."

"Yep, let's go." Pye leaped to the floor and padded to the door with an eagerness that suggested he was more than ready to leave this oppressive space.

But I wasn't quite finished yet.

Through the window behind him, I caught a glimpse of movement—something large and dark slipping between the snow-covered statues in the garden. But when I blinked, it was gone, swallowed by the storm.

"I believe the key to the recent deaths is whatever really happened the night Simone Petalsigh died," I said into that heavy silence.

"Dr. Ebonwood," he said finally, his voice barely audible, each word seeming to cost him something precious, "there are things about this place, about that night, that you couldn't possibly understand. Forces at work that go beyond simple human motivations."

A log shifted in the fireplace, sending up a shower of sparks that looked like falling stars.

"Then help me understand."

He laughed, but there was no humor in it—only a bitter, hollow sound that raised goosebumps on my arms and made Pyewacket press closer to my ankles. It was the laugh of a man who'd given up hope long ago. "Help you? I can barely help myself." He turned back to face me, and I was shocked by the haunted expression in his pale eyes. "My advice to you is to forget about Simone Petalsigh. Some secrets are buried for good reason."

His words, however gently delivered, hung in the air between us like the ghost of something dead but not yet at rest.

I opened the door and then paused before moving into the corridor, the brass handle, cold beneath my palm. The Christmas wreath of blackthorn and winterberry rustled gently. "Just one more thing. The night Simone died—where were you?"

The question hit him like a physical blow. His already pale complexion went absolutely gray. I watched his throat work as he struggled to find words, struggled to breathe. For a moment, I thought he might actually collapse. His hand shot out to grip the edge of the desk, knuckles going bone-white. But he mastered himself, though it took visible effort.

"I was... I had to step away from the Academy that evening. Personal matters." Each word came out clipped, carefully controlled.

"I see." I stood and headed for the portal that opened up in front of me, then looked back at him one final time. Snow from the windows cast his face in shifting shadows that made him look older, more haggard. "Thank you for your time, Headmaster Truegaze."

He didn't respond, just stood there framed by that window with its view of winter and whiteness, looking like a man trapped in his own personal hell.

~

"WELL," Pyewacket said once we were safely back in the Jeep, the heater running full blast against the winter cold. "He is most certainly concealing something."

"Agreed." I turned the key in the ignition.

"Beyond the obvious fact that he's employed at an educational institution?" Pye settled into his seat as I reached for his seatbelt, a requirement he insisted upon, claiming it was "civilized." "Those yellow eyes were particularly telling."

"You saw that too?"

"Difficult to miss." His tail flicked. "One doesn't survive millennia without learning to recognize curse symptoms. The sweating, the loss of composure, the flashes of amber..." He trailed off thoughtfully. "The man is fighting something."

I paused mid-buckle. "Fighting what?"

"That, my dear, is the question." His eye fixed on me. "But whatever it is, it's winning. I suggest we proceed with extreme caution. And perhaps invest in some rather robust protective charms should we visit again."

I started the engine and let it warm as I stared at the Academy's imposing facade. As we drove over the drawbridge, it groaned shut behind us—old chains grinding against older magic—locking into place with a resounding clang. I couldn't help but wonder if Truegaze was as much a prisoner there as the students. Through the rearview mirror, I watched the Academy's towers disappear into the swirling snow behind us, swallowed by white. I navigated the winding road back toward town, my thoughts churning like the snow in my headlights.

I had felt it back in that office—a heaviness settling over the room whenever I'd mentioned Simone's death. Whatever had happened that winter night twenty years ago, it had left permanent scars on everyone involved. Scars that still bled if you pressed too hard.

When the MET finally came into view, glowing warm and welcoming through the storm, I knew that this investigation was going to test more than just my detective skills. Something about both conversations today—first with Mrs. Quenleigh, now with Truegaze—hadn't felt completely truthful. As if they were each holding something back. Something that painted them in a bad light? Or something that put them in danger?

"Simone's death." I watched the snow dust across the windshield, accumulating fast. "I'm sure that's when it all started. She dies. The payouts begin. Twenty years pass, and suddenly someone's picking off students associated with her death."

I killed the engine but didn't move to get out yet.

I watched snow pile up on the hood of the Jeep, thinking about yellow eyes and scarred wrists and secrets that had festered for twenty years.

CHAPTER 15

*T*he crystal orchids on my new wreath chimed softly as a knock echoed through Fernwood's kitchen, interrupting Pyewacket and my debate about whether showing my friends the archive was brilliant or completely reckless.

Pyewacket, stretched across his favorite spot near the kitchen hearth like a furry throw pillow, cracked open his good eye.

"That'll be them," he said.

"I know."

"You're still standing here."

"I know that too."

He yawned, displaying an impressive array of teeth. "You do realize that hesitating won't change the fact that they're already here?"

"What if this is a mistake?" I twisted my watch around my wrist. "The archive is—it's a family secret. Minta kept them hidden even from you and Hilde."

"Sometimes the people who love us make decisions based on fear rather than wisdom." Pye sat up, his tail swishing in that particular way that meant he was about to deliver uncomfortable truths. "Besides, Jess has been your friend through murder investigations, supernatural threats, and that unfortunate incident with the killer in Greywolf's study. If you can't trust her with old documents, what exactly can you trust her with?"

Another knock sounded, more insistent this time.

"And Chase and Ren?" I asked.

"Chase would throw himself in front of a curse for you, and Ren can sense truth in stone itself. They're solid." He groomed a paw. "Now stop fretting and answer the door before they freeze to death on your back steps."

I pulled open the kitchen door to find all three of them stamping snow off their boots on the mat. Beyond them, Fernwood's grounds stretched white and pristine under a pale winter sky, the ancient oaks draped in fresh powder and twinkling with icicles.

Jess practically bounced across the threshold, her brilliant red hair vivid against the cream-colored wool coat she wore. A green knit scarf wrapped around her neck, and her cheeks were pink from the cold. "Finally! We thought maybe you'd changed your mind about letting us help." She unwound her scarf, revealing a thick cable-knit sweater in festive red.

Chase followed, impeccable even in winter wear—a long charcoal cashmere coat over a burgundy sweater and perfectly pressed trousers. Snowflakes dusted his golden hair. "Bonjour, *mon amie*." He kissed both my cheeks in that effortlessly elegant way he had, even as he shook snow from his shoulders. "You look troubled. Is everything all right?"

Ren brought up the rear, his quiet presence immediately grounding as he stepped inside and carefully closed the door against the cold. He wore a heavy gray parka over a thick wool sweater, jeans, and sturdy boots. His brown eyes took in my expression with that intuitive awareness mountain spirits possessed. "We can leave if this is a bad time."

"No, of course, not. I'm glad you're here. It's—" I gestured them deeper into the kitchen's warmth. "Actually, I need to show you something. But first, hang up your coats and I'll grab *the* pitcher."

As they shed their winter layers, I grabbed the magic pitcher and four mugs.

"Before we have glögg," I said, turning to face them, "I need you to understand that what I'm about to share with you has been kept secret from almost everyone for generations. Even Hilde, Sibby, and Pye didn't know about it until recently."

Chase's eyebrows rose as he smoothed down his burgundy sweater. "Well now, that's quite the introduction."

"Secret Ebonwood things?" Jess clasped her hands together, her green eyes sparkling. "Oh my gosh, is it dangerous? It's dangerous, isn't it? Is there a cursed object? Please tell me there's *not* a cursed object because we've had quite enough of those lately."

"It's not cursed," I assured her. "At least, I don't think it is. Mostly it's just...remarkable."

"Remarkable how?" Ren asked quietly, his steady presence as calming as stone.

I glanced at Pyewacket, who had padded closer to the group. He gave me what I interpreted as an encouraging nod, though with cats it was hard to tell.

"Come with me," I said. "I'll show you."

I led them through the dining room and into the sitting room. When we reached the library, soft winter light filtered through the windows, and the fireplace crackled invitingly. I felt a familiar tingle of anticipation as I approached it.

"The library?" Chase looked around appreciatively. "Darling, I've been in here at least a hundred times. Unless you've added a secret portal to—oh." His words trailed off as I raised my arms.

The wall beside the fireplace shimmered and vanished, revealing the dark stone archway and spiral stairs beyond. Cool air flowed from the opening, carrying that distinctive scent of old paper and ancient magic.

"Holy hellhound," Jess whispered.

"I've been coming to Fernwood for years," Chase said slowly. "How did I never sense this?"

"Minta was very good at hiding things." I stepped toward the opening. "Are y'all coming?"

The stairs were even colder than I remembered, our footsteps echoing against stone as we climbed. Despite my thick wool sweater, I shivered slightly as the temperature dropped with each step. Behind me, I heard Jess's small gasp when I opened the door and the turret room came into view.

"Windsor Ebonwood," Chase breathed, stepping into the circular space and rubbing his arms against the chill. "What in the name of all that's magical is this?"

"The Ebonwood archive." I watched their faces as they took in the round walls lined with shelves, the chained boxes, the impossible height of the turret with its unreachable windows. "A repository of information about our family and anyone we've ever had dealings with."

Ren moved slowly around the perimeter, his fingertips barely brushing the stone walls. "The magic here is old. Ancient. It's woven into the very foundation."

"Look at all these boxes." Jess hugged herself against the cold, her breath forming small clouds. "And the windows—how would you even reach them?"

"You'd have to fly," I said. "Which I'm sure was the point."

"Or veilshift." Chase had gravitated toward the desk, his fingers hovering over a stack of newspapers without quite touching them. His sorcerer's senses were clearly working overtime. "The preservation spells alone must be extraordinary. These documents should have crumbled to dust decades ago."

"The archive maintains itself." I moved to the center of the room, shivering. "Watch this."

I clapped twice. "May I please have four large Christmas mugs of glögg? And could you warm this room a bit?"

For a moment, nothing happened. Then four steaming mugs appeared on the coffee table, oranges slices bobbing on the surface with a dusting of cinnamon. The fireplace, which had been cold and dark, suddenly blazed to life with cheerful flames that immediately began to chase away the chill.

"Sweet baby Christmas," Jess said, her eyes wide.

"It gets better." I gestured toward the hammock that had appeared near the fireplace during my last visit. "Pye asked for a hammock and the archive gave him one that swings itself."

"Can it do anything?" Chase's eyes sparkled with the kind of mischief that usually preceded either brilliance or disaster.

"Well, it won't help me access information about my mother—there's a spell blocking that. And I assume it has other limitations, but I haven't fully explored them." Wrapping my hands around my mug, I savored the warmth that seeped through the ceramic and watched the snowflakes continue their gentle cascade onto the snow-capped village in the distance. I found myself thinking how different this felt from the humid Louisiana winters I'd expected when I first moved to Darkly.

Ren had settled into one of the plump chairs, his glögg cradled in both hands. "This is incredible, Win. Thank you for trusting us with it."

"I figured if we're going to research two murders that happened twenty years apart, we might as well use every resource available." I held my mug against my chest, grateful for its heat against my cold fingers. "Though I'll admit, part of me just wanted to share this with you. It feels wrong, keeping something this amazing to myself. Especially at Christmas—it's a time for sharing, right?"

"Can we try?" Jess asked. "Asking for things, I mean?"

I grinned. "Go for it."

Chase set down his glögg and clapped his hands together. "All right then. Archive, darling, could you provide—oh, I don't know —a comprehensive history of Creole magic in Louisiana?"

Three leather-bound volumes appeared on the desk with a soft thump.

"Magnificent." Chase moved toward them like a moth to flame. "Simply magnificent."

"My turn!" Jess clapped her hands. "Um, could I please see any information about hearth fairy magic on Darkly Island?"

A single, thick journal materialized beside Chase's books. Jess squeaked with delight and snatched it up, already flipping through pages.

Ren set down his mug and clapped, his movements deliberate and respectful. "I would appreciate any records of mountain spirits who have visited Darkly Island."

A wooden box lowered itself from one of the upper shelves, settling gently on the coffee table. The chain that had held it clattered against the shelf above before disappearing.

"Okay, that's just showing off," I said.

For the next hour, we played with the archive like children with a new toy. Chase requested fashion plates from 1850s New Orleans and got an entire portfolio of hand-drawn designs. Jess asked for recipes using fairy magic and received a cookbook that made her cry with joy. Ren, more practical than the rest of us, requested maps of Darkly Island's ley lines and got a rolled parchment that glowed faintly with magical energy.

I asked for warmer socks since my feet were freezing, and a pair of thick, hand-knitted wool socks appeared on my lap, fresh from someone's needles.

"I could stay here forever," Jess sighed, curled up on the sofa with her cookbook and glögg, now wrapped in a thick blanket that had appeared at some point. "This is better than any library I've ever been in."

"It's certainly more responsive," Chase agreed. He'd conjured himself a chaise lounge at some point and was sprawled across it like a Renaissance painting come to life, another blanket draped elegantly over his legs. The fire crackled merrily, keeping the winter chill at bay. "Though I have to ask—if the archive can do all this, why did Minta keep it secret?"

"Protection," Ren said quietly. He sat cross-legged on the floor near the fire, studying his ley line map, seemingly immune to the cold in the way mountain spirits often were. "Information is power. If the wrong people knew about this place, they could use it against the Ebonwood family."

"No doubt the archive hides explosive information about, well, everybody," I added. "And if you don't know something exists, you can't be forced to reveal it."

The playful atmosphere dimmed slightly. Chase sat up, his expression sobering. "You're right, of course. Which makes it all the more meaningful that you've shared this with us."

"You're family," I said simply. "Maybe not by blood, but by choice. And honestly, I could use your help. All of you."

"Simone," Jess said, setting aside her cookbook. "That's why you brought us here."

"Yes, I can't help but believe the key to the murders is the death of Simone Petalsigh." I moved to the desk, where the newspapers and documents I'd requested earlier still sat in neat piles. "I've been trying to make sense of it all, but there's so much information and I keep feeling like I'm missing connections."

"So we ask the archive to help us." Chase rose gracefully from his chaise and joined me at the desk. "Let's get organized. Ren, you're the most methodical. What do you suggest?"

Ren stood, rolling up his map with careful precision. "We should request everything related to Wentworth Academy first. Then anything about Arthur Vanderholt specifically. After that, we can cross-reference with information about Simone, Michey, and Letha."

"Ooh, a new mission." Jess clapped her hands. "Could I please have a notebook and pen?"

Both appeared in her lap immediately. She laughed with delight. "I love this room so much."

"Right then." Chase rolled up his sleeves. "Let's solve ourselves a murder. Or two. Or however many we're dealing with at this point."

I clapped twice, my voice steady despite the nervous flutter in my stomach. "Archive, we need any and all information related to Wentworth Academy, particularly concerning events twenty years ago involving Simone Petalsigh, Arthur Vanderholt, and student deaths."

For a moment, nothing happened. Then boxes began descending from the shelves, chains clinking as they lowered themselves to the floor. One after another they came, stacking themselves in neat rows across the room. Newspapers, leather books, and yearbooks spilled out in organized piles.

"Well," Ren said mildly. "That's more than I expected."

"Quite a lot more," Chase agreed.

Jess stared at the growing mountain of materials, her pen poised over her blank notebook. "This is going to take a while, isn't it?"

"Yes. So let's get to work," Chase said. "Someone evil has been getting away with murder for far too long. Time to change that."

The four of us settled into position around the room, each taking a section of documents. The archive hummed with quiet energy around us, while the fire crackled and popped, casting dancing shadows on the circular walls.

Somewhere in these pages, hidden among decades of secrets and lies, was the truth about what really happened at Wentworth Academy. And with my friends beside me, the archive at our disposal, and the peaceful hush of snow falling outside, I was finally going to find it.

The investigation had truly begun.

THE FOUR OF us had been working our way through boxes of documents for nearly an hour, each claiming a section of materials to review. The archive had provided a careful taxonomy of tragedy: articles mentioning Wentworth Academy in one pile, anything related to student deaths in another, and a growing third stack for pieces that made the hair on the back of my neck stand up.

Chase had commandeered the chaise lounge again, somehow

managing to make sorting through dusty papers look elegant. Ren sat cross-legged on the floor near the fireplace, his methodical approach to organizing documents almost meditative. Jess had claimed the sofa, surrounded by yearbooks and newspaper clippings, her notebook already filling with observations.

"Here's another one," Jess said, sliding a yellowed clipping across the coffee table toward me. The paper crackled like dead leaves. "This is from about six months after the initial coverage."

Pyewacket curled up in my lap as I read through the second article, my stomach tightening with each paragraph. The words seemed to pulse on the page. "Look at this—Beatrice Snarkle was already questioning the official story. She mentions students who saw things that night, evidence that was omitted from reports."

"Omitting evidence?" Chase set down his ledger, his sorcerer's instincts clearly piqued. "Deliberate intervention or simple negligence, I wonder. Neither good."

"And here," Jess pointed to a passage near the bottom, her finger trembling slightly, "she talks about students being 'marked as different' and 'singled out.' That sounds like they knew Simone was being targeted."

"Seems like Snarkle knew exactly what happened that night," Ren said softly.

Chase leaned back on the chaise lounge. "Why didn't she say anything? Why only pepper the article with clues?"

I knew why. "Fear."

The archive suddenly felt colder, as if speaking the truth aloud had invited in ghosts. The fire flickered, casting longer shadows across the circular walls.

Jess looked up, and the anger blazing in her eyes made me flinch. It was the kind of fury that had been banked for decades, smoldering beneath politeness and decency, waiting for oxygen. "Of Arthur, Win. You don't know what he was like—what he *is* like. The way he looked at anyone who didn't fit his narrow definition of 'proper magic.' The snide comments, the casual cruelty directed at those who couldn't fight back."

Her voice had risen, echoing off the archive's vaulted ceiling. Pyewacket's ears flattened slightly.

Chase had gone very still on his chaise, his elegant features hardening into something almost dangerous. "I've encountered men like Arthur before. They wrap their prejudice in tradition and call it standards."

"And they rarely act alone," Ren added quietly. "Men like that surround themselves with those who either share their beliefs or are too afraid to challenge them."

"If he did cause Simone's death," I said gently, reaching across the table to pat Jess's hand, "we'll find out. And this time, there won't be any quiet cover-ups. There will be justice."

Jess took a shaky breath, her anger deflating into something that looked more like grief. "She deserved better than to be forgotten."

"She won't be," I promised. "Not anymore."

I hesitated, picking at a loose thread in my sleeve. "Jess, what were the Charlottes really like?"

Jess's jaw tightened; her whole face hardened into a scowl. "The Charlottes? They made cruelty into an art form. You know those perfect girls with flawless hair and smiles that could cut glass? That was them. They ran this place from the shadows— spreading rumors like wildfire, sabotaging anyone who got in their way. If you dated a boy they liked, your life was over. And cheating on tests? That was their warm-up act."

She shook her head, disgusted. "No one ever called them out —they were untouchable. Just...toxic. Like venom in pretty bottles."

I blinked. That description of the group clashed magnificently with the one Eudora gave me. "Didn't they do charity events? Tutor struggling students?"

Jess snorted, her laughter sharp and humorless. "Philanthropy? Please. That was just for show—so the teachers and parents thought they were saints. Trust me, the Charlottes could charm the pearls right off a grandma, while plotting your downfall in the same breath. Playing every side was their specialty."

I frowned, unease prickling the back of my neck. "That really doesn't sound like a group Simone would've signed up for."

Jess considered, her eyes narrowing as if she were mentally sorting through old yearbook photos. "Simone? No, she was never one of them. Not her style at all. Why do you ask?"

"Interesting…Eudora told me Simone was a Charlotte."

"No," Jess shook her head. "There's absolutely no way Simone was one of those girls. Did she really tell you that?"

"Yeah. I wonder why she lied." I shrugged, trying to sound casual, though my mind was buzzing with new questions.

Moving to the third article, I quickly skimmed the headline. My eyes widened. "The headmaster firing, Truegaze's demotion—wait, Truegaze was actually demoted?"

"Oh, yes," Jess said, her voice dropping to barely above a whisper. "It was a huge scandal at the time. Headmaster Dromgoole was fired outright and assistant headmaster Truegaze was stripped of his position and demoted all the way down to groundskeeper."

"Hmm." I sat back, letting that sink in. "He conveniently failed to mention that detail when I talked to him. My word, that had to have been absolutely humiliating. From second-in-command to tending the gardens?"

"That's not just a demotion," Chase said, setting aside his ledger entirely now. "That's a public humiliation. The kind that either breaks a person or turns them bitter."

Ren nodded slowly. "And puts them in their place."

I ran a hand over Pye's back, thinking about Truegaze's careful words at the school, the way he'd avoided certain topics. His anger.

I turned back to the article I held.

"Listen to this." I read them the sheriff's cryptic quote about truths coming quiet instead of clean. The phrase had an ominous weight to it, like he'd known exactly what he was saying—and what he couldn't say outright. "The sheriff seemed to have someone in mind. Someone he couldn't directly accuse."

I scanned back to the top of the article, searching for the name of the sheriff back then. There—in the first paragraph: Sheriff Boddy Grim.

"Boddy Grim," I said aloud, a knot forming in my stomach. Of course it was Boddy. The gaunt, red-eyed coroner who currently made my life difficult at every turn had been the sheriff twenty years ago. "He investigated Simone's death."

Jess straightened in her chair. "Boddy had been sheriff since I was a child." She paused, her expression darkening. "If anyone could help us figure out what really happened, it would be Boddy. Death-sense and all."

"His abilities would have told him exactly how she died," I said. "Time of death, magical causes, injuries—everything except who did it. I wonder why none of that is in the newspaper article."

"Because someone with power told him to keep quiet," Chase said, his voice taking on an edge I rarely heard. "The Vanderholts have considerable influence on this island. Always have."

"Money and old magic," Ren added quietly. "A dangerous combination when wielded without conscience."

Pyewacket's tail twitched with interest, his eye fixing on me with feline intensity.

"I never realized what a cover-up all that was. The Vanderholts. The Lavallettes. Darkly Island royalty."

"What do you think about seeing if we can get Simone's death report from Boddy?" I said, already dreading the conversation. Boddy Grim barely tolerated my existence on a good day.

"Oh, I can get it." Jess grinned.

"Secrets can weigh heavily over time," Ren said thoughtfully as he flipped through one of the old yearbooks. "Sometimes people just need permission to finally let them out."

"*Mes amis*, I do believe I've just had a stroke of brilliance," Chase announced, one finger pointed skyward in mock triumph.

"What if we simply asked this brilliant archive to produce Miss Simone's death report?"

Jess's green eyes lit up. "Of course! Sugar, that's brilliant!"

Ren nodded slowly, a small smile tugging at his lips. "Worth trying."

I stepped closer to the center of the room, where the air seemed to shimmer slightly with magical potential. The turret's curved walls amplified sound in strange ways, making even our breathing seem louder than it should be.

"Archive," I said, trying to sound both polite and authoritative —the tone you'd use with a particularly helpful but unpredictable librarian. "Please locate and produce the death report created by Boddy Grim twenty years ago for Simone—"

BOOOOONG. BOOOOONG.

The sound erupted from nowhere and everywhere at once, two deep, resonant notes that vibrated through the stone floor and rattled my bones. It was like standing inside a church bell, if that church bell also happened to be deeply, cosmically annoyed with you. The notes held an ominous, almost theatrical quality—the sound you'd hear right before a ghost appeared in a classic horror movie.

I jumped back so hard I nearly knocked into Chase, who had also leaped sideways with a yelp that was distinctly ungentlemanly.

"What in the—" I started.

But Chase, Ren, and Jess had all broken into laughter. Chase bent forward, hands on his knees, gasping. Jess had one hand pressed to her chest, her face flushed pink with mirth. Even Ren, usually so composed, had his hand over his mouth, shoulders shaking with silent chuckles.

"Y'all!" Jess managed between giggles. "Your faces!"

"That—" Chase wheezed, "—was the most magnificently ominous sound I have ever heard. It's like the archive watched The Ghost and Mr. Chicken and said, 'Yes, that's exactly how I want to say no.'"

"What was that?" I demanded, my heart still pounding. "Did the archive just...refuse me?"

"Probably not the archive. More like Boddy. He must have put up a magical wall to protect his reports from being accessible," Jess explained, wiping tears from her eyes. "I should've thought of that. He's a former grim reaper. Reaper reports are unobtainable for the general public."

"Those notes," Ren said, his voice warm with amusement, "were definitely protective magic. Old school. Very dramatic."

"Dramatic is an understatement," I muttered, glaring at the fireplace. "It sounded like a haunted organ in a Vincent Price movie."

"Boddy does love his theatrics," Chase said, straightening and smoothing down his jacket.

"Oh, well," I said with a sigh, turning back to the table and its scattered documents. "It was worth a try."

Boddy Grim's magical protection system was the most passive-aggressive thing I'd encountered in Darkly. And that was really saying something.

Jess grabbed a yearbook off the stack in the middle of the table and opened it, the spine crackling like kindling as she turned the stiff pages. "Simone was in the year after ours, so this should have her class photos and activities, if y'all want to see what she looked like."

She flipped through pages of formal portraits and candid shots —students frozen in moments of teenage joy and possibility, completely unaware that one of them wouldn't make it to graduation.

A photo caught my attention and I stopped her page flip—a candid shot of the school's spirit squad mid-performance.

"Wait. You and Tzazi were cheerleaders?" I blinked at the image, trying to reconcile the adorable tavern owner and the sharp-tongued vampire with pom-poms. "Tzazi doesn't seem the cheerleader type."

Jess's laugh was sudden and bright, cutting through the

somber mood. "Not cheerleaders. *Screech*leaders. We didn't so much cheer for our team as jeer at the other team. You know—creative insults, perfectly timed screaming to throw off their plays, strategic heckling. It was considered an art form."

"That's the most Darkly thing I've ever heard," Chase said with genuine amusement. "Leave it to this island to turn support into sabotage and call it school spirit."

"Okay. Now that makes more sense." I studied the photograph more closely, noting Tzazi's wicked grin even in the grainy image.

That I could absolutely see Tzazi doing.

Jess gazed at the image for a long moment, something wistful crossing her face—perhaps remembering simpler times before murder and mystery had invaded Darkly and broken up their friendship.

She began flicking again, then stopped and pointed to a small photo near the back and tapped it with her finger, her expression hardening with renewed determination.

"There," she said softly. "Simone Petalsigh, junior class."

The image showed a girl with soft features and intelligent eyes, her smile tentative but genuine. She wore the standard Wentworth uniform—crisp white blouse, navy blazer with the school crest—but something about her posture suggested she didn't quite feel like she belonged in those formal halls. There was a guardedness to the way she held herself, even in a simple yearbook photo.

"She was such a sweet girl," Jess murmured, her voice thick with old grief. "Quiet. Kept to herself mostly. But when she smiled, it lit up the whole room."

Chase had risen from his chaise and moved closer to look over Jess's shoulder. "Even in a formal portrait, you can see she's holding herself back. Like she's learned not to take up too much space."

"Self-protective," Ren observed, his tone gentle. "When you don't feel safe, you pull inward."

I studied the photo, something nagging at me about the

familiarity of those features. The shape of her eyes, the curve of her jaw—there was an echo of someone else there. A person I'd recently seen. "Keep going. Let's see what clubs or activities she was involved in."

Jess turned the pages carefully, each one releasing a faint smell of aged paper and forgotten time, that particular scent of memories preserved but slowly fading. The yearbook revealed the typical collection of group photos: debate teams posed with their trophies, literary societies gathered around stacks of books, academic clubs arranged in stiff formal rows. Students who had no idea how quickly their youth would pass, how fragile their certainties would prove to be.

We were nearly through the activities section when Jess stopped abruptly, her finger freezing mid-turn.

"Win, look. Here she is again. I never realized she was a Spindler."

The page showed a group photo labeled "Spell & Spindle Society" in elegant calligraphy across the top. Six girls in matching emerald cloaks stood arranged around an ornate table draped in black velvet, each holding what appeared to be a ceremonial wand. The photograph had an almost ethereal quality, the kind of deliberate mystique that teenage witches cultivated when they thought themselves very serious and sophisticated.

Chase and Ren had both moved closer now, drawn by Jess's sudden stillness.

"Prestigious organization," Chase murmured, studying the photo with a sorcerer's attention to detail. "Old magic families only, if I remember correctly."

I flipped back to Simone's individual portrait, studying it more carefully now, then returned to the group photo. A detail I'd missed before suddenly jumped out at me. In both photographs, she wore the same distinctive accessory—a jeweled unicorn hairclip that caught the light, its silver horn gleaming.

I gasped, my hand flying to my mouth. "This hairclip. It's in Michey's pawnshop. I saw it when I was there."

"What?" Jess moved in for a better look at the photo. "Simone wore that hairclip every day."

Chase had gone very still, his sorcerer's mind clearly working through implications. "If Michey had Simone's hairclip..."

"Then he was there when she died," Ren said quietly. "Or he got it from someone who was."

Jess and I looked at each other, the same terrible question forming in both our minds. The fire crackled in the sudden silence, the only sound in the turret besides our breathing.

"Does that mean he killed her back then?" Jess's voice was barely above a whisper. "And these deaths now—Michey and Letha—are they about avenging Simone's death? Someone finally seeking justice after all these years?"

"Someone's awfully patient," Chase murmured.

I leaned back against the sofa, watching the fire burn low in the hearth. The books and papers scattered across the table caught the amber glow of the dying flames, their edges gilded with flickering light. Shadows gathered in the corners of the room, making the space feel smaller, more intimate—like we were conspirators huddled against the dark.

Pyewacket watched from his perch on the mantelpiece.

The heavy wooden door swung open, and Hilde bustled in, looking around in awe, still trying to put her head around the archive's existence. "Would y'all like anything to eat?"

When we all shook our heads, she picked up the carafe of glögg from the table and made her way around the room, topping up mugs with the steaming spiced wine. The scent of cinnamon and cloves wafted up, warm and comforting. She eased onto the arm of the sofa beside me.

"Y'all making any headway?" she asked, her Southern accent softening the question.

I sighed, rubbing my temples. "It's a tangled knot, Hilde. Every thread we pull just reveals another dozen underneath."

"It's hard to tell what's important and what isn't," Jess added, frustration evident in her voice. "Everything seems connected, but I don't see a pattern."

"We've got connections spanning twenty years," Chase said, his usual charm muted by concern.

"And three deaths that may or may not be related," Ren added quietly.

"Well, that's just the way of any mystery, sugar." Hilde patted my shoulder reassuringly. "Y'all will find the thread, then tug and yank until it all unravels." She suddenly looked around the room, her brow furrowing slightly. "Where's Tzazi? Why isn't she joining y'all tonight?"

I glanced at Jess, uncertain how much to say.

"She couldn't make it," I said carefully.

Hilde's expression shifted, that particular look of understanding that said she knew exactly what I wasn't saying. Without another word, she rose from the sofa arm and moved back down the stone steps, giving us privacy.

"Jess, I wish—" I started.

"Stop, Win." Jess held up a hand, her voice tight but controlled. "She sided with Arthur Vanderholt over me. Over us. I have nothing to say to her."

I sighed and leaned back against the sofa, feeling the weight of everything we'd uncovered pressing down on me like a physical thing.

Simone Petalsigh's face stared up at me from the yearbook page, her hopeful expression a stark contrast to the violent fate that awaited her, begging me to discover what really happened. I couldn't let her down.

I knew what I needed to do.

I needed to talk to Arthur.

CHAPTER 16

*M*y chance to talk to Arthur came far sooner than I'd anticipated, but I wasn't going to let the opportunity pass.

The crate of Jane Austens before me gave off a warm, intimate fragrance that made rushing through the work feel almost sacrilegious. Rich leather bindings worn soft at the edges from generations of devoted readers, aged paper carrying the weight of centuries in its very fibers, a scent that spoke of candlelit reading rooms and careful hands turning pages—paper that had absorbed both magic and time until it practically hummed with literary history. Every time I lifted a volume from its nest of protective tissue, the book exhaled something clever and unforgiving into the air around me.

"Emma Woodhouse would have solved this mystery by chapter three. Do keep up."

I shot the book a look. "Emma Woodhouse spent the entire novel being wrong about everything. She thought Harriet should marry Mr. Elton, that Jane Fairfax was having an affair, and completely missed that Mr. Knightley was in love with her until the very end."

"Minor details," the book sniffed.

I was halfway through cataloging the thirteenth first-edition, *Persuasion*—annotated in two distinctly different hands, no less, which made my bibliophile heart race—when movement brushed the edge of my vision like a cold finger trailing across my peripheral awareness.

Someone passed the stained-glass windows of the MET, their form distorted by the colored panes into fragments of shadow and winter light. Tall. Clean, precise lines that spoke of rigid self-control. Silver-blond hair pulled back severely with a black ribbon. A black wool coat with shoulders tailored to mathematical perfection, not a wrinkle or thread out of place.

The falling snow caught his silhouette just long enough for me to name the shape of it, to feel recognition click into place with an almost audible sound.

Arthur Vanderholt.

My pulse quickened. The Jane Austen in my hands suddenly felt heavier, as if even she was bracing for what came next.

I shoved the book cover closed harder than intended, the sharp crack of leather against leather echoing through the quiet MET. In my haste to reach the door, I stumbled over Pyewacket, who'd been napping in a nest of blankets next to the front counter. He gave an indignant yowl and burrowed deeper into his fortress of wool and fleece, muttering curses I chose to ignore.

I didn't grab my coat. Didn't pause to think. Just threw open the door and plunged into the December cold, my breath catching as winter air hit my lungs like a physical blow.

"Arthur!" The name tore from my throat, sharp and demanding in the hushed stillness that always accompanied heavy snowfall.

The sidewalk crowd stuttered to a stop when I yelled. A handful on onlookers lingered, curious and staring, before the human current swept them along.

Arthur stopped mid-stride and turned slowly, as if he'd been expecting this—or dreading it. The wind brushed silver-blond hair from his angular face, revealing stormy gray eyes that caught mine with an expression I hadn't anticipated: surprise and resignation tangled together, along with something that might have been relief.

"Windsor Ebonwood," he said, and his voice was softer than I'd braced for—careful rather than cutting, measured instead of mocking. No smugness curling at the edges. Just bone-deep weariness that made him look older than he had the night of the gala.

For a moment, neither of us moved. Snow fell between us like a curtain of white static, muffling the world beyond our small sphere of tension.

"How about a warm drink?" I asked, my voice steadier than I felt. My arms wrapped around myself against the cold, but I kept my chin up, my gaze direct. "Cocoa. Tea. Café brûlot?"

He hesitated, glancing back toward the street where footprints were already disappearing under fresh powder as if he had somewhere else to be, or somewhere safer to vanish into where difficult conversations couldn't find him. His jaw worked, some internal debate playing out behind those careful eyes.

Then he nodded once, a short, decisive movement. "Sure."

I ducked back into the MET for my coat and gloves. The jingling in my pockets—Sibby's latest warded charms, strung with swamp ash beads and a sliver of onyx—kept pace with our footsteps as we made our way down the icy sidewalk. The silence between us wasn't unfriendly. Just full. He carried himself with practiced stillness, but even that didn't hide the tension in his jaw. Up close, he smelled faintly of sandalwood, sharp mint, and a trace of something older beneath it—sadness.

The Magic Cup welcomed us in a wave of warmth, steeped in roasted chicory, almond steam, vanilla, and fresh evergreen. The fire was going strong, flames licking the carved stone hearth. Charm-lanterns hung above the booths, flickering gently, their light catching on garland draped along the exposed beams. A spell of hush settled over the shop the moment we stepped inside.

Arthur paused just inside the door, shoulders softening by a fraction as he took in the space.

Zavier was seated at the far end of the counter, shoulders hunched, hands wrapped around a steaming mug. The moment he saw us, something shifted. The angle of his jaw changed. His eyes narrowed. One tennis shoe tapped the rung of his stool once, then stilled.

Arthur didn't notice—or pretended not to.

We moved toward the counter. The barista hesitated when we approached the counter. Her gaze flickered between Arthur and the kitchen door uncertainly.

"Mint tea," Arthur said evenly. No charm. No challenge.

"Chai latte," I said. "Extra cinnamon." Then, to the barista, "Both are on me."

Arthur raised a brow.

"Consider it an investment."

"In what?"

I held his gaze, letting him see this wasn't an ambush. "The truth."

Surprisingly, he didn't argue.

Azalea appeared then, framed in the kitchen doorway like a painting someone had dared enchant. Her eyes landed on Arthur and didn't flinch. After a beat, she gave a slow, deliberate nod. The barista moved again.

Stepping back to wait, I could still feel Zavier's glare burning the side of my cheek, but when I looked, he'd turned away. Shaking his head.

We took the booth farthest from the counter and slid into opposite seats.

He wrapped his fingers around the cup without drinking. I watched the tension in his shoulders shift as he stared into the steam.

"I arrived here via book portal," he said, then took a cautious sip of his tea. "You did a great job with the MET. It still has that comfortable, welcome feel. Same as it had when Minta was here."

"Thanks." I sipped my latte, watching him over the rim. He didn't say anything more. Neither did I. The quiet wasn't awkward. Just cautious.

I traced the rim of my mug with one fingertip.

"Tzazi mentioned your work," I said at last. "The Hope Center."

His expression softened. "That place saved me. Turned me into someone worth becoming."

I nodded. "She believes in you, you know."

"She always did," he said, voice dropping low. "Even when I didn't deserve it. That's Tzazi."

He told me about the years after Wentworth Academy—the raw, unvarnished truth of them. How he'd left the island and fled to the Charming Isles with nothing but the family grimoire tucked under his arm and his grandfather's pocket watch in his coat, both heirlooms he couldn't bear to leave behind. How he'd been determined, almost desperately so, to build something that was his—untainted by inherited privilege, unpropped by family connections and old money influence.

He'd scrubbed cauldrons in apothecary basements for minimum wage. Volunteered at fire shelters where displaced magical families huddled with singed belongings and traumatized children. Took any grunt work he could find until someone—a woman who ran a small academy for magical misfits in Luneport—finally gave him a shot teaching kids with volatile magic and zero support systems. The kind of students prestigious schools refused to touch. The ones whose power manifested in dangerous, unpredictable bursts because no one had ever taught them control or given them a reason to try.

His voice went quiet when he talked about those early years. There was pride there, carefully banked, and something that looked like shame for having abandoned his principles in his youth somewhere along the way. He admitted he'd made mistakes even then—plenty of them—but they'd been smaller ones. Honest ones. The kind born from inexperience and overconfidence rather than calculated cruelty or willful blindness.

And watching him speak, seeing the way his hands wrapped around his cup like he needed something to anchor him, I began to understand. The Arthur Vanderholt before me today wasn't the same person he had been at the Academy. This Arthur Vanderholt was someone who'd tried to be better, succeeded, and was now sitting across from me trying to figure out if redemption for the past was even possible—or if he'd burned that bridge along with all the others.

"I never expected to come back," he said. "But when I saw what the gala was for— Simone would've wanted that. She loved the school."

Her name broke something.

"You knew her well," I said.

His hand paused, cup midway to his lips.

"I did."

He set it down.

"Simone was my friend," he said, each word measured and deliberate. "Not many people believed that at the time, given my reputation. But she was one of the few people who saw past the Party Arty nonsense."

"What really happened that night?"

He was quiet for a long time. The distant clatter of cups and spoons underscored the weight of whatever memory he was wrestling with.

"I don't sleep much," he finally said, his voice barely above a whisper. "That's one thing they don't tell you about guilt. It doesn't ever ask permission." His storm-gray eyes met mine. "I spent years learning to accept what harm I'd done by being passive but complicit in a system that allowed cruelty to flourish."

The fire popped in the background, sending sparks up the chimney. Arthur's gaze drifted toward the flames.

"She told me something," he said, voice quieter now. "About

her family. Something dangerous. I told her not to say anything. Said it wasn't safe."

"What did she tell you?"

"Not my story to tell."

Although he still hadn't answered my original question, I let that sit for a second.

"What do you think happened to her?"

He didn't answer right away. "Here's what I think." His thumb moved over the lip of his cup. "I don't think it was an accident."

I watched Arthur struggle to compose himself, noting how his fingers had twisted his napkin into knots.

"Do you think it was intentional?" I asked gently. "Her death?"

Arthur looked away, staring out the window at the falling snow. "I know it was. But I've never been able to prove it." He shrugged helplessly. "Who would believe me anyhow?"

Before I could press further, heavy footsteps approached our table. I looked up to see Zavier towering over us, his usually warm demeanor replaced by something tight and barely restrained.

"Why are you still here?" Zavier said, his voice low but carrying clearly in the quiet corner. His stance was wide, confrontational, like he was preparing for a fight. "You got away with it. Why don't you just leave rather than putting us all through this pain. Have you not thought about what you being here is doing to Dianthe? To me?"

Arthur didn't defend himself, didn't even look up. He just nodded slowly, letting the accusations land without protest.

Zavier turned to me. "This is the man who helped cover up Simone's death. And we're letting him sip tea in peace?"

He turned back to Arthur.

"Darkly isn't interested in your redemption arc, Vanderholt," Zavier continued, his words sharp enough to cut. "Some people don't deserve forgiveness."

"Zavier—" I tried.

He rounded on me again

"You think this is justice? Letting him walk around town like nothing happened?"

"I'm not here to be forgiven," Arthur said, quiet but steady.

"Then leave," Zavier snapped.

"I already tried that."

That's when Azalea's voice echoed across the room in a timbre low and resounding.

"Zavier Marciel Strangeland."

The temperature dropped. Even the charm-lanterns paused.

Azalea's voice cut through the tension like a blade. She appeared from behind the counter, moving with the fluid grace of someone who'd spent years managing rowdy customers and family drama. "You don't start fights in my shop, baby boy."

Her eyes were sharp, focused on her son with maternal authority that brooked no argument. Zavier's jaw worked like he wanted to say more, but he stepped back, glaring at Arthur with undisguised hostility.

"This isn't over," he muttered, but he stalked back to his seat at the counter. Azalea watched him go with arms folded across her chest.

Arthur stood. "Thank you for the tea," he said, touching the table gently with two fingers.

Then he shrugged on his coat, his hair catching a sliver of firelight as he disappeared out the door.

I sat there a little longer, fingers curled around a cup that had gone cold, turning over every word he'd given me—and wondering about all the ones he hadn't.

CHAPTER 17

The cold hit me like a slap the moment I stepped back outside The Magic Cup. Snow tumbled from the gray afternoon sky in fat, lazy flakes that caught on my coat sleeves and melted almost immediately. I pulled my scarf tighter, tucking my chin against the wind that swept down the street carrying the scent of roasted chestnuts and mulled cider from the Christmas market. A Christmas market trying to continue its festive appearance despite the deaths and demons seemingly circling its edges.

Arthur's words circled through my mind like vultures over roadkill. *I don't think it was an accident.* The quiet certainty in his voice when he'd said it. The way his hands had twisted that napkin into knots. Twenty years of guilt and secrets, and still he couldn't—or wouldn't—tell me the whole truth.

My boots crunched through fresh powder as I made my way back toward the MET. The sidewalk bustled with holiday shoppers, their arms loaded with wrapped packages and shopping bags stamped with silver bells and holly sprigs. A group of carolers had set up near the main entrance to Darkly's cemetery, their voices lifting into "Christmas All Over Again" with more enthusiasm than harmony.

I should have felt festive. Should have been swept up in the magic of a Darkly Island Christmas, with its enchanted snow globes and charm-woven garlands and the way the whole town smelled like warm marshmallows and peppermint.

Arthur thought Simone's death was murder. Truegaze blamed Arthur for destroying his career. Zavier blamed Arthur for covering up the whole thing. And somewhere in the middle of it all, Michey Stramm and Letha Marsh had been killed— methodically, ritualistically—with stones and straw and silver coins arranged in a message I couldn't interpret.

What was I missing?

"Watch it!" someone yelped as I nearly collided with them at the corner.

I jerked to a stop, blinking. A young woman with an armful of shopping bags glared at me before hurrying past, muttering something about "witches daydreaming about sexy shifters."

"Seriously?" I rubbed my temples, trying to ease the tension headache that had been building since I'd left The Magic Cup.

The MET's familiar facade appeared through the swirling snow—warm and inviting, the old Creole architecture dressed up with evergreen garlands and twinkling lights. My safe place.

I pushed into the welcoming MET, discarded my coat and hat, and slipped behind the front desk, nudging open the crate of Jane Austens I'd abandoned. After everything Arthur had said, I wasn't sure I was ready to be alone with my thoughts. But I could manage Jane. Jane had opinions, and she expressed them with all the assurance of a woman wholly unacquainted with self-doubt. Maybe some of this would rub off on me. I lifted *Northanger Abbey* from the box.

"The folly of your investigation is exceeded only by your certainty about it," the book whispered.

"Noted, Jane. Any other encouragement?"

"One ought not require encouragement to employ basic deductive reasoning, yet here we are."

Apparently, my investigation skill was up for literary review.

Pye melted into a heated cushion on the counter, his purr a soft rumble that filled the quiet spaces between us.

I blinked at the cushion. "Where'd that come from?" Then realization dawned. "Did you get that from the archive? How in the world did you drag it down here?"

He stretched one paw lazily, claws extending for just a moment before retracting. "Where there's a whisker, there's a way. Besides, gravity's more of a suggestion than a rule when you're motivated."

The bell above the door chimed, and two teens wandered past the counter, their voices hushed but thrumming with that breathless excitement usually reserved for first crushes or forbidden gossip.

"I'm telling you, Evon's not making it up. My cousin saw her too—underneath Rottwood Bridge." The first girl leaned closer to her friend, fingers twisting the strap of her messenger bag.

"She had bells woven into her hair," the other whispered, eyes wide as saucers. "Silver ones, tangled in this awful veil. You could hear them chiming even after she was gone."

A third teen popped up from behind the rotating snow globe display, startling them both. "She didn't just leave. She vanished." She emphasized the word like it held magic all its own. "Vanishing's way creepier than walking away."

The front bell jingled again, pulling me from my eavesdropping with a guilty start.

Keir stood just inside the doorway, brushing snow from his shoulders in that unconscious way of his. His hair had gone damp at the edges, dark curls starting to rebel across his brow. When he spotted me, something warm flickered in his eyes.

He crossed the shop in a few strides, and suddenly his hands were at my waist, firm and sure, drawing me close. The scent of winter air and cedar clung to his coat, and when his lips met mine, the kiss was sweet and unhurried—the kind that made the rest of the world blur at the edges.

"Missed you," he murmured against my mouth.

"I missed you too."

His arms tightened around me. "Good. Because these past few days have been unbearable."

A flutter of giggles erupted near the armillary display. Three young witches were making a spectacular show of studying portal bookmarks, though their sideways glances and poorly suppressed grins told a different story entirely.

Keir's mouth curved against mine. "We've got an audience, love."

"We always do in this town." I pulled back just enough to meet his eyes. "Want a coffee?"

His brow furrowed slightly, that perceptive gaze sweeping my face. He tucked a strand of hair behind my ear, his thumb lingering at my jaw. "Windsor. What's happened?"

The gentle concern in his voice nearly undid me.

I didn't answer—just caught his hand and led him toward the fireplace, weaving between displays of enchanted compasses and celestial maps. He followed without question, fingers laced with mine.

We settled into the deep armchairs facing the hearth, and before I could even think about summoning refreshments, two steaming mugs appeared on the low table between us—my favorite chai and Keir's black coffee with just a touch of honey.

"Show-off," I murmured at the shop's helpfulness.

"It knows what we need." Keir's eyes hadn't left my face. "Windsor."

There it was again. My full name in that Scottish lilt of his, all soft consonants and rolling warmth. It still caught me sideways sometimes. Made my chest feel too full and my stomach flutter like I needed another sip of chai just to settle it.

I wrapped both hands around my mug. "I talked to Arthur this morning. He's convinced Simone's death wasn't an accident."

Keir leaned back, crossing one ankle over his knee in that easy way he had—relaxed but attentive. "Aye, I remember when it happened. Most folk on Darkly didn't buy the accident story, even if they let it stand. The school might've wanted students to feel safe, but people saw through it."

"I'm starting to think they were right to doubt."

His expression shifted—concern threading through the warmth. "Love." He leaned forward, elbows on his knees, closing the distance between us. "You realize there's a killer walking around this island, aye?"

"I'm being careful." I reached across and squeezed his hand. "I promise."

He turned his palm up, threading his fingers through mine and holding on. "Careful's one thing. Hunting a murderer's another."

"I'm not hunting anyone. Just...listening." I took a breath. "There's something else. About Truegaze."

His thumb traced a slow circle on the back of my hand—grounding, patient. "Tell me."

I thought back to that uncomfortable visit, the unease that had settled in my bones. "When Pye and I went to see Truegaze at Wentworth..."

Keir's jaw tightened, just slightly. His thumb stilled on my hand. "Windsor—"

"I know." I squeezed his fingers before he could finish the protective lecture forming behind his eyes. "But listen. The whole time we were there, he kept rubbing his wrists. Over and over, like he couldn't stop. And when I mentioned Arthur's name?" I shook my head. "His whole demeanor changed. Went cold first, then almost...feral. And he was drenched in sweat, Keir. Like he was fighting something inside himself."

The warmth drained from Keir's expression, replaced by that sharp, focused alertness I'd seen when he was working a case. He straightened in his chair. "Show me."

I lifted my free hand and mimicked Truegaze's compulsive motion—fingers working over the inside of my wrist, pressing and circling like trying to soothe a wound that wouldn't heal.

"And his eyes." I met Keir's gaze, remembering the wrongness of it. "They kept flickering gold. Just for a second, then back to normal. But it happened multiple times."

Keir's brow furrowed, his detective brain clearly cataloging details. He released my hand only to lean forward, gently catching my wrist and studying where I'd been rubbing. "The places he kept touching—did you see any marks?"

"Thick scars. Healed, but prominent. White against his skin, like—" I swallowed. "Like restraints, maybe?"

Keir stood abruptly, already moving toward the stairs with that purposeful stride.

"Wait!" I jumped up, nearly knocking over my chai. "What are you doing?"

"We need to pay a visit to Wentworth." He was already reaching for his coat on the rack near the door.

"To see Truegaze?"

"Aye." He shrugged into the heavy wool, then grabbed mine and held it open for me—always the gentleman, even when his mind was clearly racing ahead.

"Why?" I slipped my arms into the sleeves, and his hands lingered at my shoulders for just a moment.

"Because whatever he's hiding, it's time someone helped him bring it into the open."

I turned to face him, hands on my hips. "You know that tells me absolutely nothing, right?"

His mouth quirked—just a hint of that warmth returning. He tucked a wayward curl behind my ear, then let his hand trail down to cup my cheek. "And because, love, I think I might actually be able to help him."

"Help him how?"

"You'll see." He pressed a quick kiss to my forehead, then moved to hold the door open. "Trust me?"

"Always." I grabbed my scarf from the hook. "But you're explaining on the way."

He caught my hand as I reached for the door, tugging me back just enough that I had to look up at him. His eyes held that glint—the one that was equal parts mischief and authority. "Am I?"

"Keir—"

His thumb brushed along my jaw, tipping my chin up slightly. "You trust me, aye?"

"That's not—" My breath caught as he leaned in, close enough that I could feel the warmth of him, smell the coffee and winter air clinging to his coat.

"Then trust me to handle this my way, love." His voice dropped lower, that Scottish burr wrapping around the words like velvet.

I blinked up at him, my thoughts scrambling. "Did you just...tell me no?"

His mouth curved into a devastating smirk. "Did I?"

Before I could formulate a response that didn't sound completely flustered, he pressed a kiss to my lips and guided me toward the door, his hand settling at the small of my back.

"Come on then, *mo chridhe*. Daylight's burning."

I let him lead me out into the snow, still not entirely sure what had just happened.

THE RIDE to Wentworth felt like it stretched across half the island.

I tried three more times to coax information out of Keir, but each attempt met with that same maddeningly patient response: "I need to be certain first, love."

By the time the academy's towers came into view, I'd resigned myself to waiting—though not happily.

The school had wandered toward Cradlerock during our drive, its enchanted foundations carrying it across the landscape like a ship drifting through fog. Just as Keir pulled up before the entrance, the entire structure gave one final shudder before anchoring itself in place. The drawbridge descended with a metallic groan.

Through the truck window, I studied the building with fresh eyes. The stone facade rose against the steel-gray sky, all Gothic arches and frost-laced turrets. Warm light spilled from narrow windows, but instead of feeling welcoming, it only made the shadows between them seem darker.

"Ready?" Keir's hand found mine.

"Not even a little."

His mouth quirked. "Good instincts."

Inside, the school buzzed with life. Students in crisp uniforms moved through corridors in tight clusters, their voices a hushed chorus of gossip and speculation. The stares felt heavier than my last visit—more intense, almost hungry for whatever scene might unfold.

I kept my eyes forward. "I forgot how much they love a good drama here."

"Can't blame them." Keir's hand settled at the small of my back, guiding me through the clusters of whispering students. "It's not every day someone interesting walks these halls." His voice dropped lower, meant only for me. "And you, love, are *very* interesting."

We followed the familiar path to the headmaster's quarters. The stone wall guarding his office recognized us immediately, magic rippling across its surface before the portal unfurled into swirling existence.

The scent of old leather and parchment washed over us as we pushed open the door and stepped into the headmaster's office.

Truegaze sat behind his massive mahogany desk exactly where I'd left him days ago, but with Keir beside me, I noticed details I'd missed before. The office was immaculate—grimoires arranged in precise rows, expensive artifacts displayed with museum-quality care. Everything carefully curated to project academic authority and respectability.

Everything except the man himself.

His gaunt frame seemed even more diminished today, shoulders hunched despite the rigid set of his spine. A tea tray sat untouched beside him, delicate china at odds with the tension radiating from his body like heat from a flame.

Truegaze sat at his desk, head down, scribbling on parchment, pretending we hadn't just entered his office. When he finally looked up, I watched his pale blue eyes flicker between us. His hand moved immediately to his wrist—that same compulsive rubbing motion.

But it was Keir's presence that transformed him.

Surprise flashed across Truegaze's face, followed instantly by fear. Not the uncertain wariness he'd shown me before. Real, visceral fear.

"Dr. Ebonwood." His voice carried that careful control I remembered, but now I could hear what lay beneath it—barely suppressed panic threading through every syllable. His gaze slid to Keir and held, something almost like respect warring with fear. "Lord Mac'IlleBhàin. To what do I owe this...visit?"

I felt Keir's hand tense briefly at my back, just a flicker of tension before he smoothed it away. The title always did that to him, turned him into someone he'd rather not be. But his voice remained even, almost gentle.

"I think you know exactly why we're here, Headmaster."

Keir moved deeper into the office, his presence filling the space in a way that made Truegaze press back in his chair. The air grew thick, charged with the kind of tension that preceded storms. An enchanted globe in the corner stuttered in its rotation.

"We need to talk about the night of the gala, Landavedon." Keir's voice carried through the stillness.

The intimacy of using his first name landed like a slap. Truegaze's knuckles whitened where they gripped the arms of his chair.

"I've already told Dr. Ebonwood everything I know—"

"Have you?" Keir pulled out the chair beside me, his movements unhurried but deliberate. He waited until I sat before settling into his own seat with the kind of easy confidence that made it clear he wasn't going anywhere. "Everything about where you were when Michey Stramm died? About why you fled the moment Arthur Vanderholt walked through those doors?"

The word *fled* hung in the air like an accusation.

Truegaze's mask of composure fractured—just a hairline crack, but I saw it. Something desperate and cornered flashed through his pale eyes before he wrestled it back under control.

"Arthur's arrival caught me off guard. I wasn't feeling well, so I excused myself. Surely you can appreciate—"

"To the woods?"

The question was soft. Almost conversational. But the way Keir said it made my pulse skip.

Every muscle in Truegaze's body locked. "Pardon me?"

"The woods behind Greywolf." Keir's posture remained relaxed, one hand resting on the arm of his chair, but his gaze never wavered. "The tracks I found there with Win. Boot prints at first." He paused, letting the words settle. "Then something else entirely."

So I hadn't imagined it. The shoe prints, the ones I'd second-guessed myself about, Keir had seen them too, which meant they were real, which meant...

I forced myself to stay still, to keep my face neutral even as questions exploded through my mind.

"You were there that night, weren't you?" Keir's voice gentled further, like he was coaxing a frightened animal. "Running."

"I don't—" Truegaze's protest died in his throat. His voice had gone thin and brittle, ready to shatter. Both hands flew to his wrists, fingers pressing and circling over the hidden scars with frantic urgency. "I don't know what you're talking about."

But everything about him screamed the opposite. Sweat dampened his collar. His breathing had gone shallow. And there —that gold flash flickering through his irises again, brighter this time, lasting a fraction longer before fading.

Keir saw it too. I watched recognition dawn across his features, followed by something I hadn't expected.

Sorrow.

When Keir spoke again, all the authority had melted away, leaving only understanding—raw and aching.

"Who cursed you, Landravedon?"

The question was a mercy and a knife all at once.

Truegaze's carefully constructed mask shattered. His shoulders curved inward, his spine bowing under invisible weight. The dignified headmaster vanished, leaving only someone broken and terrified. His hands moved faster now, rubbing those hidden scars with a desperation that made my throat tight.

"You can't—" The words fractured. "No one can help. It's—"

"I can." Keir shifted forward, eliminating the space between them without making it feel like pursuit. His voice stayed low, steady. "But only if you tell me the truth."

The silence stretched taut. Truegaze's breathing came sharp and shallow—a trapped animal weighing its options. Behind us, a leather-bound tome creaked open and slammed shut, pages ruffling as if disturbed by unseen hands. The magic in the room had gone restless, responding to the storm building inside the headmaster.

"I—I don't—"

"The rougarou my Enforcers tracked that night." Keir's words fell soft as snowflakes but carried the weight of stone. "That was you."

Not a question. A certainty delivered with such gentle inevitability that there was no room left to hide.

Truegaze's defenses crumbled like ash.

I stared at the headmaster.

His shoulders sagged, and suddenly he looked decades older—centuries older. The stern academic façade dissolved, leaving only exhaustion and grief etched into every line of his face.

"How long have you known?" His voice barely rose above a whisper.

"I suspected when Win described how you moved, how you

reacted." Keir's tone never hardened, never judged. "The scars confirmed it. How long have you carried this?"

Wind rattled the leaded windows, making the glass shudder in its ancient frames. The shadows in the corners seemed to press closer, as if the room itself were leaning in to hear his answer.

When Truegaze finally spoke, the words emerged hollow and broken. "Twenty-three years."

My heart clenched. *Twenty-three years.* More than two decades of living with this curse, fighting it every single day.

He stared at his hands—those elegant scholar's hands still tracing compulsive circles over his wrists. "A man named Jean-Baptiste found me in the deep swamp during my first year as assistant headmaster at Wentworth. I thought..." A bitter laugh escaped him, sharp enough to cut. "I thought he was just another researcher. Someone interested in local folklore and ancient magic."

He stood abruptly, as if sitting had become unbearable. His feet carried him to the window, though I suspected it had less to do with needing the view and more about not being able to face us while he spoke. His reflection in the dark glass looked spectral —a ghost haunting his own life.

"I'd gone into the bayou to study curse markers near one of the old ritual stones. Academic curiosity." The self-mockery in his tone made me flinch. "I was so careful, or so I thought. Following every protocol, taking all the proper precautions. And Jean-Baptiste..." He pressed his forehead against the cold glass. "He appeared out of the mist like something from a dream. Charming. Knowledgeable. So eager to share stories about the old ways, the forgotten magic."

The weight of what was coming settled over me like a shroud.

"We met several times over a month. He'd find me in the swamp, always with some new tale, some fragment of lore I'd never heard. I felt *honored*." The word dripped with self-loathing. "That someone with such profound understanding of swamp magic would take interest in my work."

"What happened?" My voice came out softer than I'd intended.

Truegaze's reflection showed eyes squeezed shut, as if he could block out the memory. "During our final meeting, everything changed. One moment we were talking about binding curses, and the next..." His hands clenched into fists against the window frame. "His eyes went gold. Feral. Wild. The change happened so fast I didn't even have time to reach for my wand."

My stomach dropped.

"The bite was..." He touched his shoulder, fingers finding a place beneath his collar. "Excruciating doesn't begin to cover it. Like liquid fire being poured into my veins. I carry the scar still— a perfect impression of teeth that haunt every reflection." His voice dropped to barely a whisper. "From that moment, I was bound. Cursed. Chained to a beast I never asked to become."

The horror of it crashed over me in waves. To be betrayed by someone you'd trusted, someone you'd *admired*. To be transformed into the very creature you'd been studying, trapped in a nightmare of someone else's making. The calculated cruelty of it—the deliberate deception leading to such devastating violence—made bile rise in my throat.

I thought of all those nights he must have spent alone, fighting the curse. All those years teaching students while carrying this terrible secret.

Twenty-three years of imprisonment in his own skin.

"Tell us what happened the night of the gala." Keir's voice remained steady, but I heard the command underneath—alpha to subordinate, but also protector to someone in pain.

Truegaze's hands shook as he pressed them against his temples. "Arthur's arrival...seeing him again after all these years..." His voice cracked. "The rage rose so fast. Not just anger —it was everything. Fury, grief, instinct, all of it scrambling together in my head until I couldn't think straight. I felt my bones start to shift, saw my fingernails elongate. The mental component is worse than the physical sometimes—you lose yourself in the rage."

"You transformed?"

"Partially in the ballroom." He looked directly at me for the first time since we'd arrived, and the anguish in his expression made my breath catch. "I've had decades of practice containing it, but that night...something unraveled. The energy at the gala, Arthur's appearance, the tension—it all hit like a storm. I fought it back, got to the woods, and made it to my chamber."

"Chamber?" I asked.

"Below the astronomy dome. There's a reinforced chamber beneath the academy—enchanted with old magic, iron, and warding stones strong enough to contain a full transformation." He paused, and something almost like a smile touched his lips, though it carried infinite sadness. "Your grandmother knew about it, actually. Minta was the only person I ever trusted with my secret. Until now."

My breath caught. "Minta knew?"

"She helped me strengthen the wards years ago. Never judged me for it. Just...helped." His voice broke slightly. "She said everyone deserves a chance at redemption, even monsters. I think about that a lot."

The revelation hit me harder than I expected. Another piece of my grandmother's life I'd never known about, another example of her quiet compassion reaching into the darkest places to offer hope.

"So you don't have an alibi." The words came out flat, but my chest felt tight. "You can't account for where you were when Michey died."

"How could I?" Something desperate crept into his voice. "What was I supposed to tell Belleclaire? That I'd been locked in a transformative episode beneath the astronomy dome while someone was being murdered?" He turned from the window to face us fully, and the resignation in his expression made my stomach knot. "I've asked myself a thousand times since that night. What if I..." His throat worked. "What if I'm the one who killed him, and I just don't remember?"

The confession hung in the air like smoke.

"You didn't." Keir's voice cut through the spiral of self-doubt with absolute certainty.

Truegaze blinked, something like hope and disbelief warring on his face. "How can you possibly know that?"

"The rougarou we tracked that night was running away from the manor, not toward it. And your timeline matches what we know about Michey's death." Keir paused, and I saw him calculating something. "More importantly, Michey's murder was methodical. Ritualistic. Someone placed stones and straw in his mouth. Left silver coins around the body. That's not the work of a rougarou in the grip of a transformation. That's the work of someone with a very specific message to send."

Something shifted in Truegaze's expression—not quite hope, but maybe the first glimpse of it in a very long time. "I've been so afraid," he whispered. "Afraid I might have done it and blocked it out. Afraid that all these years of control meant nothing in the end."

We sat with that revelation for a moment. The office felt smaller somehow, filled with the weight of twenty-three years' worth of secrets finally brought into the light.

"You mentioned that seeing Arthur triggered the episode," I said carefully. "What happened between you two?"

Would he confirm what Jess told me?

The careful mask tried to slip back into place, but there was real pain beneath it now—old wounds torn fresh and bleeding. Truegaze returned to his chair, moving like someone much older than his years.

"Arthur Vanderholt destroyed my life twenty years ago." His voice hardened to something brittle. "When Simone Petalsigh died, he threw the rest of us under the proverbial carriage to save his own skin."

"What do you mean?"

"I was Assistant Headmaster then. Young, ambitious, with a brilliant career ahead of me—everything was finally coming together despite the curse. I'd learned to manage it, built this chamber, established a life." His fingers curled into fists against the desk. "After Simone's death, the board needed someone to blame. Arthur made sure it wasn't him. I was demoted to groundskeeper—groundskeeper!—while he walked away with nary a scratch on his precious reputation."

The bitterness in his voice was raw, decades-old wounds torn fresh. I could picture it—the humiliation of being stripped of everything he'd worked for, forced to maintain the very grounds he'd once overseen as a leader.

"It took me fifteen years to work my way back up. Twenty years of being treated like a servant by colleagues who once respected me. Twenty years of watching Arthur live his charmed life in Luneport while I scraped and clawed my way back to this office. All because Arthur was too much of a coward to face the consequences of his actions."

"You think Arthur killed Simone?" I asked.

"Yes, and he let the rest of us take the blame for his cowardice." Truegaze's eyes met mine, and in them I saw a fury that had been banked for two decades, waiting. "Simone deserved better."

I could feel the rage radiating from him now, tightly controlled but simmering just beneath the surface. This was the anger that had triggered his transformation at the gala—not just seeing Arthur again but seeing him succeed while Truegaze had spent two decades clawing his way back from disgrace.

"Did you know Michey would be at the gala?" I asked.

"That little worm went to every event where he could play at being an upstanding, influential member of society." Truegaze's lip curled. "Of course, he'd be there. At the Academy, he was always trying to attach himself to Arthur—desperate for some of that golden-boy charm to rub off on him. Michey was pathetic." His expression darkened. "But he didn't deserve to die like that."

Silence settled over the office. The tea on Truegaze's desk had long gone cold, a skin forming on its surface.

I exchanged a glance with Keir. His slight nod told me he was thinking the same thing—we'd gotten what we came for. Time to let Truegaze breathe.

But just as I started to rise, the headmaster spoke again.

"There is something else." His fingers found his wrists once more, that compulsive rubbing returning. "Jean-Baptiste—the rougarou who cursed me. He's still out there. Still spreading his curse to others."

The temperature in the room seemed to drop.

"Over the years, I've heard whispers. Rumors of attacks near the old ritual sites." His voice went hollow. "Every few years, another victim. Another life destroyed. I've tried to track the pattern, but he's careful. Strategic." He looked up at us, and the guilt in his eyes was crushing. "How many others are like me because I was too ashamed to speak up twenty-three years ago?"

"Which sites?" Keir asked, his tone sharpening back to business.

"The deep swamp. The old ritual sites behind Fernwood." He nodded in my direction and I felt a chill creep up my spine. "He's drawn to places of power, areas where the veil between worlds runs thin. Places where..." Truegaze hesitated. "Places where something in the magic seems to be waking up."

I exchanged a glance with Keir. "What do you mean, waking up?"

"Haven't you noticed? The magic on this island has been...changing. Shifting. For the past few years, it's been getting stronger, wilder. Things that should stay dormant are stirring. Old protections are weakening while new powers emerge." He looked at me with something like recognition. "Your grandmother felt it too, near the end."

Grandmother knew there was something wicked in the swamps.

"Jean-Baptiste is drawn to that kind of disturbance," Truegaze continued. "He feeds on it somehow. I don't understand the mechanism, but wherever the magic runs strongest and strangest, that's where he appears. That's where he creates more like me."

As we crossed the courtyard back to Keir's Land Rover, I couldn't shake the image of Truegaze—broken but still fighting. He wasn't our killer, but his story had revealed another crack in Arthur Vanderholt's carefully maintained facade. Another life shattered by Arthur's self-preservation.

"This Jean-Baptiste troubles me." Keir's voice cut through my thoughts. "If he's still out there cursing people, and if the magic really is waking up like Truegaze said..." He shook his head. "That's a dangerous combination."

"You think you can help him? Truegaze?"

Keir was quiet for a moment, his jaw working. "Your grandmother saw something in him worth protecting. That tells me everything I need to know."

I thought about Truegaze chaining himself in that underground chamber month after month, fighting the beast within. "If you find Jean-Baptiste—"

"*When* I find him." Steel threaded through his words—the alpha who didn't accept failure when it came to protecting his people. "And when I do, I'll give Landravedon back the life Jean-Baptiste stole from him."

The sun was setting over Darkly Island, painting the sky in shades of winter fire. Somewhere in the deep swamp, an ancient evil was still hunting. But for the first time since this nightmare began, I felt like we were finally asking the right questions.

The drive back was quiet. Keir's hand found mine across the console, fingers intertwining—protective and grounding all at once. Outside, Darkly Island rolled past in shades of gray and white, beautiful and terrible and full of secrets.

Just like the people who called it home.

CHAPTER 18

*A*fter the horrors of today's revelations, I just wanted to spend some time with Keir and my friends, forgetting all about rougarous and curses and the murder of a young schoolgirl so that evening we all found ourselves back at the Christmas market. Not our brightest idea, in hindsight.

Keir laced his fingers through mine, thumb brushing slow circles over my glove, snow falling in soft spirals, dusting the cobblestones and garlands like powdered sugar over gingerbread. His soft brown eyes sparkled with contentment as we wandered past Sugarloaf's enchanted bakery, where a tiny cookie man waved at us from a waxed paper sack before biting off his own arm and cackling. A group of children watching the show laughed and ran to catch up with their parents.

The market had shaken off the previous night's terror like snow from a roof. Streets overflowed with townspeople bundled in scarves and mittens, along with a handful of visitors still lingering from the gala, reluctant to leave the magic of Darkly's Christmas Market behind.

I waved to Jess standing at Sugarloaf's booth. She squealed and fluttered over to my side, wrapping me in arms.

"I am adamant that we will have fun tonight," she said, linking her arm through mine.

"Here, here," Keir said with a grin.

Pyewacket trotted ahead of us, tail high and imperious, until the Nutcracker Brittle display caught his eye. He paused, whiskers twitching with interest, then leaned in for what I'm sure he considered a perfectly reasonable investigative lick.

The candy snapped at him with tiny, sugar-crystal teeth.

Pye shot backward with an indignant yowl, somersaulting through the air before landing in an undignified sprawl in the snow. His legs stuck up at odd angles.

Jess laughed. "Oh, you poor thing."

"The audacity," he sputtered, attempting to groom his ruffled fur while still lying on his back. "I was conducting a vital security assessment. One cannot be too careful with enchanted confections that may pose a threat to—"

"You were trying to steal candy."

"—innocent bystanders," he finished, shooting me a wounded look.

I bent down and scooped him into my arms, brushing snow from his whiskers. He made a show of pouting against my shoulder, though I felt his purr rumble to life despite himself.

We passed Abimelech's poppet stall, where the old zombie had arranged his handcrafted dolls with meticulous care. Rows of Santa-suited figures winked—or twitched—from their perches. At Mooncharms, Maisie waved as her jeweled ornaments pulsed with captured moonlight, murmuring secrets when the wind stirred them.

When Jess and Pyewacket stopped at a pretzel and popcorn booth, Keir pulled me into a darkened doorway between stalls and kissed me beneath a garland of shadow bells. They shivered with a low, musical hum, as if harmonizing with my heartbeat.

For one perfect moment, the world narrowed to sparkle and cinnamon-spiced cocoa and him.

He pulled back just enough to reach into his coat, his breath visible in the cold air. "Got you something."

The small package was wrapped in black tissue that whispered as I unfolded it. Inside, nestled against the dark paper, was a stone about the size of a silver dollar.

I caught my breath.

Clear crystal with the faintest blue tint, shot through with frost patterns that looked impossibly delicate—white dendrites branching into pale blue and lavender, like winter had crystallized its own signature inside the stone. It caught the fairy lights from the market and threw back tiny constellations.

"Keir." My voice came out hushed. "What is this?"

"A solstice wish stone." He traced the edge of it with one finger, his hand warm against mine. "From a meteor that fell during a winter solstice. Instead of burning up, it froze on the way down. Crystallized into this. They're...well, you won't find another."

The stone pulsed with gentle warmth in my palm, responding to my touch like something alive. I looked up to find him watching me with those deep brown eyes, a curl of hair falling across his forehead.

I reached up and tucked it behind his ear, my fingers lingering longer than necessary. "What does it do?"

"Once a year, on the winter solstice, you can make a wish." His hands found my waist, and even through my coat I felt the heat of them. "Nothing dramatic—it won't solve murders or raise the dead. But something your heart needs in that moment. Something real."

The stone warmed between us, the frost patterns seeming to shift and catch the light differently, as if acknowledging his words.

"One wish a year," I whispered. "That's precious."

"So are you."

The words landed soft and certain between us. I slipped the

stone into my coat pocket, feeling it settle against my heart with a contented pulse of magic that radiated warmth through my chest.

We were still smiling when *he* appeared.

The elf looked straight from a holiday catalog—emerald velvet suit, golden curls spilling from beneath a jaunty cap.

"Sweets for the especially nice!" the jolly fellow called, pulling wrapped candies from a festive basket. "Papa Noël's orders!"

Children flocked to him immediately. Parents smiled indulgently. He worked his way through the crowd with a bright smile, handing out glittering confections like a benevolent saint.

When he reached us, as he swirled his hand in the air, a small black ring with pale spiral markings caught in the lamp light, the other hand clutching a basket of foiled candies. His eyes twinkled as he posed in an exaggerated bow in front of us, then sprang up.

"Happy holidays!" He pressed candies into each of our hands. "Don't get put on Papa's Naughty List."

Jess unwrapped hers immediately. "Mmm. Cardamom."

Keir examined his with mild curiosity. "Smells like butterscotch," he said, unwrapping it and popping it into his mouth.

The elf moved on, vanishing into the chaos of the Christmas market, a crowd of children following in his wake as if he were the Pied Piper of Hamlin.

Pyewacket, sensing he was missing out, pawed at my boot.

"Discriminatory," he muttered. "I've been very good. Relatively speaking. There was that one incident with the merchant's scarf, but that was clearly self-defense."

"Fine." I unwrapped the candy, the sweet scent of vanilla and something floral rising up. "You can have mine."

He sniffed it delicately, whiskers twitching. Batted the silver wrapper with one paw. Took a tentative nibble.

His pupil dilated.

Then he collapsed.

The transition was horrifying in its suddenness—one moment

he was purring over his prize, the next he was convulsing on the cobblestones. His small body seized, joints locking at unnatural angles. His eye rolled back until only white showed. Foam flecked his whiskers, tinged faintly pink.

The sound he made wasn't anything a cat should make. High and keening, it scraped against my eardrums like nails on a chalkboard, rising and falling in waves that made my teeth ache.

"Pye?" My voice cracked. "PYE!"

I hit my knees hard enough to bruise, scooping his jerking body into my hands. He was burning up, his fur too hot beneath my fingers.

Jess screamed—a sharp, cut-off sound of pure terror.

The market noise receded like a tide pulling back from shore. Somewhere distant, I heard Keir shouting. Felt his hand on my shoulder.

Bare feet appeared in my peripheral vision. Pale against the dark cobblestones. A white dress pooled around them like seafoam.

Hands—cool and steady—covered mine.

And then the world dissolved into light and magic and the desperate, wrenching pull of the veil as I threw everything I had into saving him.

FERNWOOD'S SITTING room swam into focus around me, all golden firelight and shadows that danced too wildly across the walls. Ileana stood over Pyewacket's small form, her hands blazing with diagnostic magic that cast her face in stark relief. Wild blonde hair escaped its pins in silver-streaked wisps. Thor pressed against her leg, the massive Irish Wolfhound's ears pinned back, sensing the wrongness.

"What did he ingest?" Ileana's voice cut through my panic like a blade.

"Candy." The word scraped out of my throat. "From an elf at the market. Keir and Jess ate theirs too—"

The air cracked with displaced magic. Ileana vanished.

My legs gave out. I caught myself on the arm of the sofa, breath coming in ragged gasps as I stared at Pyewacket's motionless form.

Footsteps thundered down the hallway. Sibby barreled through the doorway with an armful of towels and a bottle of bourbon, her face bone-white. "Windsor? What happened?"

"Pye," I choked out. "He's—"

Hilde swept in behind Sibby, arms loaded with quilts that smelled like cedar and old magic. She dropped to her knees beside Pyewacket without a word, spreading blankets with practiced efficiency. Her lips moved in prayer—guttural words in a language that prickled across my skin like nettles woven into lullabies. Bear song. Ancient and sorrowful.

Pyewacket lay on the throw near the hearth, his black fur dull and lifeless in the firelight. Steam rose from his small body—or maybe it was magic, I couldn't tell anymore through my tears. His sides moved in rapid, shallow gasps that sounded like tissue paper tearing.

Then he convulsed.

Once. Hard enough that his small body arched off the fabric, legs rigid.

And went still.

Not sleeping still. Not resting still.

Dead still.

The kind of still that echoed with absence. With the hollow space where a soul used to live.

I dug into my pocket for my wish stone.

"When is the solstice?"

Sibby's brow furrowed. "Three days."

"No." The word ripped out of me. "No, no, no—PYE!"

I threw myself forward, but Sibby caught me around the waist, her arms surprisingly strong as she held me back. "Let Hilde work, honey. Let her work—"

But there was nothing to work on. Nothing left to save.

Thor's mournful howl shattered the silence, rattling the windowpanes with its ancient grief.

The air cracked open like breaking ice.

Ileana materialized in a rush of displaced magic, hauling Keir and Jess through the veil behind her. They stumbled forward, gasping, but upright. Breathing. Alive.

Relief and rage collided in my chest so violently I couldn't breathe.

"Ours were just sugar." Jess's voice came out ghost-thin, her face pale as snow. Her hands shook as she touched her lips, as if she could still taste the sweetness that had poisoned my familiar. "Win, I'm so sorry—"

"His wasn't sugar." Ileana dropped to her knees beside Pyewacket's still form, hands hovering over him. Her magic flared from white to a sickly, pulsing green that turned my stomach. "Yew berry. The poison's everywhere—in his heart, his blood, his brain. It's strangling him from the inside."

"Fix him." The words came out jagged, barely human. "Ileana, please—"

She didn't answer.

Keir was beside me in an instant, his hand finding mine.

Ileana's face had gone hard, focused, terrifying in its intensity. She pressed both palms flat against Pyewacket's tiny chest and shouted a word that felt like winter given voice—sharp and crystalline and absolute.

Kjølig!

Frost exploded outward from her hands.

It raced across the floorboards in fractal patterns, beautiful and deadly. Climbed the walls in delicate whorls. Spread across the windows like ice flowers blooming in fast-motion. The temperature plummeted so fast my next breath burned in my lungs. Keir pulled me closer, his body heat the only warmth in a room that had become a frozen tomb.

Time stretched. Seconds felt like hours.

The room held its breath.

Pyewacket's body jerked once. Violent. His small spine arching at an unnatural angle.

Then nothing.

Silence so complete I could hear my own heartbeat thundering in my ears.

Then—

A gasp. Small and wet and impossibly, miraculously alive.

A whimper that shattered what was left of my composure.

His golden eye cracked open, unfocused and glassy but there, he was still there—

"Pye?" My voice broke on his name.

His eye found mine. Held. Fought to stay open.

Ileana smiled. "He'll be fine."

My knees gave out. Keir's arms wrapped around me and caught me as I dropped to my knees beside Pyewacket.

His small body was so cold. Too cold. But his heart beat against my palm—faint, fluttering, irregular, but there.

"I've got you," I whispered. "I've got you, Pye. Don't you dare leave me. Don't you dare."

His purr started as barely a vibration. Weak. Broken. But something.

I carefully lifted him up into my arms.

The door flew open with enough force to make everyone jump. Tzazi stumbled through, coat half-buttoned, her usually immaculate hair wild like she'd run through a hurricane. Chase and Ren crowded in behind her, both breathing hard, snow melting on their shoulders.

"Win!" Tzazi's dark eyes found mine, wide with panic. "Gods, are you—what happened—"

"Someone poisoned Pyewacket." Jess's voice came out flat,

shock giving way to cold fury. "They almost killed him. He almost—"

She couldn't finish.

For a moment, Tzazi and Jess just stared at each other across the room. All the careful distance they'd been maintaining, all the awkward navigation of their ended relationship—it crumbled in the face of real danger.

Jess moved first, yanking Tzazi into a fierce hug that spoke of years of history and love that had changed shape but never quite disappeared.

Then Tzazi reached out, pulling me into the huddle with one arm while keeping the other around Jess. I went willingly, Pye still clutched to my chest, and sank into the familiar scent of my two best friends.

We held on longer than we probably needed to.

Which meant exactly the right amount.

Over Tzazi's shoulder, I watched Keir slip quietly toward the back door. He paused, met my eyes, and something passed between us—understanding, determination, rage carefully banked. Then he was gone, moving with that predatory grace that made him seem more wolf than man.

I eased out of the hug and moved to the window, Pye still trembling against my heart.

Below, Keir stepped onto Fernwood's cobbled courtyard. Moonlight caught in his dark hair, turned his breath to silver mist. He lifted his head, nostrils flaring as if scenting the wind, and raised one hand.

The shadows at the tree line rippled.

Five massive shapes loped forward—wolves the size of small ponies, their fur dappled with snow and moonlight, eyes glowing amber in the darkness. They moved with eerie silence, surrounding Keir in a loose circle.

The wolves' heads tilted in unison. Listening. Understanding.

Then they scattered, taking positions around Fernwood's grounds. One disappeared into the swamp. Two flanked the front entrance. The others melted into shadows I hadn't realized were deep enough to hide them.

Keir stood alone in the courtyard, his coat billowing in the wind, every line of his body radiating lethal intent.

That's when it hit me. Not the fear—that had been constant since Pye collapsed.

The candy had been pressed into *my* hand. The elf's eyes had lingered on *me*. I'd been the target all along.

And Pye—brave, snarky, impossible Pye—had taken the poison meant for me.

My blood ran cold.

"They weren't trying to kill Pye," I whispered.

The room went still. Even Thor stopped his pacing.

"They were trying to kill me."

HOURS PASSED. The fire in the grate burned down to glowing embers. Pyewacket slept peacefully in his nest of blankets, the protective sigil Ileana had woven still shimmering faintly above him.

A soft knock came at the front door.

Sibby answered with her usual lack of ceremony. "Come on in before you freeze your important bits off."

Ransom Belleclaire stepped inside, his face blushing red, snow dusting his dark coat while concern etched in the sharp lines of his face. His piercing blue-green eyes swept our gathered circle before settling on Pyewacket.

"How's he doing?"

"Sleeping," I said, rising from the loveseat. "Stubborn old tom. Too tough to let some amateur poisoner get the better of him."

Ransom crossed to Pye without another word, crouching beside the makeshift bed. For a long moment, he watched my familiar's steady breathing, then reached out to brush his fingers along the inky fur with surprising tenderness.

"He's lucky," Ransom murmured and then rose to speak to Ileana.

Hilde appeared with a tray of elderberry honey toddies. "Not as powerful as hearth fairy magic, but still pretty potent," she announced and handed out mugs.

Jess smiled and I felt a wave of comforting magic flow through the room.

We settled into the sitting room's comfortable chaos—Jess, Keir, and I on one sofa, Ren and Chase on the other, Tzazi by the window, Ransom in the armchair beside Sibby, who was nursing a bourbon with slow satisfaction.

"Tell me what happened," Ransom said, his enchanted notebook launching from his coat to land open on his lap, pen scribbling notes on its own.

Jess described the market, the festive atmosphere, our easy mood. "There was a man dressed as a Christmas elf. Tall, blond—though I think it was a wig."

"Lex Lavallette's behind this," I said, my voice quiet but deep.

Ransom stiffened, his eyes suddenly sharp. The room went silent, other than Ransom's pen scribbling in his notebook.

Keir's hand tightened on my thigh.

"Win, sugar, are you sure about that?" Sibby asked with unusual caution.

I sighed. "No. I'm not."

LATER, when silence had settled and the fire burned low, I stood by the window and set my solstice wish stone on the sill. The stone glowed faintly in the glass, casting soft light against the pane. Keir's Enforcers moved through the falling snow like guardian shadows.

I held the crumpled candy wrapper in my hand—silver paper that had once seemed so festive, now evidence of malice.

"He came for the wrong witch."

Everyone turned to look at me.

I faced them, feeling something cold and deadly settle in my chest. The protective magic of Fernwood responded to my mood, ancient wards rising like a tide around the property.

"Lavallette wants to see what happens when I stop being nice?"

I crushed the wrapper in my fist, watching it disintegrate like ash.

"He's about to find out."

CHAPTER 19

 evening air carried the scent of frost-kissed magnolias and woodsmoke as Jess, Tzazi, and I made our way to Briarbough Cottage, the home Arthur had rented. Last night when I walked Jess and Tzazi out to Jess's car, I asked them both to come with me to talk to Arthur. Tzazi looked at Jess and was relieved when she agreed.

As we drove down Tataille Street, Christmas lights twinkled from every lamppost, their cheerful glow doing nothing to ease the tension knotted in my chest. The cobblestones were slick with morning dew that threatened to turn to ice before noon.

"You sure about this?" Jess asked for the third time, pulling her lavender wool coat tighter around her shoulders when we exited the car in front of a house that in no way resembled the definition of a cottage. It was an old plantation house. Not as large as Fernwood, but certainly not small.

"We need answers," I said. "And, Tzazi, you have to admit, Arthur's been dancing around the truth since he got in town."

Tzazi's heels clicked against the stones with sharp precision. She'd been unusually quiet since we'd left Fernwood, but now she spoke up. "He won't want to talk about it. Simone's death nearly destroyed him."

"That's exactly why we need to hear it from him," I said, rapping my knuckles against the weathered oak door.

Arthur opened it after a moment, his silver-blond hair disheveled and his stormy gray eyes bloodshot. He wore a rumpled but expensive burgundy shirt, but it couldn't disguise the fact that he looked haggard and drawn, years older than he'd looked at The Magic Cup.

"Win. Tzazi...Jess?" He stepped back, running a hand through his hair. "I suppose this was inevitable."

We filed into his sitting room, which managed to be both elegant and cluttered. Velvet drapes of deep blue blocked most of the morning light, and half-empty teacups sat abandoned on every surface. The air smelled of mint tea.

"Arthur," I said, settling onto the huge metal blue sofa in the middle of the room. "We need you to tell us the truth."

"The truth about what?" But his voice lacked conviction, and his hands trembled slightly as he reached for a china teacup.

"About Simone Petalsigh," Tzazi said quietly. "Arthur, what really happened the night she died?"

Arthur's teacup rattled against its saucer. "I've told you—"

"You've told us nothing," I interrupted. "But we've been piecing it all together. Michey wasn't the intended victim at the gala, was he? The Lavallettes wanted you dead."

The color drained from Arthur's face. He set down his cup and sank into the armchair across from us, suddenly looking weary, like an old man.

"You don't understand," he whispered. "It's not my truth to tell."

"Arthur!" Tzazi leaned forward, her dark eyes sharp with frustration. "We believe Michey was killed by accident. You were the actual target. Whatever killed Simone is putting you in danger!"

For a long moment, the only sound was the tick of the grandfather clock in the corner. Then Arthur's shoulders sagged, and he buried his face in his hands.

"I tried to protect her," he said, his voice muffled.

"From what?" Jess asked gently and I looked at her in surprise.

Arthur raised his head, his eyes haunted. "From her own discovery. From what she'd learned about her family."

My pulse quickened. "What had she learned?"

"She'd just found out who her real father was." Arthur's voice was barely above a whisper. "Alexander Lavallette. Lex Lavallette was her biological father."

The name hit me like a physical blow. It all made sense. Protect the Lavallette family at all costs.

"Oh my god," Jess whispered.

"One day," Arthur continued, his hands gripping the arms of his chair, "she came to me so excited. She thought she could finally have a real family. She thought her half-sister might accept her."

"Her half-sister?" Tzazi asked.

I felt pieces clicking into place with an almost audible snap.

"Dora Lavallette," Arthur and I said at the same time.

He nodded grimly. "They were in the same year at Wentworth. Simone had always looked up to her, always wanted to be part of her group. The Charlottes."

Jess shook her head. "The original mean girls."

"I told her to be careful," he said, his voice gaining strength and pain in equal measure. "I told her the Lavallette family wasn't one to mess around with. I told her to let me look into things first. It wasn't safe to make something like that public. Something that could affect that family's reputation."

The bitterness in his voice could have soured milk.

"How did she find out about her father," Jess asked.

Arthur turned to her, obvious appreciation on his face that Jess was speaking to him. In a voice lacking venom, no less.

He gave an almost imperceptible shake of his head. "She heard Lavallette and the Headmaster talking about it."

"What?" Tzazi exclaimed.

"I know," Arthur said.

"What did you tell her exactly?" I pressed.

"I told her to face the truth. She'd found out she was connected to one of Darkly's most powerful families, but they'd never acknowledge her. After all, Lex knew about Simone but never helped her mother, not once." His voice broke slightly on the last words.

"I told her that Alexander Lavallette had money, power, and influence, but not an ounce of decency when it came to the children he'd fathered outside his marriage. I'd heard about what happened to others who'd tried to claim their birthright."

"Others?" Jess asked.

"There were rumors," Arthur said, still facing the window. "Other children. Other mothers. All silenced, one way or another."

I felt my anger rising. "And Dora?"

"Dora would never have accepted Simone. She would never have allowed her family name to be tainted by someone she considered beneath them." Arthur's reflection in the window looked hollow-eyed and ancient. "She'd built her entire identity around being a Lavallette. Perfect, untouchable, elite. But I don't believe she knew about Simone."

"So what happened?" Tzazi asked, though her voice suggested she already knew.

Arthur turned back to us, and I saw tears tracking down his cheeks. "I told her to stay away from Lex Lavallette, Dora, the Charlottes. Anything associated with that family. We talked about it many times. But she was so desperate to belong somewhere, to have a father who wanted her."

He returned to his chair, shoulders slumped, each movement weighted with decades of grief.

"The day of her death, she got mad at me. Threw everything she could find—books, shoes, a potted plant. Thought I was saying she wasn't good enough for the Lavallettes." His hands gripped the armrests. "I told her I thought the exact opposite. That they weren't good enough for her."

The silence stretched between us, heavy with all the words he'd never gotten to say.

"I never saw her again. Not alive." His voice went flat, emptied of everything but the facts. "They found her outside the dormitory the next morning. Frozen to death. Official statement was she'd been locked out accidentally. A prank gone wrong."

The way he said "accidentally" made it clear he'd never believed that story. Not for a single day in the past twenty years. "But you knew there was more to it," I said.

"I've always believed Simone's death had something to do with Lex Lavallette," Arthur confirmed. "But I could never prove it. And after what happened, after the way everyone looked at me..." He trailed off.

"They blamed you," Jess said softly. "I blamed you."

He shrugged. "I knew what it looked like. They needed someone to blame, and I was convenient. The boy who'd been seen arguing with her. The one with the reputation for causing trouble." Arthur met my eyes. "I let them blame me. It was easier than trying to prove the truth about what the Lavallettes were capable of."

I thought about the straw, stones, and silver coins found at each murder scene. About the careful staging of both Michey's and Letha's bodies. About the connection between past and present that seemed to wind through this case.

"Arthur," I said carefully, "do you remember when Simone told you she had found out who her father was?"

"I'll never forget," he said. "Around the first of November. Right after All Hallow's Eve."

"Do you know if anyone else could have been listening when you two were talking?"

He frowned. "Listening? I...there might have been. The quad was always full of kids."

"What was your relationship with Dora?"

He gave a slight laugh, but there was no merriment in it. "There was none. But she wouldn't leave me alone. The word 'no' has never been a word in Dora's vocabulary. At Wentworth, she followed me around campus. She'd wait outside my dorm." He gave a heavy sigh. "She even snuck into the dorm one time...I found her curled up in my bed."

"What are you saying?" Tzazi asked. ""She stalked you while we were in school?" Tzazi's eyes had narrowed to slits.

"Yeah," Arthur finally said. "I guess that's what you'd call it. And nothing's changed. Now that I'm back, so is she. She showed up here a few nights ago. Drunk. I finally had enough and asked her to leave. I thought I was going to have to call Belleclaire to get her out. Why? Is it important?"

If Tzazi answered him, I didn't hear. My mind had already moved ahead, circling back to Lex Lavallette. To the man who'd spent decades cultivating power, who controlled his family's image with the same ruthless precision he applied to his business deals. Eudora's reputation wasn't just important to him—it was sacrosanct. A reflection of his own untouchable legacy.

How far would someone like that go to keep an old scandal buried?

"One last question, Arthur." I kept my voice gentle. "Do you remember the hairpin Simone always wore?"

The change in his expression was instant—like sun breaking through storm clouds. His whole face softened, and a smile I'd never seen curved his lips. "The unicorn." His voice went tender, almost reverent. "She loved that thing."

Something in my chest tightened at the warmth in his tone, the way saying her name seemed to bring her back into the room with us.

"She found it at some vintage shop in Cradlerock," he continued, his eyes distant now, seeing something we couldn't. "Silver, with these little chips of moonstone for the horn. Probably wasn't worth much, but she wore it like it was made of diamonds." He paused, and his smile deepened. "She said it made her feel magical. Like maybe if she believed hard enough, the world would be kinder than it was."

The silence that followed felt sacred somehow. Heavy with the weight of a girl who'd deserved so much better than what she'd gotten.

"Do you remember if she was wearing it that last time you spoke to her?" I asked quietly.

Arthur's brow furrowed as he thought back, then a soft laugh escaped him—the kind tinged with both joy and aching loss. "Yes. She had on this cream-colored knit beanie, and she'd pinned the unicorn right to the front of it." His fingers moved unconsciously, as if tracing the memory in the air. "Even in the cold, even bundled up against the snow, she found a way to wear it. That was Simone. Never let the world take the small magics away from her."

Until someone did.

~

WE'D BARELY CLEARED Arthur's front gate when Tzazi stopped dead in her tracks. Her hand shot out, stopping both Jess and me mid-stride.

"Don't move," she said, her voice dropping to something low and dangerous.

Her eyes flashed red—not the warm ember glow of the fire we'd just left, but the sharp crimson of a predator who'd just caught a scent. She positioned herself in front of us, her body a barrier between whatever she'd sensed and us, her gaze locked on the dense line of trees bordering Arthur's property.

"I feel it too," I whispered.

Jess inched closer, her shoulder pressing against mine. I could feel her trembling, or maybe that was me. Hard to tell when the air itself seemed to vibrate with menace.

Something was out there, just beyond the glow of the Christmas lights.

Whatever we were uncovering about Simone's death, about Lex Lavallette, about the connection between past and present—someone didn't want us to find it.

Tzazi shifted her weight, balanced on the balls of her feet like she was preparing to spring. "On three," she said quietly, "y'all run for Arthur's door. Don't look back. Don't stop. Understood?"

"What about you?" I asked, knowing the answer before she gave it.

Her smile was all teeth and vampire confidence. "I'll be right behind you. One—"

The shadow lunged.

CHAPTER 20

The hex beast lay sprawled across Arthur's frost-covered lawn, its massive bulk still twitching in death. The thing had massive tusks and a bristled hide, limbs elongated into spider-like appendages that bent at sickening angles. Multiple tusks curved from its jaw in a crown of yellowed bone. Worst of all were the eyes—seven of them, scattered across what remained of its face like malevolent stars, all filmed over with death but still seeming to watch us with hungry intelligence.

Black ichor leaked from the wound where Tzazi had torn its throat out, staining the white Christmas lights that lined Arthur's walkway and melting the thin layer of snow beneath.

My hands shook as I lowered them, the protective ward I'd thrown up still crackling between my fingers. Tzazi stood over the creature in full vampire form, her brown skin gone pale with that bluish cast, her platinum pixie cut stark against the darkness. Those red eyes blazed as she stared down at what she'd killed, fangs fully extended and dripping with the beast's corrupted blood. Her breath came in visible puffs in the December cold.

"Everyone okay?" Her voice came out rough, still half-feral.

"Define okay," Jess managed, her wings fully visible now, shimmering orange against the porch light. She'd thrown up her own defensive magic, and the air around her still pulsed with protective warmth that seemed to push back the winter chill.

I found my voice, though it came out shakier than I would have liked. "What in the hellhound was that thing?"

Arthur leaned against his doorframe, his silver-blond hair disheveled and his face sheet-white. He pulled his black leather jacket tighter around himself. "A hex beast."

I forced myself to step closer, my boots crunching through the frost-covered grass. The wrongness of it made my skin crawl, my witch senses recoiling from the dark magic that had twisted the creature's form. "Someone sent this after us."

"They're going to be disappointed." Tzazi's voice was flat, dangerous. The vampire in her was still too close to the surface, riding the adrenaline of the kill. "They'll know it's dead soon enough."

She was right. Whoever had created this monstrosity would feel the moment their magic snapped, the connection severing like a cut string. Which meant they'd know their warning—or their murder attempt—had failed.

A sleek Range Rover pulled up behind Jess's car, its tires crunching on the shell-covered drive dusted with snow. My heart did a complicated flip as Keir Bane emerged.

His gaze found mine, and something flickered in those depths. Concern. Relief. And yes, a touch of exasperation that I could read even from here.

But he said nothing. Just gave a slight nod and approached the corpse, his movements fluid and controlled. "Arthur." His Scottish burr was more pronounced than usual. "Ladies." His eyes lingered on me for half a second longer than strictly necessary.

Keir crouched beside the creature, unbothered by the cold or the melting snow beneath his boots.

"Someone want to explain what happened here?"

Before anyone could respond, the air beside the hex beast's corpse shimmered like heat rising from summer asphalt. The temperature dropped so suddenly my breath frosted, visible in the December night, and then Boddy Grim simply appeared, his gaunt frame materializing out of nothing. His black cloak swirled around him like living shadow, and those unsettling red eyes immediately fixed on the dead creature. Snowflakes that had begun to fall seemed to avoid him, creating a small circle of clear air around his form.

A heartbeat later, another shimmer of displaced air, and Ransom Belleclaire stood beside him. The Royal Inspector's jet-black hair was slightly disheveled, those piercing blue-green eyes immediately cataloging every detail of the scene. His tailored black coat settled around him as the veil shift completed, that otherworldly fae grace evident in every line of his tall frame. A few snowflakes caught in his hair before melting.

"Inspector Belleclaire. Boddy." Arthur's voice was steadier now, though his hands still trembled.

"Arthur." Ransom's tone was smooth, professional, but I caught the steel underneath. His fae-enhanced senses were no doubt picking up every nervous tell, every hastily constructed explanation we might offer. "Though I'm curious what brings Ms. Ebonwood, Ms. Strangeland, and Ms. Wilde to your estate at this hour."

I felt Keir's attention sharpen, though he still said nothing.

Tzazi straightened, the red fading from her eyes as she pulled herself back to humanity. Her voice came out smooth as honey bourbon when she answered. "We were visiting Arthur. Having tea and discussing old academy days." She gestured vaguely toward the house. "We were heading home when that thing attacked us."

Tea. At Arthur's house. At night. With snow beginning to fall. The lie hung in the air between us, thin as gossamer, but Ransom didn't challenge it. His fae-enhanced perception probably told him Tzazi was lying, but he also didn't seem inclined to push.

Keir, for his part, remained silent, though I felt the weight of his attention like a physical thing. The alpha knew damn well we weren't there for tea and nostalgia. But whatever questions he had, he'd save them for later.

For when we were alone.

"I see." Ransom moved closer to the hex beast, his movements fluid and graceful. He didn't touch it, but I saw the faint shimmer of his fae magic as he examined it, that otherworldly perception seeing things the rest of us couldn't. "Boddy? Your assessment?"

The former grim reaper glided forward, and the temperature around us plummeted even further. He extended one pale, skeletal hand over the corpse, not quite touching, and closed his eyes. When he spoke, that hissing, guttural voice sent shivers racing down my spine. "Death came mere moments ago. The creature was transformed first, then sent to kill. Cause of death..." He paused, those red eyes snapping open. "Severed jugular. Clean kill."

His gaze slid to Tzazi with something that might have been approval.

"What was it?" Jess asked hoarsely. "Before...before someone did that to it?"

"A wild boar," Keir answered, his voice tight. "Caught in the swamp, hexed, and sent as a weapon."

"Who has the power to create something like this?" Jess asked, her voice barely above a whisper. She wrapped her arms around herself against the cold.

Ransom straightened, his coat swirling around him, sending a small flurry of snowflakes dancing. "Someone with considerable skill in transformative magic." His gaze moved between us, sharp and assessing. "And considerable malice. This wasn't a spur-of-the-moment hex. This took planning, preparation, and practice."

"Lex Lavallette," I said flatly. "He's sending a message. He knows we're asking questions about Simone's death."

Keir's jaw tightened, tension coiling through his powerful frame. He didn't like threats against those under his protection, and while I wasn't technically part of his pack, we were...together.

That made him want to shield me even when he knew I'd fight him on it.

Ransom's expression remained neutral. "That's a serious accusation, Ms. Ebonwood. Without proof—"

"The evidence is lying dead on my lawn!" Arthur interrupted, gesturing at the hex beast.

"Which proves someone has transformative magic abilities," Ransom said carefully. "Not who specifically sent it."

"I'll take the creature." Boddy's skeletal hands were already moving in an intricate pattern, golden coils of ethereal energy unspooling from his fingertips like luminous rope. The Christmas lights reflected off the magical energy, creating prismatic patterns in the falling snow. "For examination and proper disposal."

The coils wrapped around the hex beast's massive bulk, tightening until the creature's form began to shimmer and fade. With a sound like wind through hollow bones, both Boddy and the beast vanished, leaving only dead grass and melted snow where they'd been.

The sudden absence left us standing in Arthur's yard, frost crunching under our feet and Christmas lights casting cheerful colors across our grim faces. The snow continued to fall, gentle and silent.

"You should all get home," Ransom said, his Royal Inspector voice firmly in place. "Jess, do you mind if I ride with you? I'd like to ensure you arrive safely."

Jess glanced at me, a question in her green eyes. I gave a tiny nod. I'd be fine with Keir. Probably. Even if we were about to have a conversation I wasn't entirely looking forward to.

"Thank you, Inspector," Jess said softly, her breath misting in the cold air.

As they walked toward Jess's car, I heard him murmuring something to her, his voice too low to make out the words. Jess's shoulders relaxed slightly as they reached the vehicle.

Tzazi had already begun to shimmer, her form compressing and shifting. "I'll see myself home." Her voice was half-human, half-something else as the transformation took her. A moment later, a brown-furred bat launched itself into the December sky, wings beating powerfully as she disappeared into the darkness and falling snow.

Which left me alone with Keir.

And Arthur, but he'd already retreated into his house, leaving us standing in the cold with our breath misting in the air between us.

"My car," Keir said quietly, gesturing toward the Range Rover.

We walked in silence to his vehicle, our footsteps muffled by the fresh snow. He opened the passenger door for me and I slid in, grateful for the warmth of the heated seats.

The drive to Fernwood took less than ten minutes, but it felt longer with the weight of unspoken words filling the space between us. Snow fell steadily now, coating the road and making the Christmas lights from houses we passed blur into soft halos of color.

Keir pulled up next to the back porch of Fernwood, the headlights cutting through the snowfall to illuminate the dock jutting into the dark lagoon. The old plantation house looked ethereal through the white curtain of snow, Spanish moss hanging like frozen lace from the ancient live oaks.

But he didn't move to get out. Just sat there, both hands gripping the steering wheel as he stared at the dark swamp. His jaw worked, muscle jumping beneath the skin.

The silence stretched tight as a bowstring.

"What were you thinking?" His voice came out low, rough. Dangerous.

I should have felt chastened. Instead, heat coiled low in my belly at the controlled fury radiating off him.

"Anybody ever tell you you're sexy when you're angry?"

His hands tightened on the wheel. He turned to face me, and the look in his dark eyes made my breath catch—equal parts frustration and something much more primal. The air in the cab suddenly felt too warm, too close.

"Windsor." My name on his lips came out somewhere between a prayer and a warning. His accent thickened, turning the syllables into something that made my skin prickle with awareness. "This isn't—"

"I was thinking," I interrupted, though my voice came out breathier than I intended, "that Arthur needed to tell us the truth about Simone's death. Information that might help us figure out who's killing people."

I forced myself to meet his gaze, to hold it despite the heat building between us. "Before they try to kill me again."

Something shifted in his expression. The anger didn't disappear—it transformed. Became something fiercer, more possessive. He reached across the space between us, his hand finding the back of my neck, fingers threading through my hair.

"You're going to be the death of me, lass." His thumb traced my jawline, the touch gentle despite the tension coiled in his frame. "Do you have any idea what it does to me? Watching you walk into danger?"

His eyes dropped to my mouth. Lingered there.

The snowfall outside seemed to slow, the world narrowing to just us, just this moment, just the space between wanting and having.

"I have some idea," I whispered.

He pulled away.

"And it didn't occur to you that whoever killed Simone— whoever sent that beast tonight—might decide you're asking too many dangerous questions?" His voice rose, that Scottish burr rolling through the words like distant thunder. "That they might put you at the top of their list?"

"I can take care of myself, Keir."

"I don't doubt that for a second." He shifted to face me fully, and the dashboard lights caught in his eyes, turning them molten gold. "But that doesn't mean I don't lie awake wondering if this will be the night you don't come home. Every damn time you go chasing murderers, every time you throw yourself into danger without even a word to me, I—"

He cut himself off, jaw clenching so hard I heard his teeth grind.

"You what?" The challenge in my voice softened despite myself.

"I worry I'm going to lose you." The words came out raw, stripped bare of his usual control. "I've lived for centuries, Win. I've buried pack members. Friends. People I—" His voice roughened to gravel. "I cannot bear the thought of losing you too. Every time trouble stirs in this town, every time I catch the scent of dark magic on the wind, my first thought is always you. If you've pushed too far. If someone's decided to silence you for good."

My throat tightened. Snow continued to fall outside, each flake catching the headlights like tiny stars. "I can't just stand by and do nothing while people are dying."

"I'm not asking you to do nothing." His hand reached across the space between us, cupping my face with a gentleness that made my chest ache. "I'm asking you to be careful. To maybe— just maybe—tell your boyfriend when you're planning to put yourself in dangerous situations."

"I had Jess and Tzazi with me."

"Aye, and that's the only thing keeping me from completely losing my mind right now." His thumb traced my cheekbone in a slow, reverent stroke that sent warmth flooding through me. "But a hex beast nearly tore all three of you apart tonight, *mo chridhe*. What if Tzazi hadn't been fast enough? What if that thing had—"

"But she was." I caught his wrist, pressing his palm more firmly against my face. "We're fine, Keir. We're here."

"This time." His voice dropped to barely above a whisper, rough and urgent. "But there will be a next time. We both know it. So I'm asking—begging, if I have to—let me help keep you safe. Tell me where you're going. Let me send Laurent or Pup to watch your back. Something. Anything. I need to know you're protected."

I wanted to argue. Wanted to remind him I'd been handling professional threats since long before he'd walked into my life with his brooding intensity and his impossible eyes. (Academia isn't all chocolates and roses.) But looking at him now—seeing the genuine terror hiding behind the frustration, the care burning beneath the anger—my defenses crumbled like sandcastles at high tide.

"Okay," I said softly. "Next time, I'll tell you. I'll let you know where I'm going and what I'm planning."

He searched my face, probably looking for any hint I was just placating him. Whatever he found must have satisfied him, because his shoulders dropped fractionally, some of the tension bleeding out of them.

"That's all I'm asking, *mo chridhe*."

Then he was pulling me across the center console, and his mouth found mine in a kiss that tasted of relief and frustration and desperate need. His hand tightened in my hair, tilting my head back as he deepened the kiss, and I melted into him, threading my fingers through his soft hair. Trying to show him through touch what words couldn't quite capture—that I was here, alive, whole, his.

When we finally broke apart, we were both breathing hard, our breath fogging the windows and turning the world outside into an impressionist painting of snow and darkness.

"Come on," he murmured against my lips, his voice gone rough and low. "Let me walk you inside."

The cold hit us the moment we stepped out of the Range Rover. Snow swirled around us in lazy spirals, catching in Keir's dark hair and melting against the warmth of his skin. He kept his arm wrapped firmly around me as we climbed the porch steps, as if afraid I might vanish if he let go.

At the threshold, he turned me to face him. His hands framed my face, thumbs stroking along my jawline as he kissed me again

—slower this time, sweeter, like he was trying to memorize the shape of my mouth, the taste of me, the way I fit against him. Snow collected on his shoulders and in his hair, turning him into something out of a winter fairy tale.

"Be safe," he whispered against my lips. "Please, *mo chridhe*. Be safe."

"I will." I rose on my toes to kiss him once more, soft and lingering. "I promise."

He held me a moment longer, then stepped back with obvious reluctance. "I'll wait until you're inside."

I unlocked the door and stepped into Fernwood's familiar warmth, pausing to watch him walk back to his car. Snowflakes continued their silent dance around him, settling on his broad shoulders and catching in his hair like tiny stars. He stopped at the driver's door, looking back at me, and even through the curtain of snow I could see the worry carved into his features.

I blew him a kiss, trying to lighten the moment.

He caught it with the ghost of a smile, pressed his fist to his heart, then folded himself into the Range Rover.

I stood in the doorway until his taillights disappeared down the oak-lined drive, the falling snow slowly erasing even the tracks his tires left behind. Only then did I close the door and engage all the locks—mundane deadbolts and magical wards alike.

Pyewacket materialized from the shadows with his usual theatrical flair, his golden eye gleaming with unmistakable feline judgment.

"What are you doing out of bed?" I grabbed a bottle of wine from the refrigerator, shooting him a worried look. "Ileana said you need rest."

The ancient cat flicked his tail—once, twice—and fixed me with his most deliciously melodramatic stare. "I nearly succumbed to yew berry poisoning mere hours ago, but please, don't let my near-death experience interrupt the passionate farewell. I'll just lie here, slowly perishing, while you carry on."

"Well, you're alive enough to be a pain in my ass, so I guess Ileana's magic worked." I poured the wine, my hand not quite steady. "Scared the hell out of me, Pye."

"As I recall, you were the one who gave me the poisoned candy," he said primly, though his purr gave away his pleasure at my concern. "Really, Windsor, your gift-giving skills leave much to be desired."

"You begged for it, you little thief."

"I prefer 'tactical confection acquisitions specialist.'" He padded after me toward the window seat, though I noticed his gait was still a bit unsteady. "Besides, Ileana is an exceptional healer. I was never truly in danger."

"You stopped breathing, Pye."

His tail drooped slightly. "Well. Yes. There was that regrettable moment."

I settled into the window seat overlooking the swamp. Beyond the glass, that eerie phosphorescent glow pulsed in the darkness between the trees, steady as a heartbeat. Snow continued to fall, coating the twisted oaks and hanging moss in white, transforming the familiar Louisiana landscape into something from a twisted winter dream.

Somewhere out there, a murderer walked free. Somewhere, Lavallette was toasting his success with expensive champagne, celebrating the fear he'd instilled with his grotesque hex beast.

But he'd failed tonight. We were alive. We were getting closer to the truth.

I took a sip of wine, feeling its warmth spread through my chest. Pyewacket leaped onto the window seat and curled against my hip, his purr a low, steady rumble.

The question hung in the air between us, as present as the snow falling outside:

What would he try next?

CHAPTER 21

*W*armth and light poured from the Green Gator Tavern, along with the merry sounds of laughter and clinking glasses each time the heavy wooden door opened. Tonight, it seemed like half the town had gathered there, seeking comfort in numbers and familiar faces.

A perfect place to think.

Tzazi, Jess, and I found a table near the back, away from the main crowd, but close enough to overhear the conversations swirling around us. The air was thick with the scent of gumbo and cornbread. The goblin Clobber Mudkipp, the tavern's bartender, had strung lights around the exposed wooden beams, casting everything in a festive glow that felt at odds with the undercurrent of fear running through the crowd.

Clobber ambled over to take our order, his large brown eyes warm despite the tension crackling through the tavern. His green-tinged skin caught the firelight, and the small trinkets dangling from his pointed ears jingled softly as he moved.

"Ladies," he said, that easy grin spreading across his face. "What can I get y'all tonight? We got mulled wine that'll warm you right down to your toes, or Phenny just made a fresh batch of her spiked eggnog that's been known to make people forget their troubles for at least an hour."

"Mulled wine for me," I said.

"Corona with lime," Tzazi added, unwinding her scarf.

Jess glanced up at him. "My usual, Clobber."

"One warmed sweet tea vodka coming right up." He winked at her before heading back toward the bar, weaving between tables with practiced ease.

The tavern was packed tonight. Every table seemed occupied, conversations layering over one another until they became a low hum of worried speculation and forced cheer. I recognized Boone and Trixie Frick near the fireplace deep in discussion with Alvar Vache. Alvar's daughter Leidy sat beside him, absently shredding a napkin into thin strips with the practiced disinterest of a teenager who'd rather be anywhere else. At another table, Quinn Ainsley sat with several Silverfang Clan members—Ava Nguyễn and Pup Bane among them—their postures tense as they spoke in low voices.

The Christmas decorations Clobber had strung up—evergreen garland threaded with red berries, twinkling lights in gold and crimson, a massive pine tree growing right through a hole in the floorboards—should have made the space feel festive. Instead, they cast everything in an almost desperate cheerfulness, as if Darkly was trying to convince itself that everything was normal.

It wasn't working.

I was about to comment on the crowd when Jess straightened in her seat, her gaze fixed on something near the bar. Following her line of sight, I spotted Boddy Grim standing in the shadows behind the bar itself, a ledger open in front of him and a pencil in his pale, skeletal hand. Even from here, I could see the unnatural stillness in the way he held himself, that otherworldly quality that marked him as something that had once guided souls to their final rest.

"Boddy," Jess said quietly, more to herself than to us.

Tzazi followed her gaze. "Now's your chance."

"Want me to come with you?" I asked, though something in her expression made me think I already knew the answer.

She shook her head, her red curls catching the firelight. "No, this is something I need to ask him myself. He's more likely to help if it's just me."

I understood. Boddy Grim had never been particularly warm toward me, but he and Jess had known each other for years. She'd always treated him with respect when others saw only a grim reaper who'd outstayed his welcome in the world of the living. Now that she employed him, that mutual respect had only deepened. If anyone could convince him to share information about a twenty-year-old death, it would be her.

Jess stood, smoothing down her sweater. "Be right back."

Tzazi and I watched as she crossed the tavern floor, dodging servers carrying trays of jambalaya and burgers, sidestepping groups of patrons clustered near the bar. Boddy looked up as she approached, those strange red eyes catching the light. They spoke for a moment, Jess leaning in close, her expression earnest. Boddy's face remained impassive, that skeletal pallor giving nothing away. But after a long moment, he gave a small nod and gestured toward a door that led to the tavern's back office.

They disappeared through it, and I turned my attention back to our table. Clobber had returned with our drinks, setting them down with a flourish.

"One mulled wine for the lovely Miss Ebonwood," he said, placing a steaming mug in front of me. The scent of cinnamon and cloves rose with the steam. "Corona for Miss Strangeland and one sweet tea vodka for Miss Wilde when she gets back from wherever she's snuck off to."

He glanced around the packed tavern, his jovial demeanor not quite masking the concern in his eyes. "Y'all let me know if you need anything else."

As he moved away to attend to other tables, I wrapped my hands around the warm mug and let the spiced wine's heat seep into my palms. Tzazi sipped her own drink, her platinum pixie cut catching the light from the Christmas decorations overhead.

"Think he'll give her the report?" she asked.

"If it still exists." I watched the door where Jess and Boddy had disappeared. "It's been twenty years."

"Boddy doesn't strike me as the type to destroy much of anything." Tzazi's voice had gone flat, that dangerous edge that appeared when she was thinking about injustice. "I mean—he *is* an accountant."

We sat in silence for a few moments, the tavern's noise washing over us. The conversations had taken on a distinctly supernatural bent, people trading stories about strange sightings and unexplained occurrences. Fear thickened the air, mixing with the scent of woodfire and spices. Finally, the back-office door opened, and Jess emerged. Even from across the tavern, I could see the tension in her shoulders, the way her wings were tucked so tightly against her back they were invisible. Boddy glided out behind her, his black cloak billowing—all darkness and movement. He said something too low for me to hear, and Jess nodded before making her way back to our table. She held something in her hand.

She slid into her seat and picked up her drink, taking a long sip before meeting our expectant gazes.

"Well?" Tzazi asked.

Jess set down her glass and placed on the table a piece of brown paper rolled up like a scroll.

"That is so Boddy." I laughed.

"It is indeed," Tzazi said.

Relief flooded through me, quickly followed by apprehension. Whatever was in that report, whatever Boddy had documented about Simone's death all those years ago, might finally give us some answers.

"Did he say anything about what's in it?" I asked.

Jess shook her head. "Just that it was thorough. And we should be too." Her voice dropped lower. "He also said something else. Said Arthur Vanderholt visited him the day after Simone died, asking if there was any evidence of foul play. Boddy told him the same thing he told everyone else—that it looked like exposure, pure and simple. But he said Arthur didn't believe him. Kept insisting someone had to be held accountable."

"That tracks with what Arthur told us earlier," Tzazi said. "He always suspected the Lavallettes were involved. So let's see it."

Jess rolled out the piece of parchment onto the table, smoothing the page flat on the table between us.

I leaned forward, pulse quickening.

The report was meticulous—clinical in its precision, each line carefully penned in Boddy's distinctive, spidery script. His handwriting had that same ghostly quality as his voice, letters thin and elongated, as if they might drift off the page.

I smoothed the parchment flat against the scarred wooden table.

"Something's off," I murmured, tilting the document toward the amber light.

Jess leaned in, her red ponytail brushing my shoulder. "What do you mean?"

"I'm not sure yet." I squinted at the page. The words were clear enough—*cause of death, time of death, natural death detected*—but something about them felt slippery. Wrong. Like trying to read through water. Certain lines and words glimmered, almost sparkled, catching the candlelight in ways that ink shouldn't.

"I think this is glamoured."

"What?" Jess looked closer, her green eyes narrowing. Then she sucked in a breath. "Oh, I see it. It's shimmering—heat waves, the way pavement looks in August."

Tzazi grabbed the parchment and held it up to the light, her platinum pixie cut catching the glow as she examined it with vampire-sharp eyes. After a moment, she nodded and handed it back.

"It's subtle." Her dark eyes glittered with something between admiration and annoyance. "Boddy's guarding the truth."

Jess grinned, a mischievous spark lighting her face. "That tricky reaper. Just give me a second. This one's easy enough."

She held the parchment flat between her palms, closed her eyes, and took a slow breath. Her iridescent orange wings—usually invisible—flickered into view, painting the table with prismatic light in kaleidoscope patterns.

"Hearth magic," she whispered, "reveal what's been concealed. Let truth warm what illusion has frozen."

A golden light bloomed from her fingertips, unfurling across the paper in slow, golden waves. The glamour resisted at first—I watched it shimmer and ripple, fighting to maintain its hold—then began to peel away in delicate, glittering threads.

The magic rose from the parchment in wisps, swirling upward in ribbons of silver and gold. For a moment, the threads hung suspended in the air above our table, forming shapes that almost looked like words before dissolving into nothing.

"Well, well, well," Tzazi said softly, leaning forward as new text emerged on the page—dark, clear, and decidedly different from what we'd read before.

I stared at the revealed document, my stomach dropping somewhere around my boots.

Jess shifted closer, her earrings catching the light as she read over my shoulder.

DEATH REPORT

Deceased: Simone Petalsigh

Date of Death: December 12, 2005

Time of Death: 22:17 hours

Location: Wentworth Academy, The Ossuary Dormitory North Entrance

Date of Discovery: December 13, 2005, 06:45 hours

Discovered by: Maintenance staff (T. Arrog, M. Izabel)

Cause of Death: Magical exposure—freezing spell of considerable potency. Internal crystallization of major organs consistent with rapid-onset magical hypothermia. No evidence of natural environmental cause.

Physical Examination Findings:

Core body temperature: 14°F at time of examination

Extensive ice crystal formation throughout vascular system

Dermis shows characteristic silvering associated with deliberate magical freezing

Cyanosis present: lips and nail beds blue-tinged

No defensive wounds present

Trace magical residue detected: consistent with offensive frost enchantment, cast within 2-3 feet of victim

Environmental Conditions:

Weather at estimated time of death (22:17 hours): 42°F, clear skies, light wind. Storm warning issued at 21:00 hours; students instructed to remain in dormitories.

Severe snowstorm arrived approximately 23:30 hours. Body subsequently covered by 8-10 inches of snowfall by time of discovery.

Storm conditions did not cause observed injuries. Victim died before environmental temperatures dropped to dangerous levels. Ice crystal patterns and magical residue inconsistent with natural exposure.

Additional Observations:

Victim was alone outside dormitory entrance during storm warning period. Body position suggests sudden incapacitation— no signs of flight or struggle. Death would have been near-instantaneous once spell took full effect. Subsequent snowfall obscured scene but did not alter time or cause of death.

Conclusion: Death by magical means. Freezing spell, deliberately cast. Storm provided environmental cover but was not causal factor. Further investigation required to identify caster.

Prepared by: Bodderick Grim, Sheriff

Date: December 13, 2005

The silence that followed felt heavy enough to sink through the floor.

"Ten seventeen," I breathed. "She died over an hour before the storm even hit."

Jess's fingers trembled slightly as she held the page. "Everyone would have assumed the snowstorm killed her. That's why they believed it."

"Someone killed her with magic," Tzazi said, voice flat. "Then let the storm cover their tracks."

I read the line again. Freezing spell of considerable potency. The clinical language couldn't hide what it meant. Someone had murdered Simone Petalsigh, and they'd done it deliberately, viciously. Then they'd let nature take the blame.

"She was out there all night," I whispered, thinking of Simone's body, frozen in the storm, snow piled around her, while everyone slept safely in their dorms, and the killer walked free.

Tzazi's jaw tightened. "But Boddy knew. He documented everything—the time of death, the magical residue, the fact that she died before the storm arrived."

I traced my finger along the precise handwriting, imagining Boddy standing over Simone's frozen body twenty years ago. He would have seen everything—the silvered skin, the ice crystals, the blue lips, the trace of magic lingering beneath the fresh powder. And he'd documented it all with that grim, methodical thoroughness that defined him.

But someone had buried it.

"Offensive frost enchantment," I read aloud. "Cast within two to three feet. That means—"

"The killer was standing right next to her," Tzazi finished.

The image formed too easily in my mind. Simone outside, perhaps meeting someone she knew. A conversation. Then the sudden, brutal cold as magic wrapped around her, freezing her from the inside out. And hours later, the storm would arrive, blanketing everything in white, making it look like a tragic accident.

Ten seventeen in the evening. Students would have been settling into their dorms, following the storm warning. And outside in the darkness, Simone Petalsigh had died alone—murdered, not by nature, but by someone who knew exactly how to make it look like the weather had killed her.

"Arthur's right," I said. "Someone needs to be held accountable."

"But why did Boddy write a fake report?" Jess asked.

"Coercion? Fear?" I said.

"That's some power the Lavallettes have if they can force a grim reaper to do their bidding," Tzazi said with a frown.

Jess carefully rolled up the report and slid it into her bag. "Well, at least we know for certain now. Simone was murdered. And whoever did it used the storm as cover."

"The perfect alibi," Tzazi said. "Everyone indoors because of the storm warning. No witnesses. And by morning, the snow made it look like she'd simply gotten caught outside."

I met her eyes across the table, then Jess's. Twenty years was a long time to keep a secret. But secrets like this one had a way of surfacing—especially when someone started asking the right questions.

Now, if only I could get some answers from Simone's journal.

I pulled it from my bag. The coded entries still taunted me with their secrets, rows of symbols and numbers that shifted and rearranged themselves whenever I tried to make sense of them.

"I wish I could figure out what she was trying to say in these coded sections," I said, flipping through the pages. The firelight from the stone hearth made the ink shimmer. "There might be more details about what happened that night."

Tzazi slid the journal closer, and Jess leaned in beside her. They bent over the pages together, Jess's fingers carefully turning each sheet. I smiled, loving seeing my two friends together again.

After a moment, both their heads lifted, eyes finding mine with matching expressions of confusion—Tzazi's brow furrowed,

Jess's lips parted slightly as if about to ask a question she couldn't quite form.

"Mind if I take a look?"

Next to our table stood Evon Frick, his shaggy blond hair falling into his bright blue eyes. He wore a plaid flannel unbuttoned over a Velvet Static band T-shirt. A faint golden shimmer played across his pale skin in the firelight, subtle evidence of his glamour witch heritage.

"Hi, Evon," I said, angling the journal so he could see the page better. "Do your best. Think you can figure it out?"

He shrugged, that casual gesture young people seemed to have perfected that conveyed both complete indifference and genuine curiosity. But his eyes were already tracking across the symbols, and I caught the slight widening of his pupils—interest, real interest.

"This is a substitution cipher," he murmured, leaning closer. His finger traced one line without touching the page. "But there's something else layered over it. See how some of the symbols repeat in patterns that don't quite match? That's either a polyalphabetic system or—" He stopped, a slow smile spreading across his face. "Or it's a double encryption. Clever."

Jess leaned forward, her wings flickering briefly visible before she tucked them away again. "You can read that?"

"Maybe. Mind if I take this for a few minutes?" He gestured toward a table near the decorated Christmas tree. Several other young people were clustered there around a gaming system, empty mugs of hot chocolate scattered across the scarred wooden surface.

When I nodded, Evon headed over to his friends.

I watched as he showed them the journal, their heads bending together in concentration. There was animated discussion, pointing at the pages, sketching on napkins. A girl with dark purple hair pulled into two buns held up a finger and every head turned to her.

"What do you think they're doing?" Jess asked, craning her neck to see around the Christmas tree.

"Hopefully solving our cipher problem," I said, taking a sip of the mulled wine Clobber had recommended. The spices warmed me from the inside out.

Until I noticed the conversations around us had taken on a distinctly supernatural bent. At the table next to ours, an elderly man was recounting his encounter with what he swore was a rougarou just outside town.

"Eight feet tall if it was an inch," he was saying, his weathered hands gesturing dramatically. "Yellow eyes like headlights, and when it howled..." He shuddered. "Made my blood turn to ice water."

A woman across from him leaned forward. "My neighbor saw a whole pack of swamp imps dancing around her chicken coop last night. Said they left little footprints in the mud shaped like crowns."

"It's all connected to those murders," another patron chimed in. "Mark my words, when evil starts stirring, it calls to more evil."

The fear in the room was becoming almost tangible, a living thing that pressed against the warm atmosphere of the tavern. People kept glancing toward the windows, as if expecting to see glowing eyes staring back at them from the darkness.

Tzazi, Jess, and I sipped our drinks, all of us noting the fear in the room.

"Mayor Mayór needs to do something," Jess whispered.

"Before this turns into hysteria." Tzazi frowned and sipped her beer.

Fifteen minutes passed. The music switched to Nat King Cole, and Clobber brought us another round of drinks along with a plate of Phenny's famous bourbon balls, rolled in powdered sugar that sparkled like fresh snow. The Green Gator's Christmas lights pulsed gently in shades of gold and crimson. Ella Fitzgerald crooned softly about chestnuts roasting.

269

Then Evon was back at our table, journal in hand and triumph written across his features. That golden shimmer on his skin had intensified, the way it apparently did when he felt strong emotions.

"Got it," he said, sliding into the empty chair beside me. "Well, most of it. The cipher's actually pretty brilliant—whoever wrote this used a Vigenère cipher with a keyword, then added a layer of personal symbols for commonly used words. Like shorthand but encrypted."

"Can we read it now?" I asked, my heart suddenly hammering.

"Sure can," he said, "Well, most of it." He flipped to a page near the middle, where he'd made notes in careful pencil along the margins. "The keyword is 'UNICORN'—probably significant to the writer. Once we figured that out, the rest started falling into place. Listen to this entry from November second, twenty years ago: *'Why won't father accept me? I don't understand. Why hasn't he ever wanted to meet me?'"*

The temperature around our table seemed to drop. Jess's hand flew to her mouth.

Tzazi's voice had gone flat and dangerous. "Look. That's probably teardrops smearing the ink."

My heart clenched. Poor Simone.

Evon nodded. "And this section says—" He paused, checking his notes. "*'DL acts nice when others watch but her eyes are cold. I don't know if she likes me.'"*

"DL," Jess whispered. "Dora Lavallette."

The firelight flickered. Somewhere in the tavern, glasses clinked, but at our table, silence stretched like a held breath.

He handed over the journal and key he and his friends had cracked.

"Thank you, Evon."

Evon looked at us sadly. "You should have no problem reading the rest of it." He patted the table with his hands and then rejoined his friends.

Silence fell over our little group. Even the ambient noise of the tavern seemed muffled, as if the weight of Simone's final words had created a pocket of stillness around us.

"Lavallette set her up." Tzazi finally said.

A commotion at the front of the tavern interrupted our grim conversation.

"Look, Mommy! Look!" the little girl was saying, her voice high with excitement rather than fear. She pressed her nose to the frosted window glass, her breath fogging the surface. "It's a lady and she has a chicken leg!"

The mother pulled her daughter away from the window, but not before peering out herself. Her face went pale, and she grabbed her husband's arm.

"We need to go home," she said urgently.

"What did you see?" he asked, but she was already pushing him toward the exit.

"It's a lady and she has a chicken leg!" the child repeated, bouncing with enthusiasm that only children could maintain in the face of the supernatural.

The family's hurried departure had a domino effect. Other patrons began stealing glances toward the darkness outside, and several more families started gathering their things. The warmth of the tavern suddenly felt fragile—the cheerful atmosphere giving way to something tense and watchful.

"Everybody stay calm!" Clobber called out from the bar, but people were already on their feet, craning to see out into the swirling snow.

I moved to where the little girl had been standing and wiped the condensation from the glass with my sleeve. The street outside was empty, but something about the shadows between the streetlamps made me uneasy. They pooled too dark, too deep—as if something lurked within them, swallowing the light.

"Nothing there now," I said, returning to the table, but my words did little to calm anyone's nerves.

Within minutes, the tavern was half empty. Families with

children were the first to leave, followed by the elderly and anyone who lived alone going home in groups. Those who remained huddled closer together, as if proximity to others could ward off whatever lurked in the winter darkness.

We gathered our things and prepared to leave ourselves. Jess ran to the bar to talk to Clobber and Phenny the tavern's cook. I tucked Simone's journal carefully back into my bag. Thanks to the help of Boddy and Evon, we now had the key to her final thoughts, but the knowledge felt like a weight in my chest.

The snow had intensified by the time Jess returned and we stepped outside, turning the cobblestone streets treacherous and muffling sound. The usual night sounds of Darkly—the distant music from other establishments, the chatter of late-night revelers, even the ever-present whisper of wind through Spanish moss—had been swallowed by an unnatural quiet.

We stood in a tight group, our muttered conversation the only sound besides the soft whisper of snow hitting the ground. The streetlamps cast pools of yellow light that seemed smaller and weaker than usual, as if something was actively pressing against their illumination.

"There," Jess whispered suddenly, pointing toward an alley between two buildings.

We all turned, peering into the darkness where she was pointing. For just a moment, I thought I saw a silhouette slipping deeper into the shadows. But when I blinked, it was gone.

"Perchta?" Tzazi breathed.

"Maybe," I said, but I wasn't sure. Whatever I'd seen had felt different from Perchta's energy.

Jess gave me a ride home, after Tzazi flitted off into the night, but I didn't feel completely safe until I was tucked up inside Fernwood with the doors locked and warded behind me. Only then did I allow myself to consider what we'd learned tonight.

A killer was loose in Darkly. Perhaps planning their next kill. And something ancient and dangerous was stirring in Darkly, calling creatures out of the swamp and sending families fleeing into the night.

I settled into bed with Pyewacket curled warm against my side, watching the swamp light pulse beyond my window—that strange, beckoning glow that had become as much a part of my nights as the chorus of frogs and the whisper of Spanish moss in the summer. The murders, the supernatural disturbances, Perchta stalking through town with her bells and her hunger—they had to be connected. Everything in Darkly was connected, roots tangled deep beneath the surface.

The question was how.

Michey's death seemed to be connected to the corrupt activities of the Lavallette family and—I thought of the hairclip— possibly the mysterious death of Simone, while Letha's death probably had something to do with what she knew about Simone's death.

Outside snow continued to fall beyond the frost-kissed glass, and in the distance, something chimed through the winter air— almost like sleigh bells. But underneath that festive sound was something else. A low, keening wail that made the hair on the back of my neck stand up.

Darkly held its breath.

CHAPTER 22

The frost on Fernwood's windows caught the morning light in crystalline patterns, but I barely noticed. My fingers traced the decoded pages of Simone's journal spread across the mahogany table in the sitting room, each word a knife twist in my chest. The journal had given up its secrets, and a part of me wished it hadn't.

Hilde sat in her rocker next to the fireplace, sipping coffee, and gazing at me with worried eyes.

"Win." Hilde's voice was soft, careful. "You don't have to read them all aloud."

I looked up from the journal, my throat tight. "Yes, I do. We need to hear this. All of it."

Sibby flopped into her chair, wearing her favorite onesie—the one covered in Harry Styles' face. Poor Harry.

The decoded pages painted a picture that made my stomach turn. Simone's handwriting, once neat and hopeful, had grown increasingly erratic as the entries progressed. The early ones sparkled with excitement at the thought of joining the Charlottes, about discovering the identity of her father, about finally belonging somewhere at Wentworth Academy.

"Read some more, sugarbean," Sibby said. "I'm beginning to think less and less of those Lavallettes.

"Listen to this," I said, my voice barely above a whisper. "Entry from October fifteenth: *The Charlottes are soooo cool. I really really want to be one. Dora Lavallette said hi to me today!!!!!*"

Hilde made a small sound, like a wounded animal. "Oh, sweet chile."

"And this one. October 19: *I thought Dora was starting to like me, but when I asked her today about becoming a Charlotte, she laughed at me. I need to stop crying and finish my essay for spell-casting.*"

I turned the page, and my heart cracked further. "October twenty-third: *The other girls barely look at me now. Dora must have said something to them, because even Letha won't sit with me at meals anymore. I wish Dianthe would get back from her semester in the Isles. I eat alone, study alone, spend most evenings alone in my room pressing orchids between book pages. At least flowers don't pretend to be your friend.*"

The irony tasted bitter on my tongue.

I read the next entry and sat back.

"Then on November 1: *You won't believe what I found out today! I wouldn't believe it except I heard it straight from the headmaster's mouth. I mean, he didn't say it to me, of course. I was working in the orchid greenhouse when he walked in with another man. I would never ever have eavesdropped but I heard my name, as in "your daughter Simone Petalsigh." Well, then I had to peek. Can you guess who it was? Alexander Lavallette. The millionaire. They were talking about my tuition. Now I know why being a Charlotte is so important to me. My heart knew before my brain. Alexander Lavallette, the big businessman, is my father. My father! I need to talk to A.*"

Pyewacket materialized from somewhere in the depths of the house, his eye fixed on me with that uncanny intelligence he often exhibited when my soul needed steadying. He leaped onto the table, carefully avoiding the journal pages, and settled himself against my hip. His purr was barely audible, but the warmth of his small body was anchoring.

"Reading the dead's secrets never gets easier," he said softly.

"So true," snorted Sibby around the pipe in her mouth.

"Here's where it starts to change," I said, flipping forward several pages. "November thirteen: *Today Dora Lavallette said hi to me in the hall!!!*"

The raw pain in Simone's words was devastating, made worse by the knowledge that she'd been telling the truth. She'd reached out to the sister she'd never known, only to be rejected and ridiculed by the one person who should have understood.

Sibby settled back into her chair, her mug pushed up against her chest. "That psychotic little—she bullied her own sister. For what? Social status?"

"But did she know?" Hilde countered. "Nothin' in the journal says Dora knew about their relationship."

"That's true," I said quietly. "Alexander Lavallette is the bastard who knew about but never acknowledged Simone. He would have been furious if the truth came out. It would have destroyed his carefully calculated reputation, his marriage, his professional connections. He could have protected himself…"

"By destroying Simone," Hilde whispered.

"That bastard!" Sibby muttered.

I nodded, finding the next entry. "November twenty-seventh: *The other girls in the dorm are noticing me again. Trixie lent me her favorite scarf yesterday, and Letha saved me a seat at dinner. But Dora is the one who matters. She's so sophisticated, so confident. She's perfect.*"

Pyewacket's purr intensified, as if he could sense my emotional state. I scratched behind his ears, grateful for his steady presence.

"How extraordinarily peculiar," he said, his voice slightly strained. "There appears to be…moisture. Leaking from my functioning eye. Is this—good heavens, am I crying? I didn't even realize I was capable of such…sentiment."

I gave him a kiss on the top of his head, my own eyes stinging. "You've always been capable of it, you old softie."

Candlelight flickered across the journal's faded ink, pulling me back in.

"The worst part," I continued, my voice growing stronger with anger, "is what comes next. December eighth: *Something strange and wonderful happened today. Dora approached me after dinner, all smiles and sweetness. She said she'd been thinking about our conversation, about me becoming a Charlotte, and maybe she'd been too hasty. She told me I still have a place with the Charlottes. She's genuinely sorry. Maybe there's still hope for us to be sisters.*"

Fernwood was quiet as I paused, only the fire popping and a wind rushing down the eaves.

"December tenth," I read, my voice flat with fury. "The entry from two days before she died. *Dora says if I want to prove I belong with the Charlottes, I need to show courage and dedication. She's designed a special initiation just for me—something about spending time outside, connecting with the winter elements. She was very specific about the timing and the rules. She says if I can do this one thing, I'll finally be accepted. I'll finally have the family I've always wanted. As soon as I'm a Charlotte, I'm going to tell her we're sisters!*"

The silence that followed was deafening. Outside, the snow continued to fall, blanketing Fernwood's gardens in pristine white that would have been beautiful under any other circumstances.

"Hilde's right, though," Sibby said. "According to what Simone wrote, Dora didn't know they were sisters."

I turned to the final entry, dated December eleventh—the day before Simone died. My hands shook as I read: "*Tomorrow night is my initiation. Dora explained the rules carefully—I'm to spend three hours outside the dorm house, no matter what happens. I'm allowed to use any magic at my disposal. But if I move from that spot or try to come inside, I fail, and I'll never be welcomed with the Charlottes again. She says it's about proving I can endure hardship for the sake of family, about showing I understand that belonging requires sacrifice. I'm nervous, but also excited. After tomorrow night, I'll finally have a sister. I'll finally belong.*"

I closed the journal. The final entry was too heartbreaking, too naive, too full of hope for something that had been a lie from the beginning.

The weight of Simone's last words settled over us like a heavy blanket, suffocating in its implications.

"She died believing she was earning her place," I said finally. "She died thinking her sister would accept her if she just proved herself worthy."

"Who knows. Maybe she would have," Pye said.

I scratched between his ears.

"Maybe."

"So who wanted her dead?" Hilde asked.

I thought about Arthur who I now believed had nothing to do with Simone's, Michey's and Letha's death. And what about Eudora? The polished woman I'd met at the MET, with her designer clothes and confident smile. I thought about the way she'd grieved when her friend Letha died, the way she'd asked me to find the killer. Besides, Eudora may have been a horrible teenager but she was only a child herself when Simone died. I couldn't see it.

Then my mind turned to Lex. He had the power and the motivation to easily cause the death of three people who threatened his charmed life. He could easily have found out about Simone's initiation into the Charlottes. Not to mention, Lavallette Global, is all over Michey's ledger.

"The kind of person who learned early that love is conditional, that's who," I finally said. "The kind who decided that survival mattered more than connection. The kind who convinced themself that some secrets are worth killing for."

They could easily have spelled the girl or had someone else do it.

Outside, the snow continued to fall, coating the world in deceptive purity. But inside Fernwood's warm protection, surrounded by the decoded words of a girl who'd died believing in the possibility of sisterhood, I felt the cold weight of truth settling into my bones.

I knew who the killer was. Who it *had* to be. And now I was going to prove it...with the help of a young man I was already indebted to.

CHAPTER 23

$\mathcal{T}$he Christmas Market sprawled across Darkly's cobblestone streets in a maze of twinkling lights and pine-scented air. Steam rose from cauldrons of spiced cider, mixing with the smoke from roasted chestnuts and the sweet burn of Papa Noël pralines. Carolers strolled between the stalls, their voices weaving through the chatter of families bundled in wool coats and bright scarves.

The winter air carried the scent of hot toddies spiced with cinnamon and clove, mingling with woodsmoke from the braziers scattered throughout the Christmas market. I pulled my scarf tighter against the December chill and rolled my solstice wish stone between my fingers, the cool crystallized surface a small comfort against my unease.

The White Stag Inn's booth overflowed with steaming cups and festive cheer. Trixie Frick held court at the center of the chaos, her teased red hair catching the fairy lights strung between lampposts, her sequined red jacket throwing off sparks of reflected color with every animated gesture.

A cluster of teens huddled near the inn's table, their breath forming little clouds in the cold. Evon Frick stood in the center, his shaggy blond curls escaping from beneath a black knit cap, hands shoved deep in the pockets of his worn denim jacket. His friends orbited around him—two girls sharing a scarf, a tall boy with wire-rimmed glasses, another kid I recognized from the frantic entrance of the teens at the gala. They all wore that carefully constructed nonchalance of young people trying desperately to look older, sophisticated, worldly. Leaning against lampposts with studied casualness, laughing just a touch too loud, glancing around to see who might be watching.

The kind of kids who thought they were untouchable.

Simone's story proved they weren't.

One girl—maybe seventeen, with a purple streak in her dark hair—edged closer to the table while her friends provided cover, pretending to admire the enchanted snow globes in Sugarloaf's display across the street. Her hand reached out, fingers stretching toward a mug of hot toddy left unattended on the table's edge.

Trixie's head stayed perfectly still, her gaze locked on the market crowd.

The cup vanished from the girl's hand in an explosion of glittering confetti—gold and crimson and emerald green—that burst into the air like tiny fireworks before dissolving into nothing. The confetti left behind the faint scent of vanilla and sparklers.

"Nice try."

The delivery was flat. Factual. None of Trixie's usual honey-and-bourbon warmth.

The girl's cheeks flamed scarlet. Her friends howled with laughter, and someone clapped her on the shoulder.

"Mrs. Frick, I'm so sorry, I wasn't—"

"S'fine." Trixie waved a hand, then seemed to catch herself. Added a smile that didn't quite reach her eyes. "Just...be more careful, yeah? Wouldn't want your mama finding out."

She produced a tray of steaming chocolate and slid it across the table without the usual flourish or commentary about marshmallows or staying out of trouble. Just set it down and went back to organizing the mugs with surprising efficiency.

The teens grabbed their drinks, their cold fingers wrapping gratefully around the warm mugs. Steam curled up from the chocolate as they drifted away from the table, clustering together beneath the nearest garlanded streetlamp.

I tucked my solstice wish stone into my coat pocket and wandered closer to the inn's table, catching Trixie's eye.

She gave me a nod. A single, brief acknowledgment.

"Evening, Win." Her voice hit all the right notes, but the rhythm was wrong. Like someone playing a song they'd memorized without quite feeling the music.

"Hi, Trixie," I said easily. "You all right?"

"Stuck here while everyone—." She adjusted a stack of napkins with both hands, lining them up with geometric precision. "Yeah, I'm good."

I smiled, letting my gaze drift across the market, then back to Evon and his friends.

He leaned against the streetlamp, weight shifted to one hip, hand gesturing broadly as he talked, head thrown back in laughter that rang out bright and musical across the cobblestones. He touched one friend's arm, then another's shoulder, leaning in to share some joke that had them all cackling.

When he caught sight of me, his whole face lit up.

"Windsor!" He practically bounced over, moving through the crowd with easy confidence. "Sugar, you look frozen solid. Have you had any of the bourbon balls yet? The Gator is doing this divine thing with salted caramel that'll change your whole life."

His voice carried a particular lilt, effusive enthusiasm, hitting every word just a touch harder than necessary.

"Not yet," I said, keeping my expression neutral. "You recommending them?"

"Oh, absolutely." He waved one hand in the air. "I've already had three and I'm thinking about going back for more. Living dangerously tonight!" He laughed at his own joke, bright and delighted.

One of his friends called out and he spun around—heels together, almost a pirouette—and called back, "Hold that thought. I'll be right there!"

Then he turned back to me with a conspiratorial grin, leaned in close, and dropped his voice to a stage whisper. "Between you and me, I think half the town's already tipsy and it's barely seven o'clock. Gonna be a memorable night."

He winked—actually winked—and swept back toward his friends with a little wave, his stride loose and comfortable.

I glanced back at the White Stag's booth where Trixie sat picking at her perfectly manicured nails with intense focus, her shoulders square, her red lips pressed together in concentration. She looked up once, caught someone's eye across the market, and gave a small, almost shy nod before returning her attention to her nails.

I lingered near Maisie's jewelry booth, lifting a garnet brooch shaped like a cardinal to catch the fairy light. The solstice wish stone warmed in my coat pocket as I angled myself just right—close enough to admire Maisie's handiwork, close enough to hear the teens' conversation shift from fashion disasters to something far more dangerous.

"What do y'all think about the murders?" The question came from the tall boy with wire-rimmed glasses, his voice dropping low despite the market noise surrounding them.

"Perchta." The purple-haired girl wrapped her arms around herself, her earlier embarrassment completely forgotten. "My mom says we need to be on our best behavior or we'll be next."

"That's what everyone's saying." Another kid nodded, glancing toward the dark woods beyond the market's glow. "She's judging us. Picking off the wicked."

The group huddled closer, their voices falling to urgent whispers. Steam from their chocolate curled between them like ghosts.

Then one voice rang out above the others—clear, confident, carrying across the cobblestones with theatrical precision.

"It's not Perchta."

Every head turned toward Evon. He stood with his weight shifted to one hip, chin lifted, eyes bright with something that looked almost like excitement.

"How would you know?" The boy with glasses leaned forward.

Evon paused—a perfect beat of dramatic timing—and let his gaze sweep across his friends' faces before answering. "Because I know who killed them."

The word exploded from multiple mouths at once. "What!?"

"Have you told the royal inspector?" The purple-haired girl grabbed his arm, her fingers digging into his jacket sleeve.

"Not yet." He shook his head slowly, playing the moment for all it was worth.

Another friend stepped closer, voice urgent. "Are you sure? Evon, that's serious—"

He nodded, then dropped his voice to a low whisper that somehow managed to carry across half the market. The kind of stage whisper actors used when they wanted the back row to hear every word.

"I saw them."

A girl gasped, her hand flying to her mouth.

"Dude." The tall boy's eyes went wide behind his glasses. "That's dangerous. Like, really dangerous."

"I know." Evon's expression shifted—less theatrical now, more grave. He glanced around as if checking to see who might be listening, and his gaze skimmed right past me without acknowledgment. "I'm going to Belleclaire tonight."

"Why are you waiting?" The purple-haired girl's voice pitched higher.

Evon shrugged. Then, loud enough that anyone passing by would hear, "After the market closes, if I don't see him before."

The group erupted in overlapping protests—"You have to tell

us," "What if they come after you," "This is insane"—but Evon waved them off with a confident smile that looked completely wrong on his usually brooding face.

"Oh, sugars." He squeezed the shoulder of the kid nearest him —a gesture of reassurance that looked oddly maternal. "Don't worry about me. Just focus on staying safe yourselves. And for heaven's sake, don't make your mothers fret."

My eyes flowed over the booths until I found Lex Lavallette, not twenty feet away, browsing an antique weapons booth lined with faded maps and crossed swords. He'd been examining a solid gold antique bodkin, but now his hand froze. He carefully returned the blade to the table and spun around, searching the crowd.

Eudora and her husband now lolled in front of Rage, Borda Wrathfell's booth. She held a pair of delicate gold earrings, turning them to catch the light. Eliaz leaned close to her, murmuring something I couldn't hear, and Eudora glanced at her father then turned to stare in Evon's direction. She and Eliaz moved to Lex's side, Eudora whispering in his ear.

"Well, hellhound!"

Trixie stood behind the White Stag's booth, hands planted on her hips in a pose that looked right but felt stiff. Her gaze swept across the table's surface with methodical precision. "Boone, m'dear, what happened to all the cups? We can't serve hot toddies without cups."

Boone's head came up from where he'd been restocking napkins. His dark eyes narrowed, studying his wife's face for a long moment. "You okay?"

"Yeah." She blinked. "Why wouldn't I be?"

He didn't answer, just ducked behind the counter and started shifting boxes around, the sound of glass clinking against glass filling the space between them.

Trixie cleared her throat. "The cups, though—"

"They were right here." His voice carried an edge of

frustration as he straightened, empty-handed. "I swear I just restocked. I'll run inside and grab more from storage."

"No!" The word came out too sharp, and she caught herself. Softened her tone. "No, you stay here. With me...lover boy. I'll...I'll send Evon."

Boone went very still. His gaze locked onto his wife's face—searching, assessing. His head tilted slightly to one side. "Trixie."

"Mm?" She busied herself, rearranging the cups that remained, not quite meeting his eyes.

"Since when do you send Evon to do anything without at least three complaints about how teenagers these days don't know the meaning of hard work?"

Her hands stilled.

Before she could answer, Boone turned toward the cluster of teens and called out, his voice cutting through the market noise. "Evon!"

Here we go.

EVON SLIPPED AWAY DOWN a narrow path threading between Tataille and the cluster of businesses beyond, his silhouette dissolving into the darkening woods. Snow had begun to fall in earnest now, soft flakes drifting through the air like ash, muffling the market sounds into something distant and dreamlike.

I kept my focus trained on Lex Lavallette, waiting for him to reveal his hand. But, after speaking with his daughter, he only drifted through the market with infuriating leisure, pausing at each stall to chat with vendors, examining their wares with the unhurried contentment of a man with all the time in the world. The lamplight caught the gold threads in his coat as he moved, making him look almost ethereal against the white-dusted cobblestones.

What was I missing?

Did he know I was on to him?

Movement at Mr. Creech's booth snagged my attention. Eudora held one of the Papa Noël poppets, turning it over in her hands with the careful attention of someone reading a book. Now she set it down with deliberate slowness, her fingers lingering on its velvet coat. She leaned close to Eliaz, murmuring something I couldn't hear. Whatever she said made his expression tighten, concern flickering across his features like a match struck in darkness.

But Eudora was already drifting away, drawn toward the next booth. This one displaying medieval knives, their blades catching the lamplight in sharp, cold glints.

Eliaz hesitated, uncertainty written in the way he shifted his weight. Then he followed after her, keeping his distance, his troubled gaze never leaving her back.

The snow fell faster now, and somewhere in the woods beyond Tataille, something howled.

What had I done?

I slipped after Evon, keeping to the velvet shadows between stalls until I reached the narrow path. My breath clouded in the frigid air and I quickened my pace. Something flickered at the edge of my vision—a tall figure gliding between the bare trees like smoke given form. Lex.

I ran.

The faint jing-jing-jing of bells threaded through the market's chatter and carols, there and gone before I could track the source. Just the Krampus puppet show in the children's area, I told myself. But my skin crawled, tightening across my shoulders like someone had drawn a bowstring taut.

The market's warmth and noise fell away as I followed the path deeper into the woods, a shortcut to the businesses lined along Bayou Boulevard. The packed dirt trail wound between frost-silvered holly bushes, their leaves catching the lantern light in sharp, glittering fragments. Each gust of wind set the flames dancing, and the shadows writhed in response—elongating, reaching. Shades—ghostly forms of the dead who refused to leave —twisted between the dark trees.

Woodsmoke drifted through the forest, but underneath it came something else. Something sharp and metallic, coating my throat with the taste of old copper.

Evon's footsteps crunched ahead on the frozen ground, measured and unhurried. But his shoulders were rigid beneath his jacket, his spine too straight. He was performing casualness.

The temperature plummeted without warning. Cold knifed through my gloves and scarf, burrowing into my bones. A miniature cyclone of snowflakes spiraled up from the path at my feet, spinning in place despite the stillness above. The metallic scent thickened—old blood on winter iron.

I stopped. Turned slowly, listening.

Lex was out here somewhere. Watching.

The world began to muffle itself. Wind through pine needles, distant laughter from the market, even my own breathing—all of it fading, growing distant and dim. In that swelling quiet, something rumbled beneath my feet. So low I felt it more than heard it, a subsonic growl that could have been a sleigh on distant cobblestones.

Except it wasn't.

It was organic. Alive. And getting closer.

Footsteps crashed through the underbrush to my left—heavy boots trampling ferns and dead bracken. They hesitated for one suspended heartbeat.

Then came faster. Urgent.

Ahead on the path, Evon went perfectly still.

A figure stepped from between the trees.

Not from the path. Between the trees—as if the forest itself had exhaled her into being.

"Such a shame, Evon." Eudora's voice cut through the frozen air, low and almost purring. "I really liked your mother."

The world tilted beneath my feet. Simone's death. The hairclip hidden in Michey's pawn shop. Letha's desperate need to talk about something that happened twenty years ago. The pieces slammed into place with sickening clarity.

It wasn't Lex.

It was Eudora.

Evon turned slowly, one hand lifting to his hip. Eudora Quenleigh stood six feet away, backlit by the wavering lantern light, and in her gloved hand gleamed a slim stiletto. Its silver handle was worked with delicate filigree—elegant enough to pass for a lady's accessory, deadly enough to slide between ribs without catching bone.

The temperature dropped another impossible degree. Frost crawled up the holly leaves beside the path, crunching softly.

"Eudora." Eliaz's voice cracked through the cold like breaking ice. He emerged from behind a snow-dusted spruce, his usual composure shattered. He reached for her wrist, fingers circling the delicate bones. "Don't. Don't make this worse."

But Eudora's eyes never left Evon's face as she crept forward. They gleamed with something feverish, something unmoored. "He knows, Eliaz. About Simone. Just like Michey. Like Letha." Her voice climbed higher, taking on a brittle quality. "He's our ruin, Eliaz. Our lives. Our reputation. Everything."

The forest rustled around us, though no wind stirred the air. Something moved in the darkness beyond the lantern's reach— pale shapes drifting between the trunks like mist given form. The ghosts were gathering.

Evon backed up a step, but his shoulders stayed square. His voice rang out clear and defiant even as the blade caught the lantern light, its tip tracing the air between them with deadly promise. "Oh, honey, you should have stopped after Simone. But you just kept going, didn't you? Michey. Poor Letha. All because you—"

He screamed.

Eudora had lunged forward, the stiletto's tip catching the lantern light in a ray of silver.

Eliaz jerked her back, but barely. The blade stopped an inch from Evon's jacket.

"I was just a child! Your age!" Eudora's words came in a rush now, hysteria bleeding through her cultured accent. "It was a prank. A silly, stupid prank. How was I supposed to know she wouldn't be able to get back in?"

"Sugar, no." Evon's voice dropped low, disappointed. "You knew exactly what would happen."

Eudora's eyes narrowed, her head tilting as if hearing something wrong in the timbre, the cadence.

The knife trembled in her grip—but not from hesitation. She was coiled, a spring wound too tight, ready to snap.

Behind her, deeper in the woods, something impossibly tall moved between the trees. The ghost of a pale mask. The curve of antlers catching moonlight before vanishing into shadow. The jing-jing-jing of bells threaded through the darkness, closer now.

A single clear chime rang out—though no one had touched the hanging lanterns.

"Put the knife down, Eudora."

My voice sliced through the moment as I stepped into the circle of lantern light. All three of them spun toward me, but I kept my focus locked on Eudora and the deadly silver gleam in her hand.

Movement flickered behind her—impossibly fast, impossibly wrong. Something with too many joints loped through the underbrush. A swamp imp, perhaps, or something worse. The ghosts drifting between the trees had multiplied, their translucent forms creating a spectral audience to the unfolding confrontation.

The metallic scent I'd caught earlier thickened into something unmistakable now. Old blood and fresh snow and the copper tang of magic about to break loose.

She tilted her head, lips curling into something that might have been a smile if smiles could cut. "Windsor Ebonwood. The famous book conservator. The witch who thinks she can solve everyone's problems with a little research and a kind word."

"Well, bless your heart, dear, but I don't think kind words are going to cut it tonight." Evon's drawl thickened, warm as molasses and twice as sticky.

Eliaz's gaze snapped to the boy, his brow furrowing. His eyes traced Evon's face, his posture, lingering on the set of his shoulders—too square, too steady—before flicking back to Eudora with confusion creasing his features.

I decided to press our advantage while they were off-balance.

"I must tell you," I said, keeping my voice light, conversational, "that hex beast you sent after me was a nice touch. Really festive. Nothing says 'Merry Christmas' quite like a monstrous boar with a dozen red eyes trying to gore you in a friend's front yard."

Eudora's lips curved into something that wasn't quite a smile. "It was, wasn't it? Eliaz was always good at transfigurations."

Eliaz made a sound that was either a groan or a warning growl.

"So that was your handiwork," I said, turning to face him directly. "Impressive magic, Primarch. Taking an ordinary boar and twisting it into something out of a nightmare. Must have taken considerable power."

His expression flickered—annoyance, perhaps a flash of pride he couldn't quite suppress.

"Too bad it didn't have a chance against Tzazi." I let my voice sharpen. "You should choose your enemies more carefully. Some of them bite back."

Eudora's smile vanished.

"None of this is my fault, you know." Her voice turned conversational, almost pleasant—which made it infinitely worse. "My perfect half-sister Simone thought she could swoop in and take Daddy away from me. With her tragic orphan story and her big, sad eyes."

My stomach dropped. "You knew she was your sister?"

"Of course, I knew." A terrible light danced in Eudora's eyes. The stiletto caught the lantern glow, throwing silver shadows across her face. "I overheard her talking to Arthur. Planning her little revelation. Her pathetic cry for attention from Daddy."

"Oh, honey." Evon's voice carried that warm, syrupy drawl, but underneath it ran something sharp and furious. "Simone was just a girl trying to find her family. And you spelled your own sister outside to freeze to death."

The words hung strange in the frozen air.

Eudora's head snapped toward him, confusion flickering across her features before rage swallowed it whole. "Oh, shut up!"

She whirled, the blade slicing toward Evon in a vicious arc.

"Arthur said you were a stalker." My words cut through the moment, quiet and deliberate.

The effect was immediate.

Eudora froze mid-lunge, her entire body going rigid. The stiletto trembled in her grip. "What did you say?"

"A stalker." I held her gaze, my voice steady despite my hammering heart. "That's what Arthur told us. That you followed him everywhere. Watched him. Couldn't accept that he wasn't interested."

"Liar!" The word ripped from her throat, raw and unhinged. She rounded on me, the stiletto's point shifting in my direction. I saw Eliaz's face go white with horror. He still had hold of her wrist, but his grip was weakening, his fingers slipping on her glove.

We stared at each other across the frost-silvered path. The forest held its breath. Even the ghosts had gone still, their translucent forms frozen between the trees like an audience watching a tragedy unfold.

"Michey overheard daddy's little secret too," Eudora continued, her voice dropping back to that eerie calm. "Thought it was worth a few coins in his pocket. Stupid little man didn't realize how dangerous I could be."

She turned back to Evon, pressing the stiletto's tip lightly against his jacket. The dark wool dimpled under the pressure.

Evon didn't flinch. His chin lifted slightly, eyes meeting

Eudora's with steady defiance. "You're not half as dangerous as you think you are, sugar."

"We'll see about that." She turned back to me. "And Letha... Letha was clever enough to piece together what really happened that night. All these years, I was afraid she would talk."

The bells rang out again—jing-jing-jing—and this time they were answered. From somewhere in the woods came a low, guttural sound that was part growl, part laugh, part something else entirely.

"Let the boy go, Eudora."

Keir's voice rolled through the clearing like distant thunder, and relief crashed through me when he materialized from the shadows between the trees. His eyes had gone wolf-bright, reflecting the lantern light with an amber gleam that had nothing human in it. Every muscle in his body coiled with predatory readiness, and when he moved to block Eudora's retreat toward the market, his steps made no sound on the frozen ground.

"Oh, thank the saints." Evon's shoulders dropped a fraction, the tension easing from his frame. "Took you long enough, handsome."

Keir's brow furrowed. Eudora's eyes narrowed. Eliaz tilted his head—all three turned that collective confusion on Evon.

Ransom and Boddy arrived heartbeats later, spreading out to flank us. The three men formed a wall of supernatural power—werewolf, fae, and grim reaper—but Eudora only laughed. The sound cracked through the cold air like breaking glass, brittle and sharp enough to draw blood.

The ghosts hovering between the trees pressed closer, their translucent forms clustering at the edge of the lantern light. Watching.

Lex Lavallette stormed into the clearing, his usual composure shattered. "What is the meaning of—" His eyes swept across the scene: me, Keir, then finally his daughter holding a blade to a child's throat. The blood drained from his face until he looked as pale as the specters surrounding us. "Eudora?"

She didn't even seem to register her father's arrival. The stiletto's tip pressed harder against Evon's throat, drawing a tiny bead of blood that trickled down his chest. "Where was my protection when perfect little Simone tried to steal my life?" Eudora's voice climbed to a screech, raw and unhinged.

Fury ignited hot in my chest. I stepped forward, my boots crunching on frost-brittle leaves. "Are you kidding me? You killed Simone because she wanted her father to acknowledge her? Because a child wanted to belong somewhere?" My voice shook with barely controlled rage. "She didn't want to steal your life, Eudora. She wanted to share it."

"Shut up!" Eudora snarled. "She had everything—the tragic story, the sympathy, Daddy's guilt wrapped around her like a cape." Tears streamed down her face now, cutting tracks through her careful makeup. "She had Arthur. She would have taken it all from me. I couldn't let that happen. I couldn't—"

Lex made a strangled sound, his hand reaching toward his daughter as if he could pull her back from the edge she'd already thrown herself over.

"Do you even hear yourself?" My words came out hollow with disbelief.

"*L'gamine.*" Lex's voice cracked on the word. It wasn't a yell—barely more than a whisper—but it carried across the clearing like a funeral bell. "What have you done?"

I froze at the name. A nickname.

LG didn't stand for Lavallette Global. LG was *l'gamine.* Eudora. She was the one who gave Michey the hairpin. To keep quiet.

Eudora's head snapped toward her father, and in that instant, the forest itself seemed to inhale.

Thin tendrils of mist began curling in from the tree line, moving against the wind, threading between the trunks like searching fingers. The metallic scent that had been haunting the air thickened until I could taste copper on my tongue, could feel it coating the back of my throat.

The ghosts stopped their drifting. They hung suspended in the darkness, their faces turning as one toward something deeper in the woods.

Underneath Eudora's increasingly frantic breathing, I heard it —a sound that raised every hair on my body. Strange, layered humming that seemed to come from everywhere and nowhere at once. Deep masculine voices wove together with high, sharp wails in a dissonant harmony that made my teeth ache and my bones vibrate. It was ancient. It was hungry. And it was getting closer.

Evon's gaze cut toward the trees, then back to Eudora with deliberate calm. "Well now. You've really done it this time, haven't you?"

The temperature plummeted. Frost raced across the ground in crystalline patterns, climbing up the tree trunks, spreading across the lantern posts. Our breath clouded the air in thick plumes.

Then, from somewhere deep in the woods, came a sound that froze the blood in my veins.

A piercing screech—part animal, part human, part something that had never been either—erupted from the darkness. It was answered by others, a chorus of inhuman cries that built and built until the very air seemed to scream.

The lantern flames guttered violently, their light reducing to feeble sparks that barely held back the crushing darkness. Shadows surged forward like living things, eager and malevolent.

Heavy, furred shapes exploded from the tree line.

They moved with impossible speed—massive forms that shouldn't exist. Horned masks gleamed bone-white in the dying light. Antlers crowned shaggy heads. Some walked on two legs, others on four, and some seemed to shift between forms as they ran. Bells clanged and jangled with their approach, a metallic symphony that mixed with guttural chanting in languages older than memory. The thunder of hooves—or boots, or clawed feet— shook the frozen ground beneath us.

The perchten had arrived.

And they had come for payment.

They materialized from the darkness like nightmare made flesh.

Some wore carved masks of serene, almost beatific faces—smooth wood painted white as bone, crowned with evergreen wreaths. These were draped in shimmering robes of silver and white that seemed to capture and hold moonlight, making them glow with an otherworldly radiance. They moved with eerie grace, their footsteps silent on the frozen ground.

But others...the others were grotesque.

Twisted masks of snarling beasts and leering demons. Matted furs that stank of wild places and old blood. Massive cowbells that clanged and rang like funeral dirges with every movement. Through carved eyeholes, their eyes glinted—some starlike and cold, others burning like hot coals pulled from a forge.

The air turned arctic, stealing the breath from my lungs. Ice crystals formed on my eyelashes. The cold bit through my coat, my gloves, my scarf, sinking into my bones with vicious intent.

Eudora flinched at the cacophony of bells and inhuman voices, her entire body going rigid. For just a heartbeat, her grip on the stiletto loosened.

Evon moved fast—not the panicked scramble of a frightened boy, but purposeful and decisive. He twisted free with practiced efficiency and closed the distance between us in quick, determined strides.

I caught him, pulling him behind me as the creatures formed a circle around us—a living wall of fur and antler and ancient hunger. Their chanting swelled, wordless and terrible, vibrating through the ground beneath our feet.

Evon's hand gripped my shoulder—steadying, protective, the touch of someone used to being the shield rather than the one being shielded.

From the deepest shadows stepped a figure that turned my blood to ice.

Frau Perchta herself.

She was impossibly tall and gaunt, her frame draped in ragged dark furs that seemed to drink in what little light remained. Hollow eyes glowed ember-red in a sharp-featured face that might have been beautiful once, millennia ago, before cruelty had carved it into something pitiless. A hooked nose jutted above thin lips that had forgotten how to smile. At her belt hung a spindle and distaff—symbols of her ancient power—and beside them, a knife that looked hungry, its blade stained with rust or old blood.

Her burning gaze locked with mine.

She inclined her head once—a silent acknowledgment. This was her domain now. Her justice. Not mine. Not mortal law's.

The perchten closed in on Eudora like a tide of nightmare and folklore given form.

"No." Eliaz's voice was barely a whisper, lost in the jangle of bells and the rising crescendo of inhuman voices chanting in languages that predated words.

Clawed hands—some furred, some scaled, some too-pale and too-human—reached for Eudora. She screamed, high and desperate and utterly helpless, as they lifted her from the ground. Her feet kicked at empty air. The stiletto tumbled from her fingers, hitting the frost-hardened earth with a small, final clink.

"Eudora!" Eliaz lunged forward, desperation overriding every instinct for self-preservation.

But the creatures were impossibly fast. More hands seized him —dragging him alongside his wife into the seething mass of fur and horn and ancient wrath. His shout cut off abruptly as they swept him into the darkness between the trees.

Lex stood frozen, his face slack with shock. He didn't move as his daughter and son-in-law disappeared into the tumult of monstrous faces and grasping claws, swallowed by shadows that shouldn't exist.

"I...I had nothing to do with this," he stuttered as he sat down hard on the frozen ground.

Their screams rose and rose, reaching a pitch that made my ears ring—

Then faded.

Swallowed by the deeper music of the perchten—the low growl of beasts, the relentless ringing of bells, and strange otherworldly singing that seemed to rise from the earth itself, from stones and roots and things far older than humanity.

Then...nothing.

Silence fell like a curtain dropping.

Deep and absolute, broken only by the soft whisper of snowflakes beginning to fall in earnest, drifting down through the bare branches like white ash.

The perchten were gone. Vanished as if they'd never been.

Lex collapsed to his knees, a broken sound tearing from his throat. The lanterns flickered, sputtered—then surged back to full brightness, their warm golden glow chasing away the unnatural shadows. The metallic scent faded, replaced by the clean smell of winter pine and distant wood smoke. From somewhere beyond the trees, I heard it. The faint sounds of caroling, voices raised in joyful harmony as if nothing in the world had changed.

But everything had changed.

Keir's arms came around me from behind, solid and warm and blessedly real. I leaned back against his chest, feeling the wild hammering of my heart begin to slow. His warmth seeped into my frozen body.

"Is everyone all right?" Ransom's voice cut through the stillness, quiet and carefully controlled. His breath formed white clouds in the frigid air.

Evon nodded shakily, still pressed against my side. His whole body trembled. "I'm okay. I'm..." He swallowed hard, then straightened his shoulders with sudden purpose. "Actually, sugar, I'm better than okay."

The air around him wavered—ripples of starlight, bending the space between us. His form blurred, features shifting and reforming in a cascade of glittering magic that smelled of vanilla and sparklers.

When the glamour fell away, Trixie Frick stood in her son's place.

Her teased red hair had gone slightly flat from wearing a knit cap. Her sequined jacket was hidden under Evon's worn denim, but her red lipstick was still perfect. She gave a little shimmy—shoulders rolling, hips swaying—and let out a delighted laugh that was pure relief and triumph mixed together.

"Lord have mercy, that feels good." She patted her hair, trying to coax some volume back into it. "Holding a glamour that long is exhausting. And honey, teenage boys do not know how to dress for drama." Her face grew serious for a moment. "Did I really just meet the legendary Perchta?"

"Apparently she didn't appreciate being framed for murder," I said simply, my gaze drifting to the dark spaces between the trees where the creatures had vanished without a trace.

"Well, can you blame her, sugar." Trixie's voice carried her signature warmth mixed with steel. "If I'd known Frau Perchta was going to show up and handle business personally, I might've worn my good heels for the occasion." Her grin turned fierce. "But watching ancient justice served up with bells and antlers? Sugar, that's a Christmas show worth the ticket price."

Boddy and Ransom moved toward Lex Lavallette, who still knelt in the snow like a penitent. Ransom held Michey's ledger in one hand—evidence of years of blackmail and corruption by both Lex Lavallette and his daughter. Her to cover up the murder of Simone; Lex working with Michey to defraud innocent people. Boddy's golden coils unfurled like living rope, wrapping around the broken man with surprising gentleness.

Lex didn't resist. Didn't speak. His eyes remained fixed on the spot where his daughter had disappeared.

They vanished with a soft pop that echoed in the quiet.

The ghosts I'd seen earlier—pale forms drifting between the trees—pressed closer now, clustering at the edges of the clearing. More of them than before. Dozens. Their translucent faces turned toward where Lex had knelt, watching with expressions that ranged from sorrow to satisfaction to something that might have been vindication.

"Such a shame."

The voice came from directly beside me—soft, cultured, carrying that particular musical cadence of old Darkly families. I turned.

Lorinda stood not three feet away, her silver hair perfectly styled, her makeup flawless. The same measured grace, the same steel hiding behind Southern politeness.

The same clothes.

My breath caught as understanding slammed into me with brutal clarity. The way she'd appeared so suddenly in the MET. How she'd moved without sound. The scent of lavender that had lingered after she left—not perfume. Memory.

She'd been dead the entire time.

The face that looked so much like Simone's.

"Lorinda…Lavallette?" I whispered.

Her smile was sad now, stripped of its earlier sharpness. She looked past me toward the empty space where Boddy and Ransom had taken her son. "Alexander spoiled that girl. Lord knows I love them both. But he thought his name and his money could buy her out of anything."

Around us, the other shades drifted closer—a silent audience bearing witness. Some wore clothes decades out of fashion, others centuries old. They moved through the trees like mist, soundless and sorrowful.

"You can't choose your blood, dear." Lorinda's voice was quiet, almost conversational, but something in it made me pay attention. "Can't control what they do, no matter how much you love them. No matter how desperately you want to protect them from themselves."

"The chickens finally came home," I said quietly, remembering her words from the MET.

"Oh, they always do, dear. Always." Her form began to fade,

growing more translucent. "This time with talons and bells and ancient judgment."

Then she was gone, dissolving into the winter air like morning frost under sunlight. The other shades began to drift away too, melting back into the darkness between the trees until only the ordinary shadows remained.

I stood there, staring at empty space, her words echoing in my mind.

"*Mo chridhe*?" Keir's voice came from behind me, warm and concerned. His hand found mine, and the solid reality of him anchor me back to the present. "Did you say something?"

I turned to find him watching me with those beautiful brown eyes, his head tilted slightly.

Beyond him, Trixie shimmied around the clearing, head thrown back as she belted out "Santa Claus is Coming to Town" with particular emphasis on "watching out" and "being good." Farther back, I could see the market lights twinkling through the trees, their cheerful glow a stark contrast to the ancient justice we'd just witnessed.

"Just—what took you so long?" I said softly, even as Lorinda's warnings continued to whisper through my thoughts.

"Had to stop for bourbon balls." His grin was crooked, that familiar warmth chasing away some of the lingering cold. "Priorities, lass."

Despite everything, I felt my lips curve into a smile.

We joined Trixie and I wrapped my arm around her shoulders. Heat seared through my chest—sudden and white-hot—before vanishing in an instant. Trixie gasped, her hand flying to her own chest, and Keir's head snapped toward us, his eyes flashing amber for just a heartbeat.

Ransom had released the bindling.

We began the walk back toward the market. Keir stayed close, his hand warm against the small of my back. Trixie walked on my other side, still trying to fluff her hair back to its usual volume. Behind us, the dark woods held their secrets, and somewhere in that vast darkness, ancient wheels of justice continued their eternal turning.

The Christmas market welcomed us back with open arms—twinkling lights strung like captured stars, the rich scent of cinnamon and mulled cider, laughter and music spilling from every stall. The warmth hit me like a physical thing, thawing my frozen cheeks and melting the last traces of terror from my bones.

"You do realize this is the second murder case I've helped you solve," Trixie smiled at me and cocked her head. "I'm waiting for you to admit I'm your Watson."

I laughed and threw my arms around the glittery, glamorous woman. "You're my Watson, Trixie Frick."

"Thought so."

With that Trixie shimmied her way back to the White Stag's booth, her trademark confidence fully restored despite still wearing Evon's oversized jacket. She grabbed Boone's face with both hands and planted a kiss on him that would've made the perchten blush.

"Mom!" Evon—back in his own lanky body—groaned from where he stood with his friends. "Oh my god, not in public."

Boone pulled back just enough to study his wife's face, his dark eyes searching. One hand came up to cup her cheek. "You okay?"

"Better than okay, lover." Trixie's grin was pure mischief and relief mixed together, her voice dropping to that honey-warm drawl. "Best Christmas market ever."

Boone's gaze narrowed, suspicion flickering across his features. His hand dropped from her face as he looked toward Evon. "He didn't get the cups?"

"Cups?" Trixie blinked with theatrical innocence, then ducked behind the counter. She made a pretense of looking around the booth, then shifted a tablecloth with exaggerated purpose and straightened with a stack of cups balanced in her arms. "Oh, would you look at that? Here they were all along."

Her eyes found mine across the market chaos, one perfectly painted lid dropping in an unmistakable wink.

Boone looked between us, his jaw working as pieces clearly clicked into place. He shook his head slowly, a reluctant smile tugging at his lips. "You two..."

"Don't know what you're talking about, dear." Trixie patted his chest and turned to serve a waiting customer, all business and sparkle.

It was as if the horror in the woods had been nothing but a winter dream.

But we knew better.

Justice had been served. Just not by mortal hands.

CHAPTER 24

From Greywolf Manor's grand parlor, I could hear sleigh bells jingling from horse-drawn wagons carrying families to their Christmas Eve celebrations. The scent of baked ham and spiced pies drifted through the air, mixing with the pine and cedar garlands draped throughout the manor.

This was the white Christmas everyone hoped for—quiet, still, and dusted with magic.

"Another glass of champagne, *chère*?" Chase asked, already refilling my flute before I could answer.

I accepted gratefully, curling deeper into the velvet armchair by the massive marble fireplace. The grand parlor glowed with old-world Christmas charm—crystal chandelier draped in holly and red ribbons, towering tree reaching nearly to the ceiling, garlands of pine and magnolia framing the arched doorways.

"I can't believe it's finally over," Jess said from the wine-red settee. "No more murders, no more Perchta—"

"No more early nights at the Gator," Tzazi finished dryly, raising her champagne flute.

"I'll drink to that," I said, stretching my legs toward the fire's warmth. "I desperately need a night out with the girls. Dancing, drinking, zero murder talk allowed."

"Yes," Jess said emphatically. "A proper girls' night. With karaoke."

Tzazi groaned. "Not karaoke."

"Especially karaoke," Jess countered, grinning at me.

"Quiet, everyone! I have a toast!" Chase grinned slyly. "Cheers to the fact that y'all keep me around even though I'm clearly the prettiest one here."

I threw a decorative pillow at him, which he caught with one hand while somehow not spilling a drop of champagne. "Oh honey, we keep you around for your hair products," I said.

"And your endless supply of champagne," Tzazi added.

Chase clutched his chest in mock offense, stumbling backward dramatically until Ren caught him with an affectionate eye roll.

"And to found family," Ren said softly, his hand finding Chase's. "The kind that shows up when it matters most."

I raised my glass higher, warmth spreading through my chest. "Hear, hear."

We clinked glasses, the crystal singing like tiny bells. Outside, snow continued its gentle fall.

The soft chime of the doorbell echoed through the hall. Miles appeared moments later. "Keir Bane and Tal Prescott have arrived. And they've brought more champagne."

I was already rising from my chair before Miles finished speaking, my heart doing that ridiculous flutter it always did at the mention of Keir's name. He walked in with that confident stride, long dark hair loose around his shoulders tonight, and his eyes found mine immediately across the room.

"Merry Christmas, *mo chridhe*," he said softly as I crossed to him, and when he pressed a kiss to my temple, I felt the warmth of it all the way down to my toes.

"You're late," I murmured against his shoulder, breathing in his wild familiar scent.

"Worth the wait, I hope?" His hand found the small of my back, and I leaned into him without thinking.

Behind us, I heard Jess's delighted gasp as Tal made his way straight to her. When I glanced back, her face was lit up like the Christmas tree in the corner.

Chase appeared at Keir's elbow with champagne. "Drink up, *cher*. The night is young and—"

The doorbell chimed again, cutting him off. Through the frosted window, I could see multiple lanterns bobbing along the snow-dusted drive.

Miles returned, barely suppressing a smile. "It appears the rest of your guests have arrived en masse." He stepped aside with a flourish. "Zelda Merryman, Mason Beckworth, Zavier Strangeland, and Arthur Vanderholt."

The parlor door opened wider, and suddenly I was caught in a whirl of snow and laughter and Christmas cheer as four people spilled in all at once.

Zelda bounced past me, her dress jingling with tiny bells, carrying a small mountain of figgy pudding. "We all arrived at the same time. Christmas magic!"

"More like we all got stuck behind Arthur's sleigh, eh, Zave?" Mason said, and I blinked at the easy teasing in his voice. When had Mason and Zavier become friendly? "Traffic was backed up all the way to Strawbridge."

"Hey, what can I say? I'm a careful driver," Arthur said as he entered, uncertain and hesitant. Before I could get to him, Jess was there, taking his hands in hers.

"Arthur, I owe you an apology," she said, her voice steady and warm. "I let my anger cloud my judgment. I blamed you for things that weren't your fault. I'm sorry."

My throat tightened watching them, this moment of healing that had been years in the making. Arthur's eyes shone with tears, and when Zavier stood and extended a hand to him, saying something too low to catch, I had to look away before I started crying into my champagne.

"Well, *mes amies*," Chase announced dramatically, "if y'all are all done making me cry—can we please get back to drinking expensive champagne? Nobody gets to stand around looking tragic on Christmas Eve. House rules."

The room erupted with laughter and movement, and I found myself swept into the chaos. Chase pressed a bottle of champagne into my hands—"Help me, *chère*, or we'll all die of thirst"—and suddenly I was moving through the parlor, refilling glasses while conversations swirled around me.

Someone popped a Christmas cracker right behind me. The bang startled me so badly that champagne sloshed over the rim of my glass, cold and fizzy on my hand. I yelped, jumping forward, and nearly crashed into Mason, who steadied me with a hand on my elbow.

"Careful there," he said with a grin, and when his eyes tracked past me to where Tzazi stood by the fire, something soft crossed his face.

I set down the champagne bottle and grabbed a napkin, wiping my hand while trying not to laugh at the absolute chaos. When I glanced over, Tal and Keir were deep in conversation by the fireplace, and from the way Tal kept glancing toward where Jess stood, I'd bet money it had everything to do with her. That man definitely wore his heart on his sleeve.

Zelda was at the fireplace now, holding her figgy pudding high like a trophy.

"Who wants to help me set this ablaze?" she called out.

"Me!" Chase practically shouted, and I shook my head as he produced matches from thin air.

I made my way back toward the fire, drawn by the promise of warmth and the scent of caramelizing sugar as blue-gold flames erupted across the pudding's surface. Tzazi stood nearby, arms crossed, one eyebrow arched high in deep suspicion.

"Y'all are really gonna make me eat a cake that's been set on fire?" she drawled.

I bumped her shoulder with mine. "It's a Christmas tradition."

"So is getting coal in your stocking," she shot back, but when

Chase cut her a slice and held it out with puppy-dog eyes, she sighed and accepted it. "Fine. But I'm doing this under protest."

I took my own slice, the warm spices and brandy rich on my tongue. Across the room, I caught Keir's eye. He was talking to Ren, but he smiled at me over his champagne glass—that slow, devastating smile—before turning back to his conversation.

Zavier was gesturing wildly, telling some story that had Zelda doubled over. Arthur stood near the tree, paper crown askew on his silver-blond hair, looking more at peace than I'd ever seen him.

The party swirled and eddied around me like a warm tide. I found myself in conversation with Tal, then with Ren, then someone pulled me toward the piano where sheet music lay scattered. Chase started playing something jazzy, and Jess tried to sing along even though she clearly didn't know the words. I glanced over and found Keir leaning against the piano's edge, watching me with those spellbinding eyes, and the look on his face made warmth bloom in my chest.

We were all laughing so hard my sides ached, and I was reaching for the champagne bottle to refill my glass when I felt Keir's hand on my neck, warm and solid and right.

"Come with me a moment?" he murmured, low enough that only I could hear over the music and laughter.

My heart stuttered. "Of course."

He guided me toward the far corner of the parlor, past the Christmas tree with its twinkling lights, to a small alcove framed by the bay windows. Snow fell beyond the glass, and the fairy lights draped through the garlands cast everything in a soft golden glow. We were still in the room—I could hear Chase's laughter, the clink of glasses, someone's off-key singing—but here, tucked into this corner, it felt like we'd found our own private world.

"I wanted to give you this," Keir said, his voice rougher than usual. He produced a small velvet box from his jacket pocket—deep green, nearly black in the dim light—and held it out to me.

My pulse raced as I accepted it. For a moment I just held it, almost afraid to open it. Behind us, someone whooped with laughter, and I heard Chase's distinctive drawl calling out "*Mon amie!*" as he greeted another friend.

Then I lifted the lid.

Inside, nestled against dark silk, was a delicate platinum charm shaped like a wolf's fang. But as I lifted it closer to the light, I could see intricate engravings covering its surface—symbols and marks that looked ancient and powerful, flowing across the platinum surface like a story written in a language older than words.

"It's beautiful," I breathed.

"It's from my clan," Keir said, and his voice had gone soft and serious. "The markings are my personal symbols, passed down through the Mac'IlleBhàin line. My father wore one. His father before him." He paused, his eyes intense as they held mine. "When an alpha gives one to someone..." Another pause, weighted with meaning. "It means they're under his protection. Forever."

My breath caught. Somewhere behind us, the piano music shifted to something slower, sweeter. Chase's voice drifted over, singing softly now, and I could hear the murmur of conversations, the crackle of the fire.

"Forever is a long time," I said softly.

"Not long enough." He stepped closer, his hand coming up to cup my cheek, his thumb tracing along my cheekbone with heartbreaking tenderness. "Not nearly long enough when it comes to you."

The party continued around us—I was dimly aware of movement, laughter, the soft clink of crystal—but it all faded into background noise. The world narrowed to just the two of us, to the warmth of his hand on my face and the intensity in his eyes.

"I love you, Win," he said, and the words fell between us like sacred things, precious and true. "I've loved you since that first day when you tripped and fell at Mizizi's cottage. I loved you when you faced down Eudora without flinching. I loved you through every murder investigation, every moment of danger, every time you chose courage over fear." His voice broke slightly. "And I'll love you long after the stars burn out and the seas go dry."

Tears pricked at my eyes, hot and immediate. "Keir—"

"You don't have to say anything back," he said quickly. "I just needed you to know. Needed you to understand what this charm means. What you mean to me."

But I was already shaking my head, already reaching up to touch his face, my fingers trembling as they traced the strong line of his jaw. "I love you too," I whispered. "So much it terrifies me sometimes. This feeling—it's bigger than anything I've ever known."

The smile that broke across his face was radiant, transforming him from handsome to devastating. He leaned down, his forehead resting against mine, and we stood there breathing the same air, existing in the same moment while the party continued its gentle chaos around us.

"May I?" he asked, gesturing to the charm.

I nodded, unable to speak past the emotion clogging my throat.

He removed the charm from its box with careful reverence, then reached for the necklace I'd been wearing. His fingers were steady as he slid the wolf fang onto the delicate chain, the platinum gleaming in the soft light.

"There," he said softly, his fingers lingering on my wrist. "Now everyone will know you're mine."

"And that you're mine," I countered, looking up at him with a smile that felt like it might crack my face open.

"Always," he promised.

Then he kissed me—slow and deep and full of everything we'd just said and everything we hadn't needed to say. Distantly, I heard someone whistle—probably Chase—and laughter rippled through the room, but I didn't care. For that perfect moment, nothing else existed except the two of us and the love we'd finally spoken aloud.

When we finally pulled apart, both breathless, I realized the music had stopped. The room had gone suspiciously quiet.

I turned, still in the circle of Keir's arms, to find every single person in the parlor staring at us with varying expressions of delight, amusement, and satisfaction.

"Well, well, well," Chase sang out from the piano bench. "Is that—" He gasped dramatically, pressing a hand to his chest. "Is that a clan charm I see?"

Heat flooded my face, but Keir just tucked me closer against his side and smiled that confident smile. "Aye, 'tis."

Jess squealed—actually squealed—and launched herself at me, nearly knocking over both Keir and me . "Oh my god, Win! It's beautiful!"

Tzazi appeared at my other side, and I caught the suspicious brightness in her eyes as she examined the charm. "About damn time," she said gruffly, but there was warmth in her voice.

"To Win and Keir!" Chase declared, raising his champagne flute high. "May their love be as eternal as fruitcake and twice as sweet!"

"That's the worst toast I've ever heard," Tzazi said, but she was raising her glass anyway.

"It is terrible," Ren agreed, smiling.

Everyone clinked glasses, and just like that, the party swept us back into its warm chaos. Someone refilled my champagne. Zelda pulled me into a spinning hug that made her bells chime. Arthur clasped Keir's shoulder with a genuine smile. Zavier offered a fist bump that turned into a handshake that turned into a half-hug, and I felt something in my chest expand with the sheer goodness of it all.

The room buzzed with overlapping conversations and laughter and the soft strains of music as Chase started playing again.

I was standing near the fireplace, watching Mason whisper

something to Tzazi that made her eyes sparkle, when Jess appeared at my elbow. She tilted her head toward the bay alcove, where frost traced delicate patterns on the glass. Tzazi noticed and rose smoothly from her seat by Mason.

We drifted toward the frosted panes, the three of us standing together while the party continued behind us. In the glass, I could see our reflections overlaid with falling snow, and beyond that, the warm glow of the parlor with all our friends gathered.

"Okay," Tzazi said, cutting straight to the point. "What's going on? You have that look."

Jess took a breath, her fingers twisting around the stem of her glass. "I finally had 'the talk' with Jaime."

"I wondered why Tal was here," I said with a grin.

Tzazi frowned. "What talk?"

"The 'we're better as friends' talk," Jess said, her voice both relieved and sad. "I told him I care about him, but not in the way he wants. It needed to be said."

I reached out, touching her arm gently. Behind us, Mason laughed and I heard the clink of glasses.

"How did he take it?" I asked.

"Better than I expected, actually." Jess stared down at her champagne, watching the bubbles rise. "He's a good man, but we want different things."

"Hmm," Tzazi said, her eyes twinkling. "You've certainly got a type, my sweet friend."

Jess blinked. "What do you mean?"

"Brychen was a shifter. Tal's a shifter." Tzazi swirled her drink. "I'm sensing a pattern."

"Hey, don't knock it," I said, nudging Tzazi with my elbow. "Want me to set you up with Laird Kennedy?"

"Ooh, yeah," Jess said, bouncing on her toes. "He's handsome."

Tzazi's laugh was sharp. "Oh my god. We need an intervention...and I do fine on my own, thank you very much."

"We need no such thing," Jess said primly, though her grin betrayed her. "We simply have excellent taste."

"In men who shed," Tzazi added.

"They do not—" I started, then paused. "Okay, Keir does leave a lot of hair in the shower drain."

"Brychen was the same way," Jess sighed fondly. "I used to find fur everywhere."

"This is the least glamorous girl talk we've ever had," Tzazi said, "and I'm a vampire who drinks blood."

We put our arms around each other and stood there for a moment, the three of us reflected in the frost-kissed glass. Then Zelda's laugh rang out, bright and clear, and Tzazi slipped her arm through Jess's.

"Come on," she said. "Let's get back before they drink all the good champagne."

I followed them back into the warm heart of the party. Chase pressed a fresh glass into my hand. Keir found me again, his arm slipping around my waist as naturally as breathing. The conversation flowed and eddied around us—someone was telling a story about hexbees, and Zelda was distributing the last of the figgy pudding, and through it all, the fire crackled and the snow fell and the love in this room felt like its own kind of magic.

I touched the wolf fang charm at my throat, feeling its warm pulse against my skin. Around me, my chosen family celebrated together. Chase and Ren with their heads bent close. Jess and Tal stealing glances across the room. Tzazi and Mason talking quietly by the fire, rebuilding trust one conversation at a time. Arthur still with a paper crown on his head and genuine joy on his face. Zavier making Zelda laugh until tears streamed down her cheeks.

The snow outside grew heavier as midnight approached. Inside Greywolf Manor, surrounded by the people I loved most in this world, I felt something settle deep in my chest—a bone-deep certainty that whatever came next, whatever challenges awaited us in the new year, we'd face them together.

And that was enough

EPILOGUE

J should have known that peace wouldn't last.

But standing on the back porch of Fernwood with Keir's arms wrapped around me, watching snow drift like powdered sugar across the lagoon, I believed we'd earned it.

"Perfect Christmas Eve," Keir murmured against my hair. His breath warmed my neck, and I settled deeper into his embrace.

"It really is." I watched the snow swirl through the honeyed light of the old plantation house, flakes winking gold for one brief moment before the dark water swallowed them whole.

Pyewacket sat on the weathered dock planks, his eye gleaming as he batted at something in the water. Greta Garbo's massive head emerged from the lagoon, surprisingly gentle as she nuzzled the one-eyed cat.

"Who would have thought?" Keir shook his head. "A five-hundred-pound alligator playing with a cat."

"Pye would be mortally offended to hear you call it playing. He's 'engaging in diplomatic relations with a fellow guardian.'"

"Of course he is."

I laughed and settled back against Keir's chest, content to watch their odd friendship unfold. Greta Garbo disappeared beneath the water, only to surface moments later with something glittering in her jaws. She deposited it on the dock beside Pyewacket, who sniffed it delicately before batting it into the water again.

"I think they're playing fetch," I said, amazed.

Keir laughed. A deep comforting sound that resonated through the swamp.

A comfortable silence fell between us, broken only by the distant sound of Christmas carols drifting from town and the gentle lap of water against the shore. I could have stayed like that forever—safe in Keir's arms, watching my familiar and the lagoon guardian play in the snow-kissed moonlight.

Then I noticed the small, gift-wrapped package sitting on the porch steps.

"Did you leave that?" I nodded toward the gift.

Keir followed my gaze and frowned. "No."

I pulled away from his arms and approached the package cautiously. It was bound in rough brown paper and tied with hemp cord—simple, humble materials that spoke of old traditions and reverent hands.

"Careful," Keir warned, moving to stand beside me, ever wary, ever cautious.

But I could already sense what this was. The magic radiating from the package felt ancient and benevolent—nothing like the dark energy that had surrounded Eudora and her accomplices. This was something else entirely.

I picked up the package, noting how light it felt, and found a small piece of rough paper tucked beneath the cord. The handwriting was simple but elegant:

For one who weaves truth from tangled lies. The threads will show you what you need to see.

"It's from Perchta," I whispered.

Keir moved closer, his protective instincts still sharp despite the peaceful feeling emanating from the gift. "Are you sure?"

I nodded and gently tugged at the hemp cord. Inside the brown paper, nestled in what looked like raw wool, was a simple wooden spindle. The wood was smooth with age, worn by countless hands, and wound with a few silver threads that seemed to shimmer with their own light.

The moment I touched it, I gasped. Images flashed through my mind—threads of connection stretching between the people of Darkly, some bright and strong, others tangled or frayed. I could see the web of relationships that bound our community together, the lies that had nearly torn us apart, and the truth that had ultimately saved us.

"What is it?" Keir asked, concern tightening his voice.

"It's a tool." I held up the spindle, watching the silver threads catch the moonlight. "For seeing connections. Understanding how things—how people—are linked together."

There was more wool in the package, seemingly ordinary but radiating the same gentle magic as the spindle. Enchanted fiber that could be spun into thread, woven into patterns that revealed hidden truths.

"A thank you gift," I murmured, touched by the thoughtfulness of it. This wasn't just a token—it was a working tool, something that could help me in the future.

I looked across the lagoon toward the far shore, searching the tree line for any sign of our unexpected ally. For just a moment, I thought I saw a silhouette among the cypress trees—a tall, regal figure that raised one hand in farewell before disappearing into the shadows.

"Thank you," I whispered to the night.

He wrapped his arms around me again and I snuggled into his warm chest as we both gazed out over the water. Peace settled over Fernwood like a blanket, warm and comforting despite the winter chill.

"Papa Noël should be coming soon," I said, remembering the local tradition.

As if summoned by my words, a splash echoed across the lagoon. But this wasn't the gentle sound of Greta Garbo playing—this was something larger, more purposeful.

A pirogue emerged from the mist rising off the water, gliding silently through the snow. The boat was painted bright red and green, festooned with Spanish moss and tiny lights that twinkled like stars. And pulling it through the water...

"Are those alligators?" I asked.

They were. Six magnificent alligators moved in perfect formation, their powerful tails propelling the magical sleigh through the dark water.

And standing in the pirogue, one hand on the tiller was Papa Noël himself. He wore traditional red, but his coat was simpler than Santa's usual outfit—more suited to the warm Louisiana climate. His beard was snow-white, and his eyes twinkled with a mischievous light.

"Joyeux Noël!" Papa Noël called out as his gator-drawn sleigh passed in front of Fernwood, waving a hand at Keir and me.

I waved back, grinning like a child. Beside me, Keir chuckled and raised his own hand in greeting.

The magical sleigh continued across the lagoon, picking up speed as it approached the far shore. Then, just as it reached the cypress trees, the entire pirogue lifted off the water. Snow swirled around it in a glittering spiral, and Papa Noël's laughter echoed across the night as his alligator-drawn sleigh soared up into the star-filled sky.

I snuggled closer to Keir, still clutching Perchta's gift.

"Our first Christmas together," Keir said quietly, pulling me closer.

We watched until the red and green lights disappeared behind the clouds, leaving only the gentle snow and the distant sound of sleigh bells. Pyewacket had abandoned his game with Greta Garbo to sit on the dock's edge, his eye tracking Papa Noël's flight path with typical feline interest.

"Come on." Keir pressed a kiss to the top of my head. "Let's go inside before we freeze."

But as we turned toward the house, I noticed another wrapped present resting on the door facing. This one wrapped in expensive black paper and tied with a silver ribbon that seemed to absorb light rather than reflect it.

My blood chilled.

This package gave off a completely different vibe from Perchta's gift. Where the spindle had radiated warm, benevolent magic, this new arrival pulsed with something dark and hungry. The air around it seemed to shimmer with malice.

With a yowl, Pyewacket darted from the dock and launched himself onto the porch, his eye blazing with alarm.

"Win, don't—" Keir reached for me.

But I was already reaching for the black package, drawn by a compulsion I couldn't name. My fingers closed around the smooth paper, and immediately I knew I'd made a mistake.

The package felt wrong—too warm, too eager in my hands. There was no note, no indication of who had left it, but the dark magic seeping from it made my witchy senses recoil in recognition.

"Win, put it down." Keir's voice held a note of command I'd never heard him use with me.

Instead, I found myself pulling at the silver ribbon. It fell away with suspicious ease, as if it wanted to be opened. The black paper followed, revealing an ornate silver locket nestled in dark velvet.

The locket was beautiful—Victorian in design, with intricate engravings that seemed to shift and writhe in the moonlight. I turned it over—plain silver surface. I gasped. Was this the locket I saw in Michey's pawnshop?

As the locket sprang open in my hands, revealing a small mirror with a crack running down its center, the world exploded into chaos.

Dark magic erupted from the locket like a geyser, sending shockwaves of malevolent energy rippling through the air. The cracked mirror reflected not my face, but something else— something that had been waiting, watching, hungry for release.

A scream tore through the night, high and keening and utterly inhuman. It was followed by laughter—cold, cruel laughter that seemed to bubble up from the locket itself.

Pyewacket yowled and leaped to my shoulder, his fur standing on end. Greta Garbo's bellow of alarm echoed across the swamp, and even the distant Christmas carols seemed to falter and die.

"Drop it!" Keir shouted, but the locket was stuck to my hands now, the silver burning against my palms as dark magic continued to pour from the cracked mirror.

The laughter grew louder, more triumphant, and through the swirling darkness I caught a glimpse of something moving in the trees.

The locket finally fell from my numb fingers, hitting the porch floor with a sound like breaking glass. The mirror cracked further, and with one final pulse of dark energy, it went silent.

But the damage was done.

In the sudden quiet that followed, I could hear it—movement in the swamp, the whisper of something that hadn't been there before. Multiple somethings, slithering through the water, rustling through the underbrush, spreading outward from Fernwood like ripples from a stone.

Keir pulled me against his chest, his heart hammering beneath my ear. His arms formed a protective cage around me, and I felt the wolf in him rising to the surface, ready to defend against whatever had just been unleashed.

Pyewacket's eye darted between the fallen locket and the tree line, every muscle in his small body tense. "That," he said, his British accent clipped with barely controlled fury, "was a very old trap. And you just sprung it."

"I couldn't help it." My voice came out shakier than I'd intended. "It wanted to be opened."

"Aye, it did." Keir's voice rumbled through his chest, rough with his Scottish burr.

The locket lay at our feet, the cracked mirror reflecting nothing now but ordinary moonlight. It looked harmless, just an antique piece of jewelry that had seen better days. But I could still feel the echo of that dark magic, still hear the triumphant laughter fading into the swamp.

Greta Garbo's bellows had gone quiet, but I could see her massive shape guarding the lagoon's edge, vigilant in her patrols. Even the swamp itself felt different—alert, watchful, as if every creature that called it home knew something fundamental had changed.

"Whatever came out of that locket," I said slowly, touching the wolf fang charm at my throat—still warm, still pulsing with Keir's protective magic, "it's not going to stay quiet for long."

"No," Keir agreed grimly.

But then his hand came up to cup my face, tilting it so I had to meet his eyes. In the moonlight, they were more gold than brown, the wolf very close to the surface. "But whatever it is, *mo chridhe*, it will have to go through me to reach you. And I swear by the Silverfang Clan—that will not happen. You have my vow."

I leaned into his touch, drawing strength from his certainty, wrapping my arms around his neck.

Pyewacket made a sound that might have been agreement or might have been theatrical gagging—with him, it was always hard to tell. "Well," he said, hopping down from the railing to sniff disdainfully at the locket, "I suppose we should at least take this cursed thing inside. No sense leaving it out here for some curious raccoon to stumble across."

The absurdity of that image—a raccoon triggering some secondary curse—made me laugh despite everything. It came out a little hysterical, but Keir joined in, and soon even Pyewacket's whiskers were twitching with reluctant amusement.

"Merry Christmas, Win," Keir said softly, pressing a kiss to my forehead.

I looked at the locket, then at Perchta's spindle still clutched in my other hand, then up at the man who'd just promised to face whatever darkness was coming beside me. Through the windows of Fernwood, I could see the Christmas tree lights twinkling, the golden reindeer prancing within its branches, could smell the sweet scent of Sibby toasting marshmallows by the fire, could feel the warmth of home waiting just beyond the door.

"Merry Christmas," I whispered back.

Not ready to leave Darkly Island quite yet, turn the page for Chapter 1 of *Shamrocks Green & Banshee Keen*, Book 4 in **A Darkly Southern Mystery**.

BOOK FOUR, CHAPTER 1

*M*y breath caught in my throat as the massive shadow engulfed the courtyard of The Magic Cup, blotting out the twilight sky with wings that seemed to drip malevolence—and for one heart-stopping moment, I could swear I felt the scorch of phantom flames licking at my skin.

Tzazi, Chase, and I threw ourselves sideways, chairs toppling as orange flames roared through the space where my head had been. The heat seared my cheek, and the acrid stench of sulfur filled my nostrils. My prosecco flute exploded against the sidewalk in a shower of crystal and sparkling wine.

"Bloody 'ell!" Pyewacket yowled, scrambling up my back, claws digging through my shirt. "What fresh madness is this?!"

The beast circled above us with thunderous wingbeats, massive leathery wings blotting out the dusky sky and casting writhing shadows across Tataille Street. Its scales shimmered like old blood mixed with charcoal dust, each one the size of a dinner plate. When it opened its maw again—sweet mother of mercy—I could see straight down its molten throat, flames rising from the very pit of hell. The air itself crackled and shimmered with heat waves that made my skin prickle.

People in the cobbled streets of downtown Darkly screamed

and scattered like leaves in a hurricane, voices rising in terror. Dianthe Petalsigh, owner of Oopsie Daisies flower shop, flew backward, her arms windmilling wildly before she crashed into a towering display of sunflowers, sending petals exploding into the air like golden confetti. In front of Sugarloaf's, teen Evon Frick dove headfirst into a potted fern with a tremendous crash of ceramic, soil flying everywhere.

Protective wards sparked and fizzled as people crashed into each other in their panic. Someone's levitating market basket went careening down the sidewalk, jars of sweet tea and grits cascading across the pavement in a sticky, gritty mess. The dragon's roar—if that's what you'd call that bone-rattling, theatrical bellow—seemed to shake the very foundations of our little town, rattling windows and sending every familiar within three blocks into a howling, hissing, screeching frenzy.

I pressed against the brick wall of The Magic Cup, heart hammering, as the dragon banked for another pass. The rational part of my brain was already cataloging the wrongness, that instinct sharpened by life in Darkly. Dragons didn't exist. At least, not the village-razing, maiden-devouring kind. And this one moved with too much theatrical flair, like it was putting on a show for an invisible audience.

The creature dove again, jaws gaping, and unleashed a torrent of fire at the cemetery's bell tower. The flames engulfed the cursed spire completely, and I flinched from the wall of heat that rolled over the street. For a terrifying second, I thought the burning roof might collapse and send flaming timber raining down on us, releasing whatever ancient curse was trapped up there.

Then I heard it. Laughter. Three distinct voices, boyish and wild with glee, cutting through the screams like church bells through fog.

The dragon flickered. Its terrifying bulk shimmered like a mirage, then dissolved into billions of shamrock-shaped glitter particles that rained down on the panicked crowd below. Every flame vanished with it—the fire on the bell tower, the heat in the air, even the lingering scorch marks on the pavement—gone as if they'd never existed. Magic sparkled in the air like fireflies on a summer night, sweet and mischievous and utterly infuriating.

I pressed a hand to my racing heart, relief flooding through me before irritation chased right behind it. They'd scared me—really, truly scared me, the kind of bone-deep terror that made my magic flare hot beneath my skin—and it had all been special effects.

Three small figures perched on the roof of The White Stag Inn, arms thrust skyward in victory. Leprechauns, by the look of them —two with flame-bright hair, one strawberry blonde. All three grinning like they'd just gotten away with murder.

My jaw dropped. "What the—"

"Oh no." Chase Abernathy-Wyatt peeked out from behind an overturned chair, then settled back against the brick wall without bothering to stand. He took a careful sip of his Sazerac, somehow still holding the glass despite our dramatic dive to safety. His white linen suit remained pristine despite the chaos, which honestly shouldn't have surprised me anymore. But instead of his usual lazy purr, his voice carried something that sounded almost like reverence. "They're here."

"Who's here?" I demanded, brushing shamrock confetti from my hair. The glitter stuck to everything—my clothes, my skin, even Pyewacket's whiskers.

Tzazi Strangeland rose to her feet with predatory grace and raised her Corona in salute, platinum pixie cut glinting in the fading light. The half-vampire attorney studied the three leprechauns with the same sharp assessment she'd use on a legal brief. "The Hooligans. This is going to be a jurisdictional nightmare." Then her grin turned all fangs. "I can't wait."

"The who?"

"Hou-li-hans," Chase corrected, drawing out the name like it was sacred. He reluctantly stood and began righting the scattered chairs with exaggerated weariness, his movements theatrical even in cleanup. "Though everyone calls them the Hooligans. And for very good reason." He gestured toward the three leprechauns with a flourish that would've made a theater director proud. "The Houlihan brothers. Colm, Seamus, and Declan. Infamous across at least four continents, possibly five if you count that incident in Antarctica."

"There was an incident in Antarctica?" I asked weakly.

"The penguins won't talk about it," Tzazi said solemnly.

A collective groan rose from the locals who'd emerged from their hiding spots, dusting off shamrock confetti with varying degrees of annoyance. Even Mrs. Banerjee's poodles looked thoroughly offended, their pristine white coats now sparkling with green glitter.

"Oh, for the love of all that is holy," came a wail from down the sidewalk.

Mayor Fernando Mayór stumbled toward us, his mustard-yellow trousers torn at the knee and his signature feathered captain's hat sitting sideways on his head. Glitter sparkled in his magnificent red mustache like fairy dust gone terribly awry. He looked like he'd aged ten years in the last five minutes.

"Ten out of ten for the spectacle, gentlemen!" Chase called toward the roof, lifting his glass in salute. "Though perhaps a smidge heavy-handed on the sulfur effects."

The leprechauns paid no attention to either praise or the mounting irritation from the crowd. They simply vanished in three synchronized puffs of emerald smoke, reappearing in the middle of Tataille Street directly in front of our table with matched flourishes that suggested hours of practice.

Up close, I understood the strategy. These weren't just three leprechauns—this was a calculated invasion force.

The one nearest me had strawberry blond hair, the face of a Renaissance angel, and the smile of a con artist. Green linen suit, rumpled from travel but clearly expensive. Jaunty cap at a rakish angle. When he caught me looking, he had the audacity to wink.

"Ladies, gentlemen, and assorted beings of questionable origin," the tallest one announced in an accent thick as Guinness, spreading his arms wide, "the Houlihan brothers have arrived!"

Auburn hair pulled back in a leather-corded ponytail. Sharp green eyes swept across the stunned townsfolk like a general surveying a battlefield. Gold rings flashed on every finger—shimmer and brass knuckles all at once. When he smiled, infectious and dangerous, I knew immediately: this was the one in charge.

"And Darkly," the broadest brother added with a wolfish grin, "will never be the same."

He looked like he could bench-press a Buick. Barrel chest straining against a leather jerkin decorated with Celtic knots. A magnificent red beard woven with golden beads that clinked with every movement.

The streetlamps began to flicker. One by one, their warm golden glow shifted to pulsing emerald green. Then came the music—a tinny, aggressively cheerful Irish jig erupting from every lamppost at once, each playing a different tune in a dizzying collision of competing fiddles and flutes.

I winced as the lamp beside our table launched into an enthusiastic rendition of "The Irish Rover" while the one across the street countered with "Whiskey in the Jar."

"You've got to be kidding me."

But the teenagers gathering on the sidewalk were utterly enchanted. They clapped along to the competing jigs, charmed by the magical chaos. A few even started dancing, spinning in circles while shamrock confetti swirled around them like a glittering tornado.

Fernando lurched toward our table, nearly tripping over his own feet in his haste. He leaned in close, voice dropping to a panicked whisper that somehow carried more urgency than the dragon's roar.

"Win, you have to help me."

"Help you do what? Banish leprechaun muzak from the lampposts?"

"Don't joke!" His hands twisted together like nervous birds.

Actual sweat beaded on his forehead. "This is nothing. Just them warming up. You don't understand—"

My pulse quickened despite myself. I'd never seen Fernando this rattled, not even when someone defaced his statue in Oakspider Park with clown makeup. I looked at the three grinning leprechauns, still basking in the attention and chaos they'd created, then back at Fernando's stricken face.

"Wait. Why are you so—"

"They're my brothers, Win." His voice cracked on the words. "My blasted younger brothers."

The world seemed to tilt slightly on its axis.

I stared at him. Then at the leprechauns—the charmer, the mastermind, the bruiser—still grinning and soaking up the attention like they owned the place. Then back at Fernando. Our mayor. Our composed, dignified, slightly ridiculous mayor with his feathered hats and formal proclamations and endless speeches about civic responsibility and proper decorum.

Had secret leprechaun brothers.

Who just terrorized downtown Darkly with an illusionary dragon.

My mouth opened. Closed. Opened again.

"Your..." I finally managed, voice strangled. "Your *brothers*?"

"Half-brothers, technically," he whispered miserably, like the distinction mattered. I knew from experience it really didn't. "Same father, different mothers. I left Ireland fifty years ago to get away from their nonsense, changed my name, built a respectable life, and now—" He gestured helplessly at the green-lit street, the dancing teenagers, the shamrock confetti still drifting through the air like malevolent snow. "Now they've found me."

A sudden loud jangling of bells cut through the competing jigs. Brightly colored caravans rolled down Tataille Street, each one more elaborate than the last. They were painted in swirling patterns of green, gold, and crimson, with gilded wheels and shutters that sparkled in the emerald lamplight. Dozens more leprechauns perched on the caravan roofs, whistling and waving like conquering heroes.

The Houlihan brothers turned as one, faces lighting up with unholy glee.

"The party's arrived!" the youngest one shouted, and all three vanished in another coordinated puff of smoke.

Fernando looked like he was going to faint.

Pyewacket, still perched on my shoulder, leaned close to my ear. His whiskers tickled my cheek. "I want hazard pay. Japanese bonito flakes—the artisanal kind, naturally. And fresh cream. None of that dreadful boxed swill you've been palming off on me."

"Noted," I muttered.

"We should probably see what they're up to," Tzazi suggested, already heading after the caravans with the focused stride of someone who anticipated billable hours.

Chase drained his Sazerac and set down the empty glass with a satisfied sigh. "Darling, I wouldn't miss this for the world. The aesthetic potential alone is simply divine."

I looked at Fernando's pale face, then at the parade of chaos rolling down our previously peaceful street toward Oakspider Park. The air already carried the faint, jaunty notes of a fiddle and the scent of frying onions mixed with something sharper— whiskey, maybe, or that infamous green ale I'd heard whispers about.

"Come on," I said, grabbing Fernando's elbow. "Let's see what your brothers have planned."

He groaned but followed, trudging after the caravans like a man walking to his own execution.

~

ACKNOWLEDGMENTS

A special thank you to my fabulous editor, Karen "the Kraken" Block. She's the reason this book makes sense and doesn't accidentally have Win saying the same thing three different ways in the same paragraph. (Spoiler: I do that a lot. The Kraken is relentless.)

I also want to thank my beta and ARC readers. These wonderful folks catch all the typos, plot holes, and continuity errors that somehow survive multiple rounds of editing. In my defense, I have a chihuahua who likes to slap my keyboard while I write, so if you find any random symbols or the letter "q" where it shouldn't be, that's on him.

But most of all, thank you to *you*, my reader. Some of y'all have been with me since the very beginning, and I can't tell you how much that means. Writing is the best job in the world, but it can also feel a little like standing on a stage in your underwear—thrilling and terrifying in equal measure. (I held onto my first book for a year after it was finished because I was too scared to hit publish.) So thank you for making this wild, wonderful ride worth it. I hope you'll stick around to see what happens next.

With love and gratitude,

Tam xo

A NOTE ON PERCHTA

While researching Christmas folklore for this book, I stumbled down a delightful rabbit hole and discovered Frau Perchta—and I've been fascinated by her ever since.

Frau Perchta (also known as Perchta or Berchta, meaning "the bright one") is a figure from Alpine and Germanic folklore who appears during the twelve days of Christmas, particularly on Twelfth Night. Unlike our jolly gift-givers, Perchta is a stern supernatural judge who rewards the hardworking and punishes the lazy. She's associated with spinning and weaving—checking to see if households have finished their year's work—and her punishments for the idle or dishonest are, shall we say, considerably more dramatic than a lump of coal.

What captivated me most was discovering her as Santa's shadow self—the flip side of Christmas magic. Where Santa embodies generosity and joy, Perchta represents accountability and consequences. She's the reminder that the season isn't just about receiving; it's about how we've lived our lives, treated others, and honored our responsibilities. In some traditions, she travels with a group of wild, horned creatures called Perchten who enforce her judgments.

I loved the idea of bringing this darker European folklore into the moss-draped, magic-soaked world of Darkly Island, where the supernatural has always walked alongside the everyday. Perchta felt like a perfect fit for a place where swamp spirits and shape-shifters are neighbors, and where even Christmas comes with a touch of danger lurking in the shadows.

www.ingramcontent.com/pod-product-compliance
Lightning Source LLC
Chambersburg PA
CBHW032141190626
46814CB00005BA/1786